Praise for
Dire...

"Fast-paced, dark, and wickedly edgy, *Dire Needs* is a paranormal shot in the arm for the genre! No one writes a bad-boy hero like Tyler."
— Larissa Ione, *New York Times* bestselling author
of *Immortal Rider*

"Stephanie Tyler puts a unique, fresh spin on shape-shifter romance. In *Dire Needs*, she creates a raw, sexy world where werewolves make and break all the rules."
— Maya Banks, *New York Times* bestselling author
of *Whispers in the Dark*

"Stephanie Tyler has created a story that kept me on the edge of my seat. With breathtaking danger, sizzling romance, and unexpected twists, these Dire wolves are going to rock the paranormal world."
— Alexandra Ivy, *New York Times* bestselling author
of *Bound by Darkness*

"The first chapter was one of the best I've read in a while. . . . The instant the book begins, you know you are in for a great ride." — That's What I'm Talking About

"An exciting new paranormal series featuring werewolves. The theme is a classic to the paranormal romance world, but Stephanie Tyler is able to shake it up and give it a little more edge. . . . the potential to be a fantastic series."
— Romance Reader at Heart

"The chemistry between Rifter and Gwen sizzles."
— Manga Maniac Café

"A fresh and sexy take on werewolves that readers will enjoy. . . . The book moves at a clipped pace as we are introduced into a very imaginative story. . . . a great read with smoking hot scenes." — Nocturne Romance Reads

continued . . .

"*Dire Needs* creates an interesting new world, with lots of history and mythology. Great plot twists and turns, hot and steamy sex in the woods, and a bit of sweet thrown into the mix." —Sizzling Hot Book Reviews

"Riveting! *Dire Needs* hooked me from the very first page." —Shiloh Walker, author of *The Departed*

Praise for the Novels of Stephanie Tyler

"Unforgettable."
—Cherry Adair, *New York Times* bestselling author of *Riptide*

"Red-hot romance. White-knuckle suspense."
—Lara Adrian, *New York Times* bestselling author of *Darker after Midnight*

"Stephanie Tyler is a master." —Romance Junkies

"Sexy and witty." —Fresh Fiction

Also in the Eternal Wolf Clan Series

DIRE WANTS

A NOVEL OF THE ETERNAL WOLF CLAN

STEPHANIE TYLER

A SIGNET ECLIPSE BOOK

SIGNET ECLIPSE
Published by New American Library, a division of
Penguin Group (USA) Inc., 375 Hudson Street,
New York, New York 10014, USA
Penguin Group (Canada), 90 Eglinton Avenue East, Suite 700, Toronto,
Ontario M4P 2Y3, Canada (a division of Pearson Penguin Canada Inc.)
Penguin Books Ltd., 80 Strand, London WC2R 0RL, England
Penguin Ireland, 25 St. Stephen's Green, Dublin 2,
Ireland (a division of Penguin Books Ltd.)
Penguin Group (Australia), 250 Camberwell Road, Camberwell, Victoria 3124,
Australia (a division of Pearson Australia Group Pty. Ltd.)
Penguin Books India Pvt. Ltd., 11 Community Centre, Panchsheel Park,
New Delhi - 110 017, India
Penguin Group (NZ), 67 Apollo Drive, Rosedale, Auckland 0632,
New Zealand (a division of Pearson New Zealand Ltd.)
Penguin Books (South Africa) (Pty.) Ltd., 24 Sturdee Avenue,
Rosebank, Johannesburg 2196, South Africa

Penguin Books Ltd., Registered Offices:
80 Strand, London WC2R 0RL, England

First published by Signet Eclipse, an imprint of New American Library,
a division of Penguin Group (USA) Inc.

First Printing, November 2012
10 9 8 7 6 5 4 3 2 1

Copyright © Stephanie Tyler LLC, 2012
All rights reserved. No part of this book may be reproduced, scanned, or distrib-
uted in any printed or electronic form without permission. Please do not partici-
pate in or encourage piracy of copyrighted materials in violation of the author's
rights. Purchase only authorized editions.

SIGNET ECLIPSE and logo are trademarks of Penguin Group (USA) Inc.

Printed in the United States of America

PUBLISHER'S NOTE
This is a work of fiction. Names, characters, places, and incidents either are the
product of the author's imagination or are used fictitiously, and any resemblance
to actual persons, living or dead, business establishments, events, or locales is
entirely coincidental.
   The publisher does not have any control over and does not assume any responsibility for author or third-party Web sites or their content.

If you purchased this book without a cover you should be aware that this book
is stolen property. It was reported as "unsold and destroyed" to the publisher and
neither the author nor the publisher has received any payment for this "stripped
book."

For JH, always there

'Tis now the very witching time of night,
When churchyards yawn and hell itself breathes out
Contagion to this world.

— William Shakespeare

Must be the season of the witch, yeah.

— Donovan, "Season of the Witch"

Glossary

abilities: The now-immortal Dire wolves were all born with abilities, except for Rifter, who was cursed with his at birth. These abilities were looked at with fear by the Dire population at large. In fact, the Elders were once Dire wolves who were sacrificed to Hati, the creator of the Dires, because they had abilities. The abilities range from dreamwalking to communicating with the dead, and can often be seen as both a gift and a curse to the wolves trying to balance them out.

Adept: An immortal, master witch.

Brother Wolf: A Dire wolf is a dual-natured beast who lives with his Brother Wolf inside of him. These Brother Wolves are also depicted in a life-sized glyph on the Dires' backs, the glyph coming out fully after a Dire's first shift at age twenty-one. The Dires and their inner wolves have an even balance of power and a deep respect for one another. They both run the show, bowing to each other's needs and wants when necessary. This differentiates them from Weres, who, when shifted into wolf form, cannot communicate or control their wolf sides.

Catskills, NY: Place where the Dire wolves currently call home. Also home to the supernatural world of witches, vampires and other shifters who are not friendly and remain hidden; it coexists alongside the human world.

deadheads: Old Dire wolf word for vampires. Current meaning: fans who follow the Grateful Dead.

Dire wolves: (*Also see **Brother Wolf**) Dire wolves are alpha, immortal wolves who live in tandem with their Brother Wolf and take on human form to survive in the world. Dire wolves are differentiated from Weres because they cannot be killed by any means, thanks to a curse of immortality cast upon them by the Elders. When first in existence, the Dire wolves lived a long time, with an approximate one-hundred-year life span, but they were not immortal. The majority of the Dire wolf population—which was quite large, since it preceded the Were population—was killed during the Extinction, and the curse on the remaining Dires wolves with abilities was cast at that time.

However, with their gifts, immortality is exhausting for the Dires—it forces them to remain in hiding and move quite often because their human sides will not age, unlike Weres, who, although immortal in theory, can be killed and will age, albeit slowly, in their human forms.

The Dires were trained in the warrior ways. They are powerful fighters, far more powerful and violent than Weres. However, both Dires and Weres can shift at will and both are pulled by the full moon, although the Dire wolves will never fall prey to moon craze, which often happens to young Weres during their earliest shifts and can last from the age of sixteen until they are twenty-one.

Dire ghost army: These are the Dire wolves killed during the Extinction. They are raised by Seb, the master witch, through a black magic spell and are intent on harming the living Dire wolves. They then plan on spreading their destruction outward to Weres and humans.

the Elders: The Elders are a mythical group of otherworldly spirit wolves responsible for the creation of both the Dires and the Weres, and also responsible for meting out justice to both populations when necessary. One example of this was the Extinction. There were originally four Elders: Hildr, Eydis, Leifr and Meili. Hildr asked to be released from her duties (aka killed) when outvoted on an important matter concerning the Dires and their abilities rather than go against what she believed in.

the Extinction: In Norway, the Dire wolf packs committed a massacre of humans (who will later form the weretrappers) in direct opposition to orders from the Elders. The Elders killed all Dire wolves except for five Dires who were out on their Running—Harm, Rifter, Vice, Jinx and Rogue. Later the Dires discovered that another pack of non-immortal Dires in Greenland had also been saved by the Elders. Stray and Killian are immortal, since they have abilities, but the rest of their Greenland pack isn't.

fated: In the time of the Dires, their word for love was fated, so when a Dire talks about being fated, he's really talking about love.

Greenland pack: A pack of non-immortal Dires kept alive by the Elders after the Extinction so that wolves in that pack would give birth to brothers who would have abilities and thus fulfill an old prophecy.

hunters: A human antidote to the weretrappers, they're a group of humans who are on the side of good and therefore trying to weed out the bad supernaturals from the good, rather than use them or kill them at will, as the trappers do. In the supernatural world, they're seen as just as dangerous.

mating: Weres can mate with humans or Weres and sometimes with other shifter species like lion shifters. For the Dires, it's a very different story, as the old ways dictate that

Dires can mate only with other Dires and it must be cere-monial. First and foremost, a mating can never happen dur-ing first-time sex. It's too dangerous to try to mate with a new wolf because shifting for the first several times is too hard and new wolves are uncontrollable. Mating happens by consent on both sides during the third time a male and female Dire lay together—that is the Dire custom because they don't encourage sex without mating. Sex for the last remaining Dires is painful, because it goes against their mating protocol. During the mating, the non-shifted male is chained and the female will shift uncontrollably at the end. Thus mating equals danger for the male—will he be able to handle his proposed female wolf? After a mating, the Dires must come before the Elders to have the mating blessed. Mating makes Dires stronger.

the old country: The Dire wolves were created by Hati dur-ing Viking times and lived primarily in Norway, with a large pack also in Greenland.

the Running: An adult Dire has a great responsibility to his pack. Even before his shift, he trains as a warrior, as Dire culture is a warrior one. Also, because the shift for a Dire requires great strength, their lives are devoted to gaining the necessary strength before they turn twenty-one. After their shift, there is an importance placed on sensuality and play. The Running happens after their first several shifts, while they are allowed to run and play apart from the packs for six months in order to see if they are truly independent and able to blend well with humans now that their wolves have emerged.

Skinwalker: There are many myths about how skinwalkers are created. The Dire wolves know that they can become skinwalkers if they commit matricide and/or patricide. Since this killing is an unnatural act, they become unnatural beings, although they remain, first and foremost, Dire wolves. A skinwalker can shift into other beings, taking on various personas for short periods of time. Some can see the future, and others are thought to be able to curse those who speak out against them. Some are seen as witch doctors, and typically, they are cast out and live alone.

Weres: (See **Dire wolves** for more differences between Weres and Dires.) Were who are newly shifted can experience moon craze, in which they become uncontrollable and therefore dangerous to themselves, their packs and the human race. Many young wolves are put down because of this. The Dires wolves will often take in moon-crazed Weres they believe have the potential to become great warriors.

werepacks: Werepacks are scattered across the United States and the rest of the world. The main pack is located in New York City, with other large packs being in Texas, California and Wisconsin. The **outlaw pack** that forms from the New York pack is now taking in rogue wolves from other packs to join their cause. They believed that if their king Linus sold out the Dires to the weretrappers, the Weres would be left alone. They are angry wolves, not very organized, and more intent on killing than following the old ways, which makes them quite dangerous. They like killing humans and have taken to selling their own kind to the weretrappers in exchange for protection. Some of them will work as bodyguards for both the witches and weretrappers.

weretrappers: A paramilitary group of humans intent on destroying Dires and Weres, as well as using Weres for their own nefarious purposes. Their purpose had evolved over the years. At first, they were formed during Viking times; they were a tight-knit group intent on keeping humans safe from wolves. During the current century, they began to realize the power they could have if they were able to harness the power of the Weres. They capture Weres and experiment with ways to keep them under their control. They also create a pact with the witches, realizing they will need more supernatural help in order to gain domination over humans. Their goal is ultimate power and world domination, and they've begun to experiment with the dark arts (aka black magic).

witches: Witches live in covens and stay among their own kind. Widely regarded with suspicion and hatred by the rest of the supernatural world, many have started allying themselves with the weretrappers for security, which will allow their race to survive.

Prologue

The small house on the hill was silent. Typically, it was Kate's favorite time, when the moon shone through the trees and she was the only one awake, free to do whatever she wanted. Granted, most of what she did was tame—drawing or reading—but it was one of the few times she didn't feel powerless.

Sometimes, if she felt brave enough, she'd take off her nightshirt to look at the newest bruises. They often hurt for weeks until they healed, depending on if they were made with her mother's hand or the belt, but no matter what, after midnight, everything seemed better.

Tonight she snuck down to the kitchen for a couple of cookies—she knew she'd have to confess this on Sunday but she didn't care. The bruise on her arm from her mother still ached, and she'd been sent up here well before dinner.

"She deserves it. All she has to do is obey and she won't." Her mother's voice, furious, seeped through the walls.

Kate had wiped the tears from her cheeks, angry that she'd given in to them. She'd never give her mother the satisfaction of seeing them—and that, at least, was a comfort.

"She doesn't know what she's doing," her father argued back, his voice coming through the phone's speaker. He was away on business and would be back in the morning, in time for the fair and for Kate's birthday.

"I wish she'd leave and never come back," Kate whispered into the phone to her best friend, Julia, after her parents had hung up, as she prowled the kitchen with her contraband snack.

"Can you sneak out tonight?"

"I'll try."

Julia lived two doors down, an easy out-the-window-and-through-the-neighbor's-backyard walk, if Kate could manage to do it quietly. The girls would sit out on the back roof, shielded from the street's prying eyes. Julia's backyard was only woods.

Kate hung up and went back upstairs, knowing where to step so there were no creaks on the old wood. Once in the relative safety of her room, far enough down the hall from her parents', she closed the door behind her and stared at the shattered lightbulb in the corner. She fought the urge to kick over the entire lamp it came from. It wasn't Kate's damned fault a lightbulb had exploded when her mother hit her.

But somehow, everything was. The house was more oppressive than ever. Even since she'd hit twelve and a half, things had gotten worse. Her thirteenth birthday loomed tomorrow, and for the past week, her mother had been on constant edge.

They were strict Catholics. Kate went to Catholic school, church on Sundays, confession monthly. She was regularly stripped to check for markings, and she had no idea why, since she never heard this taught or preached about.

Kate also had no idea what kind of marks the devil would leave, but she'd begun to check herself too, even as she'd stopping praying, letting her mind wander to anything but Christ's teachings when in church or Sunday school, as part of her secret rebellion.

After a while, she began to wonder if she was the devil, if maybe the beatings were bringing him out in her.

"She never should've been born," her mother would mutter after each inspection. It was as though every year she descended further into some kind of madness, and Kate's father traveled more frequently to escape it.

Kate wasn't sure she didn't despise him more because he was such a coward.

She picked up her sketchpad instead and drew the moon, the ebbing shadows apparent on either side of the nearly full orb. She threw the window open to get a better view, despite the sticky night air, and got so engrossed in it that when she finished, she realized Julia would be long asleep.

She wasn't sure what startled her. At first she thought it was something in the trees outside her room. But when she closed the window, the sound was still there—and it seemed to be coming from inside the house.

She didn't want to go out into the hall, but something compelled her to. One foot in front of the other until she stood on the threshold of her parents' bedroom. The door was cracked open, and Kate was sure it hadn't been when she'd come upstairs earlier. She would've seen the sliver of light, the flashing of shadows thrown off by the muted television set.

She opened her mouth to whisper "Mom," but her voice quickly died in her throat when she stuck her head in the room, then recoiled in shock.

Her mother wasn't alone—and, although she was still asleep, she looked like she was struggling to wake.

On her chest sat a monster. It might've been a woman once, but it looked more like a thing. Greenish black lips and red eyes, a mess of tangled white hair and long nails. It straddled her mother's chest and laughed, a high, demonic sound that made Kate tremble.

"Get off her," Kate said quietly.

Her mother moaned. Her head moved from side to side, but the monstrous thing didn't budge.

"Get off of my mother!" Kate called out, and the streetlights outside the house shattered in a stunning display.

When Kate looked back, the thing was gone and her mother was sitting up, holding her chest. Kate wondered if she'd acknowledge the monster, but instead she asked, "What are you doing, Kate?" in a cold, angry voice that also held some fear.

Kate vomited on the rug before she could stop herself. "I . . . got sick. I'm sorry."

She ran and locked herself back in her room and stayed under her covers for the rest of the night.

The county fair was held in the high heat of August, and even in upstate New York, the crowds sweltered under the noon sunshine.

Kate had been sure she'd be punished for what happened last night, for not helping to clean up, for being out of bed, but oddly enough, her mother hadn't said a word. Her father had given her a brief, perfunctory hug when he'd come into the house that morning, and she was thankful there was no mention of the monster or her transgressions.

Julia rode over with them, sitting quietly in the backseat. Julia hated Kate's parents—she'd seen the bruises, although Kate refused to talk about them. She knew her best friend rode with her as often as she could so that Kate wouldn't be yelled at. Kate's parents rarely allowed her to go in other family's cars or attend any sleepovers or parties.

Her parents bought the girls tickets for rides, then went to get some lunch, making them promise to check in with them in an hour.

Giddy with freedom, the girls rode the scariest roller coaster and ate cotton candy and giggled like fools over silly things and serious things.

Kate never wanted to go home.

"This way. Come on—there's no line," Julia said as she pulled Kate toward the fortune teller's tent on the edge of the grounds, away from the children's rides, like they were trying to hide something.

"Come; get your fortune read," the woman selling tickets encouraged.

Kate shook her head, looked over her shoulder, sure her mother would come lurching across the fairgrounds.

"Come on, Kate—your mom's having lunch all the way on the other side of the fairgrounds. She'll never know," Julia urged.

Kate wanted to argue, because her mom always had the eyes-in-the-back-of-the-head thing going on.

"We planned for this all summer," Julia insisted. And while it was true, the last thing Kate wanted to do was go inside that tent now.

Yes, she'd known there'd be a fortune teller there—she'd kept the newspaper clipping that boasted the details. Had wondered for months what her future might hold.

Maybe she'll tell you that soon the hitting will stop. Or that your dad will be home more often. Or that things will just get better.

But Kate couldn't bring herself to believe any of them, and to hear it shot down by the crystal ball would make it all worse.

"I already paid!" Julia called triumphantly. "She's waiting for you. She's nice. She'll read me next. I'll keep a watch for your mom—now, go."

A small push and Kate stumbled into the small tent. The woman behind the table was bent over a layout of big tarot cards, a scarf tied around her head, silver looped earrings in her ear. But instead of looking ridiculous, she actually looked . . . pretty.

Kate had seen tarot cards once in a store, but her mother had pushed her past them in a rush.

"Work of the devil, Kate," she'd said.

Work of the devil.

Kate nearly ran. But when the woman lifted her head and smiled, a brilliantly wide and beautiful smile that lit her eyes up from inside, Kate wondered how that could be true.

God made beautiful things and this woman certainly was beautiful. Not like Kate, thirteen and still in that horrible, gangly phase, hormones running amuck, making her feel like she'd never ever be beautiful or normal.

"Normal's boring," the woman told her.

Kate froze.

"I don't read minds. It's written all over your face. Come; sit down. Let me read your past."

Past? Fortune tellers were supposed to tell the future. Still, Kate went forward and sat tentatively on the white plastic chair, her feet solidly on the ground in case she had to run. She saw the woman look at the hand-shaped bruise on her arm and she pushed down the sleeve that had ridden up.

When she looked up again, the woman's eyes held a sympathy Kate had seen before. It made her nearly gag.

"Tell me what you saw last night, Kate."

She wanted to lie, tell the woman nothing, but instead, the words tumbled from her mouth like a confession. "I think I saw a ghost. It was . . . ugly. Horrible. Green lips and mouth; red eyes; long, white hair . . . and it was sitting on my mother's chest while she slept."

"What did you do?"

"I told it to move, but it laughed." She shook her head. "I don't want to talk about it anymore. You're supposed to tell me about my future. What do those cards say?"

The fortune teller smiled, a little sadly. "It's going to change from what's laid out here in the tarot cards."

"I don't understand."

"I know. It's too soon. According to this spread, you would've married a nice boy. Lived here."

"And that's not going to happen?"

"None of it," the woman confirmed. "Everything that was supposed to be will change."

"Kate!"

Her mother's voice. Kate turned to see her face white, lips pressed together. She looked furious and frightened all at once, and she said nothing as she dragged Kate away toward the car, where her father waited.

When Kate turned to see the fortune teller as she was being pulled away, there was no one behind the table at all.

Had there ever been?

She didn't know where Julia was or why she hadn't kept Kate out of trouble. She'd find out later that her friend had gotten distracted, innocently enough, by a group of cute boys, and that being left behind at the fairgrounds would be the best thing to happen to her that day.

Kate never made it home that afternoon, and her parents would never go home again, but the fortune teller was right about one thing—everything changed that sunny afternoon when the big black truck slammed into the side of her family's car, killing them all.

Chapter 1

Two Dires will be born to aid in the great war between wolf and man. One can hear, the other, influence. Brothers who, if they don't turn their wrath on each other, will cause destruction and ruin outward.
— Prophecy of the Elders circa tenth century

The prophecy Stray had grown up hearing about himself and his brother, Killian, was coming true. Kill was coming to town and would be expected to live up to his name, and Stray needed to run to lose himself. To hunt instead of brood, to stop trying to figure out if the prophecy wanted him dead or alive.

As part of a pack of what was believed to be the last six remaining Dire wolves, he was feared and revered. Immortal and therefore invincible, they currently called Catskills, New York, home. They had come back here months earlier to aid the Weres and found themselves embroiled in a shitload of trouble.

Still, in the woods outside the Dires' secret underground lair, there was laughter under the glow of the moon. Even if it was foggy, she shone to them as bright as the sun to humans on a hot summer's day.

The nightly run would happen on the plot of land that was protected by unshifted Weres. Under normal circumstances, the Dires changed their locale as often as possible. This was anything but normal. The safe place was at the end of a tunnel that let out into a thicket of woods nearly impossible for most humans to pass through. Their leader, Rifter, was there, with Jinx and Vice.

Jinx's brother, Rogue, remained in a supernatural-induced coma back at the house, along with Harm, the Dire who'd walked away from the pack thousands of years ago and had come back just weeks earlier, bringing even more trouble with him.

Gwen was with them as well. She was Rifter's mate, a half Dire, half human. Harm's daughter.

Stray watched Vice rib Jinx for picking up a werechick the night before, and Rifter and Gwen were nuzzling each other. Business as usual, despite everything.

Except Stray had an even bigger secret than the brother he'd been keeping under wraps. Tonight, though, he was determined to shake the maudlin shit off and let his Brother Wolf run wild. And Brother growled in agreement, barely waiting for Stray to strip before the shift began. It was a pain and pleasure kind of thing, a change that took Stray to his limits every time his wolf took over.

"Stray's gone!" Vice called behind him, and Stray knew his shift would pull the others along. Sure enough, soon he was surrounded by the wolves as they disappeared into the woods, camouflaged in safety.

Stray wasn't the name he'd been given at birth. He'd adopted the moniker after he'd left his pack because he refused to use or even think his birth name. Kill refused to change his. Maybe he was too proud or too stupid—or a combination of both. Stray could be stubborn too, but living like a hermit was his specialty, not Kill's. He couldn't imagine how his brother had fared all these years in forced isolation.

Being a hermit was okay for Stray—it had been lonely as shit, but it was easier than reading people's goddamned thoughts all the time, which got old and exhausting very quickly.

The Dires had never pushed him to reveal his ability, nor had they mentioned the prophecy, but that didn't mean they didn't know about it. Fact was, Rifter and his Dire brothers might have suspected there were more of their kind out there after they discovered Stray. At one point, Rifter had asked him outright and Stray had denied it. But now that they knew about Killian, would they make the connection about the prophecy as it related to them? And when would he have to admit that there was another Dire pack, one that wasn't immortal and living quietly in Greenland?

The Elders had never forbidden him to speak on them, but he was oddly protective of a group that had been anything but kind to him.

Stray had already given up more in the past few days then he'd ever planned on doing. But this Dire pack had kept him safe, treated him like a brother for the past fifty years.

Maybe he should've let them in on all of it—the pack, the prophecy—before now. He couldn't tell if it was his guilt or their unspoken—and possibly imagined—disapproval weighing heavily on him. And so he ran faster, breaking away from the pack, Brother Wolf craving a solitude he hadn't gotten since all the shit started raining down on their heads.

He felt his brother drawing near as surely as he felt the moon's pull. There was a darkness in Killian, one that Stray brought out, and he was pretty sure he shared it as well.

And soon the pack that took him in would know too.

They all have abilities, he reminded himself. But putting his together with Kill's could turn them both into beings beyond all control.

Power was a damned dangerous thing, but not as much

as the freedom he craved. Freedom was as dangerous as anything these days to seek out, but Brother Wolf wanted to hunt. To seek, to stalk prey while relishing in the game of the chase.

He lost track of time and the trails, knew he was pushing it by running this close to the highway, but he didn't care. His Brother Wolf pushed fast, paws crunching the packed snow.

He was searching. Scenting. His body felt hot and tight and every run made things worse, not better.

He heard confusion miles in the direction he'd planned to run. Paused, listened and let the wolf take in the scene.

Human violence. One human beyond saving. Another, alive.

He still waited, deciding.

Police arriving. Which meant Brother Wolf went in the opposite direction, paws treading the wet earth until he couldn't hear anything but his own breathing. Everything inside of him relaxed, and he melded into the forest surroundings, because that's where he belonged.

He scented his prey and stalked it for miles. Sometimes the thrill of the hunt and the chase was better than the catch.

This time the catch was pretty damned good too.

Stray would be the last one back in tonight. Vice shifted and waited for him to show through the thicket of trees sometime before dawn.

The wolf would come back bloody, the way Vice had. Not unusual, but since he'd confessed how young he was — seventy-five to Vice's centuries — Vice was impressed by Stray's self-control.

The kid was really a goddamned baby.

"We've got to find out more about Killian, 'cause I've got a bad feeling about it," he said finally to Jinx, who'd come up beside him.

"You shouldn't fuck with him," Jinx said finally. "This brother thing . . . it's no joke."

He knew Jinx was speaking from experience, since his twin was currently all fucked up and lying in some kind of supernatural coma. Only the death of Seb, the witch who'd cursed him, could break the spell—and since that witch was immortal, they needed a hell of a miracle.

"Kill needs to come through with helping to take away some weretrapper power or we're fucked," Vice said.

"If Kill's ability works the way Stray says it does, with Stray reading minds and Kill able to place suggestions into a person's mind, it will work. We'll pull it out of the fire—we always do."

"Hell of a lot to pull out," Vice muttered. "And Kill can place those same suggestions in wolf minds when he's with Stray—remember that. Wolf minds. Stray doesn't know if that includes Dires or if it's just Weres. This could backfire on our asses."

"Guess we'll find out soon enough. Don't say anything in front of Rifter—he's just back," Jinx said quietly as their king and his new queen emerged from the woods, with Gwen still half wrapped around him. Vice opened his mouth to call something like *Get a room*, but Jinx stopped the comment from flying out of his mouth by literally clamping a hand over it.

"You'd think the run would've calmed you," Jinx told him, but they both knew nothing could for long.

As for Rifter and Gwen, they'd mated days earlier—and even though a mating ceremony would normally give them more time to revel, they couldn't afford to do so now.

Still, the Elders—Hati, actually—moved the damned blue moon. Scientists were calling it an aberration and astronomers were simply calling it a mistake. But April would now have two moons—a full and a blue, the perfect storm for Seb and his army, and the full moon was less than two weeks away. Seb wouldn't make the mistake of waiting for the blue moon this time—he'd take advantage of the full one.

So yes, Hati bought his wolves time, but Vice wondered what effect screwing with nature like that would have. It certainly screwed all of them up.

He leaned against the gazebo that was directly over the tunnels the Dires utilized. The protected underground lair was built beneath hallowed ground. There had once been an old church here, razed before the Dires purchased the land. Even though the building was gone, the consecration would always remain.

Vice figured there had to be some religious types flipping in their graves over the fact that wolves were living on church ground.

He wasn't sure why, other than the fact that they weren't human. But he'd never understood any organized religion. He'd fought in the Crusades not just because he liked to fight, but also because he liked the idea that everyone deserved freedom.

Well, most everyone. The weretrappers had to get over themselves. Centuries was too long to hold a grudge.

This vendetta on the part of the trappers wasn't about what the Dires once did to humankind centuries earlier and, hell, they'd paid for it with the Extinction of nearly all their kind. Over the years, the Dires had saved a thousand-fold more humans than their packs had killed. It seemed like it would never be enough. But he'd be damned if he let those fuckers use the wolves to kill. Bad enough the trappers had convinced witches to get into bed with them—although not literally, which Vice would've understood. Now the human trappers had all kinds of black magic on their side, thanks to a master witch named Seb.

Because of that, the hunt for the witch who could kill Seb and save Rogue was on. But it was more complicated than that, since killing Seb might also save their asses from the Dire ghost army Seb had raised, made up of the Dires' dead parents and various other friends and family. And if that ghost army didn't die with Seb, Rogue, who could communicate with spirits, would be able to take the ghost army down.

That was some crazy shit the witch had conjured. Vice and Jinx had seen them only once, but that had been more than enough. Jinx hadn't been able to contact the Dire ghost army since—and the Dires didn't content themselves that it had been disbanded. Seb was no doubt rallying the troops for a destructive march, trying not to give away his hand too early.

Now the sky remained unnaturally dark, as it had been for days. The supernatural influence pulled at all of them, made them uneasy. Growly. Shifty. The pull would get more intense as the full moon neared.

The supernatural storms that had invaded the town weeks earlier had receded, but they were all still vigilant, awaiting their return. The weretrappers weren't about to give up this easily.

Vice, especially, was getting tense—his shifts from one extreme to another would happen so fast his own head spun, and although he was never even close to being politically correct, the shit that came out of his mouth was worse than ever.

And Jinx was getting nowhere, except more pissed that he couldn't find the witch he'd been tracking, even though he claimed he felt her—and that she was close.

Stray had been getting more and more agitated as his brother got closer, and Vice kept having to trail him as he left the house constantly during the daylight, as if searching for something.

Between that, training Liam, the young wereking, and ghost hunting with Jinx, Vice barely found time to get into any trouble of his own. And hell, that in itself was too unnatural for him to deal with for much longer.

"Fucking witches," he muttered.

"Tell me about it," Jinx said. "Stray's coming—he just shifted."

They watched him turn from wolf to human form about thirty feet from them, still covered by the surrounding foliage.

"You're sleeping out here with him?" Vice asked.

"Yeah, think I will." Jinx motioned to the covered porch. "We'll be all right."

Vice didn't think any of them would be, but for once, he managed to hold his tongue.

Vice and Jinx were waiting for him. Neither said anything when Stray walked back to them with blood still smeared on his chest. They were all predators who believed in survival of the fittest and enjoyed the hunt as much as he did. Wolves were meant for this, and as long as they were taking down animals and not humans, they were well within their rights.

Doing so kept their predatory instincts at bay—they'd all learned long ago how important that was, but no one more than him.

You're a beast. His mother's words echoed in his ear. Why would she be surprised at that? Why would his nature be so bad when they'd been created in Hati's image?

All he knew was that he didn't want to be locked up again. Couldn't bear it. And he hated the old surge of panic that rose up in him, a sign that the street mutt inside of him had not been exorcized.

If he thought too much about it, his scar began to ache fiercely. His heart beat a tattoo against his rib cage as he ran his hand over the long, knotted swath of tissue that ran diagonally across his chest, starting just above his heart and traveling downward, as though someone tried to flay him open.

Someone had, just to see if he would die.

The only scars that won't heal on a Dire were scars made by another Dire.

Hell, dying would've been the easy part.

"Good run," Rifter said with a smile and a hand clamped on Stray's bare shoulder. He'd been behind the gazebo with Gwen, who still hadn't gotten entirely used to being completely naked in front of all the men. She already wore a T-shirt, but the rest of them were bare-assed naked.

The Dires didn't get moon crazed like Weres did, but his brothers had grown up in a time when hunting prey had been easier and more acceptable.

For as long as he could remember, he refused to be the prey, and outran and outgunned most anyone or anything that dared to come near him.

"Stray, this thing with your brother . . . how much of a fucking freak is he?" Vice asked without prelude.

Stray's way of answering was to jump toward Vice with a growl. Jinx got in between them.

"Guess I've got my answer." Vice stared at Stray over Jinx's shoulder. "We need him, so don't screw this up."

"Glad you agreed not to fuck with him," Jinx muttered, his hand shooting out to hit Vice across the back of the head.

Stray turned from them to look up at the sky as the two tussled next to him.

The moon wasn't ready to relent her hold on the world just yet. These last few hours of dawn were some of Stray's favorites, the in-between time when most creatures were quiet and everything seemed at peace.

The solitude was what Stray enjoyed the most. He knew Jinx understood that the best, as they were the only two who consistently slept in wolf form, because for Jinx, it blocked out all the ghosts who constantly needed his help.

For Stray, it wasn't that easy. His ability had been developing at an alarming rate once he left the Greenland pack. At first the other wolf's emotions had to be really strong in order for Stray to hear his thoughts. Now, if he tuned in, he could hear just about everything—from Dire, Were and human, and maybe even witch—and it made him feel like he was going nuts.

Hell, maybe he was.

Chapter 2

"Tell me what you remember," Kate Walters urged the young woman named Josie, who sat across from her on the couch. "Start anywhere."

"His hands," Josie blurted out. "They were ... hairy. God, of all things to remember."

"Keep going." Kate spoke gently as the picture began to firm up in her mind. She didn't want to see the face of the man who'd hurt Josie, but she was able to see him the exact way Josie had. The back of his hands, unnaturally furred, the face, unmasked. That wasn't always the case.

Kate concentrated on the attacker's eyes first. Windows to the soul—or lack of one. They were blue—dark—close set. Bushy brows.

The graphite pencil flew across the page as Josie talked, voice tremulous.

Eventually, Josie would find herself staring at a replica of her attacker—the man who'd also killed her best friend, Sue, in the woods early this morning, when they were walking back from a town bar to their college campus through a popular shortcut. Josie's reaction would be hard to judge— she might cry, scream or shake. The stoic ones affected Kate the most because they would simply sit there, hands balled tightly in their laps, and nod that the picture was right.

Kate wanted them to have a crack in their armor, a chip, wanted them to do something, because not reacting would come back to bite them in the ass.

It had for her. The fact that she got up daily and confronted her fears by helping others who'd lived through a violent crime was her only recourse.

And that's why, even though she much preferred to do this in the police station, she would go to the hospital and even the victims' homes if that's what it took to keep them comfortable. That was why she was at Josie's apartment instead of the hospital, where Josie had spent the better part of today.

The ultimate irony was that Kate couldn't remember the face of her own attacker no matter how hard she tried. It happened nearly three years earlier. The detective who'd helped her when she was attacked in the woods several towns over from where she currently lived had been the one who'd gotten her this job. And while she was grateful for it, some days she felt she could never—would never—escape the victimology that surrounded her.

Today was one of those days. She'd spend a long time in the shower when she was done here, trying to wash away the brutality of the attack on the woman across from her, as well as her own.

At twenty she'd already lived through what she thought was more than her fair share of tragedy. But then she was attacked and realized that there was no limit to the amount of pain someone could be forced to endure during their lifetime, no magic number that would allow them to live the rest of their life unscathed. Sometimes tragedies multiplied upon tragedies.

She'd worked with enough victims to realize the solid truth behind that.

She kept talking, small affirmations so Josie would think

she was still listening. But she didn't need to. She wouldn't stop sketching until she'd made a near-perfect reenactment of the man's face, and she wasn't there by any means.

She was always exhausted after she completed these sketches. Light-headed, like she'd left her body and was having a problem with reentry. Technically, she supposed a part of her *had* left to delve into another person's mind un-invited.

For a good cause, she reminded herself, hating to think she'd invaded a victim for the second time.

It's not like she could ask; they would think she was crazy, and she'd left all those people who'd once called her that behind. She wouldn't put herself in that position again.

The glass on the table next to her began to vibrate. Kate kept her head down, pencil moving with furious scratches, knowing all the while that she was causing the glass to move.

Josie was distracted by it, looked around nervously, because the Catskills wasn't exactly the epicenter of earthquake activity.

"Keep going," Kate urged, flicking a quick gaze on the woman. The pictures on the walls shook with Kate's nervous energy that had no other outlet. If she didn't hurry with this drawing, the woman's apartment might just explode.

This was exactly why she preferred to do her sketch interviews at the police station. No one noticed the shaking vibrations she caused when she was agitated. It was too crazy in there for anyone to notice much of anything.

At first she'd thought she was haunted. It took a psychic to tell her that all of this was a part of her, inside of her. She had informed Kate that she was more powerful than she knew and that she needed to utilize her strengths. Somehow that news hadn't been comforting at all. She knew there was something violent and dark inside of her, and she refused the psychic's offer to help her reach her potential. Instead,

Kate hoped that by helping people to exorcize their demons, she could rid herself of some of her own.

It helped a little, at least in the moment.

Concentrate, she told herself, and the image came back. Josie was still talking, but Kate wasn't paying attention to what she was saying. Instead, she focused on the picture in the woman's mind, the one she was trying so hard to relay to Kate.

It would've been impossible if Kate couldn't read her mind. She was able to capture the predator's sharp cheekbones, the cold, dead eyes, the scar on his neck that Josie didn't even remember. Identifying marks helped the police. They didn't have time or manpower for a lot of these cases. The more help Kate could give them, the better off the victims would be.

She wished she was able to erase the image from Josie's mind when she was done, take away all the horrible memories so Josie could go on with her life.

She held the sketch up. "Does this look like the man who hurt you?"

"I can't believe it—that's him." Josie put a hand over her mouth. "I didn't think I was helping you at all."

"You did fine. I'm going to bring this to the station now."

"You'll show it to Agent Young, too?" Josie pushed a business card at her. FBI Special Agent Angus Young. "He told me a picture would be important. But the police didn't seem like they held out much hope of finding this guy. I still can't believe any of this happened. It's like a bad dream that will never go away."

"I'll make sure he gets a copy." Kate slipped the card into her pocket, flipped the sketchbook closed and laid a firm hand on Josie's arm. Her voice wavered a little when she said, "Listen, you'll get through it. It's going to take time, but you'll be all right. Just don't be too hard on yourself."

Josie blinked, looked at her appreciatively. "You sound like you've been there."

Kate nodded and stood. To talk about it would tighten her throat more, and she refused to show any further weakness. Her lower back burned and she fought the urge to rub it, instead saying her good-byes to Josie and exiting the apartment building using the stairs.

Closed spaces, like elevators, hadn't worked for her since the car accident ten years ago. She liked being free. Most of the time, drawing gave her that freedom. She'd had both her artistic talents and the ability to move objects when angry or agitated for as long as she could remember, but reading minds had come only after the accident.

In the years between the accident and the attack, she'd simply hidden that new ability so she wouldn't appear to be the freak she felt she was. After the attack, when she'd sat with a sketch artist who tried patiently to get her to remember any details, she realized she could use the mind reading thing to help others. At that point, she allowed herself to use the ability for good. The victims asked nothing of her but a sketch that could help them and Kate's job was done.

She wasn't sure of her rate of success, didn't want to ask, but assumed that since Officer Shimmin continued asking her back, she must be doing a good job.

When she reached the door that led to the outside, she stepped into the cold air. She didn't call a cab, thought Josie's apartment was close enough to the police station to walk. But as dusk fell, she quickly realized she shouldn't have.

Light snow swirled on the concrete, dancing around her ankles. The white dusting on the lawns and roofs made everything look enchanting, and for a moment she paused to breathe in the slightly smoky scent that always accompanied snow.

It was then that she heard the mocking laughter. The cruelty in the sound made her brand burn again.

The group of boys looked to be in their late teens. Separately she might not have thought twice about them, but together they had a menacing, pack-like mentality that made her go cold. She turned away, but not before she unwittingly caught the biggest one's eye.

"Hey, gorgeous—looking for us?" one of them called. The others started saying things, too, that would gradually escalate to the obscene.

She was already almost a block from Josie's. It was too late to go back inside and call a cab—those boys were now nearly in front of the door to Josie's apartment and following closely. She started walking as she fumbled for her cell to call Officer Shimmin and noted the battery was nearly dead. Again.

She and electronics did not get along. Something in her body drained batteries, and it drove her crazy.

She managed to get a call through to him—voice mail—and left a message with her location. He'd come for her; she was sure of it. Whether or not it would be in time . . .

She dropped the phone, and before she could bend to retrieve it, a shape appeared in front of her. She stepped back as a man—a handsome, tall man who had her cell phone in his hand—stood motionless, watching her.

He was an impenetrable wall of protection housed in the most ruggedly handsome casing she'd ever seen. He was well over six foot six and broad, wearing all black, with a leather jacket and motorcycle boots.

He appeared aristocratic and street at the same time—he wore both looks well.

Men like him just didn't exist in the real world, and come to think of it, he was even larger than life than actors on the big screen. She didn't know if she could ever truly do him justice with a sketch, but she really wanted to try. To draw him, she would need to shadow the chisel of his cheekbones, the strong jaw, the dark hair disheveled by wind.

Something inside of her both calmed and surged simultaneously. She took the phone back from him, her fingertips brushing his.

The voices behind her grew softer, more sinister, and she realized how alone she'd been. But nothing looked like it could get through her new savior, and that's what she believed him to be.

But how could she be sure of anything?

"I'll get you home safely." His voice slammed through her like an unexpected orgasm. She took a few steps back, but somehow he was still directly in front of her. "Let me."

A command, and she immediately bristled. "I'm all right—I made a call."

"You're not safe."

She hated that he was right. The pack of boys had spooked her. "I'm not going home—I need to go to the police station."

"Because of them?" His head jerked toward the boys.

"No, I'm expected. I was headed there before those boys started calling to me." Best to let him know that, even though her body was anything but threatened by him.

"I'll escort you there." He wound his arm around her. When his hand touched her lower back, the brand so tender despite the layer of sweater and coat, she jumped.

He stepped away from her, glanced quickly at his hand and back at her. He looked like he was going to say something, but the young boys distracted him for the moment with their catcalls.

Her protector turned to them and spoke, his words too fast and too much like a growl for her to understand any of them, but the biggest held up his hands and they all stopped moving. She felt a stirring deep inside of her, longed to pull him to her, and she was embarrassed by the reaction. It wasn't the time or the place and still she wanted him to kiss her until she couldn't see straight.

She tore her gaze from him and tried to get her body back under control, but it refused to cooperate. She was hot and wanted to rip off her coat, but the man would wonder what she was doing, and so she kept it on and waited nervously.

When he turned back to her, he put his arm around her again, his hand nowhere near the brand. He was so warm, like an instant heater. He kept his pace even with hers although she knew he could move faster. There was power behind those muscles and it called to her in a way that frightened her. "Do you work for the police?"

"I'm a sketch artist," she explained.

"What's your name?" he asked, his brown eyes settling in around the color of a strong whiskey, and she was pretty sure she could get lost in them. She hadn't dated much at all, not from lack of want, but because the damned brand didn't seem to like men. It burned whenever one got too close. But now it was appeased.

She wasn't even close to being so.

"Kate. Kate Walters," she answered quickly when she realized he was staring, waiting for her to speak.

He nodded, but didn't offer his name in return. And dammit, she was curious. But they were rounding the corner the police station was located on and ahead of her was Officer Shimmin.

She wasn't sure when the man had let go of her, but she was very much alone.

"Kate, I've been calling you—I couldn't hear your location in the message," Officer Shimmin said, sounding genuinely concerned. As many times as he'd told her to call him Leo, she couldn't bring herself to do so. Although he was a good-looking man, maybe late thirties, she'd never been able to see him as anything but a boss, an authority figure, and one she was a little afraid of, if she thought about it too hard.

"I felt . . . silly even calling," she said apologetically.

"Never." He took her hand in his. "Come on. Let's get you inside."

She allowed him to steer her into the frenzy of the police station, the brand on her back humming with an energy she'd never felt before, and she knew it had nothing to do with Leo Shimmin.

The woman he'd just saved was a high-level witch—and Stray doubted she knew it. Jinx had stayed out for long hours hunting another witch who continuously eluded him, but Stray was the one to make this surprise catch.

He didn't need a picture of Kate—no, she was now branded into his mind.

She was tall—close to five foot eight—and her long dark hair hung in loose waves down her back. Her eyes were brown, but with more than a hint of copper, which matched the highlights in her hair. Natural, not store bought—he could smell that shit a mile off.

Even though she'd worn a bulky coat, it couldn't conceal her figure, more lush than thin, and his body damn near bloomed when he'd gotten near her.

He wanted to follow her everywhere, camp outside her front door or, better yet, in her bed. The lust that rose from him was like a rising smoke, visible for a thousand miles.

Wanted to press her against the wall of the nearest building and take her. Claim her.

Mark her.

Brother Wolf howled and Stray nearly dropped to his knees to join in.

Whether or not this was because of Killian coming, it was the most visceral reaction to a woman Stray had ever had.

The only one he'd ever had to a witch.

Was this a trap, a spell, conjured to yank him into the trapper's clutches?

He shook his head and realized Kate had turned to stare at the empty space he'd vacated with lightning speed and stealth once he'd come close to Leo Shimmin, in the same kind of reverie daze he'd been in before.

Good to see he wasn't the only one affected. Something had happened when he'd touched her lower back. She'd practically vibrated away from him. Whether or not she knew he was an *other*, she'd know he wasn't human soon enough.

For now he'd have to content himself with the fact that he'd actually made contact with a very powerful witch who could potentially be much more so than the one Jinx had been attempting to sniff out. He and Jinx had spent hours going over research and lore for the witches, most of which had been culled from Seb through Rifter. According to legend, when a witch gave her powers to another, it was through a brand on the person's body that typically only the witch and her recipient could see.

Jinx told him that by touching a brand of that sort, a bond could be formed, but it needed to be skin to skin. And although Jinx didn't have X-ray vision, he did know something had happened when he touched her through her coat. Even now, his hand tingled in a way it hadn't since he'd been around Killian fifty years earlier.

He rubbed his hands together as he backtracked the way he'd walked with Kate.

Her mind had been reeling when she'd first come upon him. He couldn't actively read all her thoughts, which he assumed was because of her powers, but whatever was happening, she was empathizing too much for her own mental health. He winced at the emotions rolling off her, wondered why she did this to herself over and over.

Talk about self-flagellation. Even he wasn't that bad.

He found her scarf close to where he'd first come upon her, by the building's front steps. She must've dropped it when she first noticed the young werepack. He tucked it into his pocket next to Agent Young's card that he'd taken from her pocket, trying to ignore its scent of warm sun on a spring day—the beach, salt water—all good memories he wasn't sure he ever had and was damned certain she'd never had.

The Weres had followed her for a block before he'd intervened. Stray had caught their scent immediately, but the first one he'd focused on had been Kate. Holy hell, he'd followed her just to keep smelling her. And shit like that could easily get him arrested. Women wouldn't understand.

Neither would Leo Shimmin, and Stray had no intention of going near him or the police station, especially not without the aid of nightfall or his fellow Dires.

He made a quick call to Liam to come round up the stupid young Weres who still remained in the street, harassing other young women as they passed. The young king of the Manhattan pack—the king of all the Weres—was gearing up to make his mark on the world.

He would have to start with these three numb-nuts.

"I'm on it," Liam assured him. Stray hung up and headed home through the woods. He'd walked to town, Brother Wolf trailing Kate's scent. Now he also scented fresh blood that was different than the blood of the prey he'd chased last night.

That was deer. This, what he smelled, was human. And when he investigated further, he found police tape and no bodies, but he smelled Were mingled in with the human scents.

Dammit.

Weres roamed everywhere—it was impossible not to smell them. Last night there'd been no way for him to tell that a wolf had been involved in this human kill. Today he was sure of it.

Dires were charged with protecting Weres and humans, and Weres were supposed to protect humans as well—or, at the very least, stay far away from them until they had full control.

Stray thought that a lot of the Weres never gained that

control. They were imperfect animals, far less powerful than the Dires.

He ran faster, until he got to the underground lair the Dires utilized to stay out of sight during the day. He threaded his way through the tunnel into the main Dire mansion and found Rifter, Vice and Jinx in the kitchen, their backs to him as they watched the news about the local murder on TV.

"Wolf kill," Stray confirmed.

"Just like the murders that have been following Harm," Rifter added, and Stray handed him Agent Young's card. The fed had been sniffing around them for weeks, looking for Harm to question.

"It wasn't Harm I scented," Stray confirmed, and a quick flash of relief passed over Rifter's face. "And I found a witch."

They could deal with a wolf kill later—this was far more important.

"A witch? Where? Forget it—who cares? Is she here?" Jinx demanded as Vice threw Stray a beer, telling him he looked like he needed one.

"She will be." Stray took a long drink from the bottle before saying, "I don't think she knows what she is."

"And this helps us how?" Jinx asked. "Fuck, Stray, you were supposed to be looking for the sure thing."

"Jinx, calm down," Rifter told him. "Let Stray tell us about her."

"Her name's Kate Walters—she works for the police. Sketch artist," Stray said. "I think Shimmin knows what she is. Let me do some research."

He didn't wait for Rifter to agree. He grabbed his laptop and was already typing furiously as his brothers silently moved to sit around the table and wait with a patience they didn't have.

It took him less than five minutes to find her in the victims' database. There were two separate entries, one ten years ago and the other nearly three years ago.

"She's an orphan," he managed, his voice tight, not sure why anything to do with a witch was affecting him like this.

He heard Vice's phone ring, heard the Dire talking to Liam and, in seconds, he flashed out of the room to their aid, with Rifter following just as fast. When he looked up, only Jinx remained at the table, silently watching as Stray's fingers worked.

He didn't worry about it—probably the young werepack needed some containing. Instead, he continued work on unfolding Kate's history.

"Lots of humans get thrown away in the world," Stray muttered as he paged through her history on his computer. Lots of wolves too—like him, he thought, but he didn't say that out loud.

"What about her parents?" Jinx asked.

"They were killed in a car accident when she was thirteen," Stray said. "She went to live with two different sets of relatives—which lasted less than a year combined. After that, none of her other relatives would take her in, so she went into foster care. Blew through several different homes."

"Why was she so much trouble?"

"That's what I'm trying to figure out."

"Don't try too hard. We just need her to create a spell." Jinx stared at him. "She is a witch, right?"

Stray nodded. "She has no idea how strong, though."

"We're gonna show her," Jinx promised, and Stray heard his Brother Wolf growl at the mention of *we*. "You all right?"

Stray wasn't all right at all, and there was no use pretending. "Don't touch her."

Jinx narrowed his eyes, wisely didn't say anything but, "Got it loud and clear."

By morning, all the Dires would know what Stray had said. And for the first time since he'd met them, he was glad his message was getting across.

"If she doesn't know how powerful she is, then we use that to our advantage," Jinx said.

"How so?" Stray asked.

Jinx gave him a sideways glance, like he wasn't sure how Stray would react to his words. When he spoke, Stray understood. "After she helps us, she'll need to be destroyed."

Everything inside of Stray wanted to rise up, but he forced himself to heel. If this witch fell into the wrong hands . . . "We'll discuss it when the time comes."

Jinx nodded, like he knew he wouldn't get a better answer right now. Stray forced himself not to strangle the other wolf and for the moment, all was right with the world.

Chapter 3

He'd never had love and he had no need of protection. But money? Well hell, every wolf needed that, and Killian, aka Kill to the underground world of ultimate—and illegal—cage fighting, was no exception.

"Come on, motherfucker," the Were called Champ—seriously, *Champ*—taunted Kill, revving the crowd up with his antics.

Kill had never gone for the dog-and-pony show. He would never be anyone's bitch, and he proved it when his fist connected with the wolf's cheek and the sound of shattered bone reverberated in his ears.

Fighting was easy. Natural. He pretended whoever was on the receiving end of the fists was his family—everyone except Steele, or *Stray*, as the Dire had renamed himself when they'd split.

The whole thing broke Kill's heart. And the revenge he'd taken on Stray's behalf hadn't been nearly as satisfying as he'd thought. While he didn't regret what he'd done, he did regret what he'd become.

But maybe he shouldn't. If it affected the prophecy for the better, then maybe none of it was in vain.

"Kill, Kill, Kill," the crowd chanted. Of course, the humans who ran and watched the show had no idea they were, at times, watching wolves fight. And most of the Weres around here had never seen a Dire, although they probably sensed Kill wasn't exactly one of them. But outing Kill meant outing themselves, and so they all remained hidden in plain sight, earning money from those who'd forced them into hiding in the first place.

Killian knew the stories of the Extinction—about how Jameson and his crew refused to cede his crown to Harmony or Rifter at the Elders' command and instead massacred humans. How the Elders smote the entire Dire race, save for a select few. How the Dire alphas with abilities who roamed the earth for centuries never knew about the small Greenland pack with no abilities.

Champ staggered up now. The roar of the crowd was a pumping throb in Kill's ears, a rush he had to force himself to control before things went very, very badly in front of too many people.

It took another shot at a much lower strength to make the Were go down and stay down.

He'd won. All that was left to do was collect his prize money and prepare to make the final leg of the trip to see Steele.

He left the ring with the crowd still calling for him—and he didn't look back. As he walked through the small runway, he watched women in the box seats falling over themselves, trying to gain his attention.

He didn't need to plant suggestions in anyone's mind for this. No, he'd never used it for seduction on humans or Weres, but it was an ability that made him just dangerous enough to both races when he wasn't with Stray.

Fucking prophecy.

Steele didn't want the power, which was why he'd changed his name and never tried to contact Killian. But Killian prided himself on the fact that he'd been the one to leave first. He hadn't wanted Stray to have to make that kind of decision, but still, he'd always secretly hoped his brother would seek him out. Kill thought the two of them could've had a great life if Stray hadn't been fearful of how strong they were together.

He'd figured the pup would get comfortable enough in his Dire skin and eventually return.

But then Rifter and his band of merry wolves had to get involved and ruin everything, and Killian knew that their separation was probably for the best.

More than fifty years and not a word from Stray before this. Guess Kill couldn't blame him, but was his brother going to hold a grudge forever?

Killian still couldn't tell, because Stray's phone message through Kill's manager had simply asked for help, not forgiveness. And Kill still owed him one for sure. Maybe more.

Seeing each other wouldn't be easy, but the pull to combine powers—no matter the purpose—whenever he saw his brother would be hard to resist. They were like magnets in each other's presence.

Entire states still separated them and his body had already begun the familiar tingle that had started inside of him when Steele had been born. Added to the post-fight adrenaline rush, he definitely needed a release.

A weregirl had followed him into the locker room, no doubt let in by one of the bouncers. Kill could see why—she was built and blond, sinful. Perfect for use. Perfect to keep his mind at bay for an hour or two.

He'd taken Were lovers, never humans, as he roamed nomadically through Greenland and Alaska, but he didn't rely on the Weres for help of any other kind. There were a lot of vamps in Alaska because of the short daylight hours. They knew who he was and vice versa, and they kept an eye out for one another.

He stripped his shorts as he walked, well aware of the weregirl's eyes on him. He started the shower as he waited for her to make the first move, and he wasn't disappointed.

"Hey, baby, you need some help with that?" she practically purred from behind him. She couldn't take her eyes off his ass first, and then his cock, and he certainly liked the appreciation.

He pulled her into the shower with him, fully clothed. "You have no idea."

"Good boy," she murmured, and he'd show her good, have her yelling his name and then leave her begging for more.

Because he was nobody's pet.

Chapter 4

The truck had come out of nowhere—to this day, Kate wasn't sure it had truly been an accident. One minute she'd been crying as her mother yelled at her for visiting the fortune teller, and the next, a bone-crushing slam threw her against the side window and the car was skidding off the road.

She turned over in her sleep, an attempt to stop the nightmare.

She knew she'd died that night, no matter what any doctor told her. She should've been covered with third-degree burns. At the very least, she should've been injured somehow, covered in cuts and bruises, if nothing else.

She'd been mainly fine, even though they kept her in the hospital for several days under observation. They were obviously confused as well as to how she remained unscathed except for intermittent back pain, although as the days went by and she remained in stable condition, they began to grow tired of her constant queries.

"You were thrown from the car, Kate—it's a miracle," the doctors and police told her, over and over.

She stopped asking about everything when one day she looked in the mirror and saw the unexplained handprint on her lower back that looked like a raised red brand on her skin.

It hadn't been there before the accident, and she could almost hear her mother's voice in her head.

Mark of the devil.

She'd been too scared of what it could mean to tell anyone. But shortly after that, strange things started happening, like being able to read people's thoughts. Moving objects around her when she got angry became a more frequent occurrence. She felt out of control and it seemed like her mind and body agreed.

"She lost her family—she's acting out," her aunt would say in a hushed voice, but Kate knew she didn't believe it herself. After one too many foster homes, she'd been grateful when the judge let her live on her own.

She sat up now, still trembling from the memories and not exactly sure she was out of the teeth of the dream. It used to come once a year on the anniversary of the accident. This year, she'd had one every single night since and her twenty-third birthday hovered days away.

She'd begun to dread sleep and the night, even as she was equally drawn to it.

And she rarely felt tired, which was odd. Her senses got sharper, she did her job better and the restlessness clawed at her until she felt as though she might combust.

Lately, the brand on her back burned all the time. She ran hot and cold, ached so badly at night she ended up pacing the floor of her basement apartment, flipping absently through the books on witchcraft she'd bought a month earlier, drawn to them inexplicably.

She knew it was too dangerous to go out alone at night. She knew all about the monsters. Knew they weren't relegated to only the night . . .

But the night—the moon—sometimes she'd stand and stare at it for hours. She sketched it. Painted it. Filled pages of her personal sketchbook with it.

Sometimes she swore she heard wolves howling.

Tonight's dream had been the most vivid, the most disturbing. She still smelled the acrid smoke in her nostrils. It made her go around the apartment to make sure nothing was on fire.

When the phone rang, she jumped, still in that place of half sleep, and for the first time since she'd met Officer Shimmin, she didn't want to pick up the phone and talk to him.

But she did.

"There's been another one." Something made him sound different, like he was trying too hard to keep his tone level, and fear gripped her with icy fingers. She brushed the back of her neck with her palm to wipe away the thin sheen of sweat on her skin, despite the fact that it was chilly outside and pretty cold inside this basement apartment as well.

It was dark, but the streetlamp shone through the sheer curtain on the window. Her back throbbed—she was certain the brand was now bright red. And lately that was happening more and more frequently, like something inside of her was attempting to turn on.

It scared the crap out of her.

"I'm sending men for you," Leo Shimmin continued. That was new, because he always came himself. Always. But in and of itself, that wasn't enough to make her feel the burst of fear in her chest. "Kate, are you listening?"

"Yes. Sorry—I'm just . . . I'll look for the car," she lied, then hung up and turned off the phone. For a long moment, she stared down at the sketch she'd done earlier of the man who'd protected her, and she wished he was here to help her.

Which was ridiculous. She'd learned long ago to depend on no one but herself.

She checked the clock. It was just after eleven p.m. She'd fallen asleep less than forty minutes earlier.

She dressed quickly. Left everything behind except her

wallet, her Mace and her sketchbook, not stopping to pick up the few loose pages that came out. Everything in her apartment was shaking from her stress, and it got so bad the walls started to crack. She was sure the building would come down on her head if she stayed longer.

She made it out the doorway on the other side of her small apartment, one she never used since it led to the middle of a creepy alleyway. Tonight she didn't care, but the panic threatened to overtake her. Kate forced herself to calm down before she did nothing but spin her wheels. Took a few deep breaths and then got her shit together.

She went down the alley as silently as she could and realized she had absolutely nowhere to go. No friends. Nothing.

She refused to go back. There was a motel by the hospital. She would cut through the woods so the police wouldn't see her as they cruised the streets. She knew Shimmin would send officers to look for her.

She felt the panic ease slightly when she took a momentary look up at the sky. The half-moon seemed to shimmer and she felt as if the brand pushed her toward the moon.

She was finally going in the right direction.

Stray stayed up late, broke into Kate's CPS files to read the interviews. It seemed that Kate had too many needs, like the recurring nightmares, and weird things occurred around her.

He found a video on YouTube of ghost hunters who'd helped her foster family investigate for poltergeist activity and found a significant problem. One that disappeared when Kate moved out.

There was never a poltergeist. Kate was the cause of the problems. Stray was sure of it. And Jinx agreed with him after looking at the evidence.

Stray left the house that afternoon with a sense of purpose, like he'd known he'd find something. It was dangerous for him to be walking the streets the way he had, but they'd all agreed it would be more dangerous if he didn't. Of all the

Dires, he was the least known. A tall, lean Dire killing machine with the chiseled good looks of a model wrapped up in a hell of an attitude. The chip on his shoulder was more like a cement block. Had been for as long as he could remember and he didn't see it changing anytime soon.

He managed to break into Kate's file from three years earlier, which was about an assault she survived with no memory of her attacker, according to the police report. The accompanying picture made him sit up and take notice.

There were claw marks along her calf. Four of them. Made by a wolf.

He broke into a sweat as he stared at it. He wasn't the only one who knew she was a witch, not by a long shot.

As if Kate somehow agreed, she called to him. He couldn't explain how, but she was pulling at him. Needing him. It was a strong enough sense of panicked urgency to get him up and moving, out of the Dire mansion before dusk and speeding on his custom Harley that he'd tuned to be as sleek a predator as he was.

This could be a trap, but spells didn't necessarily work on him. He'd tread carefully. Parked the bike in an alley and scented the person—woman—who needed him.

Kate lived here. He'd have known it even if he hadn't swiped the address from her files. He broke into the back door from the alley and felt the building shaking. The lights in the hallway dimmed and the floorboards quaked.

Usually, when he smelled witch, he went in the other direction. Now he was following his nose like she had him on a leash. But he stopped momentarily, because his gut told him she'd left the building not that long ago.

She lived alone. The only person who would miss her would be Leo Shimmin.

This would be his only shot. Stray was shocked the trappers left her unprotected, but maybe they didn't know what they had. Either that, or they figured the Dires had no clue as to Kate's existence.

He still needed to know what had happened inside her apartment to make her run, so he pushed forward.

It wasn't unlike last night's hunt. But this time, his prey was entirely human and surprised as hell when he slammed through the door.

The men looked from the pages they held to Stray, and Stray didn't hesitate. In seconds, he had them, backs against the wall, held by their necks, asking, "Where's Kate?"

Neither man answered, and when Stray looked down at the page the man held in his hand, he realized it was a sketch—and that he was looking at a drawing of himself.

"Who are you working for?" he demanded, and Vice came up behind him. Stray had heard his Dire brother's bike behind his, trailing him here. He'd never been more grateful to be watched over.

"Trappers?" Vice asked, and the scent of terror both men gave off confirmed it.

"Don't know, but I've got to find Kate."

Vice took the sketch and looked from it to Stray. "Nice picture. She managed to make you look good."

"Fuck you," Stray muttered as he let go of the men to grab the paper from Vice. He tucked it inside his jacket.

"Go ahead." Vice cracked his knuckles as he stared at the two men who coughed and were attempting to actually run from Vice. "We'll have fun together."

Vice liked it when they ran. All the wolves did. Stray knew these trappers wouldn't survive the next five minutes. Normally he'd want to try to get more intel from them, but this time he didn't care.

He would not let them get Kate. The instinct to save her burned hot through his blood and the intensity would've frightened him if it hadn't felt so right.

It's for Rogue. For all his brothers, he told himself, and it was, but it was way goddamned more than that.

He bared his teeth, canines elongating as he caught Kate's scent. The smell of human—weretrapper—was heavy in the air. He caught sight of police cars moving slowly up and down the street, searching.

He was faster and he had no doubt she was in the woods.

He went through the door that led to the alley, following Kate's scent, but there was more to it than that. He sensed her, as surely as if she'd called his name out loud. It was odd and had never happened to him before, beyond his brothers. And certainly that had never felt like this.

She was really scared, running for her life. His canines lengthened as he ran in human form. Brother Wolf wanted his turn, but Kate didn't need to come face-to-face with a wolf now. She was terrified enough.

He stopped. Listened. Felt her presence close by. Took several more silent steps and came up behind her, realizing at the same time that they'd been followed by more trappers.

Hopefully, Vice was on his six too. If not, Stray could handle the trappers. By this point, he was so worked up that he welcomed the opportunity. For him, hunting and sex held a similar pleasure, and the wolf was more than ready for either.

There, Brother Wolf said. He was in front of Kate in seconds, held her arm and put a hand over her mouth until she registered that it was him. Even then, she struggled, which was weird since her call still echoed in his mind. Brother Wolf growled a welcome inside his head, and Stray pulled her behind him as two weretrappers crashed through the trees and into the small clearing in front of them.

"Don't run from me. I'll make sure you get out of this safely. Just don't run," he warned her.

He turned and heard her feet crunching on the leaves behind him.

Son of a—

"Get him," the man said, and the woman with the Taser approached him, said, "Come on, little wolf."

Stray simply smiled at her. Reached out and grabbed the Taser before she could react. Read her mind.

It's a Dire, she told herself as her face drained of color.

He hated being recognized, but he wouldn't have to worry about them any longer. The Dires' no-kill rule didn't extend to this branch of humankind. They'd tortured and killed too many wolfkind for him to take pity on them.

And still, without knowing his name, Kate called for Stray inside his mind.

He Tasered the woman and then the man, broke their necks cleanly—a more humane death than they deserved—and stripped them of clothing and ID. Vice showed then, took the bundle from him. "Go get her. I'll get rid of these."

Stray ran in Kate's direction, determined not to let her go this time.

He would save her. And then ruin her life forever.

It started to pour as Kate ran deeper into the woods. She slogged through the wet earth, the only sounds, her feet slapping the mud. She could barely see.

She didn't stop even when she was sure her lungs would explode, not until she saw two figures pop up in front of her. Then she pulled up short.

"Kate, please, what's wrong?" It was Leo Shimmin. He wore his uniform, had his gun in his hand. And he wasn't alone.

"There are people . . . after me," she managed before she remembered that she should be running from him as well. The look on his face told her that things weren't right here. The fact that he'd been lying in wait for her in the woods confirmed it.

"Just let me help you," he said. "You need to come with me. For your own good."

Bitch should've stayed in her apartment and this would've gone fine . . .

She'd never concentrated on reading his mind because he was a police officer and probably thought about a lot of confidential information. And after that initial thought, she couldn't read his thoughts again, even as she tried. It was as if he knew what she'd done and dropped a brick wall between them.

Still, she absolutely knew he was responsible for what was happening to her.

"Just stay back," she told him. When he didn't, she put both hands out, fast and instinctive, her anger bubbling over to the point where she felt unstable inside her own body. Watched two grown men fly backward as though pushed by some cosmic force.

By your force.

She spoke words she didn't know—a chant, a prayer—out loud. Words the woman who'd pulled her from the fire had said, words that replayed themselves in her mind as she stared at the unconscious men, even as her protector came up next to her.

Had he seen what she'd done? If so, he gave no indication, merely put his hand out to her.

This time, she took it and didn't let go.

Chapter 5

Jinx watched the ghosts glide through the convenience store as he pretended to shop. The damned town was practically vibrating and the full moon approached too fast.

He and Vice were selective in their jobs now, focusing on those entities who might give them intel. And they just kept getting the same story over and over. Dire army of raised spirits. Unnatural. Rifter continued to dream of the ghost army, despite the dreamcatcher . . . and he couldn't get back to dreamwalk with Rogue, even with Gwen's help.

Jinx felt like half of him was missing. Tonight he'd left without telling the others, something he wasn't supposed to do, but he couldn't stay on lockdown forever. He'd waited until Rifter and Gwen had gone into honeymoon mode before he split.

Rifter could kill him later.

Now Jinx left his cart, full of crap he'd thrown in just to look like a shopper, and he pushed out into the night. There was nothing new to learn here and the feeling of unrest boiled through him like a fever.

A lot had changed in a matter of weeks. Hell, a lot had changed in the past twenty-four hours, ensuring they all needed backup wherever they went.

We've got a bead on a witch, Brother Wolf reminded him. *We're good.*

But Jinx had the strangest feeling they were far from it. He felt useless, but grateful that Stray had found a witch, since they didn't have time to waste. In the meantime, he'd done some research of his own on Kate Walters and discovered whom she'd gotten her powers from, wasn't sure when the best time was to break it to the others. If there ever was.

Vice was watching Stray, and Jinx was headed home to help him. Or he'd planned to be, until an energy buzzed through him that was too strong to ignore. He drove along as his skin buzzed, the truck taking the icy roads easily as he reached for his phone to dial Vice.

"They're here. Close. I can feel them." His voice sounded strangled even to his own ears and he ignored it in favor of chasing down the elusive army.

"I'll meet you." Vice's voice sounded slightly strained.

"Where are you?"

"Taking care of some trappers. The witch called for Stray. I think they've bonded."

"Stay close to Stray and the witch. I can do this on my own." The need to find the ghosts was more urgent now than ever. His lungs felt compressed, like he was breathing at half strength, and he pushed the pedal down harder, anxious to arrive where he needed to be and not caring if he was in one piece when he got there.

He had to do his part. He'd failed to get the witch. He couldn't fail at this.

"I don't like the way you sound," Vice told him.

"I don't like the way I feel. But they're not getting away this time. Christ, if they're back in full force this early—"

Vice spoke over him. "You're not supposed to—"

"Ghost hunt alone. I know. But I need this information. If I don't go now, I'll lose it. And you have work of your own to do . . ."

He trailed off and Vice was silent. They both knew that

disturbing Rifter and Gwen now wasn't acceptable—they'd barely gotten a proper mating time. None of the wolves would've wanted to stop that, even if it meant their lives, because Rifter would have their heads. Literally.

"We've all got our jobs tonight," he said finally, barely able to hear himself over the buzzing.

"I'll watch over the witch. You check in as soon as you can," Vice warned.

"Yes, Mother." Jinx hung up before Vice could curse at him, and let the scent of blood lead him to the scene of the crime he knew existed.

Finding out why would be the next step.

Chapter 6

Kate clung to her protector's hand as he led her out of the woods and into a huge black truck. She shivered as he started the car and blasted the heat.

He grabbed a blanket from the backseat for her before gunning the truck and putting enough distance between them and what she'd seen to feel a little more comfortable.

"I don't even know your name," she said finally, feeling more than a little stupid.

"It's Stray."

She didn't bother to ask if that was a first or last name, assumed it was a nickname because who had a real name like that? But she was in no position to question because she was soaked and freezing and being chased. "Stray, maybe we should go to the police station—"

"The police are the ones who are after you—you saw that for yourself," Stray reminded her as he numbly maneuvered the vehicle through the wet roads without the car losing speed or feeling out of control.

Unlike her, who was seriously spinning right now. She pulled the blanket tighter, put her face close to the vent so the warm air blew against her cheeks.

"We're almost there; then I can get you some dry

clothes," Stray told her as the truck began to make a slow, grinding climb up a hill. And then, suddenly, he stopped the car and turned to her. "I'm going to put a blindfold on you. It's for your own safety."

Could she even argue? Before she had a chance to, he was tying a bandanna over her eyes and securing it, and then the truck moved again. She heard a garage door open, then close, and then Stray cut the engine.

She heard him get out and shut his own door, and she had a second to reach up and grab the cloth over her eyes. But somehow he was opening her door and reaching for her hand faster than he should have been able to.

"Let's go."

He helped her down, her sneakers squishing on the floor. He put his hands on her shoulders and walked her forward ahead of him as the odd feeling overtook her. There was something in the air—if she didn't know better, she'd call it magic.

But the blindfold was making her too claustrophobic to focus on much of anything else and so she allowed Stray to guide her, his hands on her shoulders.

She forced herself to keep going, not to collapse in an embarrassing heap, but she knew she soon would. She could tell by the way her body still shook.

Before that happened, she found herself in a soft, comfortable chair. The blindfold came off and a soda was in her hands.

The light in the room was low enough to allow her eyes to adjust easily. She drank the sugared soda greedily as she got her bearings.

They were in a big living room in what she believed to be a giant house, based on how tall the ceilings were. It was clean, and dare she even say cozy, thanks to the roaring fire.

And still, the low-level hum of energy zinged through

her. The brand was reacting, but it wasn't hurting the way it normally did when she felt danger of any kind.

But you are in danger.

"You are in danger, yes. But you'll be okay here," Stray told her.

She was about to ask him if he was a mind reader when she realized she hadn't been able to read *his* mind. At all.

Maybe a better question for Stray would be, *What are you?*

"Stay here. I'm going to get you dry clothes and then we'll talk." When he left the room, she peeled off her wet shoes and socks, but kept the blanket draped over her shoulders, and padded around the living room. Her skin was clammy and she'd welcome the chance to change, but where was she?

They hadn't driven for much longer than twenty minutes. Then again, he could've been driving in circles—she'd been too distracted to notice.

The one time she really did need to break into someone's mind and she couldn't do it. What were the chances of that happening?

She turned to see him standing behind her. How such a big man moved so silently was beyond her, but he did.

He held out folded clothing to her. "I know they'll be big, but they're dry."

A T-shirt that was more than huge, a flannel shirt that was equally so and sweats she'd need to roll up several times at both the waist and the legs. She took them gratefully and followed to where he pointed at the large bathroom down the hall. She wanted to strip, dry off, change quickly. Instead, she sat on the edge of the tub and put her face against the flannel that, although clean, still smelled like Stray, and when she inhaled, the brand on her back flared ... with pleasure.

Weird.

Yeah, like the rest of the night had been so normal.

*   *   *

Stray scented Vice—and weretrappers' blood—before he heard the house unarm and rearm with the wolf's entry. In seconds, he saw the Dire round the hallway and step into the kitchen. He dropped whatever he'd been holding, followed in short order by his leather jacket.

The cold rain had washed Vice semi-clean, save for the mud he tracked all through the house. "Dude, now, that's what I call a good night. Is she here? The witch?" Vice asked as he took off the heavy black boots he'd worn for the ass kicking. Stray pointed to the bathroom. "What, did you chain her up?"

Stray sighed. "She's changing. I saw her push Shimmin and one of his men—with her mind. She threw them ten feet."

Killing Shimmin wasn't an option. Thanks to a witch's spell, Shimmin's blood was poison to Weres. And although Shimmin's blood wasn't deadly to Dires, it might have been able to incapacitate Stray long enough for him to be taken prisoner. Although it had killed Stray to leave the man behind, he had the most important piece of the puzzle safe and sound.

"Did they see you?"

"I don't think so, but I can't be sure."

"And they were both gone by the time I got there," Vice confirmed. "I'm sure by now he's gone to her apartment and figured it out partially. I didn't leave any traces of them or us, but hell, some Weres can scent me. If Shimmin brought a trained dog to the apartment . . ."

Vice trailed off and Stray figured all they could do was wait and see Shimmin's next move.

"Doesn't much matter—we have the most important thing." Stray glanced toward the bathroom door. The windows were all alarmed, and while he wasn't worried about her leaving without him noticing, he knew escape was definitely on her mind and he had to do something to change it. "She's reeling."

"Don't see how she couldn't be." Vice shrugged out of the rest of his wet clothes and strode to the fridge naked.

"Dude, you need to leave in case she comes out here—she's already on edge."

Vice looked nonchalant as he chugged chocolate milk. "Killing weretrappers makes me hungry. You gonna tell her she's a witch now?"

"Can't think of a better time. It's going to be the only explanation she'll buy. She's far from stupid."

"She's hot, too." Vice took a step back. "What? I saw a picture of her in her apartment. And I'm stating a fact. Down, wolf."

Stray hated the way his wolf reacted, but there was no denying it wasn't only the wolf. No, his other form was protective of her as well.

"Hey—I grabbed these books from her apartment." Vice pointed to two wet paperbacks with the word *witch* in the title that lay next to his jacket. "They're kind of how-to guides. So maybe she knows something."

Stray scooped them up and paged through them as he brought them into the bedroom where Kate would stay. He'd bring them up to her after he got Vice away from here. But the wolf seemed in no rush and was still eating straight out of the fridge.

"You know, if I'd seen Shimmin, his throat would've been ripped out, poison or no poison," Vice assured him, his mouth half full of tortellini salad.

It had been a seemingly perfect opportunity for Stray to do so as well, but that could've cost him Kate's trust. Besides, Shimmin wasn't the only problem they had with the weretrappers—not by a long shot. Rumors that other covens had recently joined Seb in exchange for protection from wolves and humans were more than that—the twins had reported seeing witches entering the trappers' make-shift compound, and Stray had broken into a server where the witches were discussing what they would do for the trappers.

"Go get dressed, man. I need Kate to have some privacy when I tell her everything."

Vice took the chocolate milk bottle with him and bare assed it out of the kitchen, saying, "I'll bring the others up to speed while you work your magic, young one. Do you need any pointers?"

"Fuck you, old man—I know what I'm doing."

Vice shot him the finger and turned the corner.

Kate thought she'd been holding it together really well.

She'd been wrong. Now that she wasn't running for her life, her body was rebelling. Her legs shook and her panic refreshed itself. She didn't know how long she'd just stood there, but when she decided to finally move, her head spun. She put a hand out to catch herself and then Stray was there, holding her up, despite the fact that she'd locked the door and checked it several times.

"This is becoming a habit," she muttered, even as she clutched his arms.

"Let me help you."

She wanted to tell him she could damn well dress herself, but she'd already proven she couldn't. Her cheeks burned as his hands deftly moved her shirt off her shoulders, then unhooked her bra expertly before forgoing the T-shirt and opting to help her put on just the flannel shirt.

She didn't know if his gaze settled on her naked breasts or not, because she refused to look at him until he pulled the fabric together to cover them.

His scent enveloped her. Intoxicated her. She watched, mesmerized, as he held her up with one arm and buttoned the shirt one handed, reluctant, it seemed, to button it up all the way. His hand brushed over the top of her breast and she shivered—he did too—and finally he had covered her up nearly to her neck.

But then his hands slid down to her hips, skimming her bare skin, and she almost hit the ceiling. His gaze smoldered as he hooked his thumbs in the waist of her jeans and underwear and tugged both down.

"Relax. I don't bite unless you want me to," he murmured.

God, she wanted . . .

She blew out a soft, nervous laugh and kept watching him as he maneuvered her to sit on the tub's edge again and then bent to put the sweatpants on. The top was long enough to cover her but she'd never felt more exposed in her life.

"I can run you a bath later. First you need food." His voice surrounded her like the promise of the soothing warm water.

She nodded because she didn't quite trust her voice yet—or him, entirely—but for immediate survival, it was necessary. Finally, she managed, "I'm not used to being helped."

"Except by Shimmin."

He sounded . . . jealous.

"Should I be?" he asked with a possessiveness that raced through her blood.

"No. Not at all."

He appeared satisfied with her answer. "You need to get used to help."

With that, he helped her up, gathered her wet, discarded clothing in his free hand and led her into the kitchen. "I'll wash your clothes—you need to eat."

She didn't bother protesting, because her stomach rumbled and she needed food so she could wrap her mind around whatever was happening here. She needed to keep her strength up in case she had to run—or fight—again.

"Why are you doing this?" she asked as they crossed the

first giant room and went into an even bigger kitchen with shiny stainless-steel appliances everywhere and dark wood cabinets.

"Because my brothers and I need your help."

At least he didn't lie. "With what, exactly, can I help you? Do you need a sketch artist?" Even as she spoke, her brand burned. She resisted the urge to put her hand back there and feel for it. "And how did you know I was in danger tonight?"

"You called for me."

"No, I didn't."

"You sketched me," he pointed out. She flushed as he pulled out the pages that had dropped from her sketchbook and handed them to her.

He'd been at her apartment looking for her. "You're a good-looking man. It wasn't a hardship drawing you."

He gave her a small smirk even though she swore she saw a slight rise of color on his cheeks.

"You want to tell me why you ran?" he asked.

"Which time?"

"Both." He pointed to a chair and she sat at the big, scarred oak table. He grabbed a bottle of juice from the fridge—her favorite kind—and asked, "This okay?"

She nodded. He also laid out sandwich meats and bread on the table between them and made a lot of sandwiches. Like he was expecting an army.

He pushed a sandwich toward her. In between bites, she started to talk about the phone call and her panic in her apartment. "I know it doesn't make sense, but I just felt . . . something was wrong."

"It was," he said, halfway through his fifth sandwich. He ate calmly, slowly. But, man, could he eat.

She realized her body had stopped trembling. "Will they really not find me here?"

"Not in the house, no."

"Are you some kind of . . . secret agent or something?"

He snorted. "Hardly."

"Don't get me wrong—I'm grateful you helped me. But Leo Shimmin . . . he's not going to stop looking for me, and I don't understand any of this. Maybe I screwed up a case or something? I mean, he's never been anything but good to me."

"Then why did you run when he called?" he asked.

She had no real answer for that, except that she'd followed her gut. And ultimately, that had saved her life.

Chapter 7

Seb heard Leo come into the compound, knew the head of the trappers would rush immediately to him for retribution.

The witch called Kate had escaped because of the Dires. Seb's familiar had told him the story earlier and Seb had thrown himself into his other work rather than worry about the wrath he'd face because of the loss.

He'd been bringing the Dire ghost army through their first training exercise. For tonight, they'd been let loose upon the dead only, and it took every last bit of power Seb had to keep the reins on them. Getting them to attack the living was the next step—and it would require help.

Meeting the ghosts face-to-face was like being in Rifter's past—one he'd heard so much about when they'd been best friends for centuries, Seb felt as though he'd lived it alongside the Dire king. Now he was signing something akin to Rifter's death warrant as much as he was his own.

He wished the demon that possessed his body would drag him to hell, because he'd rather that than dealing with this.

You always knew it would happen—could've taken steps to avoid it.

But he hadn't, and he was paying.

He'd been brutally punished—deservedly so—for sending Leo's brother, Mars, into the fray and letting him get killed by Rifter and Gwen. It would be the last time Seb helped any of the Dires. He'd continued to let punishments be meted out to him because the demon liked it that way.

Seb was turning into a puppet who had no control of his own strings—hand shoved into his back like a bad episode of *Angel*.

At least he'd finally gotten the demon to admit who he'd been in life—a powerful warlord who deserved to burn in hell. Problem was, the warlord liked hell far too much to think of it as punishment. As he was in life, he remained in death, and Seb was now taking the full brunt of his punishments.

The demon called himself *Kondo*, which was the Swahili word for war.

Fitting.

"The witch escaped!" Seb heard Leo Shimmin yelling as he got closer. "My best men are dead. It could've only been the Dires."

Seb agreed but didn't say so out loud. Kondo did speak, though, and Leo wasn't happy.

When the man kicked through the door to Seb's cage, as Seb thought of the octagon-shaped room at the top of the tower three towns over from the Dire mansion, Seb stood and readied himself for battle. The demon laughed softly in his ear.

"You said the brand would mark me as the one." Leo spoke through gritted teeth as he attempted to menace Seb. "You said it would work."

"*Might* work. Kate's witch is strong. Discerning. I can't change destiny." Seb pushed Leo on the chest with both hands and the cop nearly flew across the room.

Leo hadn't sold his soul the way his brother had. Mars

had been strong because he'd allowed a demon to possess him. Gwen had killed him easily because the demon had vacated Mars's body before she'd borne down on him. Leo had refused the possession option; instead, his mind was guarded against witches' spells, his blood poison to wolves, but he remained completely mortal and still in need of the immortal demon bodyguard who went everywhere with him.

"She threw Finn across the damned woods," Leo said. "You said she wouldn't be strong enough to do that to a demon at this point."

"I guess I was wrong. These powers are unpredictable."

Leo Shimmin's plans were less so, and so far-reaching, they chilled Seb to the bone. Capturing, experimenting on and killing wolves were horrible enough. But the weretrappers' reign of terror had expanded exponentially since they had gained Seb's help to include raising demons to possess, influence and use politicians for their personal gain.

So the attack against humans and wolves was many pronged. Shimmin was looking for domination by using the supernatural—and smartly left lion shifters, vamps and most witches out of the equation.

Those groups were currently flying under the radar, and word was, if they stayed out of the weretrappers' way, they'd be left alone. Since those groups had no use for humans or wolves, their way of life wouldn't be affected and their leaders were advising they turn a blind eye and let the wolves fight their own battles.

Hell, even Weres, the form of the outlaw pack, were selling out their own kind and blaming the Dires in an attempt to save themselves.

The weretrappers had succeeded in fracturing the supernatural world and using that divide for their own massive gain.

The main flaw in the trappers' plan that would return to bite everyone in the ass was the use of the dark arts. Although the Dires knew they could survive anything, going up against evil forces and legions of the dead was a deadly distraction, one that Seb had planned carefully.

But the demons and the dead could quickly override his power and take over humans themselves.

There would be no winners in this war.

Leo paced the room, muttering to himself. After several minutes, he'd regained some kind of inner calm. "What's set in motion remains. Nothing else matters."

That was a partial truth. Seb was raising an army that could capture the Dires, kill Weres and help enslave armies. "The Dire army is practicing," Seb assured him. "Growing stronger, more organized. The Dires are still working on a way to stop them."

"With this army, I can get the money I need and the power will follow. The wolves that hunted us will be under control and our ancestors will be happy," Leo said. "And then, once we have Manhattan under our thumb, we issue an ultimatum—bow to us or we'll do the same things to you. For years, we've been working to have this all come into play. Now we have all the pieces, except the female witch."

"She's too green. She can't stop an army by herself," Seb assured him. "I'm stronger—and totally under control, as you well know. The full moon will be here before we know it and I'll be able to rein in its power to assist the ghost army. The Dires are simply grasping at straws."

"They've brought in backup," Leo muttered.

"I'm aware of Killian." Seb moved to confront Leo now, some newfound sense of power coursing through him. "Now get the fuck out and let me do my job. You might think I'm your trained monkey, but you'd be sadly mistaken."

At first he thought Leo would hit him and then, just as suddenly as the cop's temper flared, his smile broke through. "You've got balls, witch. Maybe you're finally realizing my team's the one to beat after all."

Seb had played with fire and he'd gotten third-degree burns.

It was nothing compared to what would happen to the rest of the world. And he could never atone enough.

Kate looked tense, lost and tired. Her eating had finally slowed and Stray told her, "You probably need some rest. I'll show you where you can lie down for a while."

She nodded and got up from the table slowly. Her shoulders were in a tense square and she moved a little stiffly.

"Are you hurt?"

"I fell when I was running. My knee's a little stiff from sitting," she admitted.

He grabbed an ice pack from the fridge and then helped her into the first floor's extra bedroom.

"Get comfortable," he told her. He helped her up onto the bed and she moved back against the pillows and the headboard as she looked around.

"You've got a really, um, nice place here. Big, too."

"It works for us," he said as he pulled up the leg of her sweats. Her knee was bruised but not too badly swollen. He placed the ice bag on it, wrapped in a towel. "I'll have Gwen look at it in the morning. She's a doctor—she's married to one of my brothers."

The fact that another woman lived in the house seemed to ease her worries a little.

"So it's just you and Gwen and one of your brothers?" she asked.

"More than one brother. You'll meet them soon enough."

"Do they know about what happened tonight? About me?"

He nodded. "One of them was with me when we got to your apartment. You were right to take off when you did. You should always trust your gut."

"I'm beginning to understand that." She gave him a wan smile.

She looked better in his clothes than she should have

and not all that vulnerable, despite the situation. Her hair was drying in loose waves that tumbled over her shoulders and her eyes looked a little more copper than brown.

Brother Wolf gave a soft growl in his ear, didn't want to leave the witch either. He'd have to remind his wolf that they didn't like witch, but at the moment, he was having trouble remembering why.

Kate shifted on the mattress. She should've been exhausted, but she was wired on adrenaline and sugar. Stray loomed over her. She had an unnatural urge to touch his hand, stroke his jaw, run a finger along his lips.

She did none of those things, told him instead, "Look, I really didn't call you for help tonight." But . . . she had flashed to him in her mind, gave a brief thought to how protected he'd made her feel.

And then, in the woods, had he seen what she'd done?

"I did see you throw men with your mind," he said.

"What? How did you—"

Same as you.

His voice, in her head. The trembling was back. Her legs shook so badly, she couldn't think about moving.

Calm down.

"I couldn't . . . before . . ."

"You can't read my mind unless I let you," Stray confirmed. And maybe it was because of everything that happened that night or because she was tired of hiding what she could do, but she was actually excited at the thought of finding a kindred spirit.

"Why are you letting me in now?"

"It's time to explain a few things to you. But first, tell me how long you've been able to read minds and influence your environment with telekinesis."

She hadn't been thinking about that last part at all, and somehow Stray knew. "Since my accident ten years ago, I've been able to read minds. The telekinesis started before that.

I can move things—especially when I'm angry or scared—but not people."

"Not until tonight," he reminded her.

"Since you know so much about me, tell me, what kind of freak am I?"

"You really don't know," he murmured, less a question and seeming like more of an affirmation to himself.

"If you do, please share."

"You're a witch, Kate."

"A ... what?"

"Witch."

Witch.

The brand on her back flared, but it wasn't unpleasant this time. It was like a recognition. Everything swirled in her thoughts—the accident, the chant, and she couldn't deny what she was any longer.

Still, she denied it to him. "You're wrong. I'm psychic, but I don't practice witchcraft."

"You suspected what you might be." He opened the drawer and brought out the books she'd purchased two months ago. "My brother found them in your apartment—they've been well-read. Over and over, but up to a certain point. You knew, and it scared you."

"No." She backed up fast but he was on her. There was no real place for her to go anyway. "Please stop. I think you might be crazy."

"I'm not. Neither are you." He studied her for a long moment.

"How can you know this? Did you come to my apartment tonight because of what you think I am?"

"What I know you are," he corrected. "I came because I knew you were in danger. When I touched your back this afternoon, something happened between us. You felt it too."

Yes, she had. She squeezed her hands into fists as the anger rose inside of her, and she wasn't sure who it was directed toward more—herself, Leo Shimmin or Stray for what he was telling her.

"You suspected you were a witch," he repeated. "Who told you what you might be? Shimmin?"

She shook her head as memories flooded her. The psychic had told her she wasn't crazy, that she was powerful. If Shimmin knew that . . .

What if everything he'd done for her had been a ploy to gain her trust, to use her? But for what?

"Mind reading's a powerful ability in and of itself," Stray told her. "The telekinesis adds to it."

And to top it off, he claimed she was a witch.

You are, the voice inside of her said, and she'd heard it before, once, a long time ago.

She shut her eyes tight as the anger and frustration flashed through her. She was losing control. Or perhaps she'd never had any. She sank to the ground and Stray caught her. Lights flashed and she lost her sight of the present as she sank deep into the past.

She put her hands over her ears, knowing it wouldn't stop the screech of tires or the sound of metal crunching metal—and bone.

By this time, Stray's arms were around her and she was aware of being on the floor—but it was the floor of the car, where she'd gotten wedged, one arm almost pinned, useless. She'd managed to extricate it and the sight of the blood made her gag.

Her adrenaline was so high, the pain hadn't set in yet, wouldn't really until she woke again in the hospital, hooked to machines and pumped full of narcotics that made her drowsy. But now she was trapped, and the claustrophobia and complete panic had her flailing.

"We're burning," she told Stray. She opened her eyes but couldn't see him, could only feel the reassuring forearm muscles she gripped tightly as if he could save her from everything. She tried to stand, but the smell of gasoline overpowered her. The smoke was thick, cloaked her in a choking cloud when she opened her mouth to scream again for Mom or Dad . . .

Her hands went to her throat as she gagged. She screwed her eyes shut tight and the world swirled around her like the Tilt-A-Whirl she'd ridden at the county fair. She'd never get her footing again.

She was only thirteen and was sure she was going to die.

Chapter 8

Jinx drove for the better part of an hour after hanging up with Vice, bypassing the closest cemetery in town to one on the outskirts of another and finally, at a third, the intense feeling of being crushed made him slam the truck into park and step out to skid on the ice.

Brother Wolf let out a howl to wake his other half up, but Jinx was too dazed. He never lost his footing, but it was as if he'd had too much to drink. Although the night around him was calm, he smelled the scent of blood carried in the cold air. He shuffled onto the grassy area, which was soaked and a little icy from the recent rains, bypassed the locked wrought-iron gate with the flick of his hand on the old chain and lock.

His hand bled from breaking the metal, but he ignored it and moved forward.

"Father, you need to help me help you," he called out, and then said a prayer in the old language that his mother made him and Rogue say every night before bed. He'd said it every time he entered a cemetery for as long as he could remember. It was his touchstone.

Deadly silence from the dead was never good, but the buzz got so bad he stumbled and fell to his knees at some point, came up like he was praying. That's when he saw the first wave of ghosts about twenty-five feet from him.

He got up quickly, still off balance. Tensed as the random ghosts that normally circulated inside the iron gates greeted him. Well, to be accurate, they rushed toward him—and then past him. He felt their fury and their fear as cold air raced through his body, leaving him breathing ice and exhaling steam in their wake.

The ghosts were fleeing and there wasn't a Dire among them. And as much as he wanted to follow them, he pressed forward alone. Like he was never supposed to do.

Brother Wolf attempted to shift, to save his nonfunctioning half, but Jinx growled and resisted and the wolf gave in to Jinx's wants for the moment. But the wolf howled his displeasure when Jinx began to run and then stopped short when he came upon the reason for the mass ghost exodus.

He blinked through the scene in front of him, bile rising in his throat as the smell of blood became overpowering.

There were ghost corpses littering the ground next to real ones, newly buried humans unearthed and desecrated. All done on what was supposed to be the most sacred kind of hallowed ground.

They were old and young and everything in between, dressed in torn gowns and suits, battered and bloodied and terrified. Seeing the children was the worst.

He stood among the ruins of bodies ripped apart and scattered as if by an animal.

As if by *wolves.*

He moved forward to see if he could view the marks on the ghosts' nearly corporeal bodies, his legs like lead and Brother Wolf's growls in his ears.

He couldn't have missed the deep, massive wounds. He stretched a hand out and pictured Brother Wolf's paw.

These marks were made by a Dire. The Dire ghost army was back with a vengeance. This army could slaughter supernatural beings of its own kind—ghosts—as well as humans, and Jinx knew that what he was seeing was simply a practice round.

This was some kind of training ground exercise. How many cemeteries had the ghost army marched through tonight? How many more would they conquer?

There was nothing he could do to stop them, but he knew he'd have to follow the ghost army, track their destruction. The ghost corpses left out in their wake would have to be sent into the light and Jinx would need more help to get them there. For now, they would remain in the world, lost, confused and wreaking havoc on the living, although not nearly as much as the Dire army promised to do.

"Father . . . why?" he started, although there was no sign of any other Dire. "You needed to fight this. Why are you letting Seb use you this way?"

His father had been a great warrior, albeit a beta, not an alpha like his twin sons. Whether that was the reason behind his rough treatment of his boys was something Jinx often thought about.

The tingle started—there *was* someone left behind.

"Show yourself," he commanded, began the familiar chant he'd worked up to pull his father's ghost to him. It had taken four days to create the spell and, thus far, it hadn't worked for shit.

This time, it did.

He turned to see his father's form. Last time it had barely held it shape, but this time the lines were crisper. The apparition had gained strength. "Why did you stay behind?"

"I knew you were coming," his father said.

"You were a part of this?" Jinx asked, sweeping his arm over the destruction. His father nodded. God, he was going to be sick. His body trembled at the overpowering urge to get the fuck out of the cemetery and town and hide in the mountains, let the world go fuck itself.

Because suddenly everything crystallized for him, and

he understood what had happened in a way he didn't want to believe.

"It was wonderful to use the warrior ways again," his father intoned.

"You said you needed my help." Jinx couldn't keep the emotion from his voice, but screw calm, cool and collected. He was back on the edge of the field where the Extinction occurred, he and Rogue searching for and ultimately finding their parents buried among mangled bodies of their kind.

"You were punished for those ways. Taken from me and Rogue. Why do it again?"

"We had no choice."

"There's always a choice. You didn't have to follow him then and you're repeating your mistake."

"Jameson was always too strong to resist." Jameson was the Dire king who'd refused to give up his throne.

"He couldn't bend your will. He had no ability beyond brute force. Violence never used to scare the man I knew as Father."

"You were naive, Jinx. You didn't realize Jameson had poisoned everyone's mind, then . . . and now."

"Are you here to kill me, Father?" Jinx spread his arms wide. "Take your best shot."

"Rifter and Harmony have far more to worry about than you now," his father warned. "Jameson wants them dead. He placed the orders for that long before the Extinction. Had you all come back hours earlier, you all would've been killed."

"And now?"

"Nothing has changed."

"You'll lead Jameson to me, to kill me?"

His father inhaled a harsh breath. "He'll find you with or without me. But first you had a special job, one you completed days ago when you summoned me with your prayer."

The prayer. Seb had turned Jinx's prayer into a spell.

It hadn't been the chant at all that had drawn Jinx's father and the rest of the ghost army but rather the last comfort of childhood Jinx had. Now that was destroyed as well, and he couldn't tell if his father was saddened or satisfied by the development.

One you completed days ago . . .

"Do you want to see the result of your work?" his father inquired and Jinx's heart sank. He'd thought he'd already seen it all, but apparently, there was more.

The rest happened so fast there wasn't time for any more talking. Instead, he sank to his knees, his mind swimming as he tried to disbelieve what was happening in front of him.

As he watched in abject horror, his father moved aside to reveal the yowling cavern. Jinx prayed this was all a dream, that Vice had slipped him some peyote without his knowledge. That had happened before when the wolf thought he needed to relax, and Jinx had made him promise never to do it again.

One you completed days ago . . .

He'd rubbed his eyes as he watched souls dance around, not seeing him at first. They were different. They hadn't crossed over. He'd never been able to see spirits, and there was no reason for him to start now.

When they spotted him, they swarmed. He'd been able only to drop to his knees and bury his head in his hands as they hammered at him with their questions and their thoughts.

They were evil beings. Not demons, but they were spawns of Satan, nonetheless. And they'd been free for days.

He'd opened the door to purgatory, freeing the Dire ghost army from where they'd been in some kind of holding pattern. But he'd released other things from purgatory as well.

He staggered backward, away from his father's ghost and away from the desecration.

Make them go, make them go, he prayed. Then Brother Wolf took over, and they dispersed at the wolf's growl. Brother ran deep into the woods, far from the cemetery, and still, Jinx heard the ghost's laughter echoing in his ears.

Chapter 9

The force of Kate's telekinetic overload was tremendous.

It was like a mini-tornado, part wind, part tsunami as the pipes in the bathroom burst and flooded the room. Stray couldn't move either of them out of the way because he was mesmerized by what he saw.

He was experiencing everything along with Kate, as though it were happening in real time. It was fucking horrifying, more so because it was as if his body were encased in cement, unmovable, even as Brother Wolf tried to force a shift.

No, Brother, he managed as his mind cleared for a second before being bombarded again with Kate's thoughts.

He wanted to pull her out of the dream—the nightmare—but he couldn't. Instead, he held her tight as he watched the woman reach in to grab Kate from the burning wreckage of the car when it should've taken the jaws of life to do so.

And then . . . she was dying. He was dying—something he'd never do otherwise. He couldn't bring himself to look away, to tear his hands from her body, because he needed to see what happened, to experience this.

The screams and the pain receded until he felt so light he could float out of the wrecked car. He no longer smelled the smoke or burning flesh, and Kate stilled in his arms. He saw her smile a little as she stared upward, and he did the same.

It had been bright, but he hadn't needed to squint. Quiet, peaceful . . . he'd floated with her and for several moments there was absolutely no pain. He wanted to stay there, and apparently Kate did too. Together, they remained so still, so fucking happy.

And then Kate looked down and screamed. He followed her gaze, watched her out-of-body experience as a woman with long dark hair threaded with white reached into the car to grab her body out with harsh tugs.

At first Kate was lifeless in the woman's arms. But when the witch dragged her out and placed her on the concrete, the pain exploded in a flash of brilliant, blinding white-hot light.

He was seeing it from Kate's vantage point, lying on the ground, the concrete hot and uncomfortable, the burns screaming for relief.

He no longer heard her parents yelling for help and Kate sobbed as he thought that, and then there was a shadow looming over Kate. The view was fuzzy now, thanks to smoke and pain. It was the woman, her long dark hair loose around her shoulders. Her eyes were piercing. There was no sense of kindness about her despite the action she'd just taken.

Instead, she was merciless, flipping Kate onto her stomach on the pavement. When her hands touched Kate's back, Kate whimpered and tried to fight and Stray's own skin seared.

"What's done is done; now our powers are one," the woman chanted three times before removing her hands. She looked into Kate's face, smiled sadly and then disappeared.

Kate was still deep into the nightmare, so much so he heard the sirens in the distance as the car exploded in front of him, the flames and debris miraculously missing her as if she'd been placed under a protective shield.

She's immortal.

He'd suspected as much, but to have it confirmed at this stage was more than he'd thought he'd discover. She must have the brand somewhere for sure. No doubt it was what his hand had made contact with earlier when he'd touched her back.

His skin still felt burned from the fire and he smelled the smoke. He looked over his arms, sure he'd find them red and blistered, but they were fine. Kate was too—physically, at least. He couldn't say the same for the room. But hell, that was repairable.

"I knew it—knew I died. I died and she pulled me from the car ... No one believed me that I should've died," she repeated over and over. "The woman saved me. The woman saved me ... said what's done is done. I wasn't wrong."

He'd never had a mind-reading experience like that, and he never wanted to again. From the second he'd touched her, they were connected. *The witch ...*

He held off the shift as long as he could, tried to tell Brother Wolf it was all good. But the wolf was there to protect him—and it did so by forcing a shift to wolf form, leaving him able to be close to Kate without feeling the pain of her memories.

But the fact was, the pain was still so visible, visceral, that even Brother Wolf howled as she shook, unable to escape her own mind, and wolf and witch remained tangled together on the floor.

Chapter 10

Stray wasn't sure how long he sat on the floor among the ruins of the guest bedroom, Kate holding Brother Wolf's fur in her grasp. He nudged her face, her neck, licked her hand, did anything he could to try to bring her around. Finally, she opened her eyes and blinked. Blinked again, and her mouth opened and closed with no words coming out.

She was in shock. He went to rub her face with a hand, to tell her to breathe.

And then he remembered that he was in goddamned wolf form and he shifted back as quickly as possible, leaving him gasping—and naked.

Thankfully, Kate had her eyes closed and was shaking her head as if that would shake the image of the wolf—of everything she'd seen tonight—from her mind. He took that opportunity to move away from her, find a pair of sweats in the laundry room and get back to her before she got herself together.

He believed now that Kate hadn't known what she was, unless she was lying inside her own head, but it took a lot of practice to do so. He was pretty sure she hadn't met up with many people who could read her mind before this.

She was unpracticed. He'd have to be careful. She

needed to know what he was, but was now really the best time?

She opened her eyes before he got to her, and she stood, faster, much more quickly than he'd have expected. "Is this the part where you try to convince me I didn't see you turn into a wolf?"

Ah, *fuck*. "Kate, listen to me."

But she was too busy holding on to the wall behind her, edging her way around him slowly. Brother Wolf growled inside his head at the thought of her running. "Stay still."

She didn't listen, kept moving, and the logical half of him told him to let her go, that she was safe in the house.

Brother Wolf had other plans. "Kate, let's talk about this."

She sidled toward the door, said, "You're an animal. Literally. An animal."

"I'm a wolf."

"No. This can't be happening. I must've been drugged or something. I'm going to wake up and find myself alone in my bed and none of this will have really happened."

"Sorry to break it to you, but everything that's happened tonight is all too real."

Kate was almost at the door. Stray stood stock-still in the middle of the destruction, bare chested, sweats hanging low enough to be very distracting despite the very real fear piercing her.

He wasn't denying what he was. A wolf. And he said it so calmly.

He's a wolf; you're a witch.

"Yes, that's right," he agreed calmly.

"I'm . . . I can read people's thoughts, but I'm not a witch."

"You are."

"I don't understand any of this. Please, if you let me leave, I won't tell anyone."

"You're a shitty liar."

"And you're a shitty captor," she challenged. "I want to leave."

"You can't. It's for your own safety."

"And you're some kind of witch bodyguard?"

Stray licked his bottom lip. "Something like that."

The brand was responding to his voice. Making her ... squirm. After what she'd just been through, what she'd learned about her rescue from the accident, that would be the last reaction she thought she'd have.

"I won't hurt you. Let me protect you, Kate."

It was what she'd wanted to hear from him—and yet she couldn't let herself believe his intentions.

Instead, she inched closer to the door, surprised he was letting her. When he spoke, his voice sent chills down her spine.

"If you run, I'll chase you. That's my instinct. I'll chase you, and I will catch you."

"And then what?" She managed to keep the tremble from her voice when she asked.

"You really want to find out, then run."

God, she didn't know if that would be stupid—or the best thing she could possibly do. But she ran anyway, down the closest stairway and then down another, into a series of mazelike hallways.

She felt, rather than heard, Stray behind her. His heat, the soft growl of a predator on the chase reverberating through her. But still, she ran in the dark until her side cramped and her legs ached, lungs burned. She slowed, waiting for his hand on her, but it never came. She stopped, turned again, and there he was in front of her, his eyes those of the wolf but the rest of him still pure human male.

She backed up and he didn't follow, not until she turned to run again.

Finally, she pushed through an unlocked door into some sort of gym/training room. And there was no way out but the way she'd come in.

She'd really backed herself into a corner this time; Stray was already pissed at her, although the danger wasn't at her throat the way it had been with Shimmin and his men.

This time Stray didn't stop coming for her. He strode forward until only a few feet separated them. She swallowed hard, tried to ignore the way her body called out for him to touch her, and took a few steps to make her way back toward the door.

Stray gave a soft laugh. "Really, little witch? You want to bring out my prey instincts? Because you know what they say about wild animals: They can fool you because they might seem domesticated, but they can never be tamed."

God, she believed it. Right now, she didn't want him tamed at all. Walked toward him instead of away, reached her hands up to twine in his thick hair and pull her face to his. And she kissed him, reversing the roles. Because for once, she wanted to be the goddamned predator. The one who shook Stray to the core, because she was sure he'd managed to do that to every woman in his life.

But she would be different. Wanted to be, needed to be, although she wasn't sure why that desire burned so brightly hot inside of her.

She just knew it was there, and there was no stopping it.

His lips were soft, but his kiss was hard—demanding. She gave as good as she got even as she braced herself for the pain—hers and Stray's.

None came for either.

She'd tried to have sex just once and had nearly ended up killing the guy. It had been horrifying... as though something in her body had at once rejected and repelled the man.

That didn't happen, and instead her body flared for Stray. He kissed her deeper and she was helpless against him. His hands went under her shirt, touched her lower back, and the brand tingled with pleasure instead of burning.

She should be pushing him away. Pushing and slapping,

not feeling her entire body ache for him. Her nipples hardened; her body came alive. He tasted like a blend of the richest, most delicious spices. And she never wanted him to stop.

He knew it, too, the bastard, took full advantage of her sudden, inexplicable wantonness to press his body into hers, to grind his hardness to her belly. When he finally pulled back, he took in her quick breaths with a too-obvious satisfaction.

She pressed the back of his hand to her lips. They tingled—everything tingled—and if he didn't back away, she might not be able to resist reaching out and grabbing him and kissing him.

Ridiculous. Had she hit her head and not realized it?

"Is this . . . only because of your prey instincts?" she whispered, not wanting him to say yes. Because then anyone could trigger this inside of him . . . None of it would be special.

He stared at her, his eyes so mesmerizing she couldn't look away. "Yes."

He was lying, and even though she knew that, the fact that he'd deny her was worse than anything. The lights flickered, the floor began to rumble under their feet and she heard something crash.

She moved farther away from him and felt for the brand on her back, sure it was as red and angry as the first time she'd seen it. Of course, she was the only one who could, which had nearly earned her a stay in the psych ward after the accident.

She'd been traumatized, but she'd known she wasn't crazy. So she'd stopped talking about it. Tried to be good.

She'd become emancipated at seventeen and had floated around doing odd jobs until she'd met Leo Shimmin after her attack.

Leo Shimmin, who must've been watching her since then.

She was surrounded by the truths she wasn't ready to face. They made sense and fit with the dreams she'd been having, with what happened at the scene of the accident.

She'd always believed she wasn't crazy, but the rest of the world sure gave her a problem with it.

"I need to see the brand."

The door slammed loudly behind her at his request, but he appeared unfazed by any of it. She wished she could be so. "You can't see it—you don't know anything."

"I know what I saw happen to you during the accident. Control yourself and let me see the brand."

She didn't want to follow any of his orders but needed to prove to herself that she could stop the destruction her mind caused. And it took at least five minutes, with her eyes closed, whispering to herself that she could control it until she stopped hearing doors banging and glass shattering.

She opened her eyes and found Stray staring at her, approval in his eyes.

Finally, reluctantly, she turned, confident that he would see nothing. No one ever had. She lifted her shirt until the air cooled the still-too-warm area of her flesh. When she heard the sharp intake of breath from Stray, she swung her head around. "You see it?"

"It's hard to miss." She turned back, stared at the wall in front of her. She wondered if he'd touch it again, and if the same thing would happen if he did.

When he didn't, disappointment washed over her. "Show's over." She yanked her shirt down and turned to face him. "Everything got worse for me after she touched me at the scene. I should've died. You saw it, felt it. I was dying—and she branded me. I'll never be the same."

Chapter 11

The lights flickered one last time and then leveled out. The alarm system beeped in the background, but Kate wouldn't be able to hear it. It was set for wolf frequencies, not human or witch, as the case may be.

"The accident," she murmured as Stray watched. Her eyes held the faraway look they had earlier. "They said I was thrown from the car."

"You weren't."

Her next words held an urgency that broke his heart. "You saw her—the woman who saved me?"

"Yes."

"You're the first one. The only one," she murmured. "What does that mean?"

It meant so goddamned much that he couldn't even begin to understand it. Kate continued. "She did this to me. You saw when she touched me."

"She was a high-level witch."

"And she made me one too?"

"Yes. She transferred her powers to you."

"Why would she do that to a thirteen-year-old girl?" she demanded.

"She had her reasons."

"Are you going to share them?"

There was so damned much to unfold, centuries of history, and there was so little time left. "She wanted to die."

Kate swallowed hard, and he had to keep her calm. As her anger rose, the entire house sounded like it was coming down around them. "I felt what you've been through, yes. I believe you. Please let me see the brand again."

He needed to see it, an indescribable need that scratched at him until he wasn't sure he could resist touching it. He fisted his hands by his sides.

Kate hesitated briefly, but she finally turned. With her head bent forward, she pulled up the shirt, exposing a bit of unblemished skin . . . until the fabric passed her lower back.

As he had moments earlier when he'd first seen it, Stray had to fight to keep his composure at the sight of the brand marring her skin. It was a distinctly raised handprint, the mark of the witch who'd passed her powers on, in the middle of perfect, unblemished skin.

He glanced between her face and the brand as she looked over her shoulder to try to see the handprint. "You were definitely touched by a witch."

Kate was for sure a made witch, not a born one, but she'd been touched by someone very powerful. And she had to be powerful in her own right in order to handle such a transfer of power. He had a feeling she didn't look on it as a gift, and he could fully relate.

"You're sure I'm the only one who's seen this? Not even doctors?" he pressed.

"No one's ever been able to see it before, until you."

He blinked. Shook his head. "I touched your back yesterday and felt something."

"That's our link," she murmured. "That's why . . . when I need you—"

"I come to you," he finished, glad she hadn't turned to face him. His hand stretched out, his fingers nearly brushing the raised marks, but he pulled it back. If he touched that, he wouldn't be able to stop touching her, would take her, here and now on the ground, against the wall, any way he pleased. And she would let him, because she wanted him just as badly.

He drew in a deep, shuddering breath and realized he couldn't stop himself, not until Kate spoke again.

"It must . . . like you," she said. "It let me kiss you."

"What do you mean, it let you?" he demanded.

"God, this is embarrassing," she said quietly. "When I've tried to . . . you know, be with other guys—"

He growled. Couldn't help that it slipped out of his throat like an uncontrolled tic. He cursed Brother Wolf, who, in turn, bit off a sharp, howled *fuck you* in his ear.

"Sorry, keep going," he told her.

"The brand stopped me. When I'd do so much as kiss a guy . . . Okay, you're doing that growling thing again." When he didn't say anything, she kept going. "You're the first guy I've ever been able to enjoy kissing. You seemed to be enjoying yourself too. Oh wait. I forgot—prey instincts, right?"

Right then and there, he knew, somehow, that fate had socked him in the chest. "You're a virgin."

She eyed him defiantly. "Yes. And that's not going to change because you can invade my head."

"You weren't exactly trying to stay out of mine. You called for me. Drew me. Did you dream about me, too?"

"Did you dream about me?" she countered.

"I haven't slept since I met you, but I jerked off several times in the shower picturing you naked."

Whoa. Her entire body literally flooded with heat. He felt it as surely as if he were touching her. "You liked me saying that."

"I'd like it better if you meant it."

"I did. Do you want to watch me do it again?"

Without waiting for her answer, he took her shoulder and turned her. Her shirt was still raised, allowing him to cover the brand with his palm and pull her close at the same time. She gasped as their bodies jolted, and he covered her mouth with his, kissed her like he wouldn't stop.

His free hand pushed up to cover a breast. He squeezed her nipple between his thumb and forefinger and she moaned into his mouth. He knew she would be so wet for him if he pulled her pants off, and he wanted to taste her, lick her, claim her until she had only his name on her lips.

She pulled him more tightly to her, her hands wandering to grip his ass, wanting to come. And he would give that to her, would howl with pride when he did.

He bent his head and took her nipple into his mouth, tugged it between his teeth and suckled on it until the lights blew out overhead and the doors slammed open and shut, until the orgasm ripped from her with a scream, shattering her.

"Stray!"

He held on to her, forced himself not to dip his hand between her legs as the wolf howled inside his head. Not now. Later—and there would be a later.

He was never this damned possessive. He heard his own harsh breaths after he pulled away.

She run; you chased. That's all.

But it wasn't.

Kate felt completely off balance and Stray looked so calm and collected, even as the aftereffects of the orgasm vibrated through her.

"Sorry. The prey instincts are hard to control," he said easily, and she mentally called him a bastard. "I heard that."

"I wanted you to."

He was too warm and too close. She took a step to the side and sat on the mat so he wouldn't touch her again.

In reality, her legs couldn't hold her any longer.

"What else is out there?" she asked after several long moments of trying to regain her composure. But what was the point? He knew she'd come, and in reality it was the best orgasm she'd ever had, because it wasn't by her own hand. "Is this the part where you tell me that every Hollywood monster—that all those horror stories passed down through the generations are real?"

He bent down, took her palm and placed it flat against his chest. "Do I feel real enough to you? Look, you have nowhere to go that's safe. This place is."

"Only if I do what you want."

"Only if you do what's right. The witch who died and left you her powers—most likely, she died running from our enemies. Leo's one of them." Stray paused. "In your heart, you know that has to be true."

"I really want to go home and forget all of this. Pretend it never happened."

She swore a hurt look crossed his face before he told her, "We all want something."

If she didn't cooperate, what would happen to her? And, once she did, what was to stop him from killing her—or worse?

She knew exactly what could be worse. Her job working with victims of violent crimes had taught her that in many brutal and equally terrifying ways.

He stood and began to pace. "You're better off here, away from the humans."

"What do you know about them?"

"I've had thousands of years to study humans," Stray told her. "I know their ways."

"My ways," she interrupted. "I don't count myself as witch. I'm human."

"You're fooling yourself."

"I'm happy to do so and stay in la-la land," she told him. "I'm not denying I'm a witch, but I'm human still. That's how I've always lived."

"That's how you lived. Things change, Kate. Everything you know will change, too."

It already had. For one thing, she was no longer alone.

And while she couldn't be sure if this was some form of Stockholm syndrome, she realized that going back wasn't an option. It never had been. "You don't like witches."

"As a rule, no. They've never given my kind much reason to like them. And now my feelings toward them run strongly toward hate."

"You hate me for what I am. That's not fair."

"Nothing in life is."

She wanted to slap him, clenched her fist instead. He saw it and laughed.

"Go ahead and hit me," he prompted.

"The first thing I'm going to do is find a spell that works on you," she said. "If I'm that powerful, it shouldn't be too hard."

In seconds, he was on her, a palm splayed again on her brand, through the flannel shirt this time. Her entire body tingled as if on the verge of another climax. She was pleased to note by the lust visible in his eyes and the arousal against her belly that he was affected. But still angry at her last statement when he growled, "I don't take threats lightly."

She smiled, glad to have the upper hand for this moment. "Then take it as a promise."

Chapter 12

The werechick under him was asking for his number. Kill rattled off a fake one because he'd never see her again, rolled off, momentarily satiated, despite the pain after orgasm.

Fucking Elders and their mating rules. Of course they'd make sure sex hurt like a bitch after coming—they wanted mating, not casual sex, but Kill refused to mate with the female Dires in Greenland. And after Stray had been born, they were all too scared to even think about it. So he was stuck with one-night stands for the rest of his too-long life.

He grabbed his clothing and made a beeline for the door, had to get out of this cheap motel room even as the werechick cursed him for fucking and running. Slammed the door behind him and leaned against the outside wall, breathing hard after doubling over several times before he made his way to the truck, naked. Then he screeched out of the lot and turned off the GPS.

He was at the house in less than fifteen minutes; for him, the scent of Dire was unmistakable, stronger than any Were's scent.

It was like coming home, except that it wasn't.

He knew he could easily tread his way past lights and the

police cruiser he scented on the other side of the hill, toward the latitude and longitude points on Brother Wolf's inner compass.

His wolf could guide him to Steele—*Stray*—with his eyes closed.

He left the truck at the bottom of the hill, hidden off the side of the road, and slunk through the tree-lined woods toward the mansion he clearly saw outlined in the darkness, as massive as the wolves who inhabited it.

An eerie glow that looked similar to blood on the moon engulfed it.

"Witch spell," he muttered, and his wolf growled at the mention of witch. He flexed his hands to get rid of the tingling sensation that was quickly overtaking his entire body but realized it was no use. His pull to Stray was stronger than ever, and no doubt, so was Stray.

But he wasn't ready to see him or the men his flesh and blood called family now. Ended up in his truck, driving around until he happened upon a bar called Howl, with plenty of Weres and a smattering of humans.

He was aching for a fight and, when he kicked open the door of the crowded bar, he knew he'd find as many as he wanted here.

Threatening Stray hadn't been her brightest moment. But, to his credit, he hadn't said anything more, just released her and told her to follow him.

Kate did. She had no fight left in her at that moment. And she was embarrassed that, even after all that had happened, she would've given her body up to him if he'd asked.

But he didn't.

Stupid, stupid brand. It gave her a vicious stab of pain as if in retaliation, and she paused, doubled over.

Stray was at her side in seconds. He picked her up without hesitation and carried her back through the maze of hallways and up the stairs, all while she refused to look at him. Her body snuggled first against his chest and then into the soft mattress as she pretended she'd fallen asleep and he pretended to believe that. She heard the door close behind him but not lock and she breathed a little easier at that.

The pain ceded after a while and she was able to sit up, which she did cautiously in order to get her bearings. This room was as big as the other, but it was far more lived in. She looked to the left and saw clothes piled on a chair, a large dresser stacked with books and papers, a computer glowing in the darkness on a desk across the way.

This is Stray's room, she thought. She was being let in further and she wasn't sure what that meant exactly.

She'd lost track of time. The need for sleep was lacking, the way it had been for months. It was close to dawn now and, even though her body felt drained from the recent telekinetic episode, she wouldn't be able to close her eyes and drift off no matter how badly she wanted to.

And she shouldn't want to, should be trying to think of a way out of here, away from Stray . . . and to what, exactly? She had nowhere to go.

As tired as her body was, her mind raced with questions and even bigger fears than she'd had earlier. But as her eyes began to adjust to the dark, she saw that Stray hadn't left her alone—he'd simply closed the door to the room.

He was standing by the window, his bare back to her. If he heard her stir, he made no indication, and so she grabbed the sketchpad he'd left next to her and began to draw.

Her cheeks flamed as she—her body—recalled her earlier mistake of running. One that kept her body on edge every time Stray was near.

All she had to do was close her eyes to see him half naked in front of her. Abs rippled, shoulders so impossibly broad he didn't look real. And a dark tribal wolf staring at her from his right pecs.

Like it was real. The scar that bisected his chest ended right at the wolf's mouth.

Now she saw the massive portrait of the wolf taking up his entire back, its eyes alive.

The very wolf that had run her down. It had stared at her like it knew what had happened and had accepted it. It would be far longer before Stray did so.

The only people looking for her would be the police. But, according to Stray, Shimmin knew what she was, had been using her.

She was a wanted woman all around. And she couldn't be sure she wasn't wanted in the dead-or-alive way, so she did the only thing she could do right now—she drew.

Maybe they were both lulled in by the scratching sounds of pencil to paper or maybe he paid her no mind, but at least half an hour passed while she finished her drawing.

The scars. You had to be close to see them through the wolf—it was almost covering them protectively, camouflaging Stray's pain from the rest of the world. There were some along the back of his biceps as well. So many, some clean, others bumpy and all of them held a story—she was sure of it.

"Can I see it?" he asked finally, without turning. She got up and brought it to him, unable to read his expression as he stared at it.

"I never look at them in the mirror," he confessed. "I never wanted to see them."

"I'm sorry. I—"

"It's okay. It's not so bad, seeing them through your eyes. And Brother Wolf looks good."

She didn't know what to say to that; instead of words, she pressed her lips to his shoulder, then pressed her forehead to it. Part apology for earlier, part plea to continue helping her even though she couldn't bring herself to say the words.

As if he understood, he turned to her and his hand moved to caress her lower back—it was as if every time they connected like that, they grew closer.

"Who . . . did this to you?" she asked finally, her hands moving to touch the scars she'd drawn.

"My family, a long time ago, before I was a part of this pack."

"Why?"

"They marked me. I'm guessing that's something you understand."

She wanted to say that the woman wasn't her family, but technically, she was. She'd passed the gift and connected Kate's bloodline to her forever. And now, as her hands remained on Stray's back, he opened up a little more for her and she saw things through his eyes, read his mind the way she had with so many others.

But this was so very different. It was like a direct link to his every memory—and it was so easy to get lost. It felt like home.

"Bad things are going to happen," she murmured. "My God, Stray, such horrible things no one would believe. I don't want to and yet . . ."

"You know them to be true," he finished for her, his voice tight.

"We need an army to fight what's coming. I can't see all of it clearly, but I know that."

"We've got eight Dires and you. And some Weres. That's got to be enough."

Suppose it's not? she wanted to ask, but from the look in Stray's eyes, she didn't dare.

He broke her hold on him and their connection broke. He started to walk out of the room. "This is your home now, Kate. Best get used to it," he called over his shoulder. "I hope you're smart enough to not try running again."

The door shut behind him and then it opened and closed again. Even though she hadn't exactly controlled that directly, she smiled at getting in that last word.

Remember, that's how you got into trouble already.

But she swore she heard Stray's soft laugh before the door shut the second time.

"What am I supposed to do now?" she asked no one in particular before she buried her nose in his pillow, inhaling his scent deeply, the brand calming down. At the same time, she heard the door open and smelled the scent of hot chocolate. She closed her eyes again until she heard a tray being set down and Stray's footsteps and then the door closed again.

Her stomach growled and she sat up, grateful for the sustenance. Comfort food—chocolate and sugary cookies, still warm.

The snack steadied her, but the isolation wasn't sitting well. As strong as Stray was, had her powers scared him? She already scared herself and she wondered if it would always be like this.

She noted that her witchcraft books lay on the bed next to her.

Her mind flashed back to the psychic she'd visited at eighteen—the woman had handed her a book on witches and Kate handed it back and refused to think on it again. But the books Stray found in her apartment, well, she'd bought them months earlier, after browsing a store between sketches for Shimmin. She'd felt foolish for buying them, but she couldn't not.

The receipt was her bookmark in one—she'd gotten barely a third of the way through it before she'd stopped. It had made her uncomfortable, so much so that she hadn't been able to stop the lights in her apartment from blinking, to the point where the bulbs had blown out completely, shattering glass everywhere.

She reached out for them now, despite her reluctance to do so, and flipped one open to the marked page on familiars. Her face flushed as she remembered practicing calling for her familiar earlier that morning, before meeting with Josie.

Nothing had happened. She hadn't even spotted a stray cat, let alone a protector. Well, besides Stray, but that was something different entirely.

"Hey." Stray knocked on the door although he'd already opened it. "Thought you called me."

"Um, no."

"Okay. I'm right out here if you need me."

When he closed the door, something fluttered in her stomach. She didn't want to read any further. Stray might be checking up on her because he needed her help.

She curled up against the pillows and again she read the passage about witches and their familiars—a pairing as old as time and as necessary.

If she couldn't have love, she would settle for protection. *Let me protect you.* Stray's words, echoing in her ear.

And only then did she realize, for the first time, what exactly had been happening between her and Stray. She dropped the book as though it were responsible for it.

No. *Nononononononono.*

Protector. Animal. Familiar.

There was nothing in that book that said her familiar couldn't be a wolf.

Chapter 13

Jinx was still having trouble thinking straight. Brother Wolf had shifted him and run from the massacre still happening at the last cemetery because he knew Jinx was done handling it.

He'd forced Jinx to shift back, dress and drive to the nearest motel room, since it was morning light and not the best time for a wolf to be sauntering through town.

He ignored his phone in favor of sleeping in wolf form, where the ghosts couldn't get to him and the nightmares weren't as bad.

When he woke, he realized none of it had been a dream, no matter how hard he'd tried to hide from it.

His own father had sold him out in order to stay ... a ghost. A vengeful one. Jinx could've helped him cross back over—or he could've worked with Jinx to help the Dires send the Dire ghost army back to where they belonged once and for all.

But he'd chosen his side, in death, as he had in life.

Literal deals with the devil were made by humans almost every day around the world. The consequences rippled throughout the population. But the biggest loser in this case by far was probably the human who'd asked for the original bargain.

There was always a price, and it was always too high. Jinx and Rogue had heard far too many sob stories over the years. Because dead men absolutely did tell tales, none of them pretty.

Jinx always had a theory, that the more logical a person was, the more egregious their crimes.

"People need to be a little less rigid," Jinx always said. "Because that always comes back to bite them in the ass."

"Or else I do," Vice would add. Vice, who'd no doubt been calling him all goddamned night. The wolf was good enough to have scented him here, which meant he had his hands full.

If something had gone really wrong, Jinx would know it. And he comforted himself with that thought as he headed for the shower, letting the warm water beat down on his bare skin. Ignored the ghost that pulled back the shower curtain and attempted to explain why he was still there.

Jinx didn't want to hear it.

In his early years, he'd been plagued by ghosts until he realized that ultimately, his best defense against them was to ignore them, rather than trying to help them pass over. Rogue did the same to the spirits that plagued him, because they had passed over and most of them wanted to come back. It wasn't easy. Born-and-bred warriors, their abilities gave them a sensitivity not necessarily helpful to what their futures were supposed to be—warrior alpha pack leaders. The sensitivity was too distracting and the pretending soon became exhausting. The only relief they'd had was on their Running, when they didn't have to pretend they weren't different from the other Dires. Because the Dires they were running with were all as different as they were.

Jinx and Rogue had honed both their warrior skills and their abilities with ghosts and spirits over time. They'd seen some weird things, but nothing as menacing as this.

He rubbed his head against the cold tile.

Purgatory was open. And whether he'd done it or had been used as a vehicle to do it didn't matter.

It was fucking *open*.

Neither Dire twin had been allowed or able to see inside that realm and both had always supposed it to be for the best. And Jinx wouldn't tell a soul—or Vice—that he was suddenly able to see those souls, those *freaks*, as they called themselves, hanging out there in the space that wasn't heaven and certainly wasn't hell.

Jinx thought it was worse, maybe like the place Rogue currently found himself in, with a fucking mare sitting on his chest, drawing on him, marking him as hers, and all because of Seb.

After the shower, he pulled on the change of clothes he always kept in the truck and sped back to the house as dusk turned to dark, a light rain falling. There were no supernatural storms. Yet.

He pulled into the garage, letting it close behind him with the comforting, heavy thud of lockdown. Outside, there were no cop cars or signs of trappers, but inside this house was going to turn into an interrogation to beat all interrogations.

Starting with Vice, who must've slept in the damned garage, waiting for him. The wolf didn't look as much angry as . . . distraught.

"The witch is fine," Vice said by way of greeting. "And you? Can you fucking hear me now?"

He lunged at Jinx, who caught him by the shoulders, but they still went tumbling over each other on the stone floor before hitting a car to break their roll.

"Get. Up."

Rifter's voice over them. It took a long minute for Vice to obey, par for the course, but twice as long for Jinx, which was . . . odd. When his hands finally came off Vice's throat, he didn't even look at the other wolf, but stood in front of his king and waited for the dressing-down, the way he'd done so many times before in the Army for doing something not within regs.

Fuck regs. Fuck it all.

Because you've really fucked up.

He never should've come back here. Hell, he had his own bank account, plenty of places to hide. Or he could tell his Dire brothers they needed to get out of here and salvage what they could.

"Where have you been?" Rifter was demanding, shaking him by the shoulders since Jinx hadn't answered him the first several times he'd asked the question.

"Work."

"Not an answer," Rifter growled. He yanked Jinx's phone from the inside pocket of his leather jacket, turned it on and held it out to him. "Plenty of juice. You're never supposed to turn this off."

"I'm fine."

"Bullshit," Vice muttered and Rifter echoed the sentiment, then added, "I didn't tell the twins you were unaccounted for, but what the hell were you thinking?"

Jinx paused for a second, and then told the wolves the only thing he could about the night before. "It's Jameson. He's in charge of the Dire ghost army—and they're coming for us."

"It's really there?"

FBI Special Agent Angus Young looked into the empty field where Leo Shimmin insisted the wolves lived in some kind of rock-star-like mansion.

Wolves. What the fuck?

He'd been in town for a less than a month and knew his life would never be the same. He'd suspected it was coming to that the farther into his investigation he got, the one that brought him to this Catskill town in the first place. He'd been studying the supernatural and wondering if he was crazy for even pursuing that angle.

"It's there. Fifty feet in." Leo Shimmin sipped his coffee laced with whiskey and Angus shook his head.

"I don't get it."

"The witch Seb put an unbreakable protection spell on it. Not even he can break it," Leo explained. Wolves, witches . . . Angus supposed that every monster purported to live under the bed and in the closet was real.

"If I walk in?"

Leo shrugged. "We've never tried it. Any Were we've sent in said it looked like a two-room shack. No one can ever figure out what's going on."

"How can a house shift?" Angus muttered, then held up a hand. "I know. Magic."

"Unbreakable."

Angus had been surprised when the cop reached out to him early that morning. When he met Leo outside the precinct and followed his car through town and along its outskirts, he hadn't commented on the fact that the man looked like shit. Or like he'd been beaten.

"Rough night?" he'd asked instead when he'd parked and Leo let himself into the passenger's side of Angus's truck.

"You don't know the half of it," Leo had told him. "Unless you really want to."

Angus stared into the field of nothingness. It was a cold morning, dark and damp as if spring was trying to break through and winter wouldn't release her stranglehold. "You only come here in the daytime?"

"Safer that way. I don't need an ambush." The cop rubbed his bruised cheek thoughtfully. "You need to think about how far in you really want, Agent Young."

Angus had been thinking about it since he'd spoken with Shimmin yesterday. Shimmin had called Angus in to interview another woman who'd lived through a suspected wolf attack, although that was never mentioned in the official files. It fit the MO of the cases that Angus had been following for years—and Leo told him now that Harm was in fact inside this invisible house. And that Harm was a wolf.

Angus wasn't sure if he knew too little or too much about what kind of world the humans lived right alongside of—or rather, with—but either way, what he'd discovered served only to make him more on edge. "I'm here, aren't I?"

Leo nodded. "For now."

Angus stared at the emptiness again, his skin starting to crawl, which seemed to happen every time he found himself in Shimmin's presence. "I've got to bolt."

The cop smiled, like he knew. "See ya, Fed."

Fed. Not for much longer if he didn't bring on the big prize. After Shimmin left, the energy in the car got better.

According to Shimmin, he'd taken over for his brother in the fight between the supernatural and the humans—*his kind*, Leo had said.

His kind.

Christ. *He* needed to start drinking whiskey for breakfast on a regular basis if he was going to remain on this case.

He stared at the blank space and tried to imagine wolves in there. Fucking *wolves.*

And it was the best explanation he'd come up with this far. But it wasn't something he could tell his sup, who was on the other end of the ringing cell phone.

"Any leads on Harm?" his supervisor demanded.

"There was another murder. I'm close. I know it," Angus told him, knowing it was a shitty answer and nowhere near enough to justify keeping him on this case much longer. He rubbed his chin and felt the day-old rough stubble. Despite being on the road, there was nothing else to do but eat, sleep and work out, so he was staying on top of his game. At thirty-five, he had no choice. So while on the outside, he looked pretty damned good, on the inside, he felt like a house of cards that could collapse with the pressure of a strong wind.

He was restless. Horny. And pissed off. And his sup was

slow coming with a response, but Angus waited him out patiently. Sometimes, waiting was the best thing a man could do. He'd learned that in the Army and it had served him well during his sniper days.

"You've got another week, Young, and then I need to see results."

The conversation ended with a click. Angus pocketed the phone and led the truck away from the field and back through town, thinking on his next move.

When Angus had come to town and met Leo Shimmin, he'd never expected to learn what he had about the supernatural world, although he'd begun to suspect it. Having those suspicions confirmed made him feel less crazy—and way more out of control.

He'd been following his only lead, Cain Chambers, since he could actually find him. Still, Angus had a feeling everything he found on Cain was carefully crafted bullshit.

A couple of weeks earlier, Cain had been found near the body of a dead woman, killed with the same MO as the murders Harm had been accused of committing.

Angus had traced the series of murders back over a fifty-year span. If Harm was as old as Shimmin claimed—centuries—and he'd used other names throughout the ages, well shit, there were ever more murders in a pattern Angus had never thought to tie to the man—wolf . . . wolfman. But that term wasn't right, either.

Nothing human about them, Leo had claimed. Their human forms were some kind of shift thing that allowed them to blend in and trick innocent humans.

He reached for the ever-present file on the case, riffled through it and stared at Harm's recent picture and then the old album covers of other bands he'd been in.

Wolf . . . not man, and nowhere to be found.

Chapter 14

Rifter walked away from them and Jinx followed his king, Vice at his heels. They headed toward the kitchen, where they'd all learned early on that everything could be fixed.

Lately, those fixes were harder and harder to find.

When they got into the hallway near the guest bedroom, their boots squished on wet carpet. There were cracks in the plaster walls and pictures were down on the floor, but no one commented and Jinx just kept walking behind Rifter.

As he neared the kitchen, Rifter bellowed for Harm to come down, and yeah, it made sense for the wolf to be there, since this involved both him and Rifter the most.

"Rift?" Gwen looked up from the coffee she'd been pouring when they entered the kitchen, her king in the lead. She put the mug down and went to him when he didn't answer. She glanced at Jinx, her brows furrowed, but he sank into a chair instead of trying to explain what was wrong.

Because really, it was just about everything.

Vice stopped in the doorway as Rifter moved among the broken bulbs and dishes and the overturned, heavy oak table. Rifter had destroyed one just like it weeks earlier. This new one looked slightly worse for wear, but when the king righted it, it stayed in place.

Jinx got up and helped Vice collect the unbroken chairs from around the kitchen, leaving the mess scattered around them for now as the Ragnarok, an ancient Norse Prophecy circa 1000 CE, rang in his ears instead of the buzzing ceiling lights.

"Brothers shall fight, and slay each other; cousins shall kinship violate. The earth resounds, the giantess flee; no man will another spare."

It was all about the age of evil, where stealing, hoarding and fornication ruled. Even though it's the end of the world, no one lifts a hand to help the other.

This prophecy was as well known as the one they now knew was referring to Stray and Kill. Any family with brothers—especially twins—wondered if they were the ones.

Jinx hadn't thought about the prophecy since the Extinction. What was the point? At times, Rogue had wondered out loud if he and Jinx were the culprits.

But now, with Stray trotting out his brother . . . well, Jinx figured that maybe the prophecy about dangerous brothers was true after all. Together Stray and Killian could be used to wreak havoc on humans and wolves alike, utilizing total mind control.

Dangerous when apart, but terrifying together, as Stray could make sure Killian's suggestions worked their magic. And, after Jinx's announcement about Jameson and the Dire ghost army, it appeared to be only one facet of their problems.

Rifter, Gwen, Vice and Harm joined him at the table, with Liam, Cyd and Cain entering right after. Jinx asked, "Should I get Stray?"

Rifter pondered a moment, then said, "Let the wolf remain with the witch. Now, tell me what you've learned."

"The ghost army—many of them—want destruction," Jinx confirmed. "They'll be really hard to control once they start. They have a lot of unfinished business toward humans."

"I'm not sure there could be worse news, but I have a feeling there is," Harm said quietly.

"Jameson's leading the way. And he'll be looking for you and Rifter," Jinx continued. "He might not be able to kill you and Rifter, but he can torture the shit out of you for eternity."

"There are no Dires for me to lead, so what's his problem? I didn't kill him or vote myself king," Rifter said. He sighed, drank his coffee absently.

Rifter knew that something was wrong with Jinx—way goddamned wrong—but thankfully he decided against delving into it now. Jinx was relieved that Rifter preferred to use their energy to figure out the plan moving forward.

With the witch in the house, it should balance the scales more favorably. *Should.* If Stray could gain her trust.

"I've been working with Liam. Cyd and Cain have been out trying to gain support for Liam, but we all know that doesn't mean anything until Liam makes another show of power," Vice said. "Maybe we should call the pride back? We could use all the help we can get, even if the shifters aren't as strong. We'd have numbers."

"Leave them. They've made their choice." Rifter pushed the mug aside. "We'll need to pull more support from the Weres."

"What if it's not enough?" Gwen asked hesitantly.

"It has to be, baby. Has to be. I realize Seb's done something of biblical proportions and now everyone and everything in the army's path is going to pay dearly. But I'm going to make sure we're not the only ones left standing at the end."

"What if we can make the Dire army work for us?" Vice asked Jinx.

Jinx shook his head. "Even if you could grab some of them, Jameson's hold is too strong. He'd slaughter them. We don't have enough of them on the inside who'd rise up."

"Maybe you're not giving our ancestors enough credit," Rifter said, his words ending with a slight growl.

"Rift, what the fuck?" Jinx asked, his own canines lengthening in response.

"I'm asking you the same thing."

"I'm going back out, all right? I'll try to find out more," Jinx said.

"I'm going with you," Vice told him.

"I'm going alone," Jinx said firmly.

"No way," Rifter told him. "But I agree, we need Vice here. Take the twins. Liam will stay here with us, because it's not safe for him yet. Vice, if Jinx needs you, he'll call. Otherwise, we need your backup here."

Vice took Rifter's command better than Jinx would've.

Chapter 15

Half an hour earlier, Stray had left Kate alone in the room and gone through the tunnels to get outside. He'd locked the door behind him and the window was alarmed and barred. Kate would have trouble even attempting to get out without him or the other wolves hearing her. And as much as Brother Wolf's protectiveness was trying to get him to stay, he couldn't. Not without taking off her clothes and taking her in many different and inventive ways until they were all satisfied.

He'd never felt a pull like this.

Fuck.

I like her, Brother Wolf said.

"She's witch," Stray reminded him, but the stubborn wolf countered with *I like her*.

"Because you're compelled to."

That shut Brother up for a second.

Compelled to go to her, not to like her, Brother Wolf told him. *You like her too.*

He ignored that as Brother Wolf snorted softly in victory, at that and the fact that Stray was already stripping as he neared the sunroom, which was nearly bathed in darkness.

Still, he waited to strip and shift completely until he was

well into the woods, letting Brother run off some excess sexual and other energy, mainly because he couldn't deal with reading anyone's damned mind now. He could turn Kate's off, but he wasn't supposed to.

As Brother Wolf, there were no choices. He could only hear his own thoughts and those of the wolf's and he took full advantage of that. He went deeper into the woods until Brother was at least contained. But Stray knew he couldn't risk being away much longer.

When he shifted and got back into his well-worn jeans, he knew immediately that Jinx was back, could hear the confusing jumble of thoughts in his head that immediately made Stray's mood sour, although he wasn't sure why.

He strolled to the kitchen barefoot and found everyone, including Harm, sitting around the table, looking grim. They all stared at him and he remembered that the mess from Kate's breakdown had worked its way into the hallway, and he was pretty sure the pipes had leaked into the basement. The lights were also flickering, and there were some glasses that had flown off open shelves and remained on the floor, although someone had obviously tried to clean them up.

"Sorry about the mess." Fucking lame, but hell, it wasn't his fault.

"What did you do?" Vice asked, then looked up as the lights flickered. "We need to check that—been happening for hours now."

"Don't bother. It's not the electricity. It's Kate. All of this is from Kate." He sat down at the kitchen table heavily. "And she knows."

"What, that she's a witch?" Jinx asked.

"That I'm a wolf."

"Dude, what happened to easing her in?" Vice asked.

"What's wrong with him?" Stray asked instead, pointing to Jinx. He'd been purposely avoiding reading the other Dires' minds, respecting their privacy, but hell, Jinx was repeating *stay out of my fucking head* in a singsongy voice in his mind so loudly Stray couldn't help but notice. "And why wasn't I called to this family meeting?"

"I'm fine," Jinx said in the most unconvincing way possible.

"Stray, for no other reason than we didn't want to disturb your efforts with the witch," Rifter said.

"Kate. Her name is Kate." Stray heard the tension in his own voice and willed himself to bring it down several notches. "She's freaked out."

So was he. Heard her calling for him, the way she had before he rescued her. There was more urgency now, something that made his blood boil, and the need to protect her was overwhelming. He put his hands over his ears for a second, the way she had earlier, then took them off when he realized everyone at the table was staring at him.

"And you want to know what's wrong with me," Jinx huffed loudly as Stray removed his hands.

"It's weird . . . I can hear her calling for me," Stray admitted.

"We talked about a possible binding spell attached to the brand," Jinx reminded him. "A strong witch has a strong spell."

Vice broke in. "Dude, I thought you could read her mind?"

"I was trying to give her some space, but I can't shake her thoughts," he said.

Vice shook his head. "We can't afford space. And she's been reading about *familiars* in those witchcraft books I found in her apartment."

Stray knew he was right, thought about Kate and the books, the way she called to him, and it took about half a second for him to get what Vice was saying about familiars and why he'd emphasized the word—and the other half to breathe, "Fuck, no."

And then he wondered if Kate had made that connection as well. *Note to self—read her damned mind always so you're not caught unawares.*

"There's no way I'm her familiar." Then he recalled her earlier threat, her promise to create a spell that would work on him. No matter how this had happened, it was the worst possible thing for him.

"Stray, do you think that's what's happened—that you and Kate have a witch-familiar bond happening?" Jinx demanded and Stray nodded. It was the only explanation. But he wouldn't tell them that it felt like a mating, even though Jinx had already noticed that the first day Stray had met Kate.

Vice gave a low whistle. "So you're like her pet?"

Stray was on Vice in seconds. Vice was the best in a close-quarters battle, a hands-down winner in hand-to-hand combat and wetwork, his specialty, but tonight Stray could've wrung the wolf's neck easily.

"Said what you were feeling. Don't kill the messenger."

"Stray, stop," Rifter commanded. But it wasn't until the king literally put hands on him that he loosened his grip on Vice's throat.

Vice, of course, stood immediately and continued. "You're falling for the witch. You're acting like a mated Dire. What the fuck is going on around here?"

When Stray didn't deny it, Rifter jumped in. "Is she doing something to you? Compelling you because of your bond?"

He wanted to ask how this was any of their business, but fuck it all, it was. Everything any one of them did affected the pack. "She's not compelling me."

"You and Brother Wolf are just confused because of the familiar thing," Rifter told him.

"I don't think so," Stray insisted, his voice tight, body taut with anger. So much for holding back. "I think I'm in love with her. I know I'm her familiar. There's a different feel to the two things."

He wanted Jinx to understand that, mainly because Jinx had been the one who'd said they'd have to find a way to neutralize Kate when this was over. He was about to remind the wolf about that and ask him to clarify when his phone rang, loud and insistent, and he knew without looking where the call was coming from. All the wolves had this number in their phone with a distinctive ringtone, and for good reason.

It was the police station. Many young Weres ended up there and needed the Dires' help to bail them out before they were discovered. But Stray knew this call was not about Weres.

"I so do not need this shit right now," he muttered before answering.

"Steele, how's it hanging?"

"Where the hell are you, Killian?" he demanded and the other wolves stared at him, the room suddenly silent.

"Got into a slight altercation last night."

"And you need bail money?"

"Mine's a little tied up at the moment, if you know what I mean," Killian said.

Stray didn't bother to ask why his brother had remained in jail for close to eighteen hours before calling. "I'll be there. Don't cause any more trouble."

"Never, Steele."

"Stray," he said through gritted teeth before he hung up. He addressed the others. "Killian's in jail."

Vice hung up the phone call he'd just taken. "Killian was at Howl's. He was all bruised up, but witnesses say he won several fights easily. Humans started taking bets."

"Tell me he didn't shift in front of humans?" Stray asked.

Vice shook his head.

"What the hell is with your brother?" Rifter asked.

"Cage fighting is how Killian earns his living when he's not hibernating." Stray moved to grab his laptop and brought up the website for the underground chain and showed it to Jinx. "They call him Kill—he's the ultimate champ in four states now."

"Way to stay underground," Vice muttered.

"He's got to have a lot of control not to kill Weres or humans in the ring," Rifter commented.

"Money's a strong motivator," Stray said, pointed at the ultimate fighting forum he'd pulled up on his phone's browser. "And Kill is raking it in."

He supposed Killian could be doing a lot worse things to earn money. The Greenland pack didn't have anywhere close to the resources the Dire pack who'd adopted him did. Stray had been amazed at Rifter's wealth and generosity.

"What's ours is yours," Rifter had told him and Stray had never felt otherwise.

Now he looked into his king's eyes and knew the time had come. "You've been patient with me. Haven't pressured me to tell you more."

"You had your reasons, Stray. I always suspected, knew when the time was right, you would tell us everything," Rifter said. "You brought Killian back to help, even at dear cost to yourself."

"I should've trusted you."

"You did. You do. You didn't trust yourself. Fifty years might seem like a long time to many, but the fact that you could let us embrace you the way you did ... well, you're a good wolf. You just weren't ready," Rifter said.

"But now I need to be." Stray looked each wolf in the eye before he continued. "The Elders never told me anything. My pack did, from day one. They're in Greenland—kept alive after the Extinction, just like all of you."

Stray waited for the revulsion in his new pack's eyes, but none came. Instead, Jinx's eyes widened. Vice cursed quietly under his breath as Rifter asked, "How many?"

"There were thirty when I left. Not immortal. No abilities. Not until Killian and me, and we paid dearly for that."

He paused. "There are females. I guess potential mates for all of you, and I kept you from that."

Vice's face hardened. "You kept us from nothing—we don't want anything to do with females who've harmed you or Killian. I think you've always known that on some level."

Stray could only nod gratefully at him for those words as Rifter continued, asking, "That's why you and your brother left and separated?"

"Yes. They thought we were the brothers mentioned in the prophecy."

"I think you've got to tell us more about Killian," Vice said. "I want to know what we're up against."

"He won't hurt us," Stray told him. "But if the prophecy begins, you should separate us."

"Don't worry about that," Vice said.

"If the prophecy is right, this could be the end of days," Jinx pointed out.

"Or not," Rifter said. "Just because we need Killian doesn't mean that. None of those prophecies have come true—not the way they were written, at least."

It was true. The Extinction wasn't prophecy. And Stray could only hope that Rifter was right, that he and Kill and the others could work together to stop Seb and the trappers. But he couldn't ignore certain facts. "They looked on my being born as a betrayal. But my birth was what kept them from being destroyed. They were spared the Extinction so I could fulfill the prophecy. That has been passed down through the pack for centuries, through different generations of Dires."

When Stray and Killian were growing up, the small pack had always been wary of the two of them. They were kept separate and apart from the others. When Stray escaped, he'd grabbed on to technology as a way to reach out and touch somebody.

It was there that he heard rumors of other Dires—and other wolves called Weres.

He avoided them like the plague. When Rifter finally found him, Stray had been really reluctant to go back to the way things had been . . . He'd been in the process of setting free young Weres who were being hunted for fun by a group of weretrappers—or Weres themselves.

He didn't trust humans, and the packs kept trying to force him into theirs. He didn't tell them he was a Dire—and if they'd known, they hadn't said. Weres' senses weren't as keen as Dires' senses, and Stray kept himself under wraps in terms of his strength.

He couldn't hide his size, though, and that was why the packs wanted him on their side. A good mate, they kept saying. They talked about Dires in the most reverent of terms for the most part.

It was rumors of a lone Dire that brought Stray to Rogue's attention.

"You're one of us," Jinx's twin had told him, and from there, he'd never looked back. Not until now.

Stray had memorized details and facts about the time period of the Extinction and beyond from his old pack. He'd meet Weres along the way who might try to use a too-young Dire to their advantage.

He'd known that someday he'd meet up with the Dire king and others, tracked them through various exploits. And since Dires with abilities barely aged, none of them questioned his story about his pack being smote.

He didn't know why he'd kept his pack's secret for so long. "When I was younger, all I thought about was staying alive. Killian was around until I was about eight or so; then he left. I realize now that he did it for me. Before the change, so he did that on his own. Didn't want them to murder me."

"But he never told you that."

"No." He stared at Rifter. "Killian rescued me right before my first shift. Taught me how to fight in the warrior way, because my family had refused to."

And then one morning, maybe a year later, he woke and

Killian was gone. No note, although Stray knew the prophecy was at the heart of it. Stray resisted the urge to find Killian, because he knew that if he ever saw his brother again, it would mean the world was in a bad way.

Stray understood, but the feeling that he'd lost everything never left him.

Kill hadn't betrayed him, left him because of his ability and Stray kept waiting for the bottom to fall out of this pack, for them to decide that they were better off away from him.

Although they fought fiercely at times, that was never suggested.

"We tried it once, all of us being separate," Vice had told him years earlier. "Made all of us fucking miserable. Figured being miserable together's better."

A piece of Stray was definitely missing—there was no more denying that his brother was a piece of the puzzle. He'd never expected a witch to be the other, but she was. "I've got to post bail for Killian."

Rifter stared at him, his wolf barely contained. Stray couldn't blame him. Kill was supposed to help them, not make things worse. A wolf with the police on his ass would fuck them over.

"Do what you need to. Take a lawyer," Rifter said through clenched teeth, jabbing his thumb toward Jinx.

"I'll get changed and meet you in the garage," Jinx told him.

"I'll get you the money," Cain offered.

"Stray, deal with Killian now and then you need to handle things with Kate. You need your bond with both to be strong, but the witch is every bit as important as your brother. We can't move on the trappers until she's ready to eradicate Seb. We'll keep Kill close so you can concentrate on your charge," Rifter told him. Although Stray wasn't the naturally submissive type, for his king, the wolf who'd always treated him like family, he would be. He nodded as he pulled on his black leather jacket and headed downstairs, leaving Rifter, Gwen and Harm in the kitchen and, no, he didn't want to be a fly on the wall for that little family get-together any more than he wanted to go to his own.

Jinx got into the truck's backseat with him a few minutes later, dressed to the nines for his role. The truck they'd taken had blackout windows, which added to his mystique of a rich, out-of-town lawyer. Cain climbed into the front seat and drove them to the police station.

"Things okay?" Stray asked Jinx.

"Why wouldn't they be?" Jinx wasn't okay—far from it, was still doing the *keep out of my mind* bullshit song—but Stray had a bigger problem waiting at the police station. "Can Leo get to him?"

"No way. Especially when we're in such close proximity."

"Some scary shit." Jinx stared out the car window, then leaned forward and touched Cain's shoulder as the young wolf drove through town. "Hang in, brother."

Cain nodded, a tight but proud smile on his face that remained there for the ten-minute ride into town. He pulled into the back lot of the police station, keeping them as far away as possible while still maintaining a clear view of the back doors.

"You want me to go in alone? Probably safer if you think Killian will tolerate me," Jinx said.

"I don't know what the hell he'll tolerate," Stray muttered. "But I'd rather not get spotted in the police station."

"Hear ya." Jinx got out and strode into the same building Stray had walked Kate to just forty-eight hours before.

Time was flying and for the first time in his seventy-five years, that wasn't a good thing.

His skin had tingled for hours, the way it had in Killian's presence.

"Should've known that bastard was here."

Chapter 16

Jinx hated the police station, less for the humans than for the hundreds of ghosts that congregated there at any one time, hanging on in hopes of vengeance or redemption.

They'd get neither, but try telling them that.

Negativity bred in kind, and in this place, there was barely any hope. Strangled Jinx every time he walked in here playing lawyer. He adjusted his tie and showed ID to the clerk, who recognized him, pointed toward room four and said, "He lawyered up, so he's all alone."

"What are the charges?"

The clerk leafed through some paperwork on the clipboard in front of him. "Drunk and disorderly. Public nuisance. Fighting. The officer will be in to see you both soon to discuss his options."

"I'm posting bail as we speak," Jinx told him.

"Didn't doubt it, Mr. Neil."

The clerk went back to shifting through his papers and Jinx walked through the room, past the criminals and prostitutes, human and ghost and Were, and found Kill waiting for him in the small interrogation room.

The Dire resembled Stray, but it was obvious he'd lived harder. It showed not so much in his face but in his eyes, and there was a world-weariness about him that pervaded the small, depressing room.

"Aren't you fancy for a public defender?" Kill spoke in a voice tumbled hard with whiskey and no sleep. There were days of stubble on his face and his shirt was ripped half open. He hadn't bothered to wipe the blood off himself, although Jinx doubted anyone had offered to let the wolf clean up.

His hands were also chained to the table. Kill could take that table apart in seconds, never mind the cuffs, but for now he was playing nice. Like he should've been last night.

"Listen, asshole, I'm your lawyer. Your *family* hired me," Jinx told him, and the wolf across from him smiled wryly and really looked none the worse for wear, considering the rumors of just how big the bar fight he'd been involved in was.

There were still bruises, but because he was young, they wouldn't fade as fast as Jinx's would.

"Like I couldn't smell you a mile away," Killian told him. "Let's get the fuck out of here."

"I'll post bail. You'll have to—"

"I'll take care of this," Killian interrupted him. He stared down at the cuffs, then raised his arms and watched the cuffs crumple like paper clips. He waved the guard back in through the glass window and the officer came in fast.

"Hands on the damned table," the officer shouted. Killian simply stared at him for a long moment. Jinx felt the chill in the air and realized Killian was showing him his power, digging into the officer's mind and suggesting new thoughts to override his existing ones.

Fuck. And it was too late for him to do anything about it because the officer was saying, "I'm sorry, Mr. Killian. Is there a problem?"

"Yes," Killian said and then he smiled. The officer continued to stare at him and then said, "Sir, I'm so sorry you're still here. Please accept my deepest apologies."

"Not a problem."

"Please, go out the back. Don't wait another minute. I'll shred your paperwork and erase all signs that you were ever here. Better yet, that you even exist."

"That's perfect. Thanks," Killian told him, and when the officer left, said, "We'd better get out of here now, before he remembers what he's really supposed to do with me."

Jinx stared at Killian for a moment before heading through the open door and letting Killian follow him through the parking lot and into the waiting truck.

No one spoke and Cain pulled away.

"Why the hell did you put us out when you could've freed yourself?" Jinx asked finally.

"Because I never know if it's going to work correctly," Kill said simply. "Once you were there for backup, I could come out and play. Would've been better if Steele was there. Much better."

"This isn't the time for fun," Jinx said. "And his name is Stray."

"*Stray* said he was coming for me, so where is he?" Kill asked.

Cain looked in the mirror. "He said he wasn't ready to deal with you yet."

Kill laughed. "He's too ready; that's the problem. And since when do you allow Weres to get mouthy?"

"Since I respect Cain a hell of a lot more than you," Jinx told the wolf with a calm he didn't feel.

Killian snorted but remained quiet as they drove back to the house, Cain taking the back way into the underground garage, even though there were no cops or Weres in sight.

When Cain parked next to some Harleys, Jinx got out and went to the stairway, not bothering to ask Killian to follow him. If the wolf knew what was good for him, he would.

When he reached the kitchen, he noted that Gwen and Rifter had been in the final stages of cleanup when they'd gotten . . . distracted. There were garbage bags everywhere and most everything had been swept up or repaired.

"We're back," he said, hating to interrupt the embrace. Rifter didn't look bothered by the intimate position they'd been found in, but Gwen did blush a little. She was still getting used to her wolf.

Cain and then Killian walked in behind him, which gave Rifter enough time to pull off Gwen and for her to turn to the sink.

"Killian, I'm Rifter, King of the Dire Clan." Rifter stood and surveyed the newest Dire, who was slightly taller than Jinx.

"Rifter, I need a damned drink," Killian told him. Jinx grabbed the wolf by the back of the neck and slammed him into a chair.

"Cain, get our guest some whiskey," Rifter said, with a nod of approval at Killian. Cain poured a glass and left the bottle on the table next to Killian.

"Where's Stray?" Vice asked, walking into the kitchen. Jinx knew this wouldn't end well.

"My brother's not ready for our family reunion," Kill said, drained his shot and took another. Vice's wolf remained barely contained. "Can't say I blame him, but I feel like the pup should've grown some balls by now."

Vice went for him, but Rifter growled, "Down, Vice," before he pinned Killian to the floor himself. "You will have respect for my pack."

Kill put his hands up—a mock surrender, but at least he wasn't fighting. His wolf remained oddly tame.

When Rifter backed off, Killian picked himself up and drank more.

"You were supposed to come into town with stealth," Rifter told him.

"Didn't know that was part of the plan."

"It's part of any wolf's plan. It's called survival."

Kill snorted and pointed to himself. "You haven't all figured out that for us, that part's pretty damned easy?"

"Surviving well isn't easy at all," Vice broke in.

"And you wolves look like you certainly have it tough."

Rifter stared him down, but Killian was unrepentant. Jinx knew Rifter would cut the Dire a little slack—living alone for so long, it was hard to get back into the pack mentality. But Killian had better do it and fast.

"Let's talk strategy," Rifter said. "You're willing to help us, correct?"

"Wouldn't have made the trip if I wasn't. Who are we taking down?"

Rifter slid a glance toward Jinx and then back to Killian. "Trappers."

Jinx agreed silently with Rifter that now wasn't the time to bring up the Dire ghost army. You couldn't shift a ghost's or spirit's thoughts, so Kill wouldn't be any help on that front anyway.

"I'll be glad to help eradicate those fuckers," Kill told Rifter. "But Stray needs to talk to me first. I can plant whatever shit you want me to inside their heads, but if I don't know what's already in there, it will backfire. We've got to be in sync, and that shit just doesn't happen."

"I hear you, Killian," Rifter told him. "But get one thing straight—you will not use a single ability or leave this house unattended unless I give the say-so."

"I surrender myself to the king." He held up a glass. "To my Dire brothers, who've welcomed me with such open arms."

"For the love of Odin, this is going to be a long week," Vice muttered.

It had taken Killian forty-eight hours to arrive in the Catskills, another ten to party and get himself arrested and subsequently freed, and now he was inside the Dire mansion.

Stray's senses tingled and felt like fire skittering along his skin. Brother Wolf alternately pushed him toward and shied away from the man who both saved and destroyed him in one fell swoop.

If they hadn't been together the night Stray shifted, maybe their abilities wouldn't be able to work together. But it was way too late for Monday-morning quarterbacking.

"I don't want this power," he murmured, but his body, his mind refused to listen. His ability was meant to work with Killian's, had been waiting, none too patiently, to grow to its full potential. Stray wasn't all that sure what it would entail beyond completely manipulating someone's thoughts.

Stray understood Kate's fear all too well. And yet he'd been such a damned asshole to her, not caring about her plight.

He knew her nightmares. Soon she would know his as well.

He stripped and shifted, letting Brother Wolf take the reins. His wolf could hear Killian talking to the Dires without the confusion of everyone else's thoughts.

Since his confession, he'd been pushing down his ability when he was around the Dires, not wanting to hear any of his brothers thinking about how Stray had deceived them.

They haven't treated you any different.

And even though he had enough faith in them that they'd tell him how they really felt, he understood Kate's reluctance to read people's minds.

Understood her . . . and liked her.

She was sleeping—and dreaming. Of him. Of the way he'd kissed her earlier. He moved into the room next door to hers, sat on the bed and unzipped his jeans. His cock throbbed for her—he'd been half hard since he'd met her, with no relief in sight.

While she dreamed of him stripping her, suckling her nipples, entering her, he stroked himself to completion, coming with a short howl he was unable to hold back.

It wasn't enough. He had a feeling that it was never going to be enough until he was skin to skin with Kate.

Chapter 17

Kate woke to darkness outside and a small sliver of light coming from the bathroom. One of the witchcraft books was balanced on her chest and her head wasn't pounding any longer. Just the fact that she'd been able to actually sleep . . . well, it had to be because of her connection with Stray.

Stray, whom she now heard pacing outside the door. Faster steps, then they'd stop and start again, and she threw the book down and tried to center herself.

You can do this. You have to know for sure.

She got up and stared out the window at the moonlight. Her fingers tingled, itched to sketch, but she didn't see any paper or pencils in the room. She was sure Stray would bring her some, but until she got their relationship figured out, she wasn't asking for anything.

Speaking of their relationship, her subconscious had obviously worked several things out, her more-than-vivid dream leaving her slightly sweaty and wet between her legs. In her dream, he'd finished what he'd started in the basement, didn't move away and pull the prey instincts card.

She'd almost come in her dreams, but she'd startled and woke when a howl distracted her.

A howl.

You're living with wolves now.

God, could it get any crazier? She was even more off balance than she'd been before sleeping, and the odd feeling that had lodged in the pit of her stomach from the moment she'd laid eyes on Stray got stronger.

She went into the large bathroom and found that, at some point, Stray had left her more clothing, this time more size-friendly, and various shampoos and soaps. She stripped quickly and got into the large tiled shower with the water blasting her from all sides, along with the rain showerhead from above, and thought about how much everything had changed in what seemed like an instant.

Actually, everything had changed ten years ago. She just hadn't realized how much.

Stray's scent lingered on her skin, was somehow stronger now in the steam of the shower, and she breathed it in deeply. It circled her like an embrace. She wondered if that was the reason she'd finally slept—and slept well.

Or maybe it had to do with the fact that her body and mind had collapsed under the weight of everything she'd learned over the past hours.

Witch. Wolf.

She swallowed hard and tried to erase the memory of Stray's kiss. Touched her lips, which were still tender.

You dreamt of me.

Stray's voice in her head and her dream came racing back to her, making her incredibly turned on again.

She could only read his mind when he let her. Suddenly, he was.

Touch yourself for me, he told her. Her arousal flared. *I'm stroking my own cock, thinking about you.*

Thought you said it was just your prey instinct.

I don't care what it is . . . feels amazing. Touch yourself and pretend it's me, he demanded. And, as if she couldn't deny him, she did, stroked her wet folds, closed her eyes and pictured Stray watching her, wanting her.

"Please," she heard herself call out, and she didn't know what she was asking for. Her face heated with embarrassment even as Stray urged, *Say my name as you're making yourself come.*

And she was helpless not to do as he asked. The only thing that made it more intense was that he was calling her name as his orgasm pushed him over the edge. Her body vibrated as his did, their voices mingled inside her head until she couldn't tell them apart any longer.

As she caught her breath, she listened for him again, but it was completely silent.

He'd closed her out again, and all she could do was smile. *Prey instincts, my ass.*

When she finished, she dressed quickly, towel dried her hair and swept it into one long, loose braid that hung halfway down her back. With steely determination, she went back to the bed, sat down and relaxed. And then she called for her familiar—her protector.

A witch always needs her familiar to watch over her.

She resisted stopping, despite the odd feeling, like maybe she was doing something wrong. When she called out for her familiar, the animal would be bound to protect her. According to lore, each witch's familiar was already chosen for her—all she had to do was call to it and it would come to help her.

She tried. Heard Stray's pacing outside the door get more frantic. She looked around, hoping to see a cat, a bird . . . anything but what she suspected to be true.

And then Stray burst in without knocking. "Hey, sorry. It's just . . . I thought you called for me."

"I ah . . . Shit." She swallowed hard, blushed as she thought of the way she'd followed his commands. Thank goodness he could only read her mind and hadn't been able to watch her touching herself. Although the thought of him doing that . . . "I guess I did call you."

He must've suspected, although there was a slight wince on his face after she confirmed it.

"I was just . . . practicing," she explained. "Trying to see if this was all real."

He still didn't say anything, but a muscle in his jaw twitched. And then behind him were two large men, just as tall and broad and handsome as Stray but in different ways.

"I'm Stray's brother, Rifter," the dark-haired one said. "This is Vice."

She had a visceral reaction to the very blond, spiky-haired man covered in tattoos and piercings, but strangely enough, her body was responding to Stray. Again.

He moved close to her even though she hadn't spoken a word out loud. Vice whistled low, muttered something under his breath about pets.

"You keep calling, and I keep coming when you do," Stray said.

"You can't be my familiar. Only animals are familiars," she protested. Vice snorted. Rifter turned away.

Stray blanched visibly. "I guess you followed through on your threat."

"What? Wait . . . You think I did this on purpose? It's the last thing I wanted."

"Right, because you want nothing to do with me. Got it, loud and clear. But in the process of screwing me, you've screwed yourself by bonding us together."

"Let's all calm down and deal with this," Rifter commanded. Kate watched Stray bite back anything else he wanted to say and instead nod his head in deference.

"He's not an animal," she persisted. "I mean, he's— you're in human form, right? You look as human as me."

"Sweetheart, you're all witch. There's nothing human

about you *or* me," Stray told her before stripping the sweats off.

She didn't understand why he was choosing this moment to get buck naked in front of her, but before she could process anything, it was a blur of man and limbs. A low growl emanated from the spot of chaos and then Stray was gone.

In his place was a large, shaggy black wolf. And it had the same color eyes as Stray, but they were most definitely lupine, almost as if they were glowing. Otherworldly.

Rifter caught her when she fell. Vice stepped between them when Stray growled at him.

"Dude, you're the one who went all wolf," he told Stray. Brother Wolf agreed. But hell, now that Kate understood that all the supernatural shit wasn't bullshit, why not go all the way?

Besides, she'd already seen him as wolf. Who'd have thought she'd go nuts the second time?

"I'm going to kill you for doing that," Rifter told him as he brought Kate into the living room and laid her on the couch before attempting to rouse her. But Stray didn't shift back—pawed over and nosed her until she stirred. She opened her eyes and jumped back a little.

He didn't back away, forced her to look directly at him, to understand as best she could just what kind of shit she was dealing with. He rubbed his head against her arm until she touched him.

Brother Wolf liked the caress a little too much.

She looked around, a little embarrassed. "I didn't see it happen the first time. It didn't seem real until right now."

Rifter cleared his throat. "It's intense the first couple of times."

"Are you really all . . . werewolves?"

Fuck no. Brother Wolf growled and she took her hand away for a second. Stray took a few steps back and shifted. "I'm a Dire wolf."

"And there's a difference?"

"A big one."

"I never thought when I was asking for my familiar that it would be a wolf. I thought, maybe a nice cat."

She stopped talking when she heard the low growl vibrating from Vice's throat.

"We, ah, can't keep cats around," Rifter told her.

"Oh, well." She didn't know what else to say. What else *was* there to say?

She had a man—a wolf—as her familiar. And Stray was nobody's pet.

Maybe this was some kind of horrible Little Red Riding Hood dream. Then again, her dreams never really worked out all that well for her. Maybe sticking to reality, no matter how crazy it made her feel, was the best bet.

Stray turned to his brothers and asked, "Can you give us some privacy? We've got a lot more to cover."

They quickly complied and in seconds it was the two of them. Stray put on the jeans, not the shirt, and she couldn't stop staring at him. She was attracted to him—there was no denying it.

But she needed answers as well.

Chapter 18

The intimacy they'd shared in the shower was still there, somehow, rising between them like the steam had earlier. She hadn't been disgusted by the wolf, just startled by the sudden transformation.

He wasn't apologizing for it, or for anything concerning Brother Wolf. Not to a witch.

Brother Wolf howled happily to the first part and ended on a growl with the second, albeit a confused one. Witch or not, they both wanted her. "Ask your questions."

Kate did. "Earlier, you said the witch who touched me wanted to die. Why?"

Stray paused, then decided that the truth was the only option. "She knew there were powerful people ready to use her powers for evil purposes and she was tired of fighting. If she didn't pass on her powers, she couldn't die. She figured you wouldn't ever be found."

"So how was I?"

"Shimmin's been watching you. He must know about the mark, maybe because of Seb. He's a witch—used to be one of Rifter's best friends until he went over to the dark side, literally. Now he's working against us."

Her eyes flashed with palpable anger. Kate didn't like

being played and she wasn't afraid to show those feelings. "What would Shimmin have done to me?"

"If he'd captured you, he'd force you to do horrible things for the weretrappers."

"You know that for sure?"

"They're already doing it to Seb."

"So now I know what they'll do to me. Now, what will *you* do to me?"

"Protect you. Me and my brothers."

"How do you know Leo Shimmin's been after me for a while?" she asked.

"This." He knelt, touched the four deep vertical scars on her calf, and she pulled back.

"I don't remember the attack."

Didn't remember, or didn't want to. "A wolf attacked you."

She stared at him, swallowed hard. "One of your kind?"

"The marks would be bigger if a Dire had done this. And you never would've survived." Her eyes registered shock from his words as her fingers unconsciously rubbed the scar. "It was what we call a Were, and we have every reason to believe it was sent by Leo Shimmin or his brother, Mars. Did it try to touch your back?"

She closed her eyes, shook her head a little like she was trying to push the memory back and failing. "I think . . . yes. It hurt when he touched it. It didn't feel anything like when you touch me."

Holy hell. Her eyes shone when she looked at him and his hand fisted at his side instead of reaching out to hold her. "I'm glad you can feel the difference. We—neither Dires nor Weres—don't hunt humans. Or witches, typically."

"So Leo Shimmin's recruiting Weres to help him?"

He nodded. "His plans are . . . horrific. For humans, wolves. Witches. There's so much more to all of this."

Kate's head was spinning again, but she pushed through it, had to ask, "Do you have a personal stake in all of this?"

Because, in her experience, everyone did.

"Yes. We were hoping your powers could help one of my Dire brothers."

"That's all?"

"Yes."

It couldn't be that simple. It never was. "You're lying."

"I'm going slowly. You're the one who's trying to lie to yourself about the power you have."

Her anger got the best of her. She jerked away from him. Up until that moment he still held her calf in his hand. "Yes, I have some sort of power. But I have no way to control it—them—whatever. It just happens. Usually when I'm angry."

Stray looked between her and the flickering lights, and she realized that she'd caused a statue to fly across the room and bean him in the side of the head. He held his lips in a grim line and said flatly, "Noted."

She refused to apologize. Even if he'd saved her from being kidnapped, she was basically in the same position.

Granted, no one here had tried to hurt her, but what would happen when they realized she couldn't help their brother? She pushed that thought away because there was really nothing she could do about it now.

Instead, she waited to hear what Stray wanted exactly.

"You've never been able to control it?" he asked.

"No."

"You'd better be a quick study."

And just as she started to retort, he jerked his head toward the window and howled. All the men—the wolves—jumped to attention, looking far more fierce than they had moments earlier.

Warriors, all of them, and now they surrounded her.

"What's happening?"

"They're here for you," Rifter said, glancing over his shoulder at her. She touched his shoulder to see out the window and surprisingly, he allowed it. "Better that you truly believe this."

All she saw was the glow of eyes staring back at her from the bushes.

There was controlled chaos for the next few moments while Kate struggled for breath, unable to tear her gaze away from the eyes staring back at her.

"Kate, turn away." Stray did so himself, gently, his hands on her shoulders until she was looking up at him. "We've got this."

"Are they . . . ?"

"Weres."

Like the ones that attacked me.

The harsh breathing began again as her memory released what had happened on the night of her attack—she saw herself dragged into the bushes by a wolf, his claws digging into her calf as she struggled to gain some footing, her hands desperately holding on to grass and dirt that gave way far too easily.

And then . . . nothing. She was alone in the woods, her calf bleeding and the police surrounding her.

"Kate, come on. Stay with me."

She broke her reverie and saw Stray, his eyes half lupine already, and she licked her lips, her throat tight and dry. "I'm okay."

"Liam!" Rifter called. When Kate turned, she saw a handsome man stride into the living room, probably just a little younger than she was. His face bore the telltale marks of a recent fight, but his bearing was as regal as that of the men she was surrounded by, even though he wasn't nearly as tall.

It was like being in a forest of redwoods.

Stray put a hand on the back of her neck—warm and soothing. He began to massage some of the tension out even as it rose in the room.

"Liam's a Were," Stray told her.

And he was going to fight—for her. Possibly get hurt protecting her. And there was no hesitation on any of their parts. Forget lions as kings of the jungle; these wolves were spectacular. They were magnificent creatures that owned the night, the way she wanted Stray to own her.

Her cheeks blushed hot thinking about that, and Stray chuckled, and dammit, he had to stop reading her mind.

"Sorry, but that was nice," he murmured. He didn't seem concerned about the other wolves stalking the house and, as she watched, Liam shifted and went out the back door in wolf form, following Rifter.

Vice shifted too, stripping down to nothing without hesitation. His skin bore many tattoos and piercings until he shifted into a pure white wolf, the complete opposite of Stray's black-coated Brother Wolf. As she watched, Vice went out the door too, and Stray looked like he was having a hard time staying back.

"I've got to help them," Stray said quietly. "The door's locked. They can't get in. I promise. Gwen is upstairs—you're not alone."

Stray looked reluctant to leave her, but he was having a hard time holding back. "Go. I'll be okay," she promised, and only then did he back away slowly. Stripped and shifted so fast she nearly missed it.

She went to the window immediately, drawn like a moth to the flame despite all the warnings she'd been given. But it was the only way for her to be close to Stray now.

A surge went through her body as Stray leapt into the fray—mastering every wolf he came across. The other Dires and Liam were all fighting with equal measure, but it was Stray she couldn't take her eyes off, even when she began to grow light-headed. The buzzing noise in her ears made her press her palms against them, but it didn't stop.

She shook her head and realized it wasn't a buzzing—someone was calling to her. And it wasn't Stray.

Come to me, sweet one. I've waited for you for so long . . . I never thought I'd get you back.

She recognized the voice on some level, although it wasn't anyone she ever remembered meeting. No, it was a different sort of recognition, as ancient as her powers supposedly were.

"I'm staying here," she said out loud, even tore herself away from the window.

But to her horror, she turned back and headed toward the locked sliding glass door.

Please, I've missed you.

She'd missed him, too . . .

"No. This isn't right." She told herself to resist, but it was nearly impossible. She took several more steps forward and opened the sliding glass door, knowing she shouldn't be involved in this fray but unable to stop herself from moving.

Stray, please . . .

Her bare feet curled in the cold grass as she continued on a path as though she were being led on a leash.

Good, that's my girl. Leave this prison and come home to me . . .

Home. That sounded really nice. The voice was right—the Dires were keeping her in prison.

Can't trust the Dires at all.

"No. Wait, yes." She struggled to keep some sense in her head but still kept moving along the exterior of the fight, until she saw one of the wolves heading in her direction.

She closed her eyes as the wolf with the bright white coat charged, only to feel the brush of wind and fur as it flew past her . . . and into the chest of the wolf ready to attack her from behind.

And still, she walked on, toward the woods and the magical voice that caressed her like a light summer's breeze, her resolve to stay loyal to her familiar and the man who'd rescued her broken like a brittle tree branch in the dead of winter.

Chapter 19

Kate was outside. By herself, walking through the grass with bare feet and no protection.

What the hell . . .

He turned tail and bounded toward her as Vice took down the Were who'd been coming up behind her. She was still walking, though, unhurriedly and into the path of two Weres who'd come out of the woods like they'd been lying in wait for her.

As if on cue, several more Weres came up from behind and jumped him. He turned and let Brother Wolf fight viciously, until there was nothing left of those wolves but blood and fur.

But in the time it took to kill the Weres, the two who'd spotted Kate had grabbed hold of her and spirited her off toward the woods, their jaws on her arms, and she had no choice but to go.

For sure, Shimmin and Seb would want her alive—but they didn't care if she was scarred. Stray felt her pain as deeply as she did, wasn't surprised to find his own paws dripping with blood.

Brother Wolf ran to her, his gait sure and strong, got ahead of her and circled the three of them, a warning to let her go. They wanted to comply, but they had their orders.

He smelled their fear—they weren't possessed. And they were no doubt told to bring Kate to Seb and Shimmin in one piece.

And Kate remained still, not a hint of recognition in her eyes, even when she gazed on Brother Wolf.

It made no sense, but once he saw her eyes, he knew— she was in some kind of a trance.

Kate, come on—stop it, he told her. She shook her head and stared between him and the other wolves on either side of her.

There was nothing else he could do for her for the time being except kill the attacking Weres, which Brother Wolf did in clean, warrior fashion before letting out a howl of victory that matched his brothers'.

She'd called to him, even through the haze, and something inside of him surged with a combination of pride and fear. Because no matter what, he needed to protect her, whether he wanted to or not.

Good thing he wanted to.

He was enraged—couldn't see straight—and he trusted Brother Wolf to make the right decisions, because the beast knew Kate was his as much as Stray's—and neither planned on letting her get taken.

This wasn't just a fight to save the witch—it was an all-out death match to save his familiar.

The following minutes were vicious and satisfying. When he pounced, it was blood and fur and fang, sharp, lethal wounds that made the Weres cry out in pain during their death throes.

At some point, Vice was there, spiriting Kate out of the fighting, but Stray sensed her close. Watching him fight for her, kill for her.

Protecting you.

Protecting me, she answered back.

And suddenly, another black Dire was by his side, fighting as though for his life. Killian took down another couple of Weres who came at Stray from the left, which allowed him to nudge Kate out of the way of the more brutal part of the fight.

Whether or not Killian was out here protecting him or because the urge to fight was too strong, Stray didn't know. He forced his head back into the frenzy as Brother Wolf helped the rest of the Weres to meet a quick end.

When the dead Weres lay scattered around him, he howled. Then he turned to note that, at some point during the fight, Vice had shifted back and now held Kate against his very naked form.

Stray growled at that intimacy, even though it was simply a wolf helping another.

You're acting like a mated wolf.

Brother Wolf laughed in his ear, and he told the wolf to shut up.

And still he advanced toward Vice as though he were stalking the Dire.

"Easy, boy—she got a little weak. I'm just holding her up," Vice told him.

Stray and Brother Wolf weren't satisfied with Vice's answer and so Vice let her go. Indeed, when he did so, Kate dropped nearly to the ground until Stray shifted and caught her, cradled her against him almost reverently.

"There's so much more going on here it's not even funny," Vice said. "Get her in—we'll take care of the bodies."

Spelled Weres shifted back to human forms. Regular Weres who died in wolf form stayed that way. The Dires would know soon enough which they were dealing with. Not that it mattered. Seb had sent these to collect Kate.

Stray didn't sense the witch himself in these woods, but who knew what new tricks Seb had?

"Seems like I'm always saving you, baby brother."

Stray growled at Killian even as he held Kate closer to him. "You weren't needed."

"Did you want me to stand down and let the trappers take your witch?"

"Her name is Kate."

"Huh. Well, you realize you can't mate with a witch, right? Hell, I don't even think you can mate with the Dire women from our pack."

He was about to lunge at Killian when Kate woke up.

"Stray, what's going on? Why am I out here?" she asked, turned toward the house that was only ten feet behind her but that she couldn't see at all. Not until they allowed it.

He looked down at her. She looked up at him like . . .

Like she could actually love him. And that was completely ridiculous. Even so, his body stilled and for a second he couldn't hear anything beyond Brother Wolf's long, mournful howl. He fought the urge to shift, to run, to do anything but what he had to do, which was gather Kate more tightly in his arms and get her back into the house before the trappers got wind of her being outside and vulnerable.

They were all so goddamned vulnerable.

"Stray, I can walk," she insisted. But he didn't listen, got her through the open front door that he kicked closed behind them and watched her head jerk as she realized they'd gone from nothingness to house in seconds. "What's going on here? I couldn't see the house at all. Do I have night blindness or something?"

"Something like that," he muttered, keeping her in hand before letting her down in the living room, easing her to the couch gently. Her arms were bleeding, her clothing torn and she was shaking, although he didn't think she realized it.

Rifter, Vice and Kill, along with Liam, were still outside, taking care of the bodies. He glanced out the window, but Kate was tugging at his arm.

"You're magnificent," she whispered, staring into his eyes, which hadn't yet made the transition from beast to man like the rest of him. "Your eyes are—"

"Scary?"

"Beautiful."

He flinched at that, stepped back and bristled at the compliment the way he did everything unpleasant in life and pretended it didn't exist. Shoved it down if it started to bubble up, because he wasn't used to compliments. Never would be.

Goddamn, it hurt though. He liked that she seemed to accept him. But he'd learned a long time ago that people were liars. Especially witches.

He looked down and saw the blood coming through the sleeves of the sweatshirt. There were also bite marks on her hands, and he felt sick to his stomach. "They hurt you."

"But your wolf saved me. I called and you came."

"I'm not a goddamned pet," he growled, his voice rough, his eyes no doubt still full of battle.

"I can't help it. Can't control it," she told him.

"It's happening because you want me," he stated bluntly. Although it was the truth, she still flushed, but admitted, "That's not going to stop."

He yanked on a pair of jeans as she said, "You want me too. I can feel it."

"I need your help and you need mine. Lady, you're going to be wanted for the rest of your goddamned days. So welcome to my world."

She didn't look comforted at all.

There was a new wolf here and he looked a lot like Stray, but slightly harder. And he bore the same exact scar Stray had down his chest.

Kate swallowed hard when he looked at her and smiled, well, wolfishly, until Stray ordered him the hell out (Stray's words). The wolf didn't argue, went down the hall as a young woman bounded down the stairs and into the room, a bundle of clothing under her arm.

From the look on her face, she'd been worried as anything. The way she looked at Rifter—and he at her—made Kate's heart ache.

She was tall and lithe with long blond hair, and she touched Rifter on her way over, then put her hand out to Kate and said, "I'm Gwen. Let me clean up those cuts."

Stray had mentioned her earlier—she was a doctor. Still, Kate looked at Stray and Gwen understood. "We'll just be right in the bathroom there. We'll leave the door open and you can still see Stray."

That was better. Wordlessly, she nodded and let Gwen lead her toward the bathroom.

With Stray's arms around her, she felt as if nothing bad could get to her.

But something had.

She'd burrowed her face against his bare chest, wanted to do so again, no matter how angry at her he seemed to be.

What worried her most was that she had no memory of walking outside to begin with.

"I brought you another pair of jeans and a sweater and sneakers of mine," Gwen told Kate as she sat her on the closed toilet seat and began opening gauze pads and prepping ointments and what looked like a shot of antibiotics. The bathroom door was partially opened and Kate could see Stray talking with the other men. Wolves. She refocused on Gwen, who was saying, "I'll send Cain out shopping tomorrow. It's too risky for you to go back to your apartment for your things."

"So I let them go, just like my old life. But that was never really mine to begin with," she said and realized she didn't sound sad, but rather accepting.

"I was there, Kate. I mean, I'm still there," Gwen told her, putting the clothes down on the edge of the sink.

"You're a wolf, like Stray."

"Half Dire, half human," she confirmed. "Mated to Rifter."

"The king."

Gwen nodded. "Three weeks ago, I was a doctor and I thought I was dying. I would've too, if I hadn't shifted into a wolf and saved myself. It's certainly not the life I expected. I had zero preparation, but I know I wouldn't trade it."

"Because you lived?"

"Because I met Rifter," she said and Kate immediately flashed to Stray. "Rifter made everything better."

"Stray's trying, but I'm making it worse," Kate confessed.

"You're just scared."

"Shouldn't I be?"

Gwen glanced up at her, the woman's eyes glowing with a little bit of the wolf. "Not if you're our friend."

Chapter 20

Seb lit the candles, put himself in the center of the circle and let his mind wander to where Rogue's mind was being held captive.

It horrified and fascinated him that the wolf could remain still for so long, that he hadn't gone completely insane yet.

Eventually, it would happen, although it could take hundreds of years. And Seb had nothing but time.

He studied the wolf's prone body as he did his own version of the dreamwalk through the eyes of the mare.

The markings on the side of Rogue's face were growing—the dark side attempting to take hold. No doubt failing miserably. But it would keep trying with inky black marks that swirled around the wolf's eye and cheekbone, snaked down his neck as if attempting to obliterate any trace of his skin.

"Let me go, Sebastian. If you don't, my brothers will find a way. You'll just get deeper in the hole with the trappers when that happens."

"You know it's useless." The mare spell was tied to Seb's life and death, and without Rogue, stopping the Dire ghost army would be next to impossible. Rogue refused to look at him and Seb couldn't blame the wolf.

"Get her off me, Seb" was all he said. Seb traced a finger down the markings along the side of his face and scalp, saw the lines of blood the mare trailed as she laughed.

"My punishment's far worse than yours."

"Says you," Rogue bit out. "You fucking bastard. I'll rip your throat out."

The demon inside Seb bubbled up with laughter, and Rogue finally did look at him, a glance so full of hatred the demon rejoiced.

"You unleashed our ancestors against us."

"It was always going to happen. The Elders left you so much unfinished business."

Rogue closed his eyes, and Seb knew his thoughts went to the young witch. Purposefully, perhaps, because Rogue knew Sebastian could see everything he thought. Knew when Rifter and Gwen visited, knew that Gwen had touched Rogue several times and heard him speak.

Seb had the mare caress Rogue's hair, mimicking the way the new Dire queen had. But when he spoke, it wasn't about Gwen at all. "You think I can't get to her, Rogue?"

The wolf eyed him. "You couldn't stop her when she was your lover."

Seb's insides burned. If Rogue knew that, did the other Dires? And did it matter? She'd been lost to him forever a hell of a long time ago, when he'd refused to go back to the covens.

"What the hell happened out there?" Rifter demanded, managing to keep his voice down as Kate cleaned herself up with Gwen's help in the bathroom.

Stray longed to go in there and clean the wounds himself, but Gwen was the better choice. She looked up at him and nodded in his direction, as if to assure him Kate was in good hands.

He finally turned back to Rifter and answered, "Seb was pulling her. I heard the Adept's voice in her head."

"How does he have power over her?" Rifter asked as he ran a hand through his wet hair, his tone of strangled frustration mirroring Stray's feelings. Kill watched in uncharacteristic silence from the corner, his expression unreadable.

"I've got to talk to Jinx," Stray said.

"He's out hunting the ghost army—get him on the line," Vice interjected. "It sounds like Seb thinks she can really hurt him and he's trying to lure her in."

Stray glanced at the silver-eyed wolf and confirmed. "She's been to the otherworld."

Rifter blew out a low whistle, mainly of respect. Those who'd seen the light, as they called it, were to be revered. "Then she can help Jinx and Rogue for sure."

"Technically, yes." Stray pulled out his phone and dialed Jinx. The wolf answered on the sixth ring, sounded out of breath and not all that well.

He explained what happened and Jinx paused for a long moment before he spoke again. "Because the brand is there, it means her powers haven't fully integrated. Basically, as far as we know, once the brand disappears, Kate's power conversion is complete."

"It hasn't even faded a little," Stray told him. "Maybe something's wrong. I mean, has something like this ever worked before?"

"From what I've learned, several times. The witch always picks a dying thirteen-year-old and saves him or her by pouring the magic inside the body. By the time the child's twenty-three, it's ready to fully emerge. Kate just needs the right instruction and to let down her defenses."

"Good luck with that. She's half pissed and the same amount scared," Stray muttered.

"Then you fix it. You found her and your Brother Wolf doesn't want anyone else near her, so you have no choice. Seb's coven's attempting to claim her," Jinx explained. "Since she has a familiar, she can fight them."

"What do I need to do?" Stray asked.

"Make sure no one gets to her." Jinx paused for a moment and then continued. "Look, I did a little research on Kate myself and discovered something else."

"Tell me what you found. And how you did when I couldn't," Stray demanded.

"I used some old coven connections of Seb's," Jinx admitted. "They can't stand what he's done and they were only too happy to help confirm what I suspected. I was planning on telling you, just not this soon."

"Talk, wolf."

Normally, Jinx would bristle at that, but told Stray quietly instead, "In her past incarnation . . . she was Seb's lover—a witch named Lila." Stray grabbed the chair in front of him and nearly broke it with a tight grip.

"You are fucking kidding me." His voice rose and the room silenced. Because Lila wasn't just Seb's lover—she'd been the love of his life, although Seb hadn't seen her for thousands of years before she'd killed herself.

"Steady, wolf. I thought it better you know," Jinx said.

"Yeah, better," he repeated numbly.

"She's not bound to Seb. She doesn't have Lila's love for him—it doesn't work like that. She's got her powers, but she's not the same witch reincarnated."

"You know that for sure?" Stray asked. Jinx wanted to say yes, but the turmoil in his mind told Stray that his brother Dire wasn't one hundred percent sure. "It's okay, Jinx. Don't say anything else about it. Not right now."

Jinx's next words kept his unspoken promise. "You've got to go find the grimoire fast. It should bond to her—respond to her touch only. If she doesn't make an instant connection to it, Seb can definitely control her using their past bond. With it, she's got a great shot at resisting him, using it to her advantage."

Stray turned, noted the bathroom door was nearly closed. Kate must be changing into the dry clothes Gwen lent her. "We'll go now."

"Take Vice and Liam with you. I'll send Cyd back to the house."

"Where are you?"

"Busy," Jinx told him and the next thing Stray heard was silence. The wolf had hung up on him, but he didn't have the time to mull that shit over. Instead, he shoved the phone in his pocket and went to find shoes and a shirt while Gwen finished up bandaging Kate.

Kill followed him. Stray heard the wolf behind him the entire way, refused to acknowledge him. When he got to the door of his room, he turned and shoved Kill against the wall.

"You stay the fuck away from her."

"Does your new pack know you have the hots for a sworn enemy?" Killian asked as though his throat wasn't being compressed.

"My new pack knows a hell of a lot more than you ever did." He pushed away from his brother and went back down the stairs without grabbing what he'd come for. "Don't you fucking follow me, Killian."

"You can't avoid me forever."

True. But for tonight, Stray definitely would. When he got back into the living room, he saw that Gwen had moved into the kitchen with Rifter and Vice as Liam watched over Kate.

As he approached her, he noted she now wore a pair of black jeans and a black sweater. The jeans were short on her but the sweater fit her well. And when she looked up at him, she suddenly stood. Liam tensed, but Stray waved him off and watched her get that same trancelike look in her eyes.

She remained in place for a long second and then went to the door. Instead of trying to open it, she stared out the door, her palms splayed against the glass like a little kid wishing she could go outside.

It was happening again. Stray's blood went cold. There

were no eyes in the woods this time. It was just Seb's siren song, calling out to Kate. And it was working.

Come on out, Kate.

She shook her head. The voice was so clear that Stray wheeled around, expecting to see Seb in the house, when he knew damned well the witch couldn't get in. Even when Seb had been their friend, he'd never come in here. He'd kept his own place at a guest cottage that used to be a quarter mile away until Rifter burned it to the ground six years ago.

Come to me, Kate. I'll teach you everything.

Kate looked at Stray, the confusion apparent. "Can you hear him?"

"Don't listen to him," Stray implored.

"I think he's trying to help me."

"It's definitely a trick. That witch, Seb—I told you he was working with Shimmin." Stray took her hands in his. "Listen to me. You called your familiar for a reason—let me help."

"How?"

"Let me in."

She cleared her mind to allow it, to let him hear the calm, reasoning voice that urged her to step outside and meet him. Stray held her hands tightly, then pulled her into his arms.

The sensation of being wholly and completely safe enveloped her. She breathed in his scent, felt his heartbeat, fast but steady against her cheek.

Get the fuck out of her head, Seb.

Seb chuckled, an eerily demonic sound. *Not a chance, wolf.*

But then Seb was gone and suddenly Kate was back to . . . being Kate. No longer in the clutches of Seb, but she was still upset.

She looked half stunned. Backed away from him. And Stray didn't want to go back to where they were.

"You're safe now. I won't let that happen again."

"He was inside my mind."

"I know. But he won't be for long."

"He scared me." *So do you.*

He winced, hearing her unspoken thoughts, and she did too when she remembered nothing was unspoken between them. "I never want to scare you."

"I know you don't mean to. It's just—"

You're a beast, his mother's voice echoed in his ears. *You can't be trusted,* was told to him in answer to his question of why he couldn't play with the other children or live inside the house when he was two and three and four.

By the time he'd turned five, he'd stopped asking.

"Yeah, I get it, Kate." He pushed away, hated hearing the hurt in his voice. He should be past it.

Besides, she was a witch. He couldn't trust her.

No, you're just bound to her forever.

Under some circumstances, a familiar could be released from service, if warranted. But because of the depth of this bond and the power of the previous witch, it was a tenuous hope at best.

Besides, this was the best way to keep an eye on her. Keep the pack and the Weres safe. By default, the humans would be safe too.

And if she decides to move to the dark side?

He had no way to answer his own question, so he didn't bother trying.

"There's so much to take in."

"Shimmin's been calling your phone," he said. There had been undercover officers at Bite and Howl too, according to Liam's werespies.

The Dires hadn't had much time for partying—their futures didn't seem to call for it either.

Her eyes looked old as time, hunted and innocent, all at once. "You're safe with us."

She crossed her arms in front of her and, just like that,

the distance between them returned. "Seb says you're keeping me prisoner here. And I don't want to believe him."

Her unspoken words were, *Give me a reason not to.*

That was it. He picked her up, carried her to the garage and put her into the truck, even though he'd rather have put her on the back of his bike. He planned on taking her someplace to make her finally understand he was telling the absolute truth.

Chapter 21

Kate settled herself into the passenger's seat. Stray barely waited for her to buckle up before he raced out of the garage.

He also didn't take time to get dressed, save for jeans. She could do nothing but notice, although she'd thought she was being sly. Until Stray said, "I've got clothes in the backseat if this bothers you."

Shit. The mind reading thing was really a problem. "It doesn't. It's just, where are you taking me?"

"Your apartment."

"You said I couldn't go home, and now you're going to leave me there?"

"No, I'm not leaving you anywhere. I just need to show you exactly how much danger you're in, in case tonight didn't teach you," he said.

"Maybe we shouldn't be going out right now." In truth, she was partially terrified, even though his truck was built like a tank. She watched another one follow them out of the garage and down the back road in the rearview mirror.

"We're fine. The Weres have retreated. The trappers won't send more of them to attack us. They're trying to distract us instead, so they can get to you. You're the damned weak link, Kate, and until you start realizing we're here to help and not hurt, we're going to have huge problems."

She hugged her arms around herself.

"There's a sweatshirt in the back, too."

"Stop doing that," she snapped.

"What? Saving your life or reading your mind?"

She almost said *both* but stopped herself. "I'm sorry, Stray. This is all new to me."

He didn't answer her, but even as his hands gripped the wheel harder, his driving slowed to a more manageable level for her. She took a few deep breaths. It was probably a good idea to see her apartment. Although the attacks should've been enough, she still wasn't convinced this was all about her.

"It's not all about you, but you're a big part of it," Stray said. "Sorry, but, man, your thoughts—it's like you're talking directly to me."

"Is there a way out of all of this?"

"I'm it, Kate. You can't get another familiar until I'm dead, and I'm not going anywhere."

She blanched, knew she couldn't lose her one source of protection. Then again, from what she'd seen, Stray couldn't deny her when she called him. "You got upset when I mentioned that you might be human."

He glanced at her. "There's no part of me that's human. I can take this form to function in the world at large—that's the way it's always been—but make no mistake, I have no human frailties."

"But Gwen does?"

"She's been made immortal, but the mix of human in her blood along with the wolf makes her a rarity. We have no idea what would've happened to her if she hadn't been touched by the Elders," Stray said. "They're in charge of us. Our deities, so to speak."

"So this human form is . . . fake?"

"It's part of my shift. Brother Wolf's other form. His

other half." He smiled. "I know it's hard to take in. But this form is stronger, faster, and indestructible. Any medical exam you performed on me would blow your mind."

"But Gwen . . ."

"She'd show human signs. A blood type, which we don't have. Now it's my turn. Does your anger and fear always work on people the way it did with Shimmin in the woods? Because you didn't try it on me."

And you damn well deserved it, she thought, and he snorted. "You going to answer my question?"

"Honestly, I've never thrown grown men like that before."

"What exactly has happened before?"

"Well, objects can fly around. Things shake. And with people, they kind of freeze. I mean, they can talk but they can't move. But that's only happened twice in my life. I was probably the angriest I'd ever been—it happened to the same person."

"That's a type of binding spell."

"That's bad, right? That I can't control those things. Powers. Whatever."

"You'll learn, and fast. But no, anger's not always a bad thing. Sometimes it's the most valuable thing you've got, especially when it's saving your life."

"I know you think that I was trying to make good on my threat to put a spell on you, but that was honestly the farthest thing from my mind. I didn't try to make you my familiar," she said finally, after a long pause. "But suppose I do get control and I use it against you by accident—or your brothers?"

"It would take a lot to spell us."

"Okay, so I can't hurt you, and you'll keep me safe until I save your brother. At least I know I'm useful to you for a little while."

"There's so much more to it than my brother. If you'd let me explain, I think you'll understand."

"I don't seem to have a choice."

"Neither did we," Stray told her.

They rode in silence for a little while until he pulled into the alley behind her apartment. The other truck pulled in directly behind them. She waited until Stray gave her the all clear before she tumbled out basically into his arms.

"Forgot the truck was so high."

"I don't mind," he told her. His eyes shifted to the wolf's for just a second, and that hot coil in her belly threatened to unfurl again.

Seeing him fight turned you on.

And damn, he heard that too. He had the sense not to mention it, just raised his brows and gave a satisfied grin. "You should put a shirt on."

"I'm not cold." He tugged her behind him into the back doorway, no key necessary. "Besides, I might need to fight again."

Bastard.

"You already called me that," he said.

When they walked, her following him through the narrow hallway that led to her apartment, she swore his shoulders brushed the walls of the hallway. Brother Wolf's eyes watched her, and she stopped herself from reaching out to touch him, although it wasn't easy.

She brought her mind back to matters at hand. She wondered if her landlord was searching for her. Rent was due soon and she'd need to empty the place out . . .

But that thought was soon gone. Once Stray opened the still-unlocked door, the mess inside wasn't what she expected.

There was nothing left. There were scratches, deep grooves, along the floor and the walls, and there was blood, but there was nothing else left of hers. She hadn't had much of value, but it had been hers. "Where did my stuff go?"

"Shimmin's people probably came back and got rid of it."

"Why?"

"You're . . . erased, Kate. From the police databases. From social security. For all intents and purposes, you've fallen off the map."

"You had nothing to do with that?"

"No, but I would've done it if they hadn't."

"For my own safety, of course." The anger built inside of her, this time at the right people, the ones who'd tried to hurt her.

"The witch who passed her powers to me—she died so men like Shimmin couldn't use her. If she hadn't died, she might've been forced to work with them. Or she might've agreed to, like Seb did. What makes you think the same thing won't happen to me?"

"When she passed the powers, she strengthened them," he told her. "You won't be as susceptible."

But there were still no promises. "I want to know more about her. Why she picked me. I want to know everything." The lights flickered wildly and the floor began to shake under them. And for once, she didn't care that it was happening, didn't care that Stray was witnessing it this time. For the first time, she liked this power, because at least her feelings were known.

She waited for Stray to argue with her, but strangely, he didn't, just led her out of the apartment into the cold air. Before they got into his truck, he cleared his throat and said, "I need to touch the brand."

"Oh. Okay." She glanced at Vice and Cyd. Stray must've motioned to them to get into their truck and they did so. When she turned her back to him, she lifted her shirt a little and asked, "Why?"

"Because I have to find your grimoire—your book of magic. It belonged to your witch, and now it's yours."

"And it's going to help me?"

"It's a book of spells. Each witch has their own personal one, and sometimes it's passed down by generation, through families. You practice them, add to it. You make it yours," Stray explained. "It's one of the final puzzle pieces for you."

"How do we find it?"

"I can track it. I've been sensing it for half the day, but I can't quite scent it."

"You can track it?"

"That's something I'm really good at. I tracked you and look where we are now."

Where indeed. Somewhere between magic and reality, hanging on to both by a tenuous thread.

Stray was really trying not to invade her privacy, but Kate didn't realize how loud her thoughts were, how they were basically directed at him like darts to a board.

Why she wasn't able to do the same to him when he left his mind open, well, he didn't know if she was being polite or if she was simply distracted. But the fact that Seb could get to her . . . well, Stray needed to protect himself better.

Kate stood there, looking over her shoulder at him. Waiting for his touch. He rubbed his hands together, but it wasn't necessary. His body ran warm, like the wolf he was, and when he touched the mark, his fingers lined with the witch's, a current ran through him, far stronger than he'd felt earlier, a sensation of belonging, both him to her and her to him.

And that was different, a confirmation of what he'd been feeling the entire time. Everything clicked. The need for more threatened to overwhelm him, and he didn't want to be denied. Wouldn't, not for much longer.

"Ah, Stray?" she asked, because his hands slid around to her belly and his face lowered against her neck. He bent his head, suckled, marking her lightly on the side of her neck, enough to make her shiver against him in a way that had nothing to do with the cold. "Is this because of your wolf?"

"He likes it, but this is my show now." He turned her in his arms and kissed her then, his tongue stroking the roof of her mouth, teasing her until she moaned against his mouth. Her hands gripped his biceps and he pressed his arousal to her belly, wanting her to feel him. To know that she wasn't scaring him off any longer.

He'd had hours to think about the familiar aspect to all of this—and strangely enough, he wasn't running screaming for the hills.

Yeah, she wasn't scared of him any longer. No, sir, because he could smell her arousal, sweet and hot and all for him, and there was no fear. "Let's find your book."

"And then?"

"And then . . . I'm going to do this again. And much, much more."

She didn't protest. And then Brother Wolf nudged him. He caught wind of another trail, and this time, it was exactly what he needed. "Come on. I've got a lead on the book—a good one."

She scrambled into the truck and he climbed in and took off down the alley with Vice and Cyd following. He noted that she kept touching her lips with her fingers lightly.

And then suddenly the mood changed and everything shifted. "What's wrong?"

She drew in a tight breath. "That part of the dream—where I die—that's new," she said softly.

He gave a quick glance in her direction. "You never remembered that?"

"No. Is that important?"

"Very." He drummed his fingers on the wheel as the truck barreled down the highway in the dark, Brother Wolf guiding him on this hunt. "You're *other*, Kate, because you're a witch but also because you've seen the afterworld. That's going to give you a connection to the spirit world that most don't have."

He thought about Rogue. He could help her with all of this so much better than Stray could. Jinx, too.

But she chose you. She wants you.

And he wished he could believe it was of her own free will, because her scent was killing him. He wanted to stop the truck, drag her across his lap and take her until she clung to him, calling his name.

He shifted as his cock grew impossibly hard. Brother Wolf growled at him to keep it together, which he would normally find funny as shit.

But not tonight.

"Are your brothers still following us?"

He glanced in the rearview. "They're there. We'll be okay. Truck's bulletproof. Fireproof. Wereproof."

"What about witchproof?"

He sure as hell wasn't. "That remains to be seen."

"You've known a lot of witches?"

Knew them, stayed away from them. "Mainly Seb. We know a lot of lore—witches, vamps, wolves. We keep track of it."

She twisted her hands together. "Is there like a special witch's chat board or something?"

"Actually, yes. But you'll also need different resources. Internet's far from reliable—anyone can say anything they goddamned want, you know?"

He grew quiet then, because they were close. He slowed down. The urge to hunt was overwhelming, but he wasn't looking for someone. This time it was something, her magic guiding him without her realizing it. It wasn't spelling him. No, it was more like a gentle finger under his chin keeping him on track.

Chapter 22

"We're close," Stray told her. They'd been driving around for the better part of half an hour, Stray stopping every once in a while to stand outside the car, breathing in the night air. Kate longed to join him, but her legs still trembled when she realized how much was on all their shoulders.

She was secretly hoping this turned out to be some kind of crazy prank.

Why would he joke about something like this?

He wouldn't. He'd been dead serious. And her hands were shaking again.

Wordlessly, Stray reached into the backseat and pulled out an open bottle of Jack Daniel's, handed it to her. She took a sip, winced and asked, "Why does Leo Shimmin hate wolves?"

"It's a long story, stretching back to Viking times." He paused. "They started out wanting to avenge the deaths of their ancestors, but over the centuries, it's twisted into something horrible. They're called weretrappers and they want to enslave wolves and take over the world. And I realize it sounds like the plot of some horror novel, which makes it worse, because it can happen. It will, if you don't help. And humans are clueless."

"I can't believe ..." She stopped because she tried to imagine and couldn't. "I know there have been instances where humans have tried to eradicate others, but ..."

"It's going to be worse, because the wolves are strong. Coupled with the black arts, the demons, well, not only are they going to gain control, but they'll lose it just as fast to the very powers they're trying to control. They're playing with fire, and everyone is going down because of it. Except us."

"How does helping your brother work into all of this?"

"Rogue can communicate with the spirit world that Seb is conjuring. And in order to help him, we have to kill the witch who's calling to you. Many of his spells will live on without him, but not the one he placed on my brother. Seb's got other witches working spells, but he's the most important one."

"I have to kill an immortal witch. How exactly is that supposed to work?"

"You could try to force Seb to become mortal, to give up his powers."

"And hurt another girl like me."

"And save billions of people."

Another half an hour and several more swigs from the bottle, she realized two things—her head couldn't spin enough to rid her of what Stray filled it with, and she couldn't get drunk.

Stray looked sympathetic, but he hadn't held anything back. "That book of magic's looking pretty good now, isn't it?"

"Suppose I can't—"

"You can. The witch who touched you was as powerful as Seb, maybe more so. And you're almost to your twenty-third birthday ..."

"It's tomorrow," she said quietly. "Exactly ten years from the time the witch touched me. Happy birthday to me."

"You'll need a lot more than that bottle to get drunk," he confirmed. "It's your power—it absorbs ... everything."

"That sucks," she muttered, took another vicious swig in defiance. She should be saying, "I want to go home," but that basement apartment wasn't home. Nothing had been since the accident, maybe wouldn't be again. "Stray, I can't do anything you're asking of me."

"You will. I'll help you."

"If I can't—"

"A whole lot of people die. Innocent ones."

"So I take one life to save many?"

"That's the basic idea."

They rode in silence for several more minutes until Stray suddenly turned along a dirt road that seemed to lead to nowhere. Finally, it opened to a small parcel of land and a decent-sized cabin.

"That's Lila's—your witch. It's spelled still so no one can simply stumble upon it," Stray said. "The grimoire recognizes us, so that's a good sign."

"Lila," she repeated. "That's a pretty name." It was the first time she'd felt anything but anger or fear toward the witch.

Lila's cabin was well off the beaten path. As far as she could tell, they were an hour from the Dire house. As she approached the porch, lightning split the sky, a brilliant display of angry light and crackling noise as it struck the ground close by.

She swallowed hard. "That's for us, isn't it?"

Stray didn't answer, pulled her inside the cabin. When he looked back at her, his eyes were what he called Brother Wolf's—and he was hunting something.

She held tight to his hand as he navigated the pitch black of the cabin easily. She heard the scurrying of small animals, tried not to think about spiders and God knew what else until he stopped and began to dig at the floorboards.

She held the flashlight where he was working, for her benefit, not his. But then he got up in frustration and began to tap the walls, looking for hollow spots. She moved the flashlight off him and on to the rest of the room.

Before her eyes, it turned from grimy and old to new and sparkling, how it must've been when her witch—Lila— lived. She turned fast as though someone had her by the shoulders, guiding her, until she stopped in one of the corners opposite from where Stray worked.

"This is all magic," she said, her hushed tones holding a trace of awe. She touched the walls and then she went inexplicably to a place in the corner. With a touch of a finger, it opened. She reached into the dark cabinet tentatively, drew out a large, heavy box.

Her entire body flushed with heat, and she couldn't resist sitting on the dirty, dusty floor and opening it.

When she opened it, she knew she'd come home.

A book. Leather-bound with gold writing—a language she shouldn't understand but did.

Her mother's family name was written on the inside pages and her breath caught. "My mother . . . she was a witch," she murmured to herself. "Lila . . . she was related to me. It really is my bloodline. It was there the entire time."

It was too late for her to wonder if things could've been different, to wish her mother had embraced this, helped her. She could only move forward, and with the book's help, she would.

"Kate, did you find it?" Stray asked, but he knew she had. His wolf felt it, her surge of energy and power as she cradled the book of magic in her hands.

She looked up at him with a smile. "I'm not helpless anymore."

"You never were, Kate."

She let those words sink in for a long moment and then put the flashlight back on the book. She flipped through while Stray waited patiently in the dark.

She didn't know how long she sat there, drinking all of it in—her history. The writing was perfect, black ink on thick parchment paper. She traced a finger along the words that told of her destiny. "I was meant for this. She—Lila—always knew she'd pick me, out of all of the witches in her line. Do you believe in fate?"

"Yeah, I do."

His voice sounded a little odd, but she was too involved in the book to give him her attention. "It's all true, Stray. The wolves—you're mentioned here. Weres. And Dires. Your name is in this book." She stared up at him. "Did you know that?"

"No. But I'm not surprised. Good witches tend to like us."

"Because you're good wolves."

"We try, Kate." Another burst of lightning outlined his frame, and a surge of want coursed through her.

"There's more." Her finger ran down the calligraphy. "Vampires. Shifters. Weretrappers . . ."

She trailed off and read a little more about them. "That's what Leo Shimmin is."

"Yes. Look, Kate, we can't stay here. Hold tight to the grimoire. It's yours."

Indeed, the gold seemed to . . . glow, somehow, like it had honed in on her presence. "No one can take it from me?"

"No. It's part of you. Come on, now." He held out a hand, and she put the book back in the box and then under her jacket., holding it there with her arm. With her free hand, she took his help. Didn't let go of his hand until it was time to get into the truck.

Chapter 23

The lights in the truck flickered seconds later, followed by a burst of lightning.

"I didn't do that," Kate told him.

Stray looked out the front windshield at the sky. He could see perfectly in the dark. He took her in hand as he sniffed the air, and the lingering scent of burning sky filled his nostrils.

Unnatural, all of it. "We have to go now."

But even as he said it, he wasn't sure they'd make it back.

No choice, Brother Wolf said. He locked the doors and prayed the electrical system in the car would hold out.

As they backtracked through the woods, the lightning continued to flare, but somehow, the barrage of rain he expected didn't happen. When he looked over at Kate, she had her bare hands on the cover of the book and she seemed to be concentrating. Maybe getting them out of there safely had everything to do with her, or maybe not, but he wasn't questioning it.

And yet she looked so damned pale. Her breathing was shallow and when she turned to look at him, the circles under her eyes made her look wan and drawn.

He jammed the car into reverse and headed back toward

the cabin and its magical properties. That's where the current battle was being waged. He couldn't read her mind, and that scared him more than anything.

She doesn't need you if she's not calling for you.

Or maybe the opposite was true—maybe this was when she needed him the most.

As dangerous as it was, the witch in her needed to be outside. He understood that pull all too well, and he granted her wish. He got out and ran to her door.

"Stray, I—"

Her strength was crumbling. Saying *Trust me* would mean nothing. He picked her up and carried her out of the truck, because showing was always better than telling.

Her connection to the moon would be as strong as his—he had little doubt. She'd feel better outside, but she probably didn't know that.

Once out in the open air with him, he attempted to shield her with his body from the raindrops that fell, fat and uneven, like they were being held back by her power. She still held tight to the grimoire.

He noted Vice and Cyd were half out of their truck too, covering both him and Kate with guns and their wolves, if necessary.

But guns and wolves had little to no effect on magic. It was up to Kate this time, and he prayed she could see it through. Even a small victory at this point would be enough.

Kate breathed easier as soon as the open air hit her.

He placed her down under the shimmery orb and immediately her center of balance returned. She put her free hand on her belly as everything shifted right-side up again. Better than before . . . better than it had been since the accident, when every night she'd run inside at dark and wait under the covers for the dawn.

"How did you know?" she asked.

"The moon calls to wolves and witches," Stray explained. Kate was holding him, her eyes shimmering, and he wondered if this would make the brand on her back disappear. "It's not always pleasant, but it's easier if you don't fight her."

The lightning hit so close, she jumped. "We shouldn't be out here."

"We have to be—you've got to stop this. It's Seb."

"I'm not ready. I need more time."

"You don't have time," he told her. "You've got to get your shit together fast. Stop thinking. Start feeling. This month has two full moons—Seb will no doubt try to use the power of the first one, and if that fails, he's got a backup. And no one's recovered from the shit that already happened last month. Gwen's so ... new, Rifter and Jinx are battling ... We've got a lot of road to cover."

"And all I have to do is start feeling?"

"Yes."

"You make it sound so simple."

"It has to be."

Kate had protected herself from feeling anything for so long—until this wolf had come to her rescue—and now everything she felt was scaring her. It was rising up, threatening to take away every ounce of control she'd ever had—and she'd long ago discovered that her losing control was a frightening prospect.

Not for Stray, though. For the wolves, loss of control was accepted. Necessary. Wanted, even.

"I don't like feeling out of control."

"Then control it," Stray told her.

"I don't know how."

"Try."

She closed her eyes and let the thoughts swirl around her. It was too much—she wasn't grounded.

"You're ... vibrating," she called over the roar.

"So are you," he pointed out.

She wanted to be scared—should be—but with Stray

holding her, the grimoire holding her past and future, she was anything but.

The rain hadn't started again, but the lightning rolled through the sky. She waited for the familiar beats of thunder in between the bolts, but none came.

"These storms—they're man-made."

"Witch-made," Stray corrected as the electricity tingled along her skin.

She put the fingertips of one hand against the grimoire. "He's really strong."

"So are you."

Her first instinct was to deny it, but she couldn't. Stray was right. Now she just had to figure out how to utilize her powers.

The tingling continued, like the storm was calling her out, literally. Before Stray could stop her, she was out the back door and walking unprotected into the rain.

The brand flared and something . . . someone was guiding her. She tucked the book between her knees and put her hands up to the sky as if she could absorb the spell that held it there.

"Kate?"

Stray was behind her and suddenly she wasn't alone or unprotected. It made her body surge, a powerful sensation. She kept her palms up toward the sky, closed her eyes, and concentrated on trying to push the storm away. It felt so ridiculously bold and yet completely right at the same time.

"The end of the moon is the most effective time for magic. Fuck your chakras. Roll your goddamned power out," he murmured.

She felt the moon's power and Stray's protective presence, and she chanted in a language she'd never studied but knew as instinctively as she knew her own name.

She didn't see anything at all happening in the dark, but Stray must have. The low, throaty growls ripped from his throat, and she dropped her hands, grabbed the grimoire and turned to face him.

"Is everything all right?"

"Yes. Very. We're stronger than they are. Good always is."

"It really worked," she breathed.

"It's white magic, but you'll be fighting the dark arts," he told her. "It's going to be dangerous for you."

Under the heavy rain, he kissed her. Drew her close and ravaged her mouth while she clung to him, ignoring everything but the lust that rose like hot steam around them.

She heard car doors slam, remembered they hadn't been alone out here. But Stray didn't care, and neither did she as his hands traveled along her body, under her sweater. His thumbs brushed her nipples and she jolted, because they'd been aching for his touch. He rolled them lightly between his fingers and she gasped as her womb contracted, wished he would pull her sweater off and put his mouth to her breasts.

To that end, she wound her fingers from her free hand in his hair and pulled him in for a kiss, never letting go of ei ther Stray or the grimoire. Electricity that had swirled around them now danced between them, locking them together in a heated embrace.

It was a tease—a delicious, amazing, mind-fucking tease. Stray gripped her ass and rolled her pelvis against his aching cock, wanted nothing more than to drive into her. Sitting, standing, upsidefuckingdown, it didn't matter.

If this went on much longer, he wasn't going to be able to stop. As it was, Kate was in danger of going over the edge herself, and he planned on riding this out until she came to her senses.

At least Vice had the good sense to back his truck down the hill.

Maybe this is because of Vice. Whenever that Dire was around, everyone's feelings were more intense, harder to control.

But he knew it was all about him and Kate and nothing else. Animal attraction, but it was more than that. He'd been attracted to a lot of Weres over the past years, but none had ever affected him like this.

He pulled away from the kiss and buried his face in her hair—her scent killed him, flat out slayed him the way it had from day one, made every overeager, possessive alpha male need roar out of him like a freight train without brakes.

"Kate, this is—"

"Touch me," she told him. "I love when you touch me."

He didn't need to be asked twice. He pushed her shirt up to touch her with his mouth, his tongue, his teeth lightly scraping her nipples until she gasped, a sound that echoed through the now-quiet night. He was glad she wasn't wearing a bra, and his fingers trailed down her belly between her legs, finding no barrier there either.

His fingers stroked her wetness. He wanted her to come apart, wanted that above his own need, even as his heavy cock ached for release.

"Come for me, Kate. Come on, beautiful—let it all go."

His thumb circled her clit and she orgasmed instantly, her contractions making her knees weak. He held her so she didn't fall, let her ride out the pleasure until she got her breath and her bearings.

The rain that had been ferocious until that point stopped then, the sky lit up. And he knew the deluge would begin again in minutes, but it didn't matter. For that moment, they'd stopped the rain together, and he didn't know if it was because they were witch and familiar or witch and wolf—or mates.

Chapter 24

Seb's wrists were tied above his head, his face buried against a woman's breasts while another lowered herself onto his throbbing cock. A third propped him up, rubbing her wetness against his back as she did so.

These women didn't care who or what Seb was, and apparently his body didn't care either. He wanted it—wanted all of it, in a way he'd never be able to control.

He bucked his hips up, the woman's moans encouraging him to fuck her harder. The other woman replaced her breasts in his mouth with her pussy and the third began to finger his ass as he explosively climaxed, his body spasming somewhere between pain and pleasure.

He should be satiated, yet he was far from it. The smells and sounds of sex surrounded him, pushed him over the edge again and again, until his body was exhausted but his cock remained hard.

You'll always be unfulfilled.

He knew closing his eyes wouldn't block out the images of them cavorting over him, but he did so anyway. Instead of their leering, orgasmic faces, Lila's face swam in front of his vision, so realistic he extended his untied arms to grab for her.

He caught an armful of empty air, exhaled painfully and opened his eyes. The women finally collapsed around him, the possession the demon had taken over them leaving them limp and their minds permanently weakened. They'd be returned to society as shells of their former selves, dreaming nightly of Seb and this time in his bed.

With her long dark hair and beautiful, nearly obsidian eyes, Lila had been older than time and was all he'd ever wanted.

He'd given her up because she'd begged him to. And for a long time it had been the only thing keeping both witches safe.

He'd met Lila when he'd run from his family. She'd been his port in the storm—his everything. For centuries, they'd met in secret. Once a year was all they'd allow themselves, one twenty-four-hour period together, and then they'd separate so their powers couldn't be used against each other.

Lila killed herself because the trappers—and Cordelia, Seb's own sister—were trying to do just that. She refused to get caught and be the reason Seb got pulled back into his coven. And then he'd gone and let her death mean absolute shit, because he'd refused to pass his powers on to an innocent.

He hated her for leaving him, for burdening another with a gift she didn't want.

Since you want her so badly, take her, the demon Kondo urged. *She'd be easy to seduce.*

"Not with Stray as her familiar."

We'd get a Dire and a witch—not bad for a day's work. Maybe you can have both of them to play with. You'd like that, wouldn't you, Seb?

His body surged against his will. "She's not Lila any longer," he said through gritted teeth.

She's part of Lila, Kondo told him. *I thought an Adept could seduce anyone.*

As Kondo laughed, Seb prayed. Ignored the jabs, the way he did when the demon abused his body to soothe its appetites with sex and drink with men and women and Weres—it didn't matter which.

So yes, Seb might be breaking down, but he was gaining strength as well. Wasn't sure why the demon didn't notice— or, if it did, why it didn't care.

Torn between light and darkness, Seb wondered which would ultimately win, and decided it didn't matter at all.

"Dude, we're starving. Mo's is up ahead. Safe and shit," Vice said into his ear. In turn, Stray pulled into the lot and closed the phone, the answer clear.

Rifter wouldn't want them to do this, but they hadn't eaten since the fight. And Mo's was run by a family of Weres who refused to join any of the packs in the area because they were their own little army and provided a safe house of sorts to anyone who needed the protection.

Stray was starving for something a little more primal, but he suspected Kate would object to the lack of privacy. And maybe the mud.

Wolves didn't mind getting very dirty.

"You've got that look on your face again," she told him.

"What look?"

"Wolfish."

He grinned to himself as he went to help her out of the truck and escort her inside safely. The sky was still dark, stars twinkled and the familiar cold air was back. No sign of thunder, lightning or rain. Best yet, no signs of Seb invading Kate's mind.

It would've been better if there was a way to lay her out in the back of the truck and take her, but for now, food would have to do.

"Is this a regular diner?"

"Depends on your definition," he told her as he ushered

her in through the heavy glass doors. Vice and Cain came in behind them and one of the waitresses—Mo's daughter—locked it behind them.

"Safer for this time of night," she explained. Kate started to ask why it hadn't been locked in the first place, but Stray steered her away before she could.

Humans frequented the place, mainly tourists and truckers just rolling through, and they'd have no idea that the glass was bullet and wolf proof. Or that there were were-snipers on the roof twenty-four seven.

Vice waved to them and Stray waved him off and guided Kate into a private booth in the back room, leaving Cyd and Vice to eat and talk to Mo about the current situation. The less Kate knew about how bad the situation truly was right this moment, the better.

He was going to love watching her continue to come into her own. She was opening up like a blooming rose, and her scent was richer, heavier than it had been hours ago. But he still likened it to crack for his wolf, and Brother gave a deep howl of agreement.

"What'll it be, doll—the usual?" Mo's wife, Ellen, chewed her gum at a rapid-fire pace and smiled at him and Kate.

"A few of them," Stray said. "Kate, why don't you try the special?"

"That sounds great." She smiled at Ellen and when the woman left, she asked, "Human?"

"No. Were."

"Ah." She took a discreet look around. "Is everyone . . . ?"

"About half and half. I don't think it's wise to point them out."

"Can't they hear us? The wolves, I mean."

"That's why we're in the private section—we're okay to talk freely here."

He'd pushed his sleeves up and she leaned forward and

pulled his wrists toward her. "Did this happen during the fight?"

Her own bandages had come loose in the rain, but Gwen had cleaned and stitched them well enough.

"It's nothing."

"They're the exact same cuts I have."

"Technically, they're bites."

She glared at him. "You're funny when you're hungry."

He hesitated for a long moment before telling her, "We're bonded, Kate. This is what happens to familiars."

This is what happens to familiars ...

Stray had tried to spare her the answer that would make her stomach gnaw with guilt, but Kate had pushed. "I'm sorry—I didn't know that would happen."

"It's not your fault."

But it was. She'd gone outside, put herself and Stray in danger. And there was a good chance it could happen again.

Ellen brought some dishes, and for several moments, they ate in silence. Despite everything, Kate was hungry—the night's events had taken a lot from her.

Her gaze went again to the book and she said, "Tell me about Rogue. It sounds like he's under a spell by Seb, but I thought Dires couldn't be spelled."

"It's not a spell—it's a mare. She's a monster from nightmares—from hell, actually, and Seb's controlling her and Rogue's mind. But Seb, strong as he is, could never do this alone. He's entered into a very dangerous pact with the dark arts, which is why I know he'll never be the same."

"Evil seems to be unstoppable," she murmured.

"In theory."

"And in reality?"

"Sometimes the good guys win one."

"And if you don't, it doesn't matter?"

"We have consciences," Stray growled. "You have no idea how badly I wish we didn't."

She believed him. While he continued to eat, she flipped through the book, stopping on the passage about the familiars.

She'd never owned a pet, never felt particularly drawn to cats or birds, although the book said it was a bit unusual for a witch's familiar to be a bird.

"Seb's familiar's a raven," Stray told her, noting what passage she was looking at. "In case you see one hanging around."

"That's creepy."

"That's Seb for you."

"You two didn't get along, I take it?"

"I came late to the party. He did some good stuff for my brothers at one point, I guess. I just never got comfortable with him."

From what Stray had told her about the scars on his back, he hadn't even been able to trust his own family. She would imagine that trusting strangers wasn't high on his list of priorities.

"The more I know about Seb, the better," she said, and Stray began to fill her in on all things Seb. The odd thing was, it was as if he was telling her a story she knew, somewhere deep inside. His words were merely a reminder.

"So Lila was his mate?"

"In a way. But he let her leave. We wouldn't do that. We protect our mates—"

"From the big, bad humans?"

He smiled wryly. "Last time I looked, you weren't human. Convenient of you to forget."

Kate looked into Stray's whiskey-colored eyes, fringed with dark lashes and flecks of black—the color grew more otherworldly when he was in wolf form. "You hate witches more than humans?"

"It's a neck-and-neck battle," he told her. "But only certain witches."

"That's because you have to like me."

"No, not really." He continued eating—she couldn't believe the amount of food he was able to casually put away. "I normally don't put others' needs before my wolf's."

She realized he was talking about her orgasm by the cabin and her cheeks flushed with the recent memory. Her clothes were still damp and she realized she could come again easily. And that he hadn't.

She'd noted the hard bulge outlined in his wet jeans when he'd gotten into the truck, right before the blinding rain came down.

"And don't thank me—you'll have plenty of time to make it up to me," he told her.

"Stop reading my mind."

"I can't help it. I like what I hear."

"Wolves," she muttered and dug into the plate of onion rings as he let out a hearty laugh.

The Weres were back. Gwen sensed them seconds after Rifter had, and the thrill of her wolf senses getting stronger was quickly erased by the strong sense of fear.

"Don't worry, Gwen. We're not going out there to fight them this time." Rifter went into the living room and she followed. Together, through the sliding glass door, they watched the glowing eyes staring back at them.

Gwen knew they couldn't see in, but she still felt exposed.

"We're safe," Rifter repeated, and she was just beginning to believe it when something jumped in front of the doors, landing on two feet, his back to them.

Killian.

Her throat tightened and Rifter grew so tense, Gwen thought he would break. In seconds, Killian shifted to a black wolf that looked a lot like Stray's, slightly larger. He raced across the field, meeting ten Weres head-on.

"I can't let him do this alone," Rifter said, his voice already rumbling with an impending shift.

"I'll call Liam," she agreed. Until she watched Killian fight.

Kill's Brother Wolf sliced through the Weres—the *possessed* Weres—with an ease that even Vice didn't have. Kill was almost a blur as he fought. *Other*, as they were, but somehow he seemed otherworldly as well, and that was a whole different story. Because, as an immortal, Kill couldn't have gone to the other side. That would be impossible.

She continued to watch with fascination as the Weres died with a fierce howl followed by an unearthly scream, as black smoke puffed out of their mouths. It was the evil trying to escape and not die along with the mortal Weres. But as far as Gwen could tell, they didn't succeed.

He took down the wolves in a matter of minutes, then shifted immediately and walked back toward the house with an easy swagger. He looked handsome and completely unscathed, save for the blood of his kills. Instead of coming in through the sliding door, he simply saluted her and Rifter and then jumped up, presumably to the balcony he'd jumped down from.

"I thought he was staying in the basement?" she asked, not wanting to mention the issue of the bodies on the lawn.

"Who the fuck knows what he's doing," Rifter muttered. "Something's going on with that wolf. The question is what—and we'll find out soon enough."

Whether we want to or not, Gwen wanted to add, but she managed to hold her tongue.

Chapter 25

Jinx saw Cain bounding over the crest, still in human form. Cain fought the urge to shift quite well these days.

An omega would have better control than an alpha. It was why any pack would be lucky to have one. It was exactly why Cain had kept it secret for so long. If the pack that had tossed the twins out so carelessly for being moon crazed knew they'd given up both an alpha and an omega, they would've kept the boys chained up for years until they either died or grew out of it. Weres had their first shift at sixteen, which left them wild and vulnerable. Dires shifted for the first time at twenty-one—and while that was a far more dangerous proposition, they didn't fall prey to moon craze at all.

It was why Jinx had taken them in, as he'd done for Weres in the past until they safely got through their twenty-first year. But he'd never grown as close to any of them as he had these two. Five years and counting and he felt like he'd somehow given birth to them. In a non-having-female-parts kind of way.

Now they'd pledged their alliance to Liam's pack, and Jinx knew it was the right place for them.

Until then, Jinx would prepare them as best he could.

"Where've you been?" he asked Cain now.

"Recon," Cain said, and Jinx didn't believe that totally. But they were heady on Liam's new rise to power and their new positions, even if it hadn't been made official yet, and Jinx couldn't take that from them just yet. Temperance wasn't a Were's strongest point, especially not for ones who were just shy of twenty-one.

"That FBI agent's been hanging around. Watching." Cain stuck his hands into the pockets of his jeans. "He doesn't trust Shimmin."

"Who cares? I don't trust him," Jinx said.

"We can't just off a fed," Cain pointed out.

"Shimmin will, sooner or later, so at least he's good for something," Jinx told him. "You want to run, better do it now before we lock down for the day. I need to head out and check on a few things before I go back to the house." Jinx put a hand out to touch Cain's shoulder. "Talk to the fed and then get back to the house. I'll give you an hour and if you're not back—"

"I will be."

"Good wolf." Jinx ran, the wind brushing his face, his wolf longing to come out and take him away from all the shit raining down on his head.

Angus stayed in the diner until after midnight, poring over old case files on his laptop, because there was plenty of good coffee and it was far less depressing than the motel room that looked to be home for quite a while.

He continued to ignore Shimmin's calls for the moment.

Since the curtain of the supernatural had been drawn open for him, everything had changed. For better or worse . . . he guessed he'd find out which soon enough. Tangling with the supernatural didn't leave anyone alive for very long. Not humans, anyway.

He had no goddamned idea who—*what*—he could trust.

He didn't expect or want help from Shimmin's trapper group. Wanted to stay as far away from that man as he could, but he popped up like evil clockwork and kept on coming.

And Angus continued to keep an eye on Cain Chambers, mainly to find out if he was, in fact, a wolf, like Shimmin said. Angus wanted to have doubts, but, if nothing else, Cain could possibly lead Angus to . . .

To your death. Because, the thing was, as much as he was watching Cain Chambers, Cain had been tracking him since they'd met. And Angus would be lying to himself if he said he didn't like it, or the way Cain seemed to study him. It was more than simply a combatant studying an enemy, although there was definitely some of that involved. But whenever he met that boy's eyes, something inside of him burned, and in the nicest way possible. Because Cain was no boy.

He tried to tell himself it was because he'd gone without for too long, and he desperately wanted to believe his own lie. Truth was, he looked forward to the nightly stalkings.

When the hairs on the back of his neck began to tingle, he knew tonight would be no exception. He gulped his coffee and looked out the large window by his booth to see Cain was still there, leaning against the telephone pole, making no attempt to hide himself.

Angus shut his computer and stuffed it into its bag, paid his bill and went out to talk to Cain. Typically, when he tried this, Cain would vanish into thin air. But tonight Cain stayed, although he'd moved down the block, where it was quieter, more deserted.

He was smoking a cigarette—at least that's what Angus smelled as he approached, although it looked to be hand-rolled.

"That'll kill you," he said as he stood next to Cain, who now leaned against the brick building behind them. Cain gazed at him with the clear look of, *Yeah, nice try.*

What had Angus expected, for Cain to say, *I can't die*

from human diseases? He suspected most supernatural creatures didn't out themselves that easily. Instead, he watched Cain's profile. Regal. Handsome. His skin looked golden although the sun hadn't been strong enough to tan anyone in months.

"What do you think will kill you?" Cain asked, after he blew smoke into the chilled air, keeping his eyes straight ahead.

"This job," he muttered.

Cain snorted. "Dangerous for you out here."

"Not for you?"

"I didn't say that." Cain stretched. He was just over six feet, Angus's height as well, lanky but muscled. He wasn't dressed for the weather, not in a leather jacket, jeans and boots, but he didn't look cold. "This town has plenty of danger to go around."

"And you're part of that." A statement, not a question. Angus paid for it when Cain pinned him, a hand on his throat. The boy was looking him dead in the eye.

"Not a smart thing to do to a fed," he croaked. "Or are you hoping that dead men tell no tales?"

Cain laughed softly. "You've got a real flair for the dramatic, Agent Young."

He didn't back off, though. And Angus didn't think he wanted him to, because the hand wasn't pressing hard enough to do anything but keep him in position while Cain's body rested close to his. Finally, Cain released his grip. He didn't move away, though.

"What do you want from me?" Angus asked.

"You need to be careful about the company you keep."

"Present company included?"

Cain cocked his head and studied him. Angus wondered why he felt so calm . . . why this man had the kind of strength that wasn't one-hundred-percent normal.

Or maybe you've been studying the supernatural for so long, you've become too paranoid.

Cain's eyes shone under the foggy lamplight. So fucking handsome. And not all that young.

"Don't get involved," Cain told him quietly.

"Too late." He relaxed his body and then surged forward, surprising Cain. The younger man stumbled backward and Angus flew forward, knocking him to the ground. His full weight was on Cain and he got the sudden, unshakable feeling that the younger man was allowing him dominance. That he would take back control whenever he decided.

So why wasn't he?

He stared down into Cain's eyes—the boy's body was relaxed under his, Angus's knee between his thighs to hold him in place. For a long moment, all Angus could do was breathe. Stare. And then Cain broke the gaze and moved away easily, leaving Angus on his ass on the ground, his computer next to him, while Cain was back leaning against the building. He did offer his hand to Angus though, and for some reason he couldn't fathom, Angus accepted it.

"Why dance around it, Fed? Ask the question you already know the answer to."

"You're a wolf?"

"Were. Yes." Cain blinked and his eyes . . . changed. Just for a second and then they were back to his normal shade. Angus could barely breathe.

He wanted to ask if Harm was too, if they knew each other, but he didn't want to push his luck. Dancing around the subject might work better. "Were those women killed by Weres?"

He didn't think Cain would answer him, but he nodded slightly, then said, "Harm isn't a Were. He's a Dire."

"I don't care what he is. If I find out you're harboring a fugitive—"

"Those women weren't killed by a Dire," Cain persisted.

"Fine, I'll bite." He winced internally at his choice of words and Cain gave him a twisted, wry grin. "And you know that because?"

"Dires are like seven feet tall. Three hundred pounds. A bite like those on the women comes from a much smaller wolf. Someone's trying to frame Harm."

"And you wouldn't be throwing your friend an alibi."

"And give up my own kind? I'm Were, not Dire, and I'm only twenty. Twenty-one in two days." Cain stared at him. "I mean, I'm talking to you about wolves and shit. If I was trying to give Harm a cover, I'd go a different way. And for the record, he's not my friend."

"You're sharing all this why?"

"Because if you get your supernatural information from Leo Shimmin, you're going to be really fucked. He's using you."

"And you're not?"

"I don't want to see any more innocent humans get hurt. It's not what my kind's about."

His kind. This was getting far too real. Angus rubbed his forehead—the pounding pain that had occurred on and off since he'd arrived in town began anew. "Your *kind* is responsible for multiple murders."

"One of them is probably responsible," Cain corrected. "One bad apple, man. You can't let it spoil your view of the entire supernatural world."

Angus shrugged. The man—wolf—had just admitted things to him that anyone else in the world wouldn't believe. Angus did, and he wasn't sure if that made him crazy or the most sane human on the planet. "Why are you giving away all your secrets?"

Cain answered a question with a question. "You keep a lot of secrets yourself, don't you? Big pieces of yourself are hidden, but they're even hidden from you. At least they were, for a while."

"I'm here investigating murders, not for a therapy session."

"And you think I know about them?" Cain's lip curled. "I didn't touch that girl, remember?"

"Just because there was no evidence doesn't mean you're not guilty."

"True." Cain said. Then he jerked his head to the side, like he was hearing a sound Angus couldn't. And then Angus was on the ground, Cain standing over him in a protective stance. They remained that way for minutes that seemed like hours. Something was happening—Cain's muscles were tight, his face hard, like a solider preparing for battle.

"Get out of here, for your own safety," Cain told him, stepping away.

Angus got up and brushed himself off. "What about yours?"

"You're worried about keeping me safe?" Cain asked seriously, like it was something he'd never considered.

"Yes."

"And a minute ago, I was a suspect." Cain smiled wryly. "Go. I'll be fine."

Angus blinked and Cain was gone. There was only a silent winter night, too quiet for anything good to happen. But he did what Cain asked. He was too turned around not to.

"I'll be fine too," Angus echoed as he headed to his car. And even though the wolf wasn't anywhere in sight, Angus still felt Cain's eyes on him the entire time, until he got into the motel room, locked the door behind him and called Shimmin.

"I want in," he said when the cop answered. "All the way in."

Chapter 26

Stray pulled into the garage, Vice and Cyd right behind him. Stray didn't unlock the truck's doors until the heavy garage door closed and the alarm turned on.

Kate clutched the grimoire against her and Brother Wolf was able to hear her heart pounding.

"Hey, we're safe," he told her. "No one's taking the book from you."

She nodded, but didn't loosen her grip. She did let him help her out of the truck and lead her up the stairs. He was planning on putting her right into his room—his wolf wouldn't tolerate anything less—but Jinx was in the kitchen with Rifter.

Probably as good a time as any to introduce her to the wolf who knew a lot more about witches than he did. "Kate, this is another one of my Dire brothers. His name's Jinx."

It all happened at once. Jinx stood and Kate began to shake uncontrollably. The lights went nuts; glasses flew off the table; cabinets opened. She was screaming for his help but in a way only Stray and Brother could hear. It was all a jumbled mess of words and images.

"Kate, stay with me. What's wrong?" he asked, grabbing

her shoulders to try to get her to focus, and then he went as still as she was frantic when he heard her thoughts. He pulled himself together, put his arm around her to stop her from collapsing completely as he tried to reconcile the images in her mind to the wolf he'd known for so long.

It wasn't possible, but Kate truly believed it to be so.

"Him—get him away from me," she said. Although Vice and Jinx weren't completely sure who she was talking about since there were a lot of *him*s, Jinx was the new wolf in this equation.

"Dude, she's so talking about you," Vice told Jinx.

"I liked you better before the eighties," Jinx muttered, backing up only because Stray was growling at him. "Down, wolf. I'm going. But I'm not doing anything to her."

Jinx strode out of the kitchen and down the hallway, heading up to Rogue's room, no doubt, and Stray waited to see if that was enough space for Kate. Slowly, the lights went back to normal, and she finally opened her eyes and stared up at him.

"Sorry. Shit," she muttered. "You can put me down now."

But he didn't; instead he brought her into the kitchen and sat her in one of the chairs. Vice grabbed her a soda and Stray sat next to her. Her color came back slowly, but she still looked traumatized.

"Do you have any aspirin? My head feels like it's going to break apart," she admitted.

"I'll go out and get you some," Vice told her. "We don't really have a use for that."

"I do," Gwen said, coming into the kitchen holding a bottle of Tylenol. "I still get headaches occasionally." She shook out three and handed them to Kate, who gulped them gratefully with the soda. Kate started to shiver a few minutes later.

"It's a migraine," Gwen told them. "Stray, get an ice pack and move her into the guest bedroom."

He did as she said, because it was closer, because she was

queen and a doctor and she was tough as nails, despite knowing the wolves for only a couple of weeks. Besides, he didn't like seeing Kate down for the count.

She was lucid enough to grab for the book when Stray picked her up. Clutched it to her like a lifeline even as her eyes closed. "You sure you gave her Tylenol?"

Gwen smiled. "Something a little stronger. She doesn't have allergies and she won't be out long."

Indeed, being able to scent shit like that out had fascinated Gwen to no end. She wanted to go practice on humans, but Rifter had refused to allow it.

As they watched Kate sleep holding the book, Gwen looked up at him. "What the hell happened back there?"

He shrugged. "Bad reaction to Jinx."

"And you know why?"

"No clue," he lied. Gwen didn't question him further.

They were fracturing at the worst possible time; Stray felt like he was already breaking. With Kill here, any instability within him or his new pack couldn't be tolerated. And now Kate thought Jinx was evil. He'd felt her reaction and it was beyond fear.

"I'll stay with her until she wakes—you guys figure this out before Rifter gets back," Gwen told him.

"Where is he?"

"With Liam, burying the Were bodies your brother killed. Long story. Don't ask."

He wasn't about to, had enough problems already. He left Kate with Gwen and found that Jinx had returned to the kitchen. Vice was there as well, staring out the window. He didn't turn around when Stray walked in and sat down across from Jinx.

Jinx was surprisingly calm. The calm before the storm.

"Is the witch all right?" he asked.

"She will be. Jinx, can you try again, because I think you can really help her—"

"Forget it. I make her tense—and I make you tense

when that happens—and we can't give her any excuse not to help us." Jinx shrugged it off, but Stray knew his wolf was pissed and confused.

Join the club. And on that note, "What do I do?"

"Let her read the books. Her powers will recognize the spells. Make her practice. You've got to tell her the worst-case scenario so she'll understand. This isn't the time to sugarcoat anything."

"I'll make sure she's ready."

With that, Jinx pushed up from the chair and headed back upstairs.

"What's going on, Stray?" Vice asked, his back still turned to him.

It was odd that Jinx hadn't asked, which made Stray suspicious. Obviously, Vice felt the same way. "Kate thinks that Jinx is . . . evil."

"Wolves can't be possessed for long. Spirits can get in, but the wolf's too strong," Vice said, finally turning to look at him. "We'd know."

Stray nodded. "That's what I plan to tell her."

But neither of them seemed entirely convinced, which meant Kate would be a harder sell.

"Stray?" Gwen stuck her head into the kitchen. "She's asking for you."

"She didn't call me," he muttered, more to himself than to her.

Gwen put a hand on his arm. "She said she's trying not to make you feel . . . like a pet."

Vice snorted softly and Stray just nodded. "Thanks for helping."

"Do me a favor—bring her some of the tea I like," Gwen said.

When he went into the guest bedroom with the tea, Kate still clutched the book to her chest and Stray was starting to feel a little jealous of it.

"I want you to stay in my room from now on—with me,"

he told her without prelude, and in spite of everything, she gave him a small smile.

"Okay."

He handed her the mug. "Here. It's some kind of . . . soothing shit."

"Sounds lovely."

"It's Gwen's."

She accepted the mug, left the book between them on the bed as he sat down on the edge. "Did you see . . . what I did?" she asked hesitantly.

"A little. But I need to know more about the Jinx is evil thing," Stray told her. "That's what came through most clearly."

Kate took a few sips of the hot liquid before cupping the mug in both hands. "It was . . . just a feeling. Like I knew something bad is inside of him."

"You're sure it's not a premonition—a future event we can stop?"

"I've never . . . it's never worked that way for me," she said. "But with the grimoire, the new powers, how would I know?"

"Maybe it's a witch-wolf thing?"

"I don't feel it with anyone but him." She paused, then met his gaze dead-on.

"Have you ever been wrong with something like this?"

"Never," she said.

Holy hell, they were in trouble.

Kate was alienating Stray's brother. What good could come of that? She'd been taken by this wolf because they needed her help for one of his kind. They were tight knit.

They'll use you and throw you away.

"What's going on in there?" Stray tapped the side of her head gently.

She couldn't lie to him now, any more than she could lie to herself. "I've hurt Jinx."

"You looked like you couldn't control what happened."

True, but that was beyond the point. "Your other brothers, even Gwen . . . they're being nice, but when they look at me . . . I can feel the suspicion oozing from them."

"I told you—witches aren't typically a first choice of friends for a wolf. You have a lot of natural-born enemies," he said. "Vampires for sure. Shifters. Even the trappers aren't crazy about you unless they can control you. Demons don't like you, either."

"Does anyone in the supernatural world like witches? Because, honestly, it seems like even witches don't like other witches a lot of the time." She wasn't sure why she bothered asking, because she already knew the answer.

Stray shook his head slowly. "By nature, witches are solitary creatures. Always have been."

She understood why now, and she nearly crumpled. She'd been solitary for so damned long and the thought of going through the rest of her life—which was now forever—like that was unbearable. Stray might want her now, but if she continued to see bad things relating to his family . . .

A weight crushed her chest until she could barely breathe. She was vaguely aware of Stray holding her shoulders and calling for help.

"Kate, this is oxygen," Gwen told her. Kate tried to fight the plastic mask on her face, trying to see if she would die or not.

Because she wanted to.

But strong hands held her arms down and her body's survival instincts kicked in, forcing her to gasp in several deep breaths.

She didn't know how long she remained like that, but finally the grip on her loosened and she slumped forward.

"What did you do to her?" Gwen said from somewhere above her.

She wanted to defend Stray, to tell Gwen that he'd simply given her more of the truth she'd asked for, but no words came.

"Kate, are you all right now?" Gwen asked, her face set in serious lines.

"Fine. Sorry—don't mean to keep causing trouble for you and your family," she murmured.

Gwen cast a look Kate couldn't quite read her way and then told Stray, "Keep her calm. I can't give her more meds on top of what I gave her for the headache."

Kate heard the door close, felt the bed sink from Stray's weight.

"I didn't mean to do that to you, Kate. I suck at this stuff, but I'm trying to be there for you."

"Stop. I got what I asked for. I keep asking and you're going slowly, but every time you tell me something, I know you're holding back. Now I know it's witches against the world. Better I know what I'm in for, right?" She tried to give a small laugh and failed.

"It's not you against the world alone, you know. You have us, despite what you're thinking. You see what you see—you're not doing it to hurt us. It's better that we know." He paused, then said fiercely, "You have me."

She wanted to believe him so badly, but her breath came a little harsh again and she held the oxygen mask to her face for a few minutes until she was calm

"Here, drink more tea," Stray urged. She did so, mainly to stop him from fussing over her. For a minute, everything settled in and then, with no warning, she shot up, the tea spilling on the floor and narrowly missing burning her. "Stray, I have to . . . go."

"Is Seb back?"

"No. It's nothing like that. But I need to find something."

Stray stood as she did. "I'm with you. Do what you need to do."

She hoped she wouldn't run into Jinx again, but it wasn't about him this time. Something yanked at her and she had to follow it. She pointed to the book and Stray stared between it and her for a long moment.

"You're sure?"

It would be the first time he'd touched it, the first time she'd allowed anyone but her to. "I'm sure, Stray. Please."

He looked down at it with a reverence she appreciated, then picked it up carefully and tucked it safely under his arm. And just like that, they'd crossed another line, gotten in deeper.

And she knew that it was right.

Only when the grimoire was secured with Stray did she leave the room, one hand out in front of her, palm raised like it was some kind of divining rod. She took a few wrong turns and rapidly retraced her steps until she was on the right track.

She faced the wide set of stairs—she'd never officially been invited up there—and started up them, her heart beating rapidly. Something drew her this way, and it wasn't Seb's voice in her head. She was aware of Stray behind her, which calmed her somewhat.

She stopped in front of a closed door and put a hand on the knob. It gave under her touch. "Whose room is this?"

"Rogue's."

"The brother who needs help?"

"Yes. Jinx's twin."

Her throat went dry. If Jinx was in there, she would know soon enough.

With that, she opened the door and moved forward without looking, narrowing her focus before her courage left her.

When she raised her eyes, she knew exactly what called her to this room. For a long moment, she refused to look at it, stared at Rogue instead, not identical to Jinx, but close enough. Except for the markings on the side of his face, which looked as though they were a part of him, rather than mere tattoos.

Go closer, she told herself.

She did, reached out and stroked his hair with a trembling hand, swore she heard *thank you* inside her head.

It was only then that she looked up at the same kind of monster she'd once seen on her mother. This one was sitting on Rogue's chest, its wild eyes staring at her. Laughing silently. So close—and she hadn't noticed.

She hadn't backed away from it all those years ago. She wouldn't this time.

Bitch, she told it before screwing her eyes shut and turning to Stray. "How long has it been there?"

"You can see it?" Stray asked.

"Yes. What is it?"

"A mare. Typically, it's part of a nightmare—a dream you have when you feel like you can't move. Superstition says it's a mare sitting on your chest."

That thing was way more than a superstition—and it wasn't going away easily. "He's trapped like that—by her?"

"Six months now," Stray confirmed and then Rifter's voice came up from behind him.

"Get her out of here," Rifter said.

Stray walked her out and Rifter went past them and shut the door to the room behind him.

"Rifter seems angry. Was I not supposed to see Rogue?" she asked Stray.

"No. He's worried that we gave you away. The mare reports directly to Seb." Stray looked troubled. "I didn't think of it, but Rifter did. The mare shouldn't have any power over you, though. You're stronger than that."

"I hope so. She's horrible."

"Worse for Rogue, I'd imagine." Stray's voice was tight as he spoke.

"No one should have to suffer like that."

Stray's eyes were close to lupine when he said, "I guess Seb doesn't feel the same way."

Chapter 27

Stray woke from the nightmare with a start just as Killian approached him. The roar of the polar bears still rang in his ears when he sat up, covered with a thin sheen of sweat. Seconds later, Kate woke the same way he had, her eyes disoriented, staring straight ahead, but her nightmare was all hers.

When she got her bearings, she glanced at him. "Sorry."

"You didn't wake me. I have my own nightmares to thank for that." He hated the tingle that ran through his body. He'd felt it only a few times before, always when he was in physical contact with Killian.

He and Kate had slept for maybe an hour. Rifter hadn't come out of Rogue's room, and Stray and Kate returned to his room. He'd given Kate back the grimoire and she'd curled up around it. He'd curled up next to her for protection and she'd snuggled against him, her ass to his cock, and he'd willed himself to sleep, because it was either that or touch her.

And once he started, the way he had in the rain, he wouldn't be able to stop.

"Mine's the same every single time," she continued.

"Mine too. Had it every night for the past couple of

nights." He didn't add that this nightmare was twenty-five years in the making.

"I've had mine every night for a year," she admitted.

"Christ, aren't we a pair," he muttered, ran his hands through his dark hair. His chest shone, slick with sweat. "I've got to get out of here."

Kate felt the disappointment stir at Stray's declaration, assumed he meant alone. She couldn't blame him—her own nightmares made her feel exposed and raw. Stray was actually the first one she'd ever thought about revealing them to.

Granted, he'd lived them with her, so that took care of the telling him part.

"Coming?" he asked, didn't wait for her answer before he grabbed her hand and tugged her along, out of the bed and down the stairs.

She noticed he'd also picked up the grimoire and the sketchpad. The grimoire was expected, the sketchpad, far from it. How he knew her so well after such a short time together amazed her. And then he led her through the house toward a door she hadn't come across before. She walked behind him through a long, dark underground tunnel that would've spooked her before she knew what she knew now.

Finally, they ended up outside under the moon, where she and Stray both would find comfort. Actually, rather than being fully outside, they were in a screened-in section of the porch that gave the feeling of being outdoors with the added benefit of alarms. But the ceiling was nothing but the same fine mesh that threaded the rest of the area, and there was grass under her feet that came right up to the tiled section of the sunroom, where there was actual furniture.

"Since the house is spelled, no one but Dires can see it. And Weres we allow. So as long as we stay in here, we're safe, and we've got the moon. Best of both worlds."

It explained why she hadn't been able to see the house

at all when she'd been attacked by the Were earlier that evening.

He laid out the blanket he'd grabbed from one of the rooms they'd passed and motioned for her to lie down next to him. On their backs, moon shining in their faces, she began to relax. She sat up and took the pencil and paper and began to sketch the moon, the way she'd done countless times before. For many long minutes, there was a comfortable silence between them.

When she'd finished and her hand was tired, she looked over at Stray, half expecting him to be asleep.

He wasn't, remained staring at the moon, looking as sleek and dangerous as his wolf. "You're not going to draw me now, are you?"

"Not if you don't want me to."

He glanced at her. "Maybe later, all right?"

She put down the pad and laid it down again next to her. "If I wasn't here, you'd be out running, wouldn't you?"

"Probably. But this is nice too."

"Who'd have thought it so soon after the dreams. Usually, it takes me hours to feel better," she said. "I'm sure you know what my nightmare's about."

"I lived it with you, yes." He reached out and took her hand in his. Squeezed it.

"I didn't . . . tell you everything. Sometimes I have other nightmares along with the accident one. I've never told anyone about it, either. Do you think maybe sharing them would help?" she asked hesitantly.

"Like they'd cancel each other out and we'd sleep contentedly for the rest of our lives?" He snorted. "Guess it's worth a shot."

"I thought you said I'm supposed to believe in magic."

"That's not magic, baby; that's wishful thinking. And it's mostly a human thing."

"Guess I've got some human habits I won't be getting rid of anytime soon," she told him. "You're the first person I've ever told who actually believed me. Even though I technically didn't tell you."

"I've never told anyone about mine, period."

"Not even your brothers?"

He stared at her. "It wasn't time."

"And now?"

"It is."

Stray watched Kate carefully, wondering if they could both do this. Secrets weren't good for anyone, but sometimes they were completely necessary.

He'd learn soon enough if that was true in this case. "That wasn't the first time you've seen a mare."

She shook her head, pressed her lips together, like she was reliving some kind of past physical pain.

"I can't see her, but I made Gwen describe her to me," he told her.

"Gwen can see mares?"

"Only when she and Rifter dreamwalk," he explained. "That's his ability, like mine is mind reading. And she can see it only when they're together. You're the only one who's seen her outright."

"I've seen it once before, on my mother, the night before she was killed. But it left. I had no idea why. I yelled at it, but it laughed at me. I have no clue why it was there in the first place and we never talked about it afterward. And then she was dead and I wondered if there was a connection." She stared at him. "Do you think I put the mare there?"

"No, Kate, I don't. You don't have that kind of evil in you."

She was struggling to believe him. "I never wished her dead. But there were so many times I wished she was just . . . gone. I loved her, but I really hated her. My dad, too."

"They hurt you?"

"Not my father. My mom." She shook her head at the memory, and Stray nearly growled at the thought of anyone touching her in anger. "The physical pain was bad enough—it seemed to piss her off that I healed so quickly. Further proof that I was the devil's handiwork." She swallowed hard. "But she was so cold to me. It was like living with ice. It was more lonely than living alone."

She was holding back the tears—a damned strong woman.

"It all makes sense now, though. If my mother was a witch who refused to practice, who thought witchery was evil, then . . . if I showed any signs of having power, she would do anything to stop it."

She bit her lower lip gently and Stray caressed her back through her shirt where the brand was. It should be on its way to fading, never to return once her powers were fully hers, according to the lore. But the familiar tingle was still there under his palm. Kate continued. "My mother didn't want me to be what I was. But I was exactly like her."

Stray's gut tightened. "Family's a bitch."

That made her smile a little. "I guess I was always a witch. Lila just made me a more powerful one. Kept me hidden until now."

"You don't have to hide anything from me," he prompted when she paused.

"Because I can't, right?"

"I try to be respectful, but it's like you're shouting in my ear."

She told him then about the fortune teller she'd seen the day of the accident because she'd finally put the pieces together herself—and he got it immediately.

"It was Lila?"

"I didn't realize I'd met her before—not until . . . tonight. How could I not have put that together until just now?"

"Maybe you weren't meant to."

"She looked different when she was giving me her power. Wilder. Scarier. She changed my fate." She hugged her knees tightly to her chest and glanced back at the big wolf lying on his side, the moon worshipping his tawny skin. "She changed everything about me."

"No, she didn't. No one can do that, Kate, no matter how hard they try. She just changed what your mother meant to happen for you."

"And my parents had to die for that to happen."

"What if it was your mother who tried to change your fate? And Lila just reversed it to the way it was meant to be?"

She didn't answer, but she looked slightly less upset. "So that's my big secret. It's all out on the table now. No happy childhood, no matter how hard I tried to pretend everything was wonderful and normal until the accident. I don't know what's worse—that I lied to everyone or that I lied to myself."

"You did what you needed to do in order to survive. Never apologize for that," he told her fiercely as he sat up next to her. "I never have."

She hugged him then, pressed her body to his, twined her arms around him like she'd never let him go. Thing was, he never wanted her to, and that was quite a change from days earlier.

Looked like his life would never be the same again, either.

When she went to pull back, he lowered them back down to the blanket instead. Their legs twined together as if they'd just been intimate.

Hadn't they?

"You've met my brother. Killian."

"He looks like you."

"Yeah, he does. He's older. And it's the first time I've seen him in a long time."

"Why?"

"It's better for both of us that way. He came back to help us deal with the battle."

She turned to him, her face propped on her arm. He continued to watch the moon, not sure he could face her. Still, his hand remained around hers.

"His coming back has been hard for me to deal with. I've been . . . on edge."

"So it's not all about me?"

Stray laughed a little. "Very little, actually. Last night I bailed him out of jail. He was there on a drunk and disorderly. He just got into town last night and he's already screwing things up," he explained. "He's . . . necessary in this war."

"Do you two get along?"

He rubbed the long, abraded scar that ran down his chest absently, told her, "The only scars that won't heal on me were caused by another Dire."

"Your brother did that?"

"He needed to make sure I was immortal." He shrugged. "I am."

And just like that, he was back in Greenland, fifty years earlier. Except this time, he wasn't alone.

They were killing him.

Alone in the middle of a blizzard, Stray hung by his wrists, with chains wrapped around his ankles and neck to further immobilize him, the deep cuts in his skin healing slowly as they were purposely made from silver blades.

They were killing him, but he merely suffered. He wasn't dying.

He remained that way for hours as the pelting snow and ice subsided. Bright red blood fell into the white snow below him with a steady drip he could hear as the silence settled in.

The blizzard was over, but the storm was coming. And he was powerless to stop it.

He'd never doubted this day would come, even though a part of him never wanted to believe his family capable of doing this.

He would never again underestimate what fear could make a wolf do.

Younger than his brother, Killian, by twelve years, kept apart from the pack—his family—for most of his twenty years and now he was a ritual sacrifice to the Elders, the day before his twenty-first birthday. Before his first shift.

Kill had left the pack long ago, right before his own first shift. No one had heard from him since. Stray didn't even know for sure he'd survived his first few shifts, but if the prophecy was to be believed . . . he had.

Whether he'd left to make things better for Stray or for himself, well, Stray didn't know that either.

Stray didn't even have the strength to curse him now; he was too close to his first shift, his body turning into something he didn't recognize, a traitor that threatened him every time his Brother Wolf growled inside his head.

It had become too much to handle. His wolf wanted him to live, howled desperately. The voices mashed together into a painful jumble until he closed his eyes and prayed the predators would come soon.

One was close, but not the one he'd hoped for. His body tingled with power despite the pain and he cursed himself and the prophecy even as his eyes grew hazy and he couldn't see much happening around him. But his hearing remained strong—the rustling in the snow happening long before the polar bears arrived, their white fur marred by some vanilla, and they were hungry. They were dying, just like he hoped to be.

The blood scent drew them and they were coming at a run. His body would give them enough fuel to last another few weeks at most.

There was no peace to make with anyone—he'd spent twenty-one years as a pariah to his own clan, hearing what they said about him, knowing he could've escaped what they planned.

So why didn't you?

Hell, there was nothing for him to go to. A life on the streets of more alienation, well, he didn't want to deal with it.

They said he'd live forever, but nothing did. And once the polar bears ripped him to pieces, he'd find out the truth about the rumored immortality that had hung over his head from the moment he'd breathed life.

The bears approached, teeth clacking together. A few roared, and it sounded like there were hundreds of them instead of the five or so Stray counted.

A few began to fight among themselves because they didn't want to share their prey—they were, by nature, solitary creatures. Stray understood them all too well.

He'd gotten only a few minutes' reprieve. The largest bear stood on two legs, roared as it claimed victory, then brought a paw down in a slashing motion along Stray's side, opening him up as effectively as a knife.

It didn't end there. He couldn't tell if he was being bitten or flayed, but no matter what, the pain was too intense for him to remain conscious much longer. Wasn't sure why he was fighting so hard to do so, why he struggled to keep breathing even as his vision went sideways, like someone had twirled him. It hadn't helped that the polar bears had used him as a piñata.

The tingling of his skin had never retreated, but it was overshadowed by the pain. Suddenly, it reared up full strength and he heard the howl that sent a chill up his spine.

Killian moved like lightning. It was white fur smeared with red blood, silver blade against the night sky. Stray groaned as his body seemed to give way. It was nearly midnight—the change would be upon him and he'd been too weak and hurt to do it.

And if he couldn't die, as the prophecy claimed, what would become of him? Because the prophecy didn't say anything about any tolerance to pain.

"Stray, open your eyes," his brother told him. When Stray did so, he noted that the bears were all dead around them, and if Killian didn't hurry, more would soon come.

He waited, his arms numb, for his brother to help him down.

Instead, Kill moved forward and ran the sword straight through Stray's heart.

Her hand caressed the scar as he spoke. Her eyes were wide and wet as though she felt his pain as keenly as he did. "I can't believe . . ."

"We're different in the way we do things," he told her. "I would've tried to kill myself if he hadn't."

"But the fact that he did hurts you the most. Still."

He couldn't deny that, so he didn't bother trying.

"I lived alone for a long time," he admitted, afraid to say anything more about his childhood at the moment for fear of losing it. "After my pack banished me, I went my own way and my brother went his. Together, our gifts were too powerful and the pack was worried we'd draw unnecessary attention." Or take them over, he thought. He refused to say that out loud because that was the worst part of the betrayal. "I had a really shitty time on my own, had to pretend I was something I wasn't. When they found out I was a Dire, I had to prove myself. I worked whatever jobs I could to earn some money. Rifter's pack always has cash—our pack did too, I guess, but Killian and I were given nothing. So I did whatever I could to survive. It wasn't always pretty."

"I understand," she said quietly. "I was alone . . . lonely, for a long time too."

"Hard to be different."

"But you're not. I mean, your brothers are like you. They accept you."

"My own family didn't. Their families wouldn't have, either. But the Extinction happened before they discovered that." Except for Vice, who always knew his family thought his gift was too over the top. To the Dires, Vice had equaled sin personified, and even though wolves were all about primal urges, Vice's ability was feared.

"Sometimes family's not about blood."

"I still have to talk to my brother. Try to figure some things out between us. He's been alone longer than me. I don't know what he's like. He could be feral. I don't know if he's been using his power for evil purposes."

She nodded, her brow furrowed, and then asked, "Are your parents still alive?"

"As far as I know."

"Does your brother ever see them?"

"I'd be shocked to hear him say yes. Could we change the subject?"

She consented easily. "Okay. You're really seventy-five years old?"

"Rifter and the others are like ten thousand. I'm the teenager in the house who plays his music too loud. Probably why they dealt with young moon-crazed Weres so well."

"So I'll always look like this?"

"You'll age slightly. Never look more than thirty. Not sure why, but that's some kind of magic age."

"It's a big deal for humans. You're supposed to be grown up by then."

"Ah, okay."

"It doesn't sound like you really had a childhood."

"Me? No. The others did. A more typical Dire childhood, anyway. They were trained in the warrior way, but they had fun."

"They don't know how you grew up?"

"Until last week, they didn't know I had a brother." That confession would be the first of many. He started, hearing something she never could. "They're out there tonight. Circling."

He rubbed his arms and shuddered.

"Stay here with me tonight," she said, and he knew she was giving him an excuse not to see his brother if he wasn't ready.

It would be only a matter of hours, but sometimes that was all you needed.

He folded against her, warming her with the heat from his body. "Want to stay out here?"

"Will we be safe?"

"Yes." In this cold, screened-in bubble, he could hold her in his arms and she could stay close to the moon.

"Do you ever wish on stars?"

"Is that a human thing?"

"I guess so. You worship the moon; we wish on first stars, or shooting ones. I guess I used to."

"You still can, Kate."

"So I should still believe that wishes could come true?"

"Maybe now, more than ever."

"If we could stay out here like this forever . . . alone."

"Wish it were that simple. But sometimes being tied to people isn't the worst thing." He stared up at the sky, then looked at her. "I was alone for such a long time—all I wanted was contact. How can I throw away people who are trying to help me?"

"Because you're scared of getting hurt. Scared that, if your brothers make you leave, you're alone again." She stroked a hand through his hair and his libido rose. "You're close to your Dire brothers—they've stuck with you."

"What if they don't, after everything I've told them? What if, when all is said and done, they want me to leave when Killian does?"

"I don't think they're like that. They're warriors like you, and they don't turn away easily. You haven't—from me or from them."

He buried his face in her neck, breathing her in, wanting to believe every word. "If they do . . ."

She looked him in the eyes. "I won't."

Chapter 28

Kate looked luminous.

Stray could see the outline of her body under the button-down shirt she'd borrowed—braless breasts, nipples tight, her legs crossed, a darker triangle between them. The shirt hit just above midthigh, and her bared legs seemed to shimmer under the moon. Her cheeks flushed as she stared up at the white orb. Her entire countenance was one of supplication—of reverence.

He desired her more than anything he'd ever known.

He'd never had that relationship with the moon—she distressed him, troubled him, and, as he'd told Kate, she could control him if he wasn't strong.

But now, watching Kate, he began to wonder what was so wrong with letting the moon take him over for a while. Protect him. Lead him.

"I think the sharing helped," she said softly.

"I've never told anyone any of this. Fuck." He ran his hands through his hair as hers caressed his back, half massage but mainly giving comfort.

He wanted more of her touch.

"Have there been a lot of women—wolves—in your life? Your bed?"

Her thoughts told him she thought she was being selfish in wanting to be the special one for him. He was glad to be able to reassure her. "No one like you, Kate. Never."

She swallowed. "Because . . . I'm witch."

"Nothing to do with that. There's never been anyone like you—no one's ever gotten into my heart. Do you understand? No one."

He wanted her with a force he couldn't explain. Sex had always been easy for him to find. It was something he loved, unabashedly, as all wolves did.

"I'm bound to this prophecy and my brother. Now I'm bound to you. Can't escape. You know my family hurt me—abused me. I didn't tell you that they kept me in a silver-lined cage for the first twenty years of my life." Stray paused, like he was wondering how much farther he should go. But he'd gone nearly all the way, so he stepped off the cliff and told her his final fear. "I'm nobody's pet. No one's slave. Do you understand that?"

"I can't undo the familiar bond," she started.

"No, that's not what I'm saying. I'm telling you that my wolf chose you before you called me. Before all of this, my wolf knew. At first I thought I was just telling myself that to make it all okay, but I know now—Brother Wolf would never lie to me. He couldn't."

In agreement, the wolf howled in his ear.

Kate watched him carefully, her words measured. "So what are you telling me—you're okay with this? You want this?"

He tugged her close, the heat from his body overwhelming her. "I want you."

"I don't know why. I've brought you nothing but trouble."

"No, you brought me so much more."

Stray couldn't help himself. More important, he didn't want to. He pressed against her, nuzzled his head in her neck until he felt her body relent. She whispered something he probably wasn't meant to hear, but with his wolf hearing, there was no mistaking the *I'm sorry* or the hushed *yes* that escaped her.

Yes.

His hands traveled down to her hips as Brother Wolf surged. *Not your turn, boy.* No, it was all Stray's, and it was far too late to stop.

He skimmed off her lacy white boy shorts and his hand sought her sex. Wet and ready for him. He put his head back and howled.

Her fingers dug into his shoulders, like the sound excited her. She arched in to him as he traced along her folds, teasing her until she demanded more.

He would give it to her.

"Beautiful," he whispered and she tightened her arms around herself like no one had ever called her that before. And he was glad, only because he liked being the first one to put that smile on her face, the flush on her cheeks and neck. At that moment, under the moon, it didn't matter that she was witch and he was wolf. It only mattered that they were together for whatever purpose, and that this dance was as old as time.

She fitted against him, molded willingly to his body. He lifted her, arms around her hips so their mouths could meet and, to his surprise, she wound her legs around his waist.

"Yes, now. Please," she murmured, and he couldn't hold back. The air was saturated with her scent and he took her hungrily, a dying man in a desert until he drank her in.

"I want to fuck you. Mark you. Lick you until you scream, clutch the sheets, until your body is worn out from my loving you. God, I dream about tasting you, Kate. Want to spend hours between your thighs. I want to make you mine the way you've made me yours."

His words were visceral, like licks of heat on her skin.

"You're wet for me, aren't you?" He shrugged out of his pants, nuzzled her neck and she gasped a little. "Show me, Kate."

God, she couldn't do this. He was so free with his wants and needs and she was like a shy virgin.

Well, she *was* a shy virgin.

"Wolves are primal. We love sex and everything associated with it. Why not revel in it with me?" he cajoled, his hand on her thigh. "Let me all the way in, Kate."

She had nothing to lose. Her legs trembled as Stray opened her thighs, gazed at her sex and groaned. She let him strum her body with his fingers and his tongue until she was naked in the moonlight.

"This isn't about familiars. This is about me and you, not wolf and witch."

His eyes flashed something she didn't recognize, but his mouth was on hers before she could figure it out. And then it didn't matter because he kissed her like nothing else in the world mattered except her.

She felt cherished. Hopeful. And she needed him in a way she'd never thought possible.

He moved down her body leisurely, well aware he was driving her crazy with every touch and caress. When he reached the juncture of her thighs, without further prelude, his mouth locked hungrily to her core and she gasped at the intensity of the sensations that shot through her.

She knew he wouldn't stop until he'd gotten his fill. The way he held her spread open, she was helpless to do anything but enjoy the way he ravaged her. He licked and laved until her clit was a tight bundle of throbbing nerves and then something rippled deeply inside of her. She couldn't stop the perfect cascade of orgasms that flowed, one after the other with no buildup or warning in between, shocking and delighting her.

She was aware she was calling Stray's name, should be embarrassed by how loud she was, but Stray encouraged it.

He climbed back up her body, his cock jutting, heavy and hard, and she needed that now.

"Hurry—fill me," she heard herself plead. She should've been embarrassed at how forward she was, but again, Stray didn't mind, judging by the way he watched her approvingly.

He hovered over her, and then slid inside, slowly, until she jerked and took him all the way in. A heated groan escaped from his throat, and she felt the fever rise inside of her again as he made love to her.

She was taken. Possessed. Overwhelmed. "Please, Stray."

God, she could draw him looking like this. It appeared as though he ached for her, his gaze intent, cheeks hollowed and for a long, hot second she reached up and traced his lips with her finger.

He drew in a sharp breath like he wasn't used to care of any kind. And she wanted him to be.

"You deserve good things," she told him softly. When she moved her hand away, he buried himself more deeply inside of her with another long groan. And then he bent his head, whispered, "So do you—and I'll show you some good now."

With that, he began to thrust inside of her—seemed as though he was actually growing larger inside of her as she moved in complete, utter pleasure against the hard length of his body.

"Show me everything."

He did, the sex hard and fast now, like neither could hold out longer, and she didn't feel like a virgin at all. No, she was as wild and as free as he was, and she loved it. Reveled in all of it. Never wanted it to end. When his orgasm hit with hers, the look of sharp relief on his face satisfied her as much as the pleasure contracting inside her womb.

"Happy birthday," he murmured in her ear.

Happy birthday indeed.

Kate lay in Stray's arms under the moon, feeling safe for the first time in forever. It shouldn't be that way, she knew, but nothing in her life had gone as planned at all, and, at the moment, none of it seemed important.

Her hands threaded through his thick, dark hair. It hung heavy and straight to below his shoulders and she loved the feel of it. It was as silky and the same color as . . .

"Brother Wolf's coat, yes." He smiled. "Doesn't happen all the time. Just for the brothers with abilities."

She recalled Vice's shift to a wolf with a white coat and Rifter's to gray. "You said Rifter could dreamwalk."

"He was cursed with his, not born with it. But we love him anyway."

Such acceptance. A real family unit lived and breathed inside these magical walls and she was close to being a part of it.

If she was turned away when she was no longer of use, as she suspected, it would kill her. But for now, he most certainly wasn't turning her away.

His hand stroked her back and, although it was still a bit sensitive to the touch, she realized the rough feel of the mark wasn't there. She put her own hand back to touch it and her skin was nearly smooth.

"The brand . . . it's almost gone," she said. "When we were together—did you know that would happen?"

"It's not the sex," he told her. "Your brand will disappear when your powers fully integrate, and there's no way to tell when that will happen."

"But this pull I feel for you won't," she said.

He grinned, pulled back a little. "The wolf needs to run. I'll be back in a few. Stay inside here, okay?"

She nodded and, in seconds, he blurred and shifted into Brother Wolf, who was a beautifully ferocious animal.

And this time she wasn't scared at all, watched him nudge the door open and run across the lawn, his body sleek, muscles moving powerfully, rippling under his fur. Her entire body tingled, telling her they were for sure entangled in ways she could never explain.

All she knew was that she never wanted it to end, wished she could run with him through the deep, dark woods. He was all mystery and power and she burned for him.

Burned.

She stepped out onto the lawn because he was right there. Because she wanted to be closer to him.

As if he knew, Stray turned to her and ran straight at her.

If she didn't know better, she'd have thought he wouldn't stop running.

He didn't.

Instead he leapt over her, and when she whirled around, he stood, watching her. Grinning, if that was possible.

"Sneaky wolf," she muttered and Brother howled in the night, the sound echoing for longer than it should have in the dense quiet.

It was unsettling and arousing at once.

She moved back into the screened area and glanced down at the sketch she'd done of him her first night in the house. She'd seen the scars on him before, many times by this point, but they always struck her, the way they seemed to peek through the Brother Wolf glyph so the wolf and Stray both bore the marks of pain.

Kate had grown so used to pain—obviously, so had Stray. That they'd found each other under such extraordinary circumstances seemed something of a not-so-small miracle; and being a lapsed Catholic, she knew those didn't come along often, if at all.

Both their families were scared of them, clouded by their past experiences.

Both were destined to be part of a prophecy that could cause irreparable damage.

After another half hour or so of the wolf running through the yard and howling, Stray shifted back and moved to stand over her. "What are you thinking? You look sad again."

"I can't be around Jinx. This can't work. You've already had to give up one pack. I won't let you give up another," she protested.

"You don't get to tell me what to do."

"Stubborn."

He cocked a pot/kettle eyebrow and she could do nothing but concede.

"I don't see the future. I read the past and present, what's in people's minds now. And according to that, your brother is—"

"Jinx is not evil. You'll find that out for yourself," he said in a tone that made it clear he was through discussing it. "Out here, with the moon, can you show me your powers?"

Her first instinct was to give an automatic no, but then her brand tingled and her hands went out and hovered over the ground. Despite the cold and the season, warmth radiated there and a crocus appeared, purple and perfect.

Stray picked it, held it out to her. She sniffed it, then rubbed the soft petals on her cheek. "I can't believe it. I can do this with my mind?"

"Lila was alive for seven thousand years," Stray told her. "She could do a lot of things."

"Like invading people's minds." Obviously, she'd been doing her calling without even realizing it.

"For the greater good."

"So you say."

"So I know. Trust me, because you've got to trust someone. I know you realize it can't be Leo Shimmin."

Sometimes, it was about choosing the lesser of two evils. And while she'd gotten chills meeting Jinx, she'd had no such feelings about the rest of the family. Whatever she felt, she'd warned them. She had to believe that they'd do something to protect her from whatever it was. "I do."

"Good. Now use the moon. Let her help."

"Does she help you?"

"She would rule me if I let her."

"But you're stronger."

"Now I am. In the beginning, it wasn't that simple." He moved closer to her, pulled the blanket over them, tucked the grimoire close to her body as well. "Come on, let's see if we can sleep now."

And they remained there, the moon bathing them in her comfort.

Chapter 29

After a night of rifling through cemeteries and getting sick over the remains of butchered corpses and heavy demon activity, Jinx drove home to face the music, even though it was barely dawn.

He knew damned well what the witch felt. Knew that Stray did as well, by literal osmosis. What he didn't know was how to deal with it without telling the rest of the Dires what a fucking mess he'd caused.

They had too much else to worry about—he wasn't putting another thing on their heads. He'd deal with purgatory himself.

Rifter was, of course, waiting for him in the kitchen, arms crossed, his alpha wolf flag flying high. But Jinx was in no mood for any of his shit, king or no king.

"Where were you?"

"Hunting," Jinx told him.

"I told you not to go out alone," Rifter said, and yes, the wolf had, right after Kate's meltdown. *Because if there's something evil she's seeing, it could be a premonition*, Rifter had lectured.

Now Rifter narrowed his eyes. "Jinx, what's the goddamned problem?"

And that's when he fucking lost it, because he couldn't stand here and look his king, his friend, in the eye and keep lying to him. So he did what he knew would get him the hell out of the spotlight. "Right—forgot I'm *evil* Jinx. Maybe I shouldn't be allowed to do anything alone. Maybe I should be chained inside the house with Harm."

"Don't give him ideas," Vice said, coming up behind Rifter.

Jinx knew Rifter's wolf was not responding well to the challenge, and Vice's silent question—*Why the hell are you baiting him?*—hung in the air.

Since his mating, the dynamic was changing. Rifter had always been alpha, but this was beyond.

The other Dires were handling it, because it was Rifter. But now Jinx was too pissed to care that he was challenging the alpha. And on some level, he realized he might be doing this purposely as well. That riling Rifter to the point of no return would give Jinx the freedom he needed.

"You've got to get the fuck off my back, king. I'm doing this for you—for Gwen. For all of us. So you need to stay put and let me do my damned job without questioning me every time I leave this house, got it?"

Rifter's wolf growled. "You don't tell me what to do, wolf."

"Guess what, King Rifter? I'm telling you."

"Why are you pushing me?" Rift's eyes had already turned; the air held the chill of an impending Dire fight.

Jinx knew a newly mated alpha king was not to be challenged if you wanted to keep your head on your body. And he definitely needed his head, but he needed to get the hell out of this house more, before Kate had another crazy vision and figured out what he was dealing with. Hell, Stray might've already read his mind, but Jinx hoped he was too caught up with his witch to read too much into Jinx's tension.

Jinx was pulling a tiger by the toes—wasn't smart,

wouldn't be pretty, but he pressed on. "Because I'm tired of you making shit decisions for this pack."

The growl ripped from Rift's throat. Jinx's own Brother Wolf was confused, was used to bucking the alpha king occasionally, but never this hard.

"Jinx, stand down," Rifter warned one final time.

"Fuck off," he replied, and the fight happened in a blur, the mated alpha far more unpredictable than Jinx had expected.

It had been a long time since he'd seen one of them up close and personal. Everything was raw, right on the surface. It was almost like dealing with a newly shifted Dire, except a mated alpha had complete control over his fighting abilities and that made him even more deadly and unpredictable.

Jinx barely held him off, still ended up with deep, bloody scratches down his neck that would scar and cracked ribs that would heal before the night was over.

He'd given as good as he'd gotten, but Rifter was too amped up to care. The only thing that stopped them from coming as close to killing each other as they possibly could was Vice's Brother Wolf, who jumped in and nearly decimated them both.

And still Rifter kept coming for him. Jinx watched the white wolf shift into his tattooed Dire brother in order to hold Rifter at bay. With Vice's pull, he and Rifter both shifted back as well, and Vice was saying, "Rift, come on—tone it down."

Jinx should've let it go then, could've walked away with his scratches and his dignity, but he knew he'd have to push it to get the results necessary for him to keep his secret.

He lurched forward, past Vice, put his finger close enough to Rifter's face for the wolf to bite it off, and managed, "I'll be goddamned if I'm going to walk around here, subject to your scrutiny. I'm not following special rules because you all trust some crazy witch over your own brothers."

He couldn't stop himself, figured this was how Vice must feel all the time. But the suspicion in his brothers' eyes was too much to take. Obviously, he'd gotten careless, allowed his own charm in the form of the prayer to work against him, something Rogue would probably have warned him about, if he weren't being held unconscious by a fucking hag mare.

"You get the fuck out of this house—and you don't come back until I invite you." Rifter's words roared, shook the walls of the house. Everything seemed to stop then, including Jinx's heart for a brief second before it began the familiar, fast beat of the wolf's again.

"Fuck you and your house, King Rifter," he spat.

"Jinx, get out—now," Vice told him, his voice low, his eyes turned lupine, his body shaking.

This was probably harder on Vice than anyone, and Jinx felt another pang of guilt stab him squarely in the chest. It was what finally made him turn and leave the house with nothing but the clothes on his back.

You got what you wanted.

It was still like a knife to the gut. Brother Wolf wasn't happy, wanted to run back and make peace with the king, despite the fact that there wasn't a submissive bone in Jinx's body.

All those alphas under the same roof . . . Shit, it wasn't the first time they'd split, but it wasn't the right time for it.

This wasn't the right time to be connected to purgatory, either. Asking for help would make things worse—he'd figure it out himself. Because if he'd been able to push his king, the one he'd ceded to centuries earlier, there was something evil inside of him, like the witch had seen.

Seb could be manipulating him somehow. Jinx had considered that, but he didn't feel that pull. Besides, he'd already cast a spell to protect the rest of them from a mare spell, even though none of them could ever be pulled in that deeply. Rogue had because of his connection to the spirit world—he walked a very thin line between life and death.

Thankfully, the rest of the Dires wouldn't find themselves enslaved that way, but who knew what else Seb had in store for them.

Gwen had watched the fight from the safety of the next room, struggling the entire time not to let Sister Wolf out. And her wolf wanted out bad. But fighting with the men wasn't going to do anything except get her hurt. This was a show of testosterone that ended badly and it was only once Jinx slammed down the stairs and left the Dire property alone on his Harley that she let herself react.

"You can't let him go alone like that."

Rifter had been watching Jinx's bike roar down the driveway. He turned to her in a flash. "Enough. It's done."

"We're all in danger and we need to stay together," she protested, and Rifter growled at her. "You did not just growl at me, did you?"

He had and he did it again.

Vice took her shoulder and pulled her back a little. "Gwen, it's an alpha thing. Newly mated male kings are ... well, let's just say, it's not the time to question his decisions."

And as pissed as she was, Sister Wolf was strangely aroused by Rifter's commands and his attempts at domination—of both her and the entire pack. She didn't know if Vice's proximity was adding to her feelings, but Vice's canines were elongated, his eyes changed to lupine, like Rifter's.

Come to think of it ...

She touched her tongue to her teeth and found herself in the same predicament. If she looked at her eyes in the mirror, she knew wolf's eyes would greet her back.

"Jinx will be fine. Staying here now is not an option," Rifter repeated.

"I would think you'd make an exception," she started,

but quickly stopped. Obviously, Rifter knew it wasn't the best time, but if he was having trouble controlling himself, it might actually be in all their best interests for Jinx to be on the outside.

"He'll handle himself," Vice promised. "He'll stay at the apartments. No one's going to know where he is. Might give us an upper hand to have someone on the outside if there comes a time we can't leave. I'll call to check in on him in a few."

He left and Gwen realized this was probably harder on Vice than anyone. She turned back to Rifter.

"The building's not spelled."

"If he's careful, no one will know he's there," Rifter said.

"Hopefully it's not permanent."

"That's up to me," Rifter said, giving no indication either way.

Gwen felt a surge of desire run through her, which was odd, considering her anger. But the wolf part of her was growing stronger on a daily basis and surged in appreciation of her alpha and his ways. And he knew—the bastard knew how conflicted she was and how turned on, and his eyes changed to lupine.

"I want to hate you for doing this," she told him.

"Pack law," he murmured before nipping her neck. "King's rule."

"Doesn't the queen get a say?"

"You've had yours," he reminded her. "But right now Brother Wolf's not handling resistance."

She'd seen it happening over the past week, but she'd been so buried in her own wolf things that she didn't stop to think it had to do with their mating. "This will pass?"

"Eventually." Rifter yanked her closer. "Stop questioning me."

The alpha authority in his tone infuriated her, but it excited her more. "And if I don't?"

"You will, little wolf."

Any guise of polite behavior was gone, vanished as if

Rifter let the facade go completely. He pinned her to the ground and she knew she'd pushed too hard one time too many.

She would pay now. But the funny thing was, she didn't think she'd mind it, especially not when his thigh pressed her sex, holding her open. He ripped her top open with his canines and she felt the pleasure surge through her.

"I'm going to take you, right here and now."

"Do I have a say?"

"You have the next two seconds to say no. Otherwise, I'll keep your mouth occupied."

She yielded to him, pulse racing.

If he'd ever been civilized, any trace of it was completely gone, replaced by his raw physicality that threatened to consume her.

She would let it.

Rifter grabbed her, stripped her pants down with efficiency and tore his own as well. He entered her before she could draw another breath, holding her to him with one arm as he stood with her and propped her ass against the nearest table. And then he took her with a force that overwhelmed her. It was nothing like mating sex, which had been a wild thing on its own. No, this time Rifter had complete control and there was no pain for him involved, only pleasure, an intent on proving himself alpha to her.

And he did. Every time he rocked into her, her womb contracted and the orgasms were fast and furious. She couldn't recover in between as Rifter showed his dominance and she accepted it gratefully, crying out her king's name in the process of complete surrender.

Afterward, Gwen and Rifter remained splayed on the floor of the living room, covered by a blanket Rifter pulled from the couch.

Gwen blushed as she realized how loud she'd been—and how exposed.

"You're never going to stop blushing, are you?" Rifter asked, and he didn't look unhappy about it in the least.

"We're just so out in the open."

"Everyone stayed away, Gwen. They know better."

Every wolf except Jinx knew better. And she couldn't let it go, despite Rifter's warning. She only hoped the sex had mellowed the newly mated alpha male syndrome he had going on.

"Maybe Kate's splitting you up on purpose," Gwen pointed out. "What if she's smarter than we think about all of this? She's been working with Shimmin for years."

"Shimmin sent a Were to attack her—to control her," Rifter countered. "When that didn't work, he got her a job to keep an eye on her and her powers. They didn't think they'd need her. They just didn't want us to have her."

"I don't like my family being separated." Rifter might be alpha, but Gwen's mother alpha instincts were shining through, along with the human desire for family.

"I'm not taking them away, Gwen. It's—"

"Pack law." She pushed away from him. He studied the Sister Wolf glyph on her back, almost as beautiful as her wolf form.

He knew what she was really worried about. What if Jinx really was evil? If the weretrappers found a way to turn the Dires . . . would the Elders help?

Would they care? From what she'd seen of the hierarchy who ruled both the Dires and the Weres, she didn't think so.

"We need him here," Gwen said.

"Not now," Rifter told her.

"Because of Kate, or because he defied you?" she asked.

"The latter."

The wolf part of her understood that immediately. The human side that hated to see these wolves separated for any reason, didn't. "He belongs here."

"I can't expect you to understand."

"We have limited time. Seb is gearing up the army again

for the blue moon and you're kicking him out when we need to work together—now more than ever."

Rifter's fists unclenched. "As much as I needed him to go, Jinx wanted to go more."

"Why?"

"I guess we'll find out. But I think it's best he's working from the outside, and the key is that he's still working for us. That much I know. Eye on the prize." Rifter paced, but his stance, his voice, were strong.

He was right. Gwen mentally calculated the number of wolves on their side. Liam, in particular, was amassing a great deal of respect with both the Manhattan packs and the others across the country as well. That put their numbers up substantially, but going up against the ghost army . . . well, all of it was risky.

And you're powerless.

She stared at her hands. *Or maybe not.*

Chapter 30

Jinx flew down the road on his Harley, headed to the bank of buildings the Dires owned on the other end of town. It was the best place for him to stay, and the Were who acted as the building manager assured him that there was an empty apartment under the penthouse.

No one wanted it and Jinx knew why—it was under the damned vampire, and Weres never trusted vamps. Jinx wasn't about to be the exception to the rule.

He parked in a hidden space in the underground garage, went through the double-reinforced door with his code.

Brother Wolf would buck if Jinx attempted to use the elevator. The wolf trusted his own legs and jumping ability rather than a machine, and Jinx conceded, took the stairs.

He'd been inside the apartments before. Cain and Cyd kept one in the building next door, just in case there was a night they couldn't get to the safety of the Dire house. The apartments been reconfigured and upgraded to make the rooms larger—and reinforced to handle wolves, although not Dires. Jinx, at six foot six, had needed to duck to enter some of the rooms in the twins' place, and Brother Wolf wasn't looking forward to the confines of the apartment at all.

Finally he reached number nine, the penthouse that had exclusive use of the rooftop.

It was time for the vamp to go. Right now, Jinx had no love for any kind of supernatural creature except his own. Well, some of his own kind.

It was time to start eviction proceedings.

In seconds, he was pounding on the vamp's door. Jez answered, looking like his typically bored British tight-assed self. "Go away, wolf. I don't need company."

"I'm moving in."

"I don't bloody well remember advertising on Craigslist for a roomie."

"You're out."

"I don't think so, wolf. I have a lease."

"And I have ownership papers."

"Papers? I figured house training wolves would be a bitch, but after several centuries, I would hope you'd get it down pat." Jez smirked. "There's only one top dog here, and it's me."

"I'm not a dog and you're going to have to move one floor down."

"Make me."

The fight that had been building inside of Jinx burst forth until he couldn't hold back any longer. He needed this and it didn't matter who was on the other end of his fury.

It only mattered that someone was.

Jinx dove for Jez, knocking the vamp to the floor and feeling the solid muscle he'd connected with. It might possibly be the fairest fight he'd ever had with another species of supernatural—and the most complicated.

He was already banged up from going head-to-head with Rifter—and still, his body was chock-full of enough adrenaline to choke a vampire. Which he did on multiple occasions, only to find himself slammed across the room.

He bounced right back, though, and even succeeded in putting the vamp's head through the bathroom door at one point. He'd laughed at that, although his success was short-lived when he found his head shoved into the fridge and the door closed on his neck.

It could go on for fucking ever, and hours later, Jinx wasn't sure it hadn't. Wolf and vamp lay next to each other on their backs, panting.

The penthouse was a wreck, though not as bad as it would be if not built for this kind of abuse. Doors were pulled half off hinges, the fridge was dented with an imprint of Jinx's body—a neat vamp trick—and Jez in turn was slowly healing a broken leg.

"Round eighteen?" Jez asked, and Jinx rolled his eyes.

"What—for another draw? I think it's time to put our dicks away." Jinx pushed up onto his shoulders.

"I never knew wolves could be as strong as you," Jez told him.

"Ditto. Fucking deadhead," he muttered and Jez threw something at him—a lamp, he was pretty sure, as it whizzed by his head. Jinx ducked and something shattered against the wall. "Neither of us can stay here now."

"I'll stay with you downstairs until this gets cleaned."

"First of all, this is my place, not the— Ah, fuck it. How's that going to happen? You've got a vampire cleaning fairy?"

"Something of the sort," Jez said. "I'm starving."

"My blood's staying in my body, thanks."

Jez snorted. "I don't like wolf. I'd prefer a good fried rice and wonton soup."

"I know the best place," Jinx said, hearing the exhaustion in his own voice. He looked over at Jez, who was already sleeping. "Ha. I fucking win, deadhead."

"I heard that," Jez muttered. "Why are you even here in the first place?"

"I'm going fucking crazy."

"Can you do it quietly? I've got to get some rest."

Instead of flipping the vamp off, Jinx and Brother Wolf agreed that rest was a really good idea and won out over food. Too tired to strip and shift, he slept instead.

When he woke, ten hours had passed and he still lay on the floor of the penthouse, Jez next to him. Both were covered by blankets, and Jinx sat up on his elbows as Jez stretched.

"Aren't we cozy?"

"Don't get any ideas, wolf," Jez told him. "Are you ready to discuss purgatory?"

Jinx sat up like a shot. "You see it too?"

"Help with the going crazy thing?"

"A little." Jinx lay back and stared at the ceiling. "Since when?"

"Since you opened it."

Angus watched Cain get out of the police cruiser's backseat, handcuffed and escorted into the station house.

Shimmin hadn't called him about this, which made Angus suspicious about the officer's real motives. Nothing in this town was as it seemed, and he wasn't sure if that meant things weren't on the up-and-up, but something about Cain turned him protective.

Like the wolf really needs your help.

Still, he shoved his hands in his pockets and waited anyway. Ruminated on the fact that Shimmin had given him very little information in the few days since he'd agreed to work for the trappers.

Sure, the cop had outlined more about Were culture and the like, the way Cain had started to. Angus had also met a group of trappers who taught him the best way to take a Were down.

In their eyes, a Were should be killed no matter what. *You spot one, you kill it, even if it's doing no harm—that's the only way we can be sure it will never do any harm*, one of Shimmin's men told him.

Instead of comforting Angus, it chilled him. And when he'd tried to question them about their motives for joining the trappers—and what the trappers stood for in general, they'd gone quiet.

"Sorry. The questioning thing is ingrained in me—it's part of my job," he'd lied.

"This isn't your job, Angus," Leo had chided him later, after the group had reported every damned thing Angus had said. "It's our purpose—your purpose now. You'll have to trust me."

Angus didn't trust him worth a damn, and for good reason. When Cain hadn't stalked him that evening, he'd actually gone out looking. And then he heard on the scanner that a young man had been taken into custody for questioning.

What were the chances? And yet Leo mentioned that they brought Weres in for questioning as often as they could. Especially the young ones.

Angus could hear Leo's lies now. "Fed, we didn't arrest the kid—just needed to talk to him on another matter." Because Leo had promised to keep Angus in the loop on anything and everything concerning the murders, which included Cain.

And Cain looked arrested to him.

He waited half an hour, drumming his fingers on the steering wheel, and then got out of the car to go inside. It was only then he spotted Cain walking through the back lot toward the woods, weaving slightly. Last time Angus checked, there weren't kegs inside the station house and he was relatively sure Cain wasn't a drug user.

He got back into his car and drove it around so it was closer to the woods. Got out, made sure no one saw him, followed Cain and called his name quietly when he got close. Cain went to swing, but when he saw Angus he stopped.

"What the fuck?" Cain asked.

"I was about to ask you the same thing."

"Get me away from them," Cain slurred, jerked his head toward the building. From their hidden position, Angus could see some of Shimmin's men looking out the back door, then exiting the buildings holding shotguns at their sides.

"Did you escape?" Angus demanded.

"They let me go," Cain insisted.

And now they were hunting him. Literally.

Cain didn't protest at all when Angus slid an arm around him to hold him up. His breathing was fast, his face flushed. There wouldn't be time to walk him out. If he didn't move now, they'd be spotted.

He slung Cain over his shoulder—damn, the kid was heavy—and he got him to the car before the officers turned in their direction. Shoved Cain in the back and put a blanket over him, because the wolf was completely passed out.

He dug into Cain's pocket first to look for an address beyond the invisible house and recalled it immediately, the one listed on his arrest report. Not safe. Angus had kept his motel room—the one Shimmin knew about—and rented another one under a different name.

He'd take Cain there.

After making sure no one was following him, he managed to get the young wolf safely stored in the room, curled up on the bed. His color was good, but he was definitely drugged. Angus paced, wondered if he should call someone about this and decided it was ultimately better to let Cain make that decision when he woke.

Whenever that would be.

Which ended up being two hours later, with Angus passed out on the bed next to him. He'd started out propped against the headboard but ended up closer to Cain. He knew he was taking a chance being this close to the wolf, but chance had served him well until this point.

Cain had to get up and moving. Out of here. Away from humans of any kind. But when he tried to stand, he and his wolf felt the room spinning.

He thought about shifting, but then he'd be totally out of control. And a drugged, totally out-of-control, once-moon-crazed Were didn't mix well with humans of any sort.

And he really shouldn't give a shit.

"Cain, come on. Down, boy."

"That supposed to be funny? Because I'm not a damned dog." He moved to hit Angus, but the fed moved out of the way easily. "I'm . . . fine." Damn. Finding the words wasn't easy. Especially when Angus's big hand clasped with an unexpected gentleness on the back of his neck.

"Not even close. Lie down."

"Can't stay here."

"And you can't leave in this condition. I can't take you to an apartment Shimmin knows about or a home that technically doesn't exist."

"Point taken."

"We're in a motel room rented under an alias. Shimmin doesn't know about it."

"You sure, Fed? He's good."

"I'm better."

Cain could believe that. "Cyd must be frantic."

"You should call. Keep it short, though, in case they're watching the number."

Smart man. Cain dialed the number, not bothering to mention the secure line, and Cyd answered on the first ring with "I'll rip his head off if he hurt you."

Not an empty threat. "I've been drugged by Shimmin, but Angus is keeping me safe."

"Have you taken a blow to the head?"

"I'm fine. Gotta sleep this shit off." There. He'd finally relented. Angus obviously approved, because the massage on the back of his neck started again, and he nearly howled at how good it felt.

"Where are you? Because if you're not back in the morning—"

Cain closed his eyes and thought about the address. The spooky twin thing wasn't always reliable, but it typically worked in these situations.

"Got it. Be safe, brah," Cyd told him.

Cain hung up the phone and handed it to Angus, who was staring at him oddly.

"What?"

"You're . . . glowing a little."

Cain nodded. Strange that the fed could see it. "I'm omega."

"Omega," Angus repeated. "Isn't that usually the lowest rung on the wolf ladder?"

"Not for my kind," he murmured. "Special."

Angus gave him a grim look. "Don't tell me any more, Cain. Shimmin gave you truth serum."

"No shit." Cain closed his eyes and then opened them again. Pulled Angus in for a kiss. At first the fed froze, and Cain realized he couldn't fight the truth with or without the serum.

His wolf instincts were never wrong about this shit, but what was wrong was wanting a human male. And a fucking fine specimen he was.

He waited, his lips against Angus's until he heard, "Cain."

It was a whisper. A plea. And it was spoken half captured by Cain's mouth covering his. But Angus responded after he froze for a second, gave as good as he got, pulled Cain closer.

Yeah, Cain hadn't been wrong about this. He kissed the fed fiercely, and Angus's hands fisted in Cain's hair gently as Cain struggled to stay the fuck awake.

Wasn't going to happen for much longer. When he woke, there might be regrets on both ends, but for now the truth overtook him.

"Wanted to do that . . . for a while," he managed before the drugs won. He should've shifted to get them out of his system faster, but it would've meant less time with Angus . . . and more danger for him as well.

Fuck, he was in trouble.

Chapter 31

Since you opened it.

Jinx didn't say anything for a good long while after the vampire called him out. Not until his phone rang and he knew he couldn't avoid Vice for much longer. "I'm okay," he started.

"Good for fucking you, but Cain's not. He's been drugged by the fucker Shimmin," Vice told him.

Jinx shot up. "Where is he? I'm going to get him."

"He's with Angus Young."

"The fed or the rock star?"

Vice snorted. "Cyd talked to them both—says Cain's all right, sleeping off the drugs."

"Suddenly we trust the fed now? He's on Shimmin's side."

"Cyd doesn't think he is or Cain would be in the trappers' hands by now. He said his twin antennae would be blowing up if there was a problem."

Well, hell, Jinx couldn't argue about that. He knew the twin connection was way more powerful than anything. "Call me the second he gets home."

"Got it, *boss*." Vice hung up on him, rightfully so. Jinx shoved his phone in his pocket and wondered when he'd become such a dick.

"Let's go. I'm starving."

They ordered takeout to be delivered to the completely empty apartment below, so Jez's vampire cleaning staff or whoever the fuck he hired could clean it up. Jinx wasn't paying attention most of the time, not until they dug into the food and Jez said, "You can stay with me upstairs, wolf."

Jinx snorted. "I don't need a roommate."

"Well, you need fucking furniture. And you need protection. Without your pack, you're—"

"Fucking immortal." Jinx grabbed the lo mein and dove in, and for many minutes there was only the sound of chopsticks and quiet chewing from both wolf and vamp. "Didn't think you guys ate."

"Most don't. I'm from the older generation."

"Yeah, ditto. And the present sucks. Nothing is the way it was. It stayed pretty much the same since the tenth century and now it's going to change?" Jinx asked, not really expecting an answer.

He didn't get one. Jez shrugged and asked, "Want something to drink?"

"If you offer me blood, I'm going to punch you."

"Wolf, please." Jez handed him a beer and Jinx took it grudgingly. "I understand there's a war brewing."

"A fucking mess is more like it."

"So why are you here instead of with the Dires?"

Jinx smiled. "Haven't you heard? I'm an evil son of a bitch."

Jez clinked his beer against Jinx's. "Welcome to the club."

After they both took long drinks, Jinx asked, "So where's your vampire nest?"

"Don't have one."

"You're rogue?"

"Not exactly. I'm not the only vampire in town, but I'm the most powerful."

Jinx wasn't feeling powerful at all. In fact, this whole thing had taken a turn he hadn't quite expected.

"You're worried they're right—about you being evil?" Jez inquired.

"Why would the witch lie?" Jinx asked.

"Maybe she's not lying, just misinterpreting what she sees. Nonetheless, we can't be separate entities any longer," Jez said. "There's too much at stake."

"So all the deadheads are getting into bed with the wolves?"

"You won't get help on this from the vampire community—just us," Jez said.

"Who is *us*?"

Jez smiled. "For now, be content with me. The rest are working in ways you won't see, waiting for the right time to strike—although that might not happen for years."

"And you?"

"I will strike as soon as you need me to. I'm here to watch you, Jinx."

"For thirty years?"

"It's been longer than that."

"So there's more than just one prophecy floating around."

"There's more to that wolf prophecy," Jez conceded.

"There's no prophecy about me."

"That you know of," Jez added.

"Didn't know vamps were so into wolf business."

"Don't flatter yourself. We kept up with you to save the humans." Jez didn't look happy about that as he sniffed, "Inferior race."

"You weren't ever one of them?"

"I was a born vampire, not a made one," Jez said. "We're far superior, and we've been around longer than the Dires."

"I'm sure we have history to disprove that." Jinx wasn't in the mood for yet another pissing contest with the vamp. His body ached, Brother Wolf was uncomfortable and he longed for a good, hard run. Or a fuck. Or both, and he wasn't getting either thing here. "Look, in case you haven't noticed, our kinds don't exactly work together."

"That's because you have more wolves per capita in this area than anything. You've got some shifters, like the pride who come and go when things get too rough. Basically, they're lazy." The vamp dismissed them with a wave. "Your clan is as powerful as mine, both body-wise and ability-wise. If our clans were to spar, it would be a draw. Together, we would be most powerful."

"My clan isn't interested in power," Jinx said evenly.

Jez laughed. "Everyone's interested in power. What differs is why and how it's used," the vamp corrected.

Jinx had to agree. "What's Kate interested in?"

"The witch? She's good. She's got an old soul and she can help, but Rogue . . ." Jez trailed off and shook his head.

"Did you know the one who did this to him?"

"Quite well." Jez threaded his long fingers together and paused. "Seb loves the Dires."

"He's got a funny way of showing it."

"He did choose, Jinx. It could've been worse."

Jinx wasn't sure how, but he'd been around long enough to know that jumping to conclusions never got you anywhere.

They ate the rest of the meal in relative silence, with Jez mentioning his nighttime routines.

Jez certainly did more than stay in his penthouse. The Dires should've been paying him, since the vamp did nightly patrols in both the buildings and the neighborhoods, often stopping the trappers from ensnaring unsuspecting young wolves.

"You always sleep in wolf form?" Jez asked him finally.

Jinx shrugged. "The ghosts leave me alone that way."

"They don't bother me."

"I wouldn't think the undead would bother themselves."

Jez gave a small smile that didn't reach his eyes. "You'd be surprised."

Angus had finally fallen asleep, still half pressed against the young wolf and trying not to hump him in his dreams. He'd been out maybe a few hours when his ringing cell phone woke him.

He fumbled in his pocket, the proximity between him and Cain still somewhat startling to him.

It was Shimmin. All he said was "Bring Cain Chambers to me immediately."

How the cop knew he was with Cain bothered Angus. He'd been discreet, and he was damned good at his job.

"The scent—they can track us," Cain said sleepily.

Shit. "What do I do, rub us in mud?"

"Such a fucking soldier," Cain mumbled. "Hang on. I can take care of it. But you have to move closer. Unless you want to call Shimmin back and turn me in."

The wolf's eyes were wide open now.

"If I do that, you'd kill me before I could dial the number," Angus said.

"If I thought your answer would be yes, I'd have already flayed you, human, drugs or no drugs."

Angus pressed his lips together as his phone began to ring again. He held it in his hands and moved closer to Cain. The young wolf nestled Angus against him, his cock brushing Angus's ass, his arms around his chest. The heat rose around them; the air changed—it smelled like sunshine, the beach. Everything wonderful.

He turned his cell phone off and fell back to sleep, until Cain shoved him. He woke with a start and stared down at eyes that were still out of it, but much clearer than earlier.

"What the hell happened to you?" Angus asked him.

"I drank the water," Cain said with a coherence that was a relief.

"I'm guessing that's not a drank the Kool-Aid euphemism, right?"

Cain shot him a dirty look. "That fucker drugged me."

"Why?"

Cain shook his head, and Angus knew he wouldn't get any more intel, even though he felt he was owed for sticking his neck out.

You were never on Shimmin's side to begin with. And still, no part of him was ready to admit that everything in him was telling him to root for the damned wolves.

When Stray left her bed, Kate slept, restlessly at first, and then she'd reached for the grimoire. Holding it, she'd had her first easy slumber in forever. It was as if the magic eased inside of her and covered her protectively. She felt reborn, renewed when she woke, having no idea how long she'd been out for.

She sat up and paged through the book—and she recognized what was written, knew all of it. As she'd dreamed, the pages had become a part of her, and now the power that coursed through her frightened her. The lights flickered. She didn't know if it was only in her room or happening throughout the entire house, but she couldn't control it.

Yes, you can.

The voice was hers, quite rational, and the instant she thought it, calm settled on her like a warm blanket. The lighting situation stabilized immediately.

"Good, that's good," she told herself. How could she feel crazy any longer after what she'd learned about Stray and from him?

There are monsters out there, and right now, they were actually the good guys. She had no reason not to believe him. She didn't feel any sense of evil in his presence or in the house and she'd definitely felt it from Leo Shimmin. The man had been sent to kidnap her.

Stray hadn't told her exactly what her role would be, but

she felt a bit like a superhero, like Wonder Woman, her favorite, in this great war. And the fact that she could help eased her apprehension. Because this was big, life-altering, world-changing stuff.

She wished she had Wonder Woman's bracelets or at least the Lasso of Truth.

As she got to the chapter she'd stopped on originally a few weeks back, the one on familiars, the same nervous feeling she'd gotten before fluttered in her stomach and she almost put the book down again.

Almost.

It was only then that she realized Stray was in the room with her, his wolf curled on the chair in a tight ball by the door. Guarding her. Protecting her.

She had to accept that and knew also that to accept this new world, her powers, her place, was to surrender to it.

For so long, she'd maintained her sense of careful balance that the outside never matched the inside. Now that would change, and she was actually relishing the feeling that allowing her tight grip on self-control to release would make everything right in a way it hadn't been in a long time.

She decided she needed to stop reading the book because by doing so she avoided having to actually practice magic. She wasn't ready to face this, but with this supernatural war happening, there was no time for further procrastination.

"Start simple," she whispered to herself. There was such a need to prove that she wasn't what Stray told her she was, and somehow a greater one to prove that she was powerful.

She'd never had power in her life—moved from circumstance to circumstance, helping people. But that always drained her.

She wanted to do something that made her feel good.

Her fingertips tingled as they remained close to the candle's wick. Too close, because she had to pull back fast when the flame shot up. She sat back and rubbed her hands together, watched the white light flicker. Then she extended a hand and concentrated on making the flame higher and finally extinguished it completely with a snap of her fingers.

Pretty cool. But certainly not enough to break an Adept's spell.

She paged through the book she'd been avoiding. There was an entire chapter devoted to the witch whose powers coursed through her. With a shaking hand, she turned the page and stared at the picture of someone she'd been told never existed.

"Lila, I wish you'd told me who you were when we met. I wish you'd saved me earlier." Kate knew none of that could've happened. Lila had been beautiful, with strong features and a small smile, not unlike the *Mona Lisa*, which belied the hint of secrets untold. "But in the end you did save me."

And dropped her into a world she might never have known otherwise. Wolves. Witches. Vampires.

Don't think about that now, she lectured herself.

"I'm meant to do this. It's right," she told herself. The candles raised their flames for that moment of agreement before going back to their normal size.

She would never have normal again, and she needed to be strong enough to handle it. The choice to be otherwise just wasn't there.

Chapter 32

Stray needed to meet with Kill alone first. Since the Dire relationships were tense within the pack even as plans came together, Stray would put things as right as they could be between himself and his brother before inviting the rest of the clan in.

He needed to do his part to keep his family together. He would get what was necessary from his brother and then he would force Killian to leave town, no matter what that took. Oh, and hope that working together wouldn't trigger an apocalyptic type of prophecy, as Vice had so kindly reminded him of moments earlier.

With a last look behind him, to where Rifter, Vice and Gwen sat around the kitchen table with Liam, he opened the door to the room in the basement Killian stayed in. He pushed the guilt aside that his brother was down there all alone, because it was by the wolf's own choice.

"He asked to stay alone in the dark—said it was like his hibernation period," Vice told him.

Even so, the area where Killian resided was a mini-apartment, complete with kitchenette, plasma TV and plenty of entertainment to keep anyone happy.

He knocked once and then went in, because Killian would be waiting for him.

"Brother." Kill stood in the middle of the room, his arms open with a drink in one hand, the bottle in the other, his voice mocking.

"Put the drink away," Stray told him in lieu of a greeting. "We have a job to do."

Kill smirked, but he shelved the bottle behind him, threw the remains of his drink down the drain before placing the glass on the table that separated them. "Peace, Stray. That's all I want."

"Bullshit."

Kill kicked the chair out to sit, did so with his arms folded on the table. "You didn't tell your new Dire family about us? Our family? I'm so hurt."

"You have no right to talk about my past."

"Our past," Killian reminded him.

"Let's just stick to talking plans, all right? We need to use our abilities together to program as many human weretrappers as we can to get out of the business of trapping and killing wolves."

"Consider it done."

"And that's it, Killian. That's all you're putting in their minds. Just that they need to leave the weretrappers, leave the wolves alone and go on with their lives."

"Forever?" Kill asked. "Because alone, I can plant new thoughts. Working with you, it's different."

"You told me you needed me to make sure the thoughts you planted worked."

"Yes, that's what I told you—and that's true. But when we work in tandem, I don't just plant thoughts. I can erase memories and create new ones. It goes beyond the power of suggestion—takes it to a whole new level."

"And you never told me?" Stray demanded, and Kill shrugged.

"Somehow, I didn't think you'd take it well. Besides, it was more dangerous for you to know. I didn't trust your new family not to use you."

"And now?"

"Now you asked, so I told you."

"How can I tell if something is a permanent memory?" Stray asked.

"You'll listen to the difference. You'll have to help me, because it's a delicate procedure, and delicate and I don't exactly mix." Killian smiled wryly and Stray's gut churned. "You know, these abilities are inside of us for a reason."

"To help. And to destroy," Stray muttered without thinking.

"You still believe in that prophecy?"

"You know you do too. I called you because the great war is starting."

"Steele—"

"Don't call me that," Stray growled. "Ever."

Killian held his hands up in mock surrender. "Got it, *Stray*. So, great war. We help and then . . . we destroy?"

"We help and then separate again so we don't have to destroy."

"You stay with your new family and I slink back into the night, is that it?" Killian rubbed his hands together.

If Stray closed his eyes, he could see Kill's hand wrapped around the hilt of the knife. "You could try to kill me again, but it didn't go so well the first time. Maybe you could turn the knife on yourself instead."

Killian stood so quickly the chair he'd been sitting in flew back, hit the wall and toppled with a loud crash. Stray braced himself, but his brother remained in place, his only movement to unbutton his shirt.

When Kill pulled the fabric apart to expose his chest, Stray saw the same knotted scar he had.

When his eyes met his brother's again, the understanding—and the explanation—he'd always wanted to see was there.

Turns out, it hadn't come too late after all.

Killian spent forever rehearsing for this moment and he still hadn't known how to tell his brother what he'd wanted to say for fifty years. Turned out, showing him had been simpler.

Kill hadn't told him anything earlier about the mixing of the abilities or the scars because what would it change? They had great power together—yes. And he'd sliced the knife through his younger brother with the intention of killing him. There was nothing he could say that would change that, or the fact that he'd left Stray to rot in that damned cage his parents kept him in.

He'd been only twelve when he'd first visited the newly born infant, named Steele at birth, howling in the bassinet outside the damned house. Even then, his parents couldn't show his brother any kindness or consideration.

"He'll get used to it," his father said.

Killian and the rest of the Greenland pack trained hard in the warrior ways, hardened from an early age to fight, not feel. But what they were doing to his brother, well, that was something altogether different.

His parents were scared shitless of a baby.

There had been talk of killing Steele—or secreting him away because of fear of the prophecy.

Killian had also heard the discussion among the pack before the baby had been born that their mother had done everything in her power to rid herself of the baby. The fact that nothing had worked made them even more fearful. They gave Steele only the most basic of necessities to not let him die and anger the Elders.

Kill made sure that Stray reached an age where he could fend for himself before he took off, figuring they wouldn't dare try to harm him.

He'd been so very wrong. And when he'd come across his brother, trying to die and unable to, his blood had boiled. Actually, his body had begun to tingle days earlier, alerting him to Steele's impending birthday, as if he could've ever forgotten it. He'd traveled back from Alaska to find him, and when he'd tracked Steele, his heart broke for both of them.

Goddamned fucking prophecy. Leave it to the Elders to be purposely obtuse. Help or no help, he and his brother were here to stay, and the world would just have to deal with them in kind.

To see Steele being mauled . . . well, he couldn't sit and watch. No, because then he'd have to wait and see if an immortal Dire could regenerate.

But even as the polar bears tried to rip and bite off Steele's limbs, they wouldn't give, not the way they would've if he'd been born regular Dire.

Rather than letting Steele remain under their torture, Kill figured he could put an end to everything.

He wasn't sure if Steele knew that he'd also run the knife through his own heart, fell to the snow and suffered there for several hours until his wound healed.

Steele had been unconscious, but he'd healed too. Killian had cut him down and carried him out of the danger, away from the pack who'd held him hostage for twenty-one years. He would never send his brother back there.

But when his younger brother woke, he was definitely going to be pissed.

"I know why you changed your name, but you were never a stray to me," Killian told him now, felt a jolt of emotion he hadn't been sure he was capable of anymore.

"I can't believe . . . you never told me." Stray's eyes were full of an emotion Killian had never seen directed at him before—kindness.

"Does it change what I did?"

"It puts it in perspective." He moved forward, touched his brother's chest. "You have two scars here."

He looked Stray in the eye. "I tried to kill myself before I came to you. When it didn't take, I thought . . ."

"Maybe if we were together . . ."

"Seems we're entangled for life, brother, no matter how much you hate it."

"And you stayed away then . . . just like you've been staying away for the past fifty years." Stray grabbed his brother's shoulder and pulled him closer. Killian wanted to resist, didn't want to get used to this touchy-feely shit because soon it would be over. Stray would realize they couldn't stay together as a family and he'd be alone again.

Not knowing what he'd been missing made everything a lot easier. But still, he allowed Stray to hug him.

Chapter 33

Stray felt the initial resistance, but then Killian embraced him back willingly. When they pulled apart, Stray told his brother, "Let's go talk to the others about the rest of the plans."

Killian shrugged like it didn't matter one way or the other, but Stray knew far better. The wolf followed him into the kitchen and the talking ceased.

It was only Rifter and Gwen now.

"Vice is going to check on Kate," Rifter explained. "I thought it best to keep this small. Sit, please." Rifter gestured to the seats across from them. "I'll brief Vice, who'll will fill Jinx in on our plans."

"And the witch?" Killian asked.

"Kate," Stray corrected him, and Killian nodded and repeated, "Kate."

"I think it's best she concentrate on her part in all of this, rather than muddy her mind with the entire plan," Rifter said diplomatically, and Killian smiled.

"You don't trust her either."

"Ah, fuck, Killian—give it a rest, all right?" Stray took a slug from the water bottle Gwen pushed in front of him.

"No one's going to talk about the fact that my brother's

bound to a witch?" Killian demanded, the protectiveness in his voice hard to miss.

"It's something we can figure out later," Rifter said. "Can we focus on the fact that Seb and the trappers are determined to take over the goddamned humans? The fallout in the supernatural world will be tremendous."

"And where are the rest of them?" Killian demanded. "The packs? The vamps? Heads in the sand, I'm assuming."

"I kind of like him," Gwen said with a small smirk.

"Let's talk about the Greenland pack." Rifter covered Gwen's hand with his, and he wasn't the least bit upset with her. Obviously, their queen was learning to straddle the fine line of a mated alpha king's unpredictable temper.

Now if she could just talk him into bringing Jinx back.

"They're not like us," Kill practically hissed. Stray heard the hatred behind his brother's words, one he himself felt every time he thought about them. "They have a shelf life. No abilities." *Fucking cowards.*

Dial it back, Kill, Stray told him.

"But they're self-sustaining, procreating Dires, and they should be under my rule," Rifter said steadily. Gwen couldn't help but nod at the truth of his words.

"Rifter, I don't think we can get the Greenland Dires on our side before the great war goes down. Let's get through that and then you can deal with Greenland," Gwen suggested, taking over a role usually filled by Vice.

Rifter bowed his head for a moment. Stray scented an imminent shift and then it passed. Rifter's eyes were still changed, but his countenance was calm. "Agreed. But I want the exact coordinates of the pack. And everything you know about them. Everything. Start with how many are left."

"Last I checked, still probably thirty Dires. Two alphas in charge of different packs, but they live in the same village for safety reasons," Killian told them. "They live for at least several hundred years. Most of them die from hunters when they're in wolf form. None have lived as long as you."

"But they knew of us?"

"You're legend," Kill admitted without a trace of sarcasm. "I'm glad Steele—Stray—found you."

"We found him," Rifter corrected.

"And you took him on without question. Don't be angry that he's never spoken about me to your pack."

"I understand why he didn't. But if you and Stray work together, the prophecy is set in motion."

"It already is." Killian stared at Rifter. "We'll fight the trappers and then I'll leave."

Stray hadn't asked him to do that—had wanted to, but now everything had changed. Before he could protest, Gwen said, "You'll be hunted."

"I'll manage," Kill said.

"It doesn't seem fair," Gwen murmured.

"No one ever promised fair," Killian told her. "I'll live."

She looked so sad at Killian's words. "There are so few of us. We should be together."

"When's the last time you saw your parents?" Rifter asked both of them.

"I haven't seen them since the day you tried to kill us both," Stray said to Kill, his voice steady as he looked between his brother and Rifter. He noticed the surprise in Rifter's face, but there had been no rancor in Stray's tone.

"I haven't seen them in fifty years." Kill rocked back in his chair and stared at Stray. "And I made sure you'll never see them again."

"What are you talking about?"

"They're dead."

"How?" Stray demanded.

"Murdered in cold blood by another Dire. Turnabout's fair play, I figure." Kill looked as though he understood the seriousness of his words and the actions he'd taken. He didn't look particularly proud or cocky, but there was no remorse either.

"Why?" Rifter asked. Killing one's parents in the Dire

community meant a sentence of death. The execution was traditionally a beheading.

Kill seemed completely unconcerned. "They tried to kill my brother, so I killed them for that transgression."

Stray didn't doubt he was telling the truth. Kill might be dark, but he didn't lie.

Rifter stood, the chair falling behind him, a hand pulling down the neck of his shift to reveal the tribal wolf on his chest.

Killian looked up at him and nodded in silent confirmation to whatever Rifter was attempting to ask. Stray was as confused as Gwen until Rifter said tightly, "Killian's a skinwalker now. A powerful one at that. A consequence of killing one's parents."

The implications of that were phenomenal. Beyond the powers that he and Stray had together . . . Stray couldn't wrap his mind around it. Didn't want to. "This should never have happened."

Kill stared at him, his expression momentarily softening. "It had to, Stray. They'd never have left you alone otherwise."

"They came looking for me?" Stray asked.

"While you were recovering, they tracked us. Dad and some of the other pack alphas. Mom too. You were still in and out of consciousness. You'd healed and then you shifted twice in the space of an hour."

Stray remembered part of that—the total and complete confusion, the pain . . . Brother Wolf attempting to comfort him and failing miserably for those first days.

Extenuating circumstances, Brother pointed out with a haughty sniff.

"They broke into my hiding place when you were still recovering from everything—the mauling, the knife, your first shifts. I killed the lot of them before they laid a hand on you again. And then I left their bodies for the bears." Kill's voice was tight again, and Stray finally understood what

Rifter had been saying all along—sometimes you have to cause a lot of damage to avoid hurting people.

"Holy hell, Killian—I'm worried about you," Stray told him.

"You're worried about me?" Kill sounded incredulous. "You're the catalyst to our powers. Without you, my words wouldn't take permanently. When you were born, it was all set in motion. You thought you needed me to help, Stray. Turns out you were wrong—you've been the necessary one all along."

Stray's throat tightened at the truth in his brother's words. He looked down to catch his breath as Killian explained the jolt in powers that would happen now that they were together.

"And the skinwalker ability?" Rifter asked.

"It makes everything I do . . . stronger," Kill said.

"That explains how you took out the possessed Weres," Rifter said. "Thank you, Killian. For that. For saving your brother."

Killian got up and went to the window, turning his back to them as the emotion grew heavy around them. And Stray knew then he'd always really been part of Killian's heart.

Chapter 34

Night cycled around. Cain didn't feel all that much better, knew he had to wait, play possum until darkness settled and so he remained close to the fed, pretending to sleep soundly under the cheap motel quilt. Wondered again why Angus would risk his life for him.

Realized how much he owed the man. Cain didn't like owing anyone.

Now he felt his twin was close, waiting to pick him up. And he could swear the ground under his feet was shifting a little, but that was probably a leftover effect of the drugs.

He stood, still a little shaky, and pulled his shirt on as Angus watched. "Look, thanks for this. I owe you."

"And I'll collect."

"I figured as much." Cain pocketed his phone. "But you still need to be careful. I'm not the most dangerous thing out there."

The wolf was almost out the door before Angus told him, "You're the most dangerous for me."

Seb leaned against the stone wall, watched the man go down on him as Seb's hand fisted his hair, moving his head faster.

He'd come four times already and still he needed more. He felt as though he was ready to burst through his skin. His body's appetites were suddenly ferocious, and the women Leo brought him weren't enough. No, they were like sacrificial lambs laid to slaughter and they gladly sacrificed themselves for what they considered the cause.

Earlier, he'd watched the Dire army slaughter yet another cemetery full of corpses and ghosts. They were bloodthirsty and bent on revenge.

They were perfect. Leo was pleased, as was the demon Kondo.

Lila wouldn't be pleased at all, a voice he didn't recognize at all spoke inside his head.

"Who the fuck is that?" he demanded of the demon, but the only sounds were the furious sucking ones. He yanked the man away from him disgustedly and began to prowl around the otherwise unoccupied room with the bed in one corner and the small bathroom in the other.

He hadn't been allowed out since Mars was killed, not even to glimpse the sunlight.

Now he decided he'd make it rain all the time, since he didn't care.

A brilliant white light flashed before his eyes. He turned away, momentarily blinded as though he'd just run across a flash-bang grenade from his Navy days. Kondo scrabbled madly inside his head, like it was unable to gain access to Seb's mind. For the first time in weeks, Seb's mind was momentarily all his own.

"I can't promise it will stay that way," the white light explained. He blinked and stared at it, shielding his gaze a little with one hand above them. He could make out some kind of figure within, but it was like she wore a purposeful shroud.

"Who are you?" he asked.

"For every demon, there's one of us," she explained. "Even though you brought this on yourself with hubris—and power combined."

"Fuck you," he told her. "And that's not the demon talking. That's all me."

"What you need . . ."

"Is sex," Kondo growled through him, cutting her off.

"Can you get this bastard out?" Seb demanded of the white light.

"Out, yes, but you'll still be half controlled. I'm here for balance."

"Can everyone see you?"

"Just you and demon-breath. If you want it out, you have to help me."

He closed his eyes and focused on that black ball of negative energy inside of him, imagined it growing smaller and smaller until he was able to force it out of himself.

It came out through his mouth in a huff of smoke, causing him to choke, fall to his knees. When he looked up, there was black smoke next to the white gauzy shroud.

Somehow, he'd gotten strong enough to force Kondo to live outside his body.

"Doesn't mean I don't have control," Kondo pointed out.

"How did I do that?" Seb asked.

"It's too cursed inside your body for him to gain a foothold," the white shroud answered. "You've become your own worst enemy."

That couldn't be good. "Why are you here?"

"Lila sent me," the white shroud answered.

Kondo laughed and said, "You can't believe her."

Seb knew at that moment that he couldn't trust either of them. He also couldn't trust himself, but he'd known that for much longer.

Playing both sides against the middle was always a risky move, but Angus hadn't gotten as far as he had in life and his career by being safe. And so going back to Shimmin and telling him that he'd taken Cain on purpose, that Shimmin didn't realize the Were was so much more useful to them alive because of his semi-relationship with Angus could've meant certain death for him. But Shimmin wasn't completely stupid—and not all that hard to convince.

"The trappers, especially Al, think you talk too much," Shimmin told him now.

"I get results."

"What results did you get from Cain Chambers?"

"He's not an omega."

"He's lying to you, then."

"He's lying to everyone—including the Dires—so they'll keep him. The only one who's supposed to see his glow is Liam, and Cain's convinced that would-be king that he hasn't seen it because he's so new," Angus lied.

Shimmin nodded, and Angus began to wonder if he'd told an actual truth. He must've, because Shimmin said, "Only his alpha king *and* his mate can see the glow—it's an omega's protection very few know about. And he doesn't have a mate."

Angus swallowed hard. "Right."

"So you're the only one he trusted with his deception?"

"I heard him convincing Liam, and then I did some research. I can spot a fraud, Shimmin."

"Well, then, welcome to your initiation. Al will walk you through it." Shimmin pointed to the small group of trappers coming through the trees, clapped Angus on the shoulder and began to walk to his car. "If all goes well today—and it should—you'll be official."

Angus watched Shimmin drive off before turning his attention to Al, who narrowed his eyes at him. "I don't trust you fully, Angus, but Shimmin said you have a plan."

He had a plan, all right. It involved all these assholes getting hurt.

But obviously, so did they. Two trappers dragged a young, terrified boy wrapped in silver chains and dropped him to the ground in front of Angus.

The boy's skin was smoking where the silver touched it.

They weren't even giving the poor bastard a chance to run, to be hunted. That would've evened the playing field, but the trappers weren't about fair.

"First, you practice on this. And then you get to take down Cain Chambers. It'll be tougher, because the Dires are training him. But he's taken a liking to you—shouldn't be hard to get him alone."

Angus didn't show any emotion on his face. He hadn't needed training for that—he'd learned very early on that emotion got you in trouble, that it was always misinterpreted. That it showed weakness. And he was far from weak.

It was time for the trappers to know that. "Bring the Were here."

They dragged the wolf, trussed in silver, smoke coming from his skin, and shoved him to his knees in front of Angus.

"What did he do?"

"Do?" The trappers started laughing, and Al said, "Like we told you before—he didn't need to do anything. He's a fucking Were. A killer. He will kill. It's his nature."

And then Al handed him the long silver blade. "Killing is your initiation. Part one, anyway. Do it right, Angus."

Chapter 35

Vice came into Stray's room, where Kate sat alone on the bed, flipping through the grimoire. She'd been doing so for the past hour while Stray was with Killian.

Stray was purposely keeping her out of his mind during this time, which she appreciated. It didn't stop her from worrying, though, and the words swam on the page.

Frustrated, she closed the grimoire and put her palm on it as she stared up at the silver-eyed wolf.

"Waiting on Stray?" he asked.

"Yes—did everything go okay?"

"There's no bloodshed, so I'm guessing yes. There's some strategizing going on now. Sometimes it's better I'm not there when they're discussing fighting. I tend to rile everyone up." He carried two sodas, walked in and handed her one. "I'm going to hang with Rogue—wanna join me?"

She hesitated. "I think I'll stay here and work."

"Suit yourself." He left without pressuring her any further, but she couldn't get Rogue's *thank you* out of her head.

She tucked the book under her arm, walked into the hallway and saw Vice waiting for her at the top of the stairs.

"What, you read minds too?" she called up to him.

"Just people."

"Witch, remember?" She climbed the steps to close the gap between them. When she stood on the landing next to him, she continued. "Rifter's worried—thinks I shouldn't go in there because the mare reports to Seb."

Vice shrugged. "Hell, it's not like he doesn't know you're here. And you've got the book—and Stray is right in the house."

He opened the door wider, almost a dare, and she took it, walked in and went right to Rogue.

It was hard to ignore the mare, but she did. Stroked Rogue's hair again, heard the same *thank you* echo inside her head. And then everything felt peaceful, despite the mare's horrid presence.

"I'm guessing you're on board."

She glanced at Vice and back to Rogue. "Yes."

"You're connected to Stray."

"Yes."

"Don't hurt him."

The words were a soft growl, less of a menacing threat than a simple statement of fact.

"I don't want to." She tightened her grip into fists in her lap, watched the color blanch from her knuckles as the lights flickered.

"I know you're doing that. And it's all right that you are," Vice told her.

"I keep forgetting I don't have to hide anything anymore."

"You don't have to hide anything from us."

"I'm used to freaking people out," she said.

"Not much worries us here," Vice told her. "Feel free to fly your freak flag high and proud."

His upper body—and his bare feet—were covered with tats, but when she looked hard enough, she saw the tribal wolf looking at her through the maze of black-and-white symbols.

She'd seen him strip to shift the other night, knew his entire body was tatted and pierced in some interesting places.

The weird thing was, as attractive as Vice was, being around him made her only hotter for Stray. Although maybe that was not so weird for a wolf whose abilities centered on vice.

She made a mental note to ask more about that and then she moved closer to Rogue, kept a hand on the book and chanted the spell to rid a person of mares. A person, *not* a wolf.

Still, what could it hurt to try?

It did nothing but make the mare laugh at her harder.

"I'm sorry, Rogue. I'm trying."

Distracted by the brothers.

"Yes," she agreed.

Both will walk the earth forever, but one will remain cursed for all days.

She had no idea what that meant, but it couldn't be good.

More to the prophecy than meets the eye.

"Like what?" she asked Rogue.

"Kate."

It was Stray. She turned from Rogue to go to him. He looked tired, but there were no visible signs of a physical fight. She guessed progress had been made.

"Rifter's waiting to prep you downstairs," he told Vice.

"I'll leave you two alone," Vice told them. "I'm going to check on Cain first and then I'll catch up with Rift."

He sank to the floor next to her and she hugged him hard. His arms wrapped around her and she whispered, "Proud of you."

"Thanks." He brushed the hair back from her face. "What were you trying to do here?"

"I think Rogue can talk to me. Or, at least, I can hear him. I'd like to try again with you here, if you're up for it."

"No time like the present."

This was all so important—for the war between man and wolf, for her and Stray, for their families. "Vice said all of you have abilities. I know what yours is. What's Killian's?"

"I read minds and my brother manipulates thoughts separately," he told her. "When I'm physically with him, we can erase and cement new memories. Which means that together, we're—"

"Unstoppable."

"Dangerous," he corrected.

"Could you use it on me?"

"Yes, but I wouldn't." He paused. "You have to believe that."

"I do, Stray." She stared up at the moon thoughtfully and then back at him. "You can read minds; so can I. Kill can manipulate—if we all work together, there has to be a way we can use what Seb did against him."

"No. As much as I forgive Killian, I'm not about to let him go roaming in your mind."

"I can roam in Seb's, though."

"Yes, and you can let him back into yours at will. But even though you're strong, that will be dangerous."

"But if you're there, you can stop me if things go too far."

He nodded. "I don't know if I want to. I'm not in a sharing mood. With you, I'll never be again."

"I don't plan on being shared. I promise. The only one I want is you."

Stray stared at her for a long moment, the look of complete ownership warming her in ways she never thought possible. He wanted her—all of her—and that was the best thing to happen from all of this.

"Ready?" he asked finally.

She nodded. Blew out a breath and linked her hand with Stray's. Opened her mind the way the book taught her to, imagining the protective lining opening like a zippered purse to let Seb have access to her.

He did, almost immediately, like he'd been waiting for

this opportunity. For a moment, she almost felt sorry for him.

Lila, come back to me. I'll lead you—show you the way. It's so hard for you now, but with me, it will be so easy.

Stray's hand on her elbow squeezed as she answered, "What do you want with me? You know who I am."

You're part of Lila, and I want her back.

"You gave Lila up. That's part of why she died—you betrayed her." With her free hand, she reached out to touch the mare, who was intricately and intimately connected with Seb, and she recoiled in horror. Hissed. Ran her nails in a raking motion down Rogue's chest as the wolf remained stoic and unmoving, even though she swore she heard his moans in her head.

Stray started, like he did, too.

"I can see you, Sebastian," she whispered, knowing that's what Lila called him as her connection to the witch flared. "I will stop you."

The mare shrieked, a sound like nails on a chalkboard as Rogue did a silent writhe of pain under her.

Seb pushed back, hard. *Silly witch. You can't do this.*

In another time and place, this wouldn't happen; they would be friends. Seb would be her mentor. "You know it's wrong."

Of course I know. But sometimes you have to cause great damage to do the most good.

"You're not doing any good—and I'm here to stop you."

No. That was Rogue, his thoughts clenching hers so tightly, her head began to throb. *Stop. This isn't your place—this isn't what you were meant to do.*

"Then what?" she asked.

Stop the army. You and Jinx together can do it.

"How?"

Lean in to me.

She did, and Rogue whispered things about the dead, their path, their crossings . . . Over the mare's screams, he told her secrets about the dead no one should know, things buried by the rushing River Styx, and it felt right and wrong at the same time. It confused her—like what he was telling her didn't match the truth he was giving her.

But he did tell her what was wrong with Jinx. And by the time he'd finished, his voice was fading, and she was exhausted and dizzy. But fortified.

Your witch knows what to do.

"It will hurt your brother," she said.

Yes, it has to, Rogue agreed. *He knows it. Put yourself in his presence and work together. Don't be distracted by the wolf in sheep's clothing.*

Seb went insane that a new witch was disrespecting him. He used to have everything, including and especially Lila. Now Lila's new witch had made him look like a fool.

And he was no fool.

The girl might have Lila's power, but she knew nothing. *Nothing.*

Ah, so that's what it takes to get your ire up, the white shroud whispered, and that's when Seb realized he couldn't tell the difference between angels and devils at all.

Let it go, Sebastian. Show them all what you can do, Kondo urged, and for the first time, Seb listened to his dark side wholeheartedly.

He'd been afraid of it his entire life. Now he had nothing to fear. He could be all-powerful, let people bow to him. The jig was up, the worry gone.

And it felt good.

Chapter 36

Jinx was lying on his back on the couch, willing himself to get up and out and into the shit waiting for him just outside the apartment door. Brother Wolf wasn't going to push him, didn't want to deal with the plethora of ghosts that circled the building.

But they were tame compared to the other things that hovered. Jinx could feel them so deep down, like they were attached to him, yanking at him. Attempting to force him out into the darkness he normally loved.

Jez finally pulled a chair over and sat next to him, staring directly into his face, fangs elongated. A show of violence, of domination, but it had come out of nowhere.

Jinx jumped up, prepared to fight, Brother Wolf rising to the challenge. "What the fuck is this, Jez?"

"Just waiting for you to get up off your ass and notice that the building's shaking," Jez said, seemingly unconcerned, but his glowing eyes told a different story. Unlike wolf's eyes, deadhead eyes seemed to lose their pupils; the ring circling the iris was an odd glow around the blackness inside.

That ring was the only thing that differentiated the deadhead from a demon—and it was unlike any vamp he'd ever seen. Good info to know, and Jinx put that in the back of his mind as he hightailed it to the window.

The building was moving, like some kind of earthquake that wasn't stopping. The streets were cracking and humans ran into the streets, looking at the sky, like the answers could all be found there. "Gotta be Stray's witch—"

"Not her," Jez said, and Jinx felt the skitter of cold fear wrap his spine when he realized the vamp was right.

"We've got to get out there," he breathed as he watched humans continue to pour outside and begin fighting—out of fear, mostly. Mixed in with the humans, he noted Weres in human form and the horrors of purgatory flew over them. Circling and watching. "Gotta figure out what's going on."

"I know exactly what this is. Seb's having a temper tantrum," Jez said. "And it's nothing compared to what the Dire ghost army can and will unleash on us."

"But for now, if the trappers can't even control him—" Jinx started.

"Then he's vulnerable—and so are they," Jez finished. Jinx was already calling Liam and the twins.

"Time for reinforcements."

Vice burst into Rogue's room, where Kate still sat, recovering from talking with Rogue. Stray immediately stood, because something was really wrong based on the fact that Vice was ready for an imminent shift.

"We've got to get downtown—big trouble."

As he spoke, the house began to shake. "Is that just us?" Stray asked as Kate said at the same time, "That's not me."

"It's not you—it's Seb," Vice said. "That's what Jinx said, anyway. What the hell happened in here between you guys?"

"Seb's angry because I talked to Rogue," she said.

"Rogue told her to help with the Dire ghost army—to work with Jinx, not to worry about him," Stray added.

Vice whistled. "Yeah, that's gonna work out well. Look,

Liam's rounding up whatever Weres he can trust to try to help get the humans under control—Seb's got them in the streets, fighting. We need you and Kill."

Stray looked back at Kate. "She'll have to come with. I can't leave her alone with Seb this angry."

"Do whatever you need to, brother, but let's roll."

There was no time to waste—Stray helped Kate up and ushered her down the stairs and into the garage, stopping only to collect shoes and a jacket of Gwen's for her.

Killian was waiting by the truck. He nodded to Stray and Kate and got into the front seat next to Vice. Liam and the twins had already taken off.

Rifter, as much as it pained him to send his men out without him, would remain home and keep Gwen safe.

"What's the plan?" Stray asked.

"Same plan—just a smaller scale this time. You and Kill reverse Seb's message inside the humans' minds. I realize we're giving away our hand, but Seb already knows what Kill can do. I'll watch out to make sure he's not laying other traps. Stray, you made sure it's working, weed out any trappers. Liam's Weres will usher the humans back to safety with Cyd and Cain helping. Jinx is close to the area as well."

"I guess we're jumping into the fire without practice," Stray said.

"Believe in us, brother, the way you do your witch," Kill told him. "I'm going to have to plant some earthquake story to the network news, too. In the scientists' minds as well, or people are going to get really suspicious."

"Witch, you need to stay close to Stray—you can't defend yourself."

"I can fight," Kate insisted. "I've taken a lot of self-defense courses."

Vice turned to hand her a covered silver-bladed knife. "This can hurt a Were, kill a demon or human. Use it if you need to."

With that, he blasted the truck out of the garage.

*   *   *

Ten minutes later, Kate stood and watched Liam talking to a small group of Weres, including Cyd and Cain, his voice loud and firm over the chaos just outside the woods.

"We don't hurt the humans—we herd them back to safety, understood?" Liam told them and one of the Weres called out, "What about Seb's spells? They work on us, remember?

"Killian won't let that happen," Liam assured them. "The newest Dire has my trust, and that means he has yours as well."

She watched Killian nod in appreciation. Whatever had happened between Stray and Killian went a long way toward Liam's sentiment, and she hoped it would be enough to control this situation.

And then the unshifted Weres begin to move toward the rowdy crowd.

She wondered if she could distract Seb, give the wolves enough time to clean this up. She'd started this mess in the first place, and it should be her job to end it.

She realized she was trembling a little, with the threat, the crowds, the smell of violence that permeated the normally more peaceful city.

Although there was gang violence and other crime here, this particular section of town wasn't usually a hotbed of activity.

Things were getting darker now, and not just because of nightfall.

"Don't use your powers out here," Stray admonished. "You don't know who's watching. Bad enough we had to bring you out."

"I can't stay locked inside forever."

"It's not the time to argue with me. Stay close," Stray told her. "Stay right between me and Kill. Tuck your arms in ours and keep your eyes peeled for trouble."

He turned to talk to Stray for a minute, his hand still on

hers. She jerked away fast. "You're worried Seb's going to call to me again, and that I'm not strong enough to resist."

He wheeled back around to her, said fiercely, "I'm worried you're going to let him in, in some misguided attempt to save everyone."

"I wouldn't do that. There's too much at stake."

But the fact that he didn't trust her at all . . . that nearly killed her. "You said you wouldn't read my mind unless I invited you to."

"Or if we were in a dangerous situation. This shit counts." He lowered his voice. "I'm with you, distracted. You could get us both into a really bad place. Do you understand? I'm tied to you, in more ways than one."

If I go down, you go down.

When he nodded, the monumentality of that hit her, probably for the first time since she'd met Stray and discovered what she was.

"Let's do this," Killian interrupted them. "You can deal with your personal issues later."

Neither argued. She threaded her arms through the big wolves' arms and let them lead her into the mob.

Stray had wondered if this would be too much, if Kill's skinwalking curse would interfere with their abilities.

If anything, it made their bond stronger, more effective. Kill had been right—Stray could see the difference between a permanent memory and a suggestion, as Kill had demonstrated to him when they picked their first human to fix.

A dark gift turned darker by default, and Stray listened in to the humans' minds and told Killian what he needed to say to quell their confusion and fear and turn them calm and docile.

An army of docile humans. He was sure this wasn't what the Elders had in mind, and he also knew this was nothing compared to the battles to come.

"Concentrate, brother," Killian muttered now, his hand

in the air as he and Stray pulled Kate along through the relentless crowd. Kate had her head down, her hand gripped both his and Kill's biceps tightly and he tasted her worry.

Stray couldn't delve into her thoughts at the moment and risk Killian getting to them, and so he hoped she was doing as she promised, staying out of it. He continued to read minds and make sure the suggestions were implanted.

"He's resisting." Stray pointed to a man in overalls walking away from the crowds.

"Trapper," Killian said, baring his canines ever so slightly. He closed his eyes and his body shook from the effort—and Kate and Stray's by default.

In seconds, the trapper turned, slowly, dazed and disoriented. "He's Shimmin's bitch," Stray caught Liam and told him. "Leave his memory intact and take him alive. Bring him to Vice to interrogate later."

Liam sent Cain over to collect the confused man, and Stray and Kill continued, even as the crowd began to surge again, like Seb was starting new with his violent attempts at control.

Chapter 37

Some of Kill's attempts were too aggressive. These powers had never been used and trying to hone them among the masses of humanity wasn't working well. Time after time, he'd bend a group's brains too hard, take them too far, erase too much until they collapsed like husks on the floor, bags of bones encased in skin.

Weak. Mortal. And still he pressed on to help them because he'd promised the Dires and the Elders he would. Because not doing so wouldn't gain him death. Because Stray believed in him, guided him, as he'd promised. Told him when to rein it in. Killian put all his trust into his brother and together they worked their brand of magic on the crowd.

He fisted his hands as thirty more rushed at him, watched them drop to their knees. Only then did he ease the pressure, remind them, *It's an earthquake—we should be inside, helping one another.*

Like lemmings, they stood, shakily, as the earth still shook under their feet, and made their way toward buildings and homes and cars.

*   *   *

Jinx and Jez stayed along the outskirts of the fighting, watching to make sure that the humans and Weres who came their way were nonviolent.

Jinx was clawing to get into the fight—Brother Wolf as well, although he knew that staying out of it was the best thing he could do.

He hated being helpless, now more than ever, and he could only imagine how Stray felt at points in his life. Even now, watching the power he and Killian had over these people—it was both reassuring and frightening as hell.

"I should be out there," he muttered.

"I'm sure Rifter and the others feel the same way. You can do more good when this is over. Your Dire brothers have it under control," Jez pointed out.

Jez was right. Kill and Stray moved through the crowds, Kate between them, subduing herds of humans. Kill was changing the crowd's memories so that they'd always remember this as merely Mother Nature, a small earthquake, and nothing to get violent about, while Liam's Weres were acting as crowd control under his leadership, stopping fights and keeping themselves calm, pushing the humans back to their homes and businesses.

The Weres appeared unaffected by the mob violence, but Jinx would bet anything that all of them would shift if pushed just slightly further.

And that would truly be madness.

"It's not only happening here," Jez said as he checked his iPhone. "CNN and other affiliates reported riots all across New York State. Reports of an earthquake are unconfirmed."

"At least what Kill's doing is working," Jinx muttered.

As he watched, Killian stood in the middle of the empty street, still holding Kate, who clung to him and Stray like her life depended on it. Killian closed his eyes and for a long, tense minute, Jinx wondered what the wolf was doing.

"Skinwalker," the ghost who floated in front of the partially opened window whispered, and Jinx jerked his head toward it, as did Jez.

"Is he right?" Jinx asked Jez.

"Do I have encyclopedia of the damned stamped across my forehead?" Jez demanded. "What the hell did you wolves do before I got involved?"

"Looks like you've always been involved."

What Kill and Stray were doing was working, but not fast enough. The crowd swirled around her, and Kate felt choked by the thickness of the hatred. All of that was directed at her.

Defying Stray wasn't first in her mind, but she needed to help, to stop being powerless.

Maybe she was strong enough to do this. If Kill could gain control as she watched, why couldn't she do the same?

She opened her mind and focused her thoughts. *Seb, please, stop this.*

Stray jerked his head to stare at her. Yelled something, but she'd already made the decision to stop this on her own.

Come to me and I'll stop this, Seb told her.

She suddenly had more strength than before, extricated herself from the wolves and began to walk through the crowds that seemed to part for her.

"Kate!" Stray's voice was behind her, but she ignored him, walked faster even as she felt the heat from his body behind him.

If you run, I will catch you, Stray warned.

Tell your pet to follow, Seb instructed.

She was helpless to resist, and had realized too late that Seb was far more insidious than she'd have thought. "Stray? Please?"

If she was doing it for Stray or Seb, she didn't know, wasn't sure it even mattered.

If you come to me, I'll end all of this. Keep walking.

"Bullshit. Kate, don't believe him."

Keep coming, Kate—just a little farther.

She listened to Seb's voice, since the riot seemed to be calming, or maybe it wasn't, but she couldn't stop now. She was in too deep.

Kate was leaving, against orders, and hell, he was being dragged along with her. Helplessly, because of their bond. Stray would never let that happen again. Not for anyone.

He tore his mind away from Kate's and called, "Help me, Killian."

He felt his brother reaching into his mind. It hurt like a headache from hell as he allowed his brother to manipulate his mind. He felt a tearing inside, like the bond with Kate was ripping apart, and no, he didn't want that, not completely.

He stared at his brother as the realization of what Killian could do to him—for him—in this regard dawned on him. And then he shook his head no.

Kill understood, eased up so the bond was stretched, not broken. It was enough to stop him from walking behind Kate, although she continued along.

Stray turned to see Killian. His brother looked . . . different, like he was morphing into something other than himself. But then his entire body shook and Stray heard him tell Kate, *Turn around and go back to Stray.*

She stopped and dropped to her knees and he knew Killian was inside her mind as well. She cried out, "I can't. This is the only way—"

"He'll kill you, Kate. Look straight ahead at what's waiting for you," Kill told her even as she struggled to her feet.

Stray made the mistake of looking and saw Shimmin, waiting at the edge of the woods, holding a semiautomatic by his side . . . and a hypodermic needle tucked into his free fist.

Kate gasped and then she turned, hard, right into Stray.

He grabbed her and ran with her, back into the crowd, toward Killian, as the humans around them began to close them in.

And the shaking began again.

Kate had closed her mind against Stray—and Stray only. He dropped away from following her; in essence, she was saving him.

But he's bonded to you forever.

When she looked up again, she saw a man with dark hair and a fierce expression. *Seb.*

She stopped in front of him. "I'm here."

"Good. Shut your mind to me—now."

She did, and the silence was deafening. Wonderful. She waited to be taken away, to see Leo Shimmin, but none of that happened. Instead, Stray was tugging her and when she looked back, it wasn't Seb who stood there, but Kill.

"How did he do that?" she asked.

"This isn't the time or place to talk about any of this," Stray told her. "Don't do it again."

But nothing had changed—nothing stopped. The earth still shook hard and people were screaming. Shots rang out and it felt like the world was ending.

I'm so much stronger than any of them. Don't worry about Shimmin. I won't let him hurt you. Go to him now.

Kate believed him because she had to stop this. And so she broke away from Stray's grasp when he was distracted and she ran toward Shimmin, like Seb had directed. Stray's voice came from behind her just as shots rang past her head.

"No!" she shouted, broke the contact with Seb at that moment when she realized everything had gone so very wrong.

In retrospect, it was the stupidest move ever. But her instinctive need to protect Stray and his kind overtook her. She'd never had anyone to care about that deeply, and now.

And now she'd killed him. And it didn't matter that he

couldn't die, because she watched him collapse to the side, blood streaming from his chest. She opened her mouth in a silent scream. Tried to sink to her knees toward him, but someone pulled her up from behind.

Friend? Foe?

"Stray? Stray!" she called. And he opened his eyes, but they were cold. And for the first time, she totally understood the consequences of Stray being bound to her. "I'm so sorry. I just couldn't be helpless anymore."

"Don't talk." *Don't think. Do nothing until I have you in a safe place.*

It was fair, and maybe more than she deserved.

Chapter 38

After he'd managed to give Kate an order, Stray went unconscious, although it wasn't for long. Maybe he even died, but he never knew exactly what happened during that time. All he knew was that, for those brief moments, there was no pain, no nothing, except Brother Wolf's short whine in his ear, because Brother did not want to end things this way.

Brother Wolf liked immortality. He'd found his mate and he wasn't letting go. Stray wasn't either.

It hurt like a motherfucker. Stray groaned inwardly as his inability to just lie down and die propelled him upright, despite the sucking chest wound.

At least he had all his limbs, because regeneration took a while and that was a real bitch and a half.

And, just like the last time he'd died, he saw his brother standing over him, watching with that look in his eyes.

Unlike last time, Stray now knew he meant no further harm. "I don't want you to ever erase my memory of the familiar bond between me and Kate."

Kill stared at him intensely. "You're sure? I can fix it so even if she calls, you'll never remember a thing about it. Your wolf will never be vulnerable to her again."

"No. Leave my memory intact." Stray took the knife strapped to his ankle and cut his palm. "Blood oath."

"She tried to save you, no matter how badly it turned out. She's good in my book." Kill took the knife and did the same, grasped his brother's hand so their blood mingled. "Blood oath. On my honor."

"Thank you. Now get me back in there," he growled.

"At least now you've got some fucking bite behind that bark," Killian told him as he helped him stagger into the middle of the crowd. "Don't worry about her. She's out of here, safe and sound. Just worry about this."

And for the next two hours, Stray did.

He and Kill took out dirty cops, weretrappers, outlaw Weres, and it was like blowing ash off a ledge. His conscience didn't ache this time; his body and mind weren't on autopilot, but rather, focused with the purpose of saving innocents, like he'd been charged with from birth.

Jinx didn't need to hear or see the shot to know what happened. He doubled over as he felt a pain in his own chest, which always happened when one of the immortal Dires was mortally wounded. It was all he could do to not drop to the ground the way Stray had.

All the Dires would be affected and he hoped they were well protected, as he was.

For the first time, he realized he needed to be grateful to a goddamned vampire, even as Brother Wolf bucked that thought away.

It's time to allow for new alliances, Brother. The future's not pretty.

Brother Wolf howled and Jinx stumbled from the pain. Gasped for breath as Stray died and was reborn. It took only seconds—maybe a full minute, if that, but it wasn't fun.

"Jinx, you all right?"

"Fine. Help me up."

"Kill's still going," Jez said.

"Fucking skinwalker," Jinx managed as the deadhead dragged him to his feet.

"Stray's up too."

Jinx looked out in the crowd that was starting to calm again. "Get the witch out of there before she hurts someone."

"The twins have her. They're bringing her this way."

"That's going to work out well. Tell them to take her to Vice," Jinx said, taking his hold off Jez and holding on to the building instead.

Jez did as he asked but not before telling him, "I'll meet you at the cemetery later."

"Which one?"

"Pinewood," Jez said as he left. Jinx waited to leave until he saw Kate safely with Vice. He didn't allow a shift, and Brother Wolf calmed the farther they got from the violence.

The twins found him about an hour later outside Pinewood, Cain bounding up to him like nothing had happened, Cyd lagging behind him, watching both their sixes.

Dusk was coming. Jinx had come to despise the night as much as he loved it.

"Jinx, you all right?" Cain asked.

"I should be asking you that."

Cyd sniffed the air. "I smell vamp."

"I smell it too. He's close." Cain moved closer to Jinx as if protecting him and then stilled. "What the fuck, Jinx?"

Jinx ran a hand through his hair, his frustration peaking. He didn't want to take it out on the twin—never did—but this was all bullshit. "I've been staying with Jez."

"You got kicked out because you defied Rifter and you're living with a vamp," Cain mused. "How long was I out for?"

"Was the witch right about what's happening with you?" Cyd asked.

"No. And yes. But mainly, no."

"That's reassuring," Cyd said with a small frown marring his handsome face.

He ignored the wolf, instead tipped Cain's chin to look his wolf in the eyes. "You all right? Seriously?"

"Shouldn't have had the water at the station, but yeah, I'm all right. Angus saved my damned hide this time."

"You don't owe him shit," Jinx told him.

"Let's just run and hunt for the ghost army, all right?" Cain said in response.

"You start. I'll join you in a minute," he said, ignoring Brother Wolf's aching need to shift and run immediately. He watched the twins strip and shift and bound away, and he ached inside, managed to call, "Don't approach them— recon only."

"Hey." Vice clapped a hand on his shoulder, and Jinx whipped around, baring his canines.

"Who the fuck are you posturing for?" Vice shook his head. "The twins are going through a lot of shit. Don't lock them out, hear?"

Jinx's aggression waned. "I hear," he echoed. "Where's Kate?"

"Safe with Jez, coming up with some kind of spell. I guess he knows about that shit. He told me you needed help."

Fucker. "I don't. What do you think of Kill?"

"He's kind of a dick." Vice shrugged. "I think I like him."

"His powers are intense." Jinx stared at Vice. "If we didn't trust Stray—"

"But we do," Vice emphasized. "He's brought Killian here to fight all this shit."

Jinx flicked his eyes toward Vice's. "Or to make the prophecy come true."

"I know you've always been a suspicious son of a bitch—"

"But this time, I'm wrong?" Jinx prompted.

"What's Kate talking about?" Vice asked instead. "Do

you feel evil? You can't stay possessed for long, so what the hell?"

"I'm not possessed."

"Then what? You were in the cemetery all alone. I know you're never supposed to do that, even if you are a big, bad wolf."

"Just stay focused on keeping Rifter and Harm safe and alive."

"I bet you never thought you'd say that about Harm."

"Vice—"

"I know, you're handling things. But you're supposed to work Kate through this witch thing."

"No more spells for me," Jinx said, and Vice cocked a brow. "That's all I'm saying."

"Jinx—"

"I'm here to help, any way I can. But it's better if I don't get too close. Kate's powers know what to do—she needs to be receptive to them."

"And if she can't convince or force Seb to give up his powers?"

Jinx stared up at the moon. "She doesn't have a choice."

"Well, actually, she does. That's not her plan anymore. Instead, your twin wants you to work with her to defeat the ghost army. Says there's no way she can beat Seb, so to forget about him and work with you."

"First of all, that's bullshit. She can't work with the dead unless she goes dark herself. Rogue was born to talk to spirits—he's the natural choice and that's the whole goddamned reason we were looking for the witch in the first place. And how's it supposed to work again, when she can't be in the same room with me without screaming?" Jinx demanded.

"Don't shoot the messenger, hear?" Vice took a long drag on the special hand-rolled cigarette, the blue smoke forming an incongruous halo around his head. As if he knew, Vice grinned sardonically. "I'll be there to help. Stray too."

"I'll call you." No confirmation. He couldn't risk opening Vice up to purgatory. The Dires needed him and the others primed and ready to fight.

And just like Jinx wanted him to, Vice walked away. Jinx felt the hurt rolling off the wolf in waves and he wished he could do something to settle him down. But letting Vice go was for the best—for Vice, anyway, and that was all that mattered to Jinx at the moment.

When the twin Weres and Vice left her behind with the tall man named Jez, Kate quickly learned he wasn't a man at all, not with those canines. They were sharper than a wolf's, his eyes were different and he didn't have the same scent.

"Vampire," he said shortly, extending a hand to her.

"Witch. Correction—fucked-up witch." She shook his hand and looked toward the crowd.

"You can cry about it or get on with creating the spell. You've got to convince everyone in this town that this was a fear-based reaction to an earthquake, not just the ones outside in this particular crowd."

"I don't have the book." Stray had convinced her it was better to leave it in the Dire mansion, and she'd agreed.

"You don't need the damned book, witch. It's inside of you."

She closed her eyes and heard Stray's voice. *I'm alive, Kate. Do your job.*

She turned to the crowd and watched Killian and Stray continue to work their magic. Stray had closed his mind to her, and while she deserved it, that didn't make it hurt any less.

And then she began to chant words she didn't know, but they flowed out of her as easily as her native tongue. She began to sway, felt the vampire there to steady her and she continued until her mind told her it was done.

She opened her eyes and blinked. Dusk had come and gone and she had no idea how long she'd been casting the spell. It appeared to be working, but she refused to give voice to that hope and tempt the fates.

"What do I do now?" she asked of Jez.

"First you'll go back with the Dires and Stray. Later you'll go to the cemetery with Jinx," Jez told her.

"I can't be around him."

"You can. You will." Jez checked his phone and held it out to her. "It's slowing down."

She watched a news video that showed reports were coming in from all over New York that the mobs were caused in reaction to strange earthquakes. There were reports of people hurt, but no more mention of fights or rioting.

She turned back to Kill and Stray. "Their powers are that far-reaching?"

Jez wasn't smiling when he said, "Your power, not theirs. Lucky you're on their side."

Chapter 39

When the dust settled and the humans appeared to be back under control, Liam ordered the Weres to scatter, lest they be called by the police or the local media to describe their experiences during the faux earthquakes.

Cain watched over his king with Cyd by his side as they regrouped in the woods for a few minutes.

"We've got to blend better. Become nearly invisible," Liam lectured the group before he let them go. "We've got to go back to the old ways, because the outlaw ways will get us all killed."

No one argued. Liam didn't have all of them—not yet—but Cain knew it was only a matter of time before his king got control again.

But now . . .

Liam furrowed his brow. "I smell it too," Cyd agreed as Cain also caught the scent of death.

"Let's find it before the police or the trappers," the young king said. The three Weres moved through the woods as one, unshifting and scenting until they came to the steep slope of the ravine that led to the river.

This time of year, it was nearly still, partly frozen. Icy limbs cracked around them, snow crushed under their heavy boots as they threaded down the slippery hill, the wolves in them helping them hold their footing easily enough.

The bodies were halfheartedly hidden, like it had been done quickly or the trappers had wanted these Weres to be found.

They were still in human form. Young—sixteen if they were a day. Cyd cursed and kicked the nearest tree. Liam moved forward with Cain as he bent to check the bodies.

"They haven't been dead long. And two of them hadn't even shifted," Cain said. As the omega, he felt the emotions strongly. Maybe that was why Cain spent as much time with Vice as he could, because Vice and emotional swings went hand in hand.

"These are the Weres from Kansas. Their pack leader called me yesterday, said they insisted on coming to meet me. They wanted to fight for my cause—heard I was looking for new blood. They had their alpha's blessing and I promised I'd teach them," Liam explained, his voice guarded. "This can't keep happening."

"You do need new blood, Li. They were answering the call. They knew the dangers." Cain picked up a body and walked him to the truck. Liam did the same. Once all three bodies were loaded into the back, Cyd called Rifter to report what happened.

"He wants us to stay put," Cyd confirmed. "He's not one hundred percent convinced it's trappers."

"Shit," Liam muttered. And when Rifter pulled up, alone, about fifteen minutes later, he called, "Liam, you're with me."

"Now I get an escort?" Liam muttered.

"Damn straight," Rifter said from inside the truck.

"I'm not going into hiding," he argued with the Dire.

"You're going to do what's best for the pack," Rifter told him. Cain supposed that having a Dire come as an escort meant things were going from bad to worse. And then Rifter focused his attention on Cyd and Cain. "You two, track, but that's all. I want to know if it's wolf, witch or demon."

After Rifter and Liam pulled away, the twins went to where they'd found the bodies.

"There's no scent here but theirs," he said. Cyd had a nose like no one's business—if he couldn't scent anything, that meant there was nothing to scent. "We'd be able to scent trappers."

"There were no marks on them. Could be demons," Cain pointed out. "We could call Jinx."

"Let's find them first and then call him. Let's do this unshifted—it's definitely a safer move."

Cain walked deeper into the woods, his wolf wanting out. It was still hard for him to push down the shift, no matter how much control he had these days. The scars that stretched the length of his back pulled now, as they did when he shifted, so that it would always be extra painful.

Those marks had been placed there purposely by his old pack. Cyd bore the same scars. The twins had taken beatings for being moon crazed, which had only made the affliction worse. If it hadn't been for Jinx's intervention, they would've been put down at sixteen.

Most thought that omegas were the weak ones, and in a traditional wolf pack, that was certainly true. But for the Weres, an omega was the best-kept secret of any pack.

His omega was far from weak—in a fight with Cyd, the men would come out equal, despite Cyd's emerging alpha status.

Cain's claim to fame as an omega was similar to what Killian's influence was to humans—and Harm's too, when he sang. In his presence, calm spread over whoever he was with, which certainly helped where Cyd's moon craze was concerned. It just hadn't helped until his own was under control, although his was never as bad as his twin's was.

He was as close with Cyd as Jinx was with Rogue. He could only imagine what Jinx was going through.

"This way." Cyd tracked just as well in human form, and Cain trusted his lead. It certainly helped their relationship that he was content to take the backseat because of Cyd's alpha status,.

But halfway through the woods, they picked up trapper scent, right before they spotted a human body. Angus. And he'd been badly mauled.

"A wolf did this." Cyd confirmed what Cain knew as he got closer, threading his way down the ravine while Cyd stood watch. The scent was strong even though the man was covered with dirt and leaves.

He felt a weak pulse on the man's neck. "He's alive," Cain whispered, more to himself than Cyd.

"He doesn't look like he will be for much longer. And he knows too much," Cyd pointed out.

Angus was a beautiful man, ravaged by the recent stress and the mauling. Cain laid his hand on him and let the heat run through him in order to heal the broken man enough for Angus to wake up and tell him what the hell was going on.

His eyes opened and Cain demanded, "Who did this to you?"

"Don't remember."

He was lying—why was an entirely different story.

"Need to hide. Can't go back to . . . my hotel," Angus managed.

"How's this my problem?"

"I . . . met with Shimmin," Angus said. "Working . . . with him. Pretending to . . ."

Cain didn't bother to tell him he was delirious—and an idiot. The man hung with Shimmin—and whether or not Angus was really pretending or actually was on Shimmin's payroll, Angus knew what Cain was.

Proving it would be a different story and Angus wouldn't get that chance. He put his hands out and moved them toward Angus's throat, ignoring the man's struggle.

Chapter 40

"What were you thinking?" Stray demanded of her, and Kate fought to keep her composure.

She didn't answer him immediately. Instead, she checked on Killian, who looked pale from the exertion. His abilities obviously took a toll on him, and because of her, he'd need longer to recharge. Or at least that's what Stray told Kate on the ride back as his brother slept in the very back of the truck and Vice pretended he wasn't in the middle of a very big fight.

"If Kill hadn't been there," Stray started.

"But he was."

"You distracted him—and me. Dammit, Kate—"

"Rogue told me—"

"He's wrong, Kate. Dammit, I don't know what he was thinking, but there's no way you can do much against this ghost army. It makes no sense at all."

"You don't believe in me. Have you been blowing smoke up my ass just to make me work harder? You keep telling me how strong and powerful I am."

"I guess you proved me wrong," he yelled and then he softened. "You've been at this only a little while. Seb's had centuries."

"I'm not strong enough to help you. Seb knows all of Lila's weaknesses, obviously. And I'm a big one."

"Kate, come on."

She turned away from him. She was ashamed and angry—at herself and him.

Thankfully, they pulled into the garage. Vice got out and helped Killian to do the same, leaving her and Stray alone in their misery.

She slammed out of the truck as well, but Stray was right behind her. He took her by the elbow. Even though her body yearned for his touch, she forced herself to pull away, to fight back against the one person who'd saved her life several times over the past few days. "You resent being tied to me."

"We got past that."

"You don't have to. I almost got you killed, and you'll never trust me again."

"That's not what this is about at all," he told her. "You call me for protection. You call me when you need me. Only then. What about when I need you?"

"You don't," she burst out. "You need me for helping your brother, but you don't need a damn thing from me for you."

He blinked, a predator's gaze as he considered her words.

"Maybe you're the one who doesn't give a shit about me," she finished, hating to hear the raw emotion in her voice, hating that she cared so much.

When he didn't say anything further, she knew she needed to leave before he saw her cry. There was a lot she could handle, but her tears . . . she would not give him those. She'd given too much already. "Please, I just want to be alone now. I don't need you nosing at me every five seconds."

"Maybe you picked the wrong familiar," he said, his voice oddly quiet.

"I didn't pick you—"

She stopped, but not quickly enough.

"I get it, Kate. You don't have to spell it out."

"Stray—"

She quickly realized his name had never seemed so apropos as now.

He simply stared at her. "Stop. Quit while you're ahead."

It was a turning point—one that turned Stray's stomach as well. All the closeness they'd had over the past days seemed to crumble.

He thought about how close he'd come to being in the trappers' clutches—both of them—and how Killian had been the only thing preventing that.

He'd hated his brother all these years and all the man had done was save his life. And he'd done it again.

"I don't need you nosing at me every five seconds."

"Maybe you picked the wrong familiar."

"I didn't pick you—"

The look on her face told him she knew she'd gone too far. What he couldn't decipher was if she cared. But he did. You didn't back down from a blood oath promise and the worst part was, he still didn't want to.

You're a beast . . . and that's just how she sees you.

He'd never minded being a wolf—but the fact that he could possibly bring so much trouble to the packs nearly killed him.

He walked out without another word.

His brothers were shocked at the amount of power he and Killian wielded together. Maybe they weren't scared of him but they had to be afraid of what kind of destruction he could cause.

He wondered if they were thinking about caging him, putting him in silver chains the way they had Harm at first.

And then he decided that if they were, he didn't want to know.

He was a fucking witch's pet. Reduced to an animal.

You're nothing but a beast.

In Kate's eyes, that's all he would ever be, and even though there was no escape, his Brother Wolf ran until Stray couldn't see or hear himself thinking anymore, until he was all wolf.

It rarely happened that the two weren't working together in tandem. During these times, Brother Wolf had to be especially vigilant to keep Stray safe.

Brother Wolf had taken over many times for Stray, especially on his first several shifts when he was still dying from the polar bear attack. He'd been too weak to deal with anything. As Kill watched over him, Brother Wolf shifted over and over until Stray came back out.

Stray didn't plan on coming back out ever. And Brother Wolf would watch out for him until the end of time.

Chapter 41

Cain couldn't take the fed to the mansion, but with Cyd's help, he got Angus to the apartment they rented near town for cover, in the building next to where Jinx was staying.

Cyd left them there to report back to the Dires, and Cain called Jinx, who arrived at his doorstep in record time, with the vampire in tow.

"What the hell is going on here? You don't owe him shit—we discussed this," Jinx told him.

Jez was circling the unconscious man. "Human?"

"Not to be touched," Cain said.

Jez frowned and retracted his fangs. "You take all the fun away."

"I know." Cain shrugged.

"Hear you wolves are in trouble. Too much pack shit. Stay solitary; you're better off."

"A little late for it, but I'll pass that advice on to Rifter," Jinx told him.

Jez smiled. "I like Rifter, but Vice . . ."

"Yeah, yeah, he brings the party. I know," Jinx muttered before turning his attention back to Cain. "I don't know if we can let the fed live."

"I know that."

Jinx paused for a long moment and Cain swore his fucking heart stopped beating for a split second. "See what he knows. If he's useful, he can live."

He left, taking Jez and Cyd with him.

"Stupid, stupid human," Cain muttered, his touch much gentler than his words. "What were you thinking?"

Angus couldn't form the words, was pretty sure he was dying.

Just as before, the young wolf was touching him, hands over his throat and chest. Angus felt the heat radiate through his body, overriding the pain and somehow intensifying it at the same time. He groaned, despite his best efforts to be stoic, but hell, he'd been literally thrown to the wolves.

"Why are you doing this?" he asked, and it took nearly all his strength.

"I made a promise to help the innocent."

"I'm not."

"I know. You're lying to me about who did this. Why?"

"Have to. Your safety."

Cain looked like he was going to say something angry—his mouth twisted and Angus braced himself, but all the wolf said was "Stay still."

"Trying." And he was, until Cain put his hands on Angus's chest and it burned worse than any beating could've. The wolf was killing him, it seemed. How would Angus know the difference at this point?

"Stop moaning and it'll be done faster. Fucking humans," the wolf muttered, but Angus couldn't say anything back. At first the pain seemed to eat at his mind until he couldn't form a coherent thought, never mind speech. And then, when the pain receded slightly, he was too fascinated by the fact that Cain was glowing again, the way he'd been the night Angus had rescued him. Holy hell, he guessed this was calling in the favor chip big-time.

He thought momentarily about what Shimmin mentioned earlier, about omegas and who could see their glow and he decided it must be bullshit.

Cain put a hand on his neck and the fresh, ripping pain began anew.

He managed to wind a hand around Cain's wrist. "First . . . in case . . ."

"You're not going to die."

Sure felt like it. By this point, he was either in pain or floating away into some white light. Neither option was great news. "Shimmin . . . said . . . wolves . . . so busy . . . with magic that they . . . won't do . . . what's . . . obvious."

Jesus H. Christ on a stick, that nearly killed him. He wanted to double over, but he couldn't move.

Shimmin would kill him for leaking this, once he found out Angus hadn't been killed by the wolf. Either way, Angus figured he was a dead man.

"What's obvious, Angus?" Cain demanded.

"Fight. Supposed . . . to . . . fight them. Battle. Like . . . old . . . times." After he finished, he closed his eyes and knew he'd pass out again. But he'd given Cain more than enough.

He heard Cain make the call with the intel, leaving someone a detailed message. And then he hung up and continued healing Angus's broken body as Angus finally let himself slip into unconsciousness.

The wolf and the vamp roamed the night. Jinx's Brother Wolf stopped protesting when he realized that the bloodsucking deadhead wasn't going to be eating innocent humans.

In fact, Jinx wasn't sure how or when he fed, but as long as he didn't see it, he was cool with it.

Even though Brother Wolf was dying to come out, Jinx had to keep him tamped down, promising that he'd shift for a much-needed run later. Now he strode into the cemetery,

Jez behind him in a long black leather coat and a buzz cut reminiscent of a military one, although a series of tattoos showed through, intricate patterns that reminded Jinx of the ones that had shown up on Rogue's face recently.

He really had more to learn about this deadhead. This could all be a trap. But Brother Wolf was the best judge of a supernatural's character and, so far, no hells bells were ringing.

Except for you.

"You ever go out during the day?" he asked Jez.

The vamp shook his head. "Not unless there's an emergency. But the sun's not going to hurt me. Neither will cutting off my head, so don't get any ideas, wolf."

"So nothing can kill you?"

Jez shook his head. "Sucks to be us, doesn't it?"

Yes, it certainly does, Jinx mused as he approached the newly smashed mausoleum, care of Vice. The spell had been broken by screwing with its origins, but Seb hadn't let it go.

The ghost army hadn't been defeated, just momentarily delayed, but it bought them the time they needed.

"Are you just saying it sucks, or do you really feel, vamp?"

Jez smiled. "When we came back, we were given souls. Stupid little buggers, if you ask me."

"*That's* gotta suck."

"You have no idea. But at least I've also now got an appetite and needs."

Jinx looked out the window and wondered how the hell this was all supposed to work. "We've got to kill this Dire ghost army, and the witch won't let me near her."

"We've all got some repenting to do," Jez told him. "Suck it up and move on. What's happening with the Dire ghost army is nothing."

"That's why you were brought back?"

"You can't do it alone."

Jinx snorted. "The Elders think we should."

"Hey, I've got my own problems with higher beings. Let's just get this started."

Jinx didn't see any ghosts except for the few odd ones that hovered around the gates of the cemetery. The Dire ghost army had already blown through here for a practice round, and the news of desecrated corpses was just one more thing New York was buzzing about.

"It's too damned quiet," the vamp said.

"Anyone here?" Jinx called, his voice echoing eerily. Usually, there were stray ghosts nattering in his ear at any opportunity, and this was a prime one.

He heard marching—an overpowering sound that echoed through his brain, made him cover his ears in the vain hope of blocking it out.

It only made the sound louder. It was like every single literal thing from purgatory had decided to march.

He managed to stand, wheeled around, expecting to see his ancestors marching toward him, but there was only ... nothing.

And that was worse than anything.

"Jinx, move." Jez's voice boomed over the other sounds. Brother Wolf forced Jinx to drop and roll just in time for the vamp to slice through a demon with a long silver blade that glowed with an eerie light, similar to the ring around Jez's eyes.

The demon screeched, stared at Jez like he was a devil the thing hadn't seen before, but one in particular it feared. It burst into flames and then disintegrated into a pile of ash.

The vamp stared at Jinx, who asked, "You gonna share your heritage now? I'm thinking you're part demon."

"No, but I am from hell." Jez stared at him. "I can take down the possessed ones, and there are a lot of them."

"You were really sent here to wait and watch for thirty years for purgatory to open?"

"For however long it took. I'm a patient thing. I knew it

would happen. No matter how much I tried to find a way around it, you had to do what was meant to be."

Jinx studied the vampire and wondered if trusting him was the stupidest thing he could've done. "Tell me more about yourself."

"I'm from an entirely different race of vampires. An ancient one that none of these young, vulnerable fangers remember," Jez told him. "You already know I can't die. I can influence humans and other supernatural beings except Dires. I can influence you, but I can't force you to take my advice. And I can kill. Well. But I can't get rid of your Dire ghost army problem. I will, however, fight with you and then force you to deal with the purgatory issue. And yes, I'll keep your secret until you decide your kind should know about it. Is that enough sharing? I typically like to play this a little closer to the vest, but considering we slept together—"

"Next to each other," Jinx told him. "Are you king?"

"There are twelve of my kind left, scattered about."

"You didn't answer my question."

"I know."

Jinx sighed. "I think you need to come back to the house and talk to Rifter."

"I can do that, if he'll listen."

"Am I possessed?"

"No, but you're purgatory's conduit. The spirits that emerged are going to keep track of you, make sure you don't try to close their passageway. The ghost army was just there temporarily—some of those other spirits had been there for years, and they can't just rush out. Many of them have to claw their way to the opening, which is why we need to close it before everything manages to escape. Because that would be . . . horrific."

Meaning, if Jinx thought the ghost army was angry, he hadn't seen anything yet. And with that thought, he threw up, heaved his goddamned guts out. When he stood, Jez handed him a bottle of water.

Where he'd gotten it, Jinx hadn't a clue.

"Looks like I'm going to severely disappoint them," he managed. "So what, you're like my big, bad vampire guardian angel?"

"Something like that, wolf. Hell knows you needed one."

"I need my twin back."

"Can't help you there. But once the Dire army's defeated, there's a whole new presence to deal with."

"What if I hadn't come to the apartment and talked to you?"

"You have an interesting way of talking, wolf. But I would've worked on my own," Jez said. "I'm helping you, but we didn't need to be a team. The walls are coming down. We've got to build them back up again, and the Dires are the closest thing to us there is."

"I'll call Rifter on the way over."

An unlikely alliance would be forged between vamp and wolf. There was already one between wolf and witch, but that had gone so badly before.

Chapter 42

So much had happened over the past weeks—the past twenty-four hours—that Gwen's Sister Wolf was urging her to shift, to stop thinking and start letting her beast side take over to handle things.

It seemed like an awesome idea, but first she needed to communicate with Rifter, and that had to be through talking.

"I'm worried about Stray," Gwen told him, the words tumbling out as he emerged from the shower, before he could take her to bed again. It didn't stop him from coming over to her, nuzzling her neck before answering. "You're worried because of Killian?"

"Killian, the witch . . . there's a lot of pressure on him."

"On all of us."

"Yes, but you're all old," she teased. Rifter grabbed her and tickled her for a few seconds until she sputtered, "Uncle—I'll remember to mind my elders."

"Yes, you'd better." Rifter nipped her neck gently. "I'll keep an eye on him, Gwen. And you—promise me."

"You're going to make me do this on a daily basis, right? I won't go anywhere without you or one of your brothers.

I'd never put myself into a position where I could be used as a weapon against you."

"I know you wouldn't. But in the heat of battle, if something goes wrong, your Sister Wolf's first instinct will be to save me. You have to fight that. Know that I'll always come back to you. You're safest in here, you and Sister Wolf. And I hate having to cage you in."

"I have everything I need—I have family," she said quietly. "This seems a small price to pay."

Finding out that her blood had the capacity to kill the Dires—that it was the one, the only thing that could end their centuries of immortality—was a sobering discovery for all of them. Gwen couldn't imagine them being taken from her, since upon her mating, the Elders had granted her immortality as well.

She would do everything in her power to keep her new mate and his family safe. Being watched over when she was allowed out seemed a small price to pay for getting rid of the seizures that had been killing her.

Maybe in a century, she'd feel differently.

"Anything more happening with the clinic?"

"I've been ordering more supplies, stocking up," she said. She couldn't help thinking about Rogue telling her she was both healer and destroyer.

Healer. If she could actually heal, if that was her ability, the clinic could handle the load it might see when the Dire ghost army marched through town.

But if Kate could stop it . . . Well, it seemed like a long shot no matter how Gwen looked at it.

"Hey, we'll be okay," Rifter told her. "We'll find a way—we always do."

"Are you ever going to let Harm fight with you again? Or at least, run with the pack?"

"I think he'll work the clinic with you for the time being. With the fed still around looking for him, it's too dangerous for him to show his face and risk our exposure." He paused. "Will you be okay working with him?"

"We need to repair the relationship between all of us," Gwen said. "That starts with me."

"Good. Harm's open to it."

She knew Rifter would still prefer to barbecue Harm over an open pit, but maybe that would ease somehow. Before she could say anything else, Rifter's phone beeped and he pulled away reluctantly. He read the text message with a serious look on his face, and then he showed it to her.

It was from Jinx—and he had information. "Let's go hear him out, Rift."

"Jinx and a vampire—this better be good."

Jinx and Jez both rode their own Harleys, the vamp's quiet next to Jinx's noisy ride. The two, Jinx was sure, were quite a sight tearing through the streets and up the private road to the Dire house.

Brother Wolf howled, grateful to be home. Jinx didn't have the heart to remind the wolf that wouldn't happen yet. Instead, he led Jez toward the gazebo where the wolves, Dire and Were, waited for them.

They parked, and Jinx led the way to his family, feeling strangely out of place. Rifter was the only one who waited outside the sunroom for them, but Jinx could see inside to the others. Kate and Stray were there, on opposite sides of the crowd. They weren't all right yet, which was a shame, because they needed that damned bond to get through this.

"Keep your cool," Jez told him. Jinx wanted to snap at him, but he didn't. Instead, he continued along with a deep breath and jumped right in.

"We've got some intel from Cain on Leo's plans," he reported.

Rifter didn't say anything, moved tensely to one side and allowed them to walk past him.

"I can see your goddamned house, wolf," Jez told Rifter by way of greeting.

"I can beat the shit out of you, vamp," Rifter replied haughtily. Then the two shook hands. Two centuries-old supernatural creatures. Jinx didn't know if Jez was a king or not, but he sure as hell acted like it. Jez immediately sat in an empty spot on the couch next to Kate while the others stared at him. "Tell them what you told me, Jinx."

Jinx did and Vice clarified. "Cain's still with the fed, Angus, making sure he's safe from Shimmin."

"Because he's so trustworthy?" Stray muttered.

"Anyway, I think we've finally got intel we can use, and the fed nearly lost his life over it. I don't know if he'd go that far for the trappers," Jinx said.

"Could be a trap," Stray pointed out.

"Angus saved Cain—why go to all that trouble?" Jinx asked. Stray shrugged. "Look, he said that Shimmin basically has us where he wants us—chasing our tails, looking for a way to defeat the Dire army that involves Rogue and witches and magic."

"What the hell else are we supposed to defeat them with?" Vice asked.

"Us," Jinx told them. For a long, astonished second, no one spoke.

When Rifter did, it was with the calm purpose of a leader. "Then we fight, using the old ways."

Vice nodded in agreement. "It makes so much goddamned sense. That's what Jameson has always wanted—a fight from Rifter."

"And Harm," Stray added. "You're going to have to let him out to fight."

"It's not a matter of me letting him any longer. Now it's up to him," Rifter said. He stared at Harm, who held out his hands, wrists ringed in silver.

"Take this shit off. I'm going to kill that motherfucker," Harm said with such command in his voice, it left no doubt that he could've led the Dires as the Elders wanted centuries ago. "And that is not a challenge to Rifter—he's the rightful king now."

"What about Seb?" Stray asked.

"He's turned," Jinx said. "The demons are making him push things too far. Seb had to know it would all start backfiring, that soon no one would control the demon-possessed humans but the demons themselves."

"What if we can't save enough of them?" Stray asked. "Maybe we should have some kind of contingency plan."

"What, take all the Weres we can and hide on some deserted island until this is all over?' Vice asked.

"Not a bad plan," Kill said. "Maybe this is like survival of the fittest."

"Or maybe the Elders will have our heads," Jinx said darkly.

"Not necessarily a bad thing," Vice pointed out.

Rifter began to laugh, long and loud, and the others joined in, even Jez. Jinx knew it would be the last time they shared this for some time. He pretended that everything was fine for the moment, because he desperately wanted it to be.

Chapter 43

Gwen knew what Rifter would want to do directly following the meeting. The mood was somber, although she finally felt as if everything was settled. The Dires had a true direction, a plan that seemed right, if not completely dangerous.

Jinx and Jez left. Gwen wished Rifter had invited both of them to stay, but knew he wouldn't. Cain was still with Angus, and Cyd went with Liam to do some more scouting.

Harm went back upstairs. He'd looked more like a warrior than a rock star during that meeting, and she wondered if her father was finally accepting himself as wolf. If she had more courage, she might talk to him about it. But her husband—her love—was her first priority.

Rifter came into Rogue's room and found her there. Vice was behind him. She realized it had been one of the first meetings they'd had that didn't center literally around Rogue.

She reached out and stroked his hair.

"Vice, you stay here with us," Rifter told the wild wolf. "Gwen and I are going to see Rogue."

Gwen knew Vice noted the determination in Rifter's

eyes. There was no talking him out of this. "We have to confirm what Jinx told us."

"Because you don't trust him?"

"Because Rogue might be giving Kate misinformation," Rifter growled.

"Jinx thinks it's the best way to give Kate help," Gwen explained. "We can't put this all on her."

"What do you want me to say—you know it's the most dangerous thing you can do now," Vice told her.

"I'm more afraid of losing my family than anything," Gwen said softly. She took Vice's hand in hers. "We'll be careful."

She tried to reassure Vice, who walked away without being very reassured at all. Still, she had no doubt he'd watch over them.

She did, however, have other doubts. "We haven't been able to do this since Rogue helped to save me," she reminded Rifter, although he hadn't needed it.

"We haven't been able to because he hasn't let us," Rifter growled. "He goddamned will now, because I'm his king—he will remember that."

Gwen didn't doubt Rifter's words at that moment—the alpha was large and in charge, his eyes lupine, the growls coming so fast she was sure she'd be holding Brother Wolf's paw at any moment. And as usual, Sister Wolf wanted in.

Down, girl, she told her wolf, who whined impatiently.

In the privacy of Rogue's room, she and Rifter joined hands and she grabbed Rogue's cool one. They were sitting on the floor next to the bed and Rifter pulled her into a deep slumber easily.

His powers were getting stronger. Hers seemed stagnant, beyond the fact that, because of their bond, she was linked to his dreamwalking into Rogue's mind. And from what they said, it was no trip to Disney.

She moved through the familiar bowels of what looked like hell to her, stayed away from the walls dripping with blood and entered the room where Rogue lay, the mare on his chest, marking him and cackling. The familiar torture of random people went on all around him, the way it had the last time.

"Too dangerous for you to be here. I told you not to come back."

"Jinx moved out," Rifter said instead of dealing with Rogue's statement.

Rogue glanced at him. "Your alpha's really showing, isn't it?"

"Kate says Jinx is evil," Gwen blurted out. "I can't believe that's true, but . . ."

"If that's what the witch sees . . ." Rogue trailed off and shut his eyes. The markings on the side of his face were darker now. He muttered something under his breath. "Tell the witch to leave the mare. I sing to her and she seems to like it."

Rogue had gone too long without a shift. The mare had started scratching him along his neck and chest, and the marks were showing up on Rogue's motionless body.

"What about the ghost army?" Rifter asked. "Is what we think true—we should fight them?"

"You can defeat most of it, but some will escape, no matter what. And the demons are turning bad. Well, turning against their makers—Seb and by extension, the politicians and the Weres who are possessed. Kate needs to do what she can against the army—it will be enough for now."

At Rogue's words, Rifter jerked away from Gwen. "There's got to be something more we can do."

"For me? Not likely. Not soon, anyway. Let Kate focus on the ghost army now," Rogue insisted.

"We can't leave you here like this."

"You have no choice. Just fucking go, and don't come back." Rogue closed his eyes and he started to sing, low and sweet. The mare began to giggle in a psychopathic way and clap her hands.

Rifter tugged Gwen back from the abyss and for a long while, they held on to each other in Rogue's room, feeling like they'd already completely lost him.

Physical strength, when combined with emotional fortitude, was unbeatable. Over the past twenty-four hours, Kate trained both as if her life depended on it. She still wasn't quite sure what would happen to her if she failed.

Vice helped her in the gym room she'd run to that first night—her cheeks burned with those memories every time she walked in there, and if the wolf noticed, he never said.

Jinx went over spells with Stray and Gwen and they helped her. Gwen was *new,* she'd called it. A little hard to control, Stray said. Kate watched with more-than-mild jealousy the ease with which Gwen and Rifter climbed all over each other.

Stray was still standoffish, but she swore he was thinking about her an awful lot.

As his weapon. No matter how she tried to pretend there was more, she couldn't.

He comes when you call him . . . because of magic.

She was pretty sure he hated her for it. She tried not to call on him without warning him, but sometimes it just happened and he was there at her side. Glowering.

He was glowering now, even though she couldn't see him, since he rode in front, Vice in the back with her. Kate wondered if insisting on going to the cemetery had been the best of ideas.

Trust yourself.

That was her voice, or maybe it was Lila's, but either way, she needed to listen. And as they walked in through the opened iron gates, she spotted Jinx and Jez together by the ruins of what was once a mausoleum.

"I've got to talk to him," she said, was surprised when neither wolf protested. She walked toward them and Jez nodded and took leave, while Jinx remained rooted in place, watching her warily.

"You're . . ."

"Evil, I know," Jinx said tightly.

"No, that's not it."

"Well, at least you're not collapsing this time," Jinx said wryly.

"This isn't right—not at all," she murmured. "I want to help . . . but I can't."

Jinx nodded. "I agree."

"It's not . . . because of you."

"Why can you suddenly stand being in my presence?"

"I spoke to Rogue," she said. His eyes widened. "I'll keep your secret for now."

He turned away, stared up at the sky.

"I know it's not your fault—you were tricked," she continued.

He turned. "Guess you were, too, since Rogue told you to help me with the Dire ghost army."

She frowned at the truth of that statement. "Maybe I misinterpreted something with him. I definitely did with you. You're not evil—you're a pawn. I know one when I see one."

"I should be offended by that, but I don't think you mean it that way."

"I don't, Jinx. I really don't." She held out her hand for him to shake. "We can work together, okay?"

He grasped it firmly and she noted the pain in his eyes, the burden from the secret he carried.

It was then that the others joined around them, because Jinx had ripped his gaze from her and gone still, his hand still on hers. She heard Stray's growl of possessiveness and tugged her hand away, not wanting to be the cause of any further strife.

Stray's wolf relaxed momentarily. She was surprised he hadn't shifted forms yet. It seemed to be the only way he could handle being around her at this point. But that thought soon faded as something whooshed by her head.

"I don't normally see ghosts. Can witches see them?"

"No," Stray told her.

"Maybe being with me and Jinx is like the perfect storm," Vice said. "Besides, do you really think we're going to question when weird, unexplained things happen among us? I don't give a shit how or why it happens, just that it does. You want to figure out how, good luck. But the unexplained is usually that way for a reason, and sometimes it makes things a hell of a lot more fun to just roll with it."

Kate didn't have time to ponder before the apparitions floated around her. She fought the urge to swat them away, because it made her uncomfortable as anything.

Jinx looked so relaxed, used to it, but his eyes were lupine, belying what she saw on the outside. "It's not the ghost army."

"Rogue told me I could help with them—with you. But I think he was lying."

Jinx's eyes went to hers. "What makes you think that?"

"The words he spoke in my head didn't match the movement of his lips. It was like he was layering thoughts to keep me off balance."

"Or to keep Seb from knowing what he was saying. The mare reports directly back to the Adept," Jinx said. "You've got to go back over what he told you and figure out what to do. But you and I both know, we can't stop the ghost army with your powers, no matter how strong. Your job lies in dealing with Seb. No question."

Chapter 44

After Kate got back from the cemetery, she sat in the middle of the bed in the guest room and stared at the grimoire. Put her hands on it and knew that what Jez told her was right. It was inside her—she had the answers.

And Stray still wouldn't deal with her.

A knock on the door made her look up. Her heart leapt, even though she knew it wasn't Stray. "Come in."

Gwen stuck her head in. "Sure you're up to this?"

Kate nodded and Gwen came in. Kate could see the wolf working in tandem with the woman. Still half human but yet somehow immortal, Gwen was the closest thing to her ally in this house now that Stray had locked her out.

Gwen sat on the bed next to her, tucking her bare feet under her. "You were at the meeting. You know what needs to be done."

"I do. And I'm planning. I'll be ready."

"The full moon's so close—days away," Gwen said. "The time for action is now."

"Suppose it doesn't work?" she asked. Gwen's face drew tight because she understood—Kate was asking if the Dires would kill her.

"It was the general plan, either way," she admitted.

"Witches and wolves, well, let's just say there's very little trust left there. And if you're as powerful as everyone says . . ."

"You've painted a lovely picture," Kate said. "So why has the plan changed?"

Gwen looked surprised that Kate didn't know the answer to that. "Stray's in love with you. And If I'm not mistaken, you're in love with him, too."

"It's the spell."

Gwen sat back on her heels. "A month ago, if you'd asked me about magic, I would've laughed at you. Now I believe anything's possible, but I don't think magic can force a heart to love what it doesn't."

Kate shook her head, wanted to believe her, but she couldn't. After everything that had happened the other day, her vulnerability, the fact that she could take Stray down with her. "I thought I'd be safe now that I have the grimoire."

"You are. You let Seb in and you locked him back out. You're in control. You just didn't fully understand the implications of the familiar bond."

"I had to distract Seb to save Stray."

Or Seb had gotten to her because Stray wasn't with her.

"We're each other's weaknesses now—don't you understand?"

Gwen lowered her eyes for a long moment and then looked Kate dead in the eyes. "Yes, I know something about that. My blood has the power to kill the immortal Dires. I'm the only thing on this earth and in the heavens with that power—and Rifter loves me anyway. Sometimes you have to shove back your fear and go for what you want. So Stray won't come to you. You go to him."

You go to him.

Stray had been acting like the perfect soldier—stalwart— one who'd accepted his charge and did his duty coldly. Too coldly, especially because she knew just how warm he ran.

Now he stood in the doorway of the guest bedroom, the wolf staring at her. She wanted to run her fingers through Brother's fur, but she didn't know if she'd be accepted. She settled for talking instead. Because she realized that she'd never apologized, and she was ready to let down her pride first for both their sakes.

"You've got to shift back and talk to me, Stray. I need you and not just as my familiar. We're bonded and in more ways than this. You know that or maybe it's scaring you. It's scaring me, too."

Kate tried to hold back tears, but her voice caught anyway. She turned her back to him, pressed a hand against her mouth to stop herself from saying anything more.

She heard something behind her and she turned toward Stray, expecting to see his wolf.

Instead she saw a very naked Stray. And while he didn't look exactly happy, he had shifted back, and all because she'd asked.

That had to mean something, right? Or maybe . . .

"I didn't switch because you made me. I do still have the power of free will," Stray said.

Sometimes it was convenient that he could read her mind. Other times she could see the downside. Still . . . "Good, I'm glad."

Stray moved closer to her in stages, like he wasn't sure he was ready for that yet, but he remained naked. Unabashedly so, and she tried to stop herself from staring, because it seemed a really inappropriate time to be turned on.

His easy smile told her otherwise. "This is natural—for me, at least. I'm a beast, Kate. You said so yourself."

"I didn't mean it."

"Don't back down now. Not your style."

"I can lash out, yes. I'm sorry. I was just—"

"Telling the truth."

"Angry. At you. At these circumstances. You don't understand."

"Right." He sighed, stared at the sky. And yes, it was time for her to do some serious groveling. She took a few steps toward him, hoping he wouldn't back away.

He didn't, but that wasn't going to make this any easier.

She started again, needing to find a way to make him understand. "I've never had anybody. And I've never had any say in what I do, not since the accident. And then you tell me what I am and that you hate me."

Speaking of hated, she hated that her voice cracked.

Stray put a hand on her shoulder. "Stop."

"No. I'm apologizing. Let me."

"You already did."

"It's not good enough."

"It's going to have to be," he told her. "For a long time, I didn't have anyone either. I do now. So do you."

She couldn't speak. Her throat constricted and she believed him. But the words she'd said . . . no matter what he told her, she needed to do more.

So she kissed him gently, first on the cheek, then kissed a path along his jaw. He stiffened, drew a harsh breath, like a tender touch was the most alien sensation in the world.

He froze for a moment, and then his arms wound around her, held her tight as he returned the kiss.

It didn't stop at the kiss. Couldn't. Stray had to kiss Kate everywhere—neck, breasts, belly. Had to taste her, spread her legs and take her with his tongue while she moaned his name, gripped his hair. Really let herself go for him.

When she came against his mouth, he made it happen again, because he could. And then he took her while she wrapped her legs around him and undulated her hips against him in a rhythm that drove them both right to the edge.

In the aftermath, Stray lay next to Kate on the floor. The post-orgasm screaming pain ceded, but it was getting worse each time he made love to her. Until this point, he'd managed to hide it among her blazing orgasms and his mind block, but she was getting stronger. Soon he wouldn't be able to keep her out. Such was a necessity between a familiar and her witch. Still, the pain was worth it.

"That was some apology," he told her.

"I can apologize again, if you want," she told him with a grin.

"Cheeky witch."

"I can't help it—you're that good."

He shrugged. He'd had lots of practice and had no shame about it. "Sex for us is life. We have no worries about too much of anything."

"That must be nice."

He pulled her closer. "You didn't find this nice?"

She laughed and his wolf soared. "More than."

"We're going to be doing a lot more," he told her. "Is that going to be a problem for you?"

"No. Being around you seems to bring out . . . something raw and primal inside of me."

"It's the wolf—you can't resist him."

"No, I can't. I'm glad both of you forgive me."

"I didn't forgive myself, Kate. Don't you get it? I was angry because I let you get hurt."

"You let me get hurt?" she asked incredulously. "I got you killed."

"I'm still here."

"I never want to see you like that again."

"Yeah, well, I could go a long time without that too."

"I understand now why you don't think too highly of witches or humans. I have to tell you that, from what I've seen of both, neither do I." She hugged herself tightly, a shield from everything. "There's so much bad in the world— even in people's thoughts. It's exhausting."

He knew it all too well. That's why he hung with wolves, because their thoughts were primal and far more comfortable.

"If I could turn it off, make it go away, I would."

"You're not going to do that," he told her.

"Your original plan was to let me die."

"That was the original plan, but it was never mine. And it was before."

"Before what?"

"Before I knew you. Met you. Smelled you." He did release her then, but he stroked her chin with his thumb. "It was before I fell for you. Humans call it love—I call it fate. Whatever you want to call it, I'm in."

"Sometimes love means having to make hard decisions," she whispered. "You have to help me make the right one when all of this is over—for us, for your family. For the good of everyone."

He stared at her with unblinking wolf's eyes, and she knew she had an uphill battle.

Chapter 45

When Angus woke, darkness surrounded him, but he most definitely wasn't dead, unless heaven was a two-bedroom loft apartment with stainless kitchen appliances and a wolf.

He sat up tentatively. He wore no shirt—or pants, for that matter—and a thin blanket covered him. The couch was leather, but Cain had laid him on a blanket. "What's going on?"

"Business as usual," Cain commented.

"You're going to tell me what you did for me is normal?"

Cain gave him a crooked smile. "Not for you, it's not."

Angus looked down at his arm and saw the fading bite marks. "I've been bitten. What does that mean?"

"Means you tasted good."

Angus stared at him. "Seriously?"

"You're not going to howl at the moon, if that's what you're asking. That's old lore. You'll heal and you'll be fine. One hundred percent human. It's going to leave a hell of a scar, though. That's one thing I can't get rid of for you."

Angus stared at him for a second before deciding to continue the lie. "A wolf attacked me. I saw a man change into a wolf and then he attacked me, dragged me into the woods and left me for dead."

"I hate to be the one to break this to you, but that Were had to have had orders not to kill you, Angus." Cain paused. "Shimmin was probably waiting to see what you'd do—who'd come for you. He doesn't trust you're on his side completely."

For good reason. Angus stared down at his arms again. Both forearms were covered with bites. On further inspection, there was also one on his side, his thigh and claw marks on his shoulder.

When he reached up to his cheek, he felt the indents of more claw marks running down the right side, passing his neck.

"You're still beautiful," Cain whispered. Maybe he didn't say it out loud, but it came through Angus's head as clear as day.

Then again, he'd been given pain meds—couldn't be feeling this good this close to nearly dying. "Shimmin doesn't trust me—do you?"

"Not completely," Cain told him, then shut down the conversation by turning on the TV. Angus stared at the reports of earthquakes that shook New York City and her surrounding areas today. "Did this really happen?"

"You don't believe your own kind?" Cain asked.

"Where I grew up, we were taught never to believe anything we didn't see with our own eyes—God performed miracles."

"Where'd you grow up?" Cain asked.

"Foster care. Nuns took me in until I went to military school."

"You don't act like you were raised by nuns." Cain handed him water and more pills that Angus gratefully accepted. No point in acting like Superman when you weren't.

"You don't act like anyone I've ever met, so what's your point?"

Cain smiled, like he'd heard it before. "Yeah, there's something about you too, human." He touched Angus's forehead with a light hand, and Angus wanted him to leave it there forever.

Human. He stared into Cain's eyes and watched them change—fiercely lupine and then back to normal. He wasn't sure if it was the strong medicine or a trick of light.

"I know what I saw tonight," he said finally.

"You believe in fate, human?"

"I believe in fighting like hell to get what you want," Angus countered. He'd been doing it his whole life and it hadn't gotten him all that far. Didn't stop him from trying, though.

Cain settled on the couch across from Angus, continued flipping channels restlessly. Outside, a storm began to rage that shook the building, and the studio apartment was suddenly much too small, bathed in the half-light from the moon shining through the clouds.

Before he could ask more, the power shut with a hard slam, as though someone took a violent fist to a power lever.

"You finally believe, don't you, human?" Cain asked.

"In what?"

"*Others.*"

The word came out like a growl and Cain's eyes shone lupine through the darkness again. Angus fully expected to find a wolf leaping on him any second, but Cain remained frustratingly far away.

"Yes," Angus admitted. "I believe."

"Does it scare you?"

"Sometimes. But I think humans scare me more."

"Smart man. Too smart to think I believe your story. Tell me what the hell really happened to you, Angus. Because if Shimmin sent a possessed Were after you, you'd be DOA. This was the work of a new, uncontrolled Were. So tell me now."

The words were like a command, although they weren't loud, but almost whispered. It was like Cain was gripping his insides, forcing an answer Angus hadn't wanted to give. "I went back to Shimmin, to get more intel. To be initiated, they wanted me to kill a Were."

"They brought the wolf to you, chained."

"Yes. How did you—"

"I'm asking the questions—you're answering. They brought the wolf to you, chained and helpless. Unshifted. They gave you a silver blade. What did you do next?"

"I told them I wanted to do it alone," Angus told him. The trappers hadn't given him much trouble with that. In retrospect, maybe they'd known what he'd planned on doing.

"Did the wolf escape?"

He stared at Cain. "No. I freed him."

"What the hell were you thinking?"

"I got your intel. It was the only way."

"Wait a minute—the Were gave it to you?"

"His name was—is—Jamie," Angus said. "He told me . . . *Cain knows me*."

Cain didn't hesitate to say, "He was from my original pack. Younger than I was. Got beaten often, the same way I did."

"Because he's an omega?"

"Because they could." Cain's voice sounded as dark as the room they sat in now. "He wouldn't lie—not to me."

"Why not?"

"I was the one who snuck back to our old pack last year and freed him. Hooked him up with the Manhattan pack. He wouldn't betray me."

"You're sure?"

"Yes." Cain sounded tired. "Tell me what really fucking happened."

"I was going to kill him. It was the only way. But he begged me not to—said he had information for you. That he could tell I wasn't like the trappers."

"He's a beta. They're good at reading people," Cain agreed.

"He told me about the Dire ghost army—what I told you before—that's all straight from him. He heard Shimmin talking to the other trappers about it when they thought he was passed out. He said the drugs hadn't worked on him because—"

"Because he hadn't shifted yet. But he was about to, so his metabolism would've been running like a freight train." Cain sounded tired. "You freed him, then, in exchange for what you told me about the Dire ghost army, right?"

"I did." Angus hadn't expected what happened next. One minute, the young boy was limping off toward the woods. Angus waited and began to pretend chase him. And that's when he heard the shots.

"The trappers shot him. It brought on his first shift," Cain explained. "He didn't mean to attack you, necessarily. It's why Weres aren't supposed to be out that close to their first shift."

"It wasn't nighttime," Angus said.

"The moon's always around," Cain told him. "You've got to stop believing all those fucking myths—nothing happens exactly as it's written. Trust what you saw."

"That's all I remember."

Except his own screams. He didn't have to tell Cain about those.

"And the trappers never came back to check on you?"

"They found me . . . afterward. Told me the only way I'd ever be fully trusted is if I brought them your head on a stick," he finished. "I don't know what happened to your friend."

Cain was silent for a long moment and then said, "Cyd found Jamie's body about five miles from where I found you."

"I'm sorry, Cain," Angus whispered.

Lightning flashed, exposing them both. They stared at each other as darkness fell again, and Angus's chest tightened at how damned beautiful the wolf was. Thought about telling Cain that and then decided to hold off.

"These storms . . . Shimmin said they're electrical. *Other*," he started hesitantly.

"Shimmin says a lot of things."

"He says he's the one pulling the strings to do it. Is he . . . ?"

"He's human, but he's working with the devil," Cain said bluntly. "And people think Weres are evil. Far fucking from it."

"Except when they're murdering women or working for Shimmin," Angus pointed out, not so helpfully.

"Fuck you, Fed."

"Might not be one for long." Angus sat up, the sheet half off, and Cain pointed him in the direction of the bathroom. "Sweats in there for you."

Angus took him up on the offer, closing the door and staring at the scars in the mirror, probably for too long, because Cain called to ask if he was all right.

"Far from it," he muttered. "I'll be right out."

He used the new toothbrush and took a quick shower. Assessed the rest of the cuts and bruises and realized how lucky he really was.

He looked out the window but couldn't see much. It was thick glass, double paned and probably bulletproof. He'd driven by these apartments many times since he'd gotten into town, but he'd never have believed wolves lived here.

"Thought you drowned," Cain commented.

Angus ignored him and looked out the big windows to the street. "What is this place, a supernatural flophouse?"

"Pretty close, except everyone pays rent." Cain studied him. "Are you really thinking of resigning from the FBI?"

"I don't know. Shit, I don't even know what side is up right now." He ran a hand through his hair, his injuries still aching as the young wolf—wolf, for chrisssakes—studied him.

Angus suddenly knew what prey felt like.

"Shimmin's been calling you." Cain held Angus's phone in his palm. "If you don't answer, he's going to get suspicious, since obviously he couldn't find your body."

"What am I supposed to say to him?"

"I guess it's time to decide whose side you're on."

"Is that the only reason you're being nice to me, because you need my help?"

Cain snorted. "You've got a weird idea of what nice is. And I don't need your help, human. You do need mine, though. So it's all up to you."

Cain tossed him the phone in a perfect arc and he caught it, wincing as the muscles in his right arm protested. That made Cain smile, for whatever reason . . . and it made Angus's decision infinitely easier.

There were no words, not this time. Cain's mouth covered his, and Angus felt the breath suck out of him and a hard body rubbing his.

And he was fully found, not lost.

Cain wouldn't stop, not this time, but Angus didn't want him to. The phone dropped. The sweats he'd borrowed pushed down easily and he lay under a fully clothed wolf, vulnerable and willing, not caring that his body still ached. Because the kiss was that good—what he'd been dreaming about over the past weeks.

He felt pinned, trapped—and he liked it. He gripped Cain's hair as the kisses grew more intense, moaned into the wolf's mouth as their cocks ground together.

Fuck, he could come, just like this. Especially when he felt the brush of sharp teeth against the most sensitive part of his neck. A loud groan escaped his throat, because the rush of fear was nothing compared to the one of equal pleasure.

The teeth scraped and then a rough tongue soothed. "Don't worry; you can't be turned."

"But I can die," Angus whispered, and immediately wondered why the fuck he'd say something like that. Especially when Cain pulled back and stared at him oddly.

Surely that was something the young wolf knew. Hell, it was a given. Angus caught his wrist before Cain moved away completely.

"Don't go. Stay," he told Cain.

The young wolf nearly relented, but his expression shuttered again and he pulled away. "I'll be back later. There's plenty of food in the fridge. Don't leave. With the intel we have from Shimmin, it's only a matter of time before he figures out that you're the one who screwed him." With that, Cain grabbed Angus's phone and shoved it in his pocket. So much for decisions.

"And then what, Cain? Do I stay in this place forever?"

"Didn't realize you had a whole lot of places to go," Cain said coolly.

"Fuck you, wolf." He jumped up, stood toe-to-toe with Cain, now angrier than he'd been in a long time. "I'm leaving in the morning."

Whether Cain would let him do that, Angus didn't get a hint of a clue. The young one just brushed past him and left the apartment without a backward glance.

It was only when Angus heard the lock turn that he realized, for the first time, that there was no turn lock on his side, just a place where a key would fit.

He'd always been a prisoner. Cain had been making a fool of him, purposely, and he'd fallen for it like he was some novice without years of training.

In this world, you are.

Not for long, he promised himself. Not for fucking long.

Kate left Stray sleeping, slid out of the room while pulling a shirt over her head. Rogue was calling to her—or maybe she needed him. But either way, she had to go there.

Kate?

Going to Rogue—I'll be fine, she assured Stray.

Stray didn't say anything further and she felt him go back to sleep. His trust warmed her.

She stopped with her hand on the doorknob, knowing what she'd face when she went inside. And she was ready.

The mare turned her head sharply and smiled.

"I'm not a kid anymore," she told her. "You can't scare me."

She cackled, like she knew better, but when Kate met her gaze and refused to blink, the mare turned away first and continued marking Rogue's skin.

Hate for the creature burned through Kate. She paced the floor of Rogue's room, unable to stop talking to herself. She kept her mind closed, the way she'd learned to, even though she ached to go back and converse with Rogue again. But it was best this way. The brick wall ensured the mare wouldn't read her thoughts—and the mare could read only internal thoughts, not Kate's external ones.

"You wouldn't send me into a battle I couldn't win, dammit. Why would you tell me to do something you don't want me to?" she whispered finally. "What am I missing?"

She touched the book. "Lila, come on, you have to help me out here. I've messed things up so badly for the wolves— for Stray."

Nothing. Dammit. She let go of the book, closed her eyes and concentrated. *I know you lied to me, Rogue. I know it . . . But why . . . ?*

She thought back over what he'd told her and the events of the past days.

Something about *a wolf in sheep's clothing . . .*

She let out a small gasp and turned to Rogue. "Okay, I've got it. It's a long shot, and it's all got to be done in tandem, but I've got it."

She touched his hair and heard the word *thanks*. Not *thank you*, as Rogue usually said to her when she'd made the same exact gesture twice before, and she knew she had it right this time.

Then she exited the room as she wiped a few tears from her eyes. She planned on keeping this to herself for the moment. Because none of it would be easy. It would have to be planned perfectly.

And it could all go so horribly wrong.

Chapter 46

After the meeting with Jinx and Jez happened and plans were set, Jinx ordered Cain to stay away from Angus. Now, in the rooms at the end of the Dire tunnels, Cain argued with Cyd.

"He's not a bad guy. He's not like Shimmin. He's just . . . human," Cain told his brother.

"Then friend him on Facebook, but in real life, avoid," Cyd told him. He stripped and headed toward the bathroom. Cain stood there for a few minutes and pondered on whether his brother was right.

The intel Angus had given him could be a big fat trap, although Rifter and the other Dires didn't seem to think so. Still, Cain had done what Jinx said, systematically avoiding Angus's many urgent phone messages that all said the same thing.

Come back and let me the hell out.

Where the hell could the human go that he wouldn't be marked for death?

When Cyd came out, shaking off water droplets like the wolf he was, he grabbed his phone. "Text message from Jez. Angus is gone. Jez claims he heard a racket but didn't investigate. Found the door yanked off its hinges—must've done it with a knife when he couldn't get through the bolts."

"Vampires," Cain muttered. "Why the hell not?"

"He said he thought it was the Were couple—you know, Sharon and Mike Muha and their new werepups, Stephen and Annie? Talk about moon crazed," Cyd explained. "Jinx wants to know if you can scent Angus. We'll go together, but you spent more time with him."

There was no rancor in his twin's tone—he was simply stating a truth. He'd never cared that Cain's preferences ran toward men. Maybe because they'd spent a lot of time with Vice, who didn't discriminate. Wolves in general weren't picky—most just also came equipped with the strong urge to procreate. "Let's go make sure he's not with Shimmin."

"You don't think he is, do you?" Cyd asked as he threw clothes on.

"I don't. I wish I did," he muttered, because it would be a hell of a lot easier to reconsider his feelings for a human.

They drove one of the trucks through town. The rain had started that morning, the air warm and supernatural lightning scored the darkening sky.

Cain caught Angus's scent right up to the building's parking lot. "He stole a car. I doubt he's still in town."

He didn't want to think about *why* the human had left. *You drove him away.* And Angus was safer for it. Unless . . .

"We need to check Shimmin," Cain said after they scoured the apartment. The fed had gotten out of the steel door using brute force Cain's wolf would've approved of. Cain felt the swell of admiration for the man even as the anger rose hot inside of him. He didn't scent Shimmin anywhere around, but they couldn't be sure.

"Shouldn't we bring a Dire?" Cyd asked.

"No. This is my problem."

"Yours is mine," Cyd growled. Younger by ten minutes, Cyd was as overprotective of Cain as any big brother.

"And both of yours is mine," Vice said from behind them as he surveyed the apartment.

"We're Jinx's."

"You're all of ours," Vice corrected.

"We still have work to do," Cain said, tried to slide out past the Dire.

"What happened between you and Angus?" Vice asked, but Cain just shrugged and kept moving. "Don't make me hurt you."

Cain turned. "I got too close."

"And stupid. Remember, we don't get close to humans."

"Tell that to Rifter."

"Gwen's a wolf," Vice said. "No human I know can shift like that, so unless Angus has some superpowers—"

"He's gone. He won't work for Shimmin. Can we drop it?"

"You know that for sure?"

"Yes." He was lying. Vice knew it but didn't call him on it. Cain just had to pray he was right about Angus, and that the agent would stay far away from all his newfound discoveries.

Together the three wolves roamed the woods around the apartment, catching no scent of Angus and a little of Shimmin's, which wasn't surprising.

And when they'd finished and the skies opened up, they dried inside the truck as they drove back.

Vice put his phone on speaker when Stray called.

"As of several days ago, the FBI claims Angus Young no longer works for them in any capacity. The man's officially dropped off the face of the earth," Stray reported.

Cain nodded, like it didn't matter. Wished it didn't. And when he got home, he went into his room and shut the door and returned the message.

Angus had been calling him all fucking afternoon. Cain had avoided him, hadn't been ready to hear what the human had to say.

Now he had no choice. "Did you tell me the truth?"

"You know I did." Angus's voice sounded far away. Cain could hear the wind whipping through open car windows over the line, the heavy beat of rock music in the background. Angus was very much alone.

"He's going to come after you."

"I've got people to watch my back, all right? They'll keep me away from Shimmin."

"You're too fucking trusting." Cain fisted his hand around the phone. "Where will you go?"

"Gotta do what a man's gotta do, Cain." A pause. "Stop worrying about me."

"Then do something to make me."

"That's exactly where I'm headed," Angus told him. Cain didn't push him further.

"What does Shimmin know?" Cain asked.

"What you are," Angus said. "Look, he's one of those guys who wants all my intel and barely gives any of his own. But I gave you the best intel I got. Nearly died for it. Now I have a job to do."

"According to my sources, not anymore."

"It might not pay me, but it's a job. Watch out for yourself, wolf."

Angus didn't wait for Cain to answer before he hung up, but the emphasis on the word *wolf* was softer than the rest of the man's words.

Chapter 47

Stray slept until Kate called to him. There was no danger but rather an urgency and he was out of bed and in the bathroom in seconds, slamming the door open to find her facing him. The way she looked, hair tumbling over her shoulders, the towel she held across her front barely covering her, steam curling around the edges of the room ... all of it took his damned breath away.

"Didn't mean to bust in. But you call, I come."

She gave a small smile, but it wasn't all that shy. "I know."

Jesus, he was slow sometimes. "Wait, you called me in here on purpose?"

"Yes."

"But you're not in danger. The rule was—"

She dropped the towel and fuck the rule. *Fuck the rule.*

He didn't give her a chance to beg off or change her mind. Couldn't. Her body called to him in a way he'd never be able to forget, even if he needed to.

And he would need to. He was sure of it.

She didn't hesitate to put her hands on his shoulders, to accept the hard kiss that brought their bodies together in an embrace that made them both gasp.

The fire between them was undeniable. He ran his fingertips over her back where the brand once was and watched her face mist over with pleasure. The touch hit him as a stroke to the groin. If he hadn't known it before, he did now. They were connected. Bonded.

She didn't know if living with wolves made her more feral or if it was the acquisition of the powers, but she couldn't shake the need to go to him and she didn't try to.

He slaked her need just like that night in the rain outside of Lila's house. And he seemed to be the only one able to truly make her feel.

Her nipples tightened, skin tingled as Stray howled and she didn't care that the others would know what was happening. She realized she was the prude—the wolves found all of this natural.

Her mouth suckled a tender spot she'd discovered right behind his ear and he growled, his grip tightening on her hips.

"I want you," she purred against his ear, and she was lifted and carried without hesitation to the bed and then whisked her shirt off.

He mouthed her nipples, biting them gently, his sharp canines sending waves of pleasure through her.

Naked, writhing under him, her core bloomed for him as he got as naked as she was.

"I want this, Kate. I've been wanting it, you," he told her before he dipped his head between her legs and licked her, brought her to the edge and didn't stop when she whimpered with frustration laced with pleasure. She wanted him—all of him—and he didn't make her wait long, entered her with a long, slow stroke and then let her lay claim to him. They rocked against each other, pulling and writhing until their climaxes swelled together, and they murmured each other's names into their mouths as they kissed. It was a greeting, a good-bye to all things past—a welcome to whatever was to come, good or bad.

It was everything.

*   *   *

Kate snuggled in Stray's arms in a way she feared she was getting far too used to. They didn't have long before the battle would begin, but Stray insisted they make the most of this time.

And they had.

"Kate?" he asked now, and she heard slight surprise in his tone.

"Yeah?"

"We're floating."

"What?" She looked over her shoulder and saw they were hovering above the bed. "Good. It's about time all of this kicked in."

She stared at the bed and concentrated on bringing them down again, slowly. They lowered and then fell the last foot with a hard jolt. "Shit—sorry. I'll work on that."

He was staring at her, not caring about the landing. "Something's changed."

"I have a plan. I understand what needs to happen to defeat him."

"Don't tell me," Stray said. "Keep me the hell out of your mind, for your sake."

"I will. That's why I called for you. I wanted to make sure I could."

It was his turn to concentrate now, tried to break into her mind, so to speak. But based on what Rogue told her days ago, she finally realized what she needed to do.

"I can't hear a damned thing," he said regretfully. "I don't like not being able to hear you. Everyone else, yes, but you . . ."

"I know. I'll let you back in as soon as I can. When I need to. And then I won't lock you out again. I promise."

"Never again," he said.

"That's a really long time, you know."

"I'm still getting used to the concept myself," Stray said.

"It's one thing not to die when you're killed. Another to think of a sprawl of centuries that lie ahead."

"What do your brothers say about it?"

"They don't talk about it much. It is what it is. The hardest part for them was going all this time without mates."

"So Rifter waited centuries for Gwen?"

"He thought he'd never have a mate, so it was a surprise," Stray admitted. "They didn't think there were any Dire females left to mate with. I knew there were some, but based on the way they treated me, none of these wolves would have them."

"So you can only mate with Dires."

"Gwen's an exception, since she's half Dire, half human."

"Are there other exceptions?"

He pressed his lips together in a grim line for a few seconds, then said, "The mating rules are pretty specific. And they involve the female shifting into wolf form to complete it. It also involves pain for me. But then again, orgasms without mating always cause pain."

She stroked his cheek. "I don't want to cause you pain."

"It's worth it. It's left over from the old ways. The Elders never thought we should be having casual sex—mating was the way to go."

"So they left you with no mates and in pain? They sound cruel."

"I think they've just lost sight of their charges. They were Dires once too, lived among us." Stray shrugged. "Maybe one day they'll realize they need to change some things, but I'm not holding my breath."

"You can understand what the witch did," she said quietly. "Because you might have done the same thing if it were possible."

He paused, considering that. "I couldn't imagine passing on my legacy to a young child, but, for me and the rest of the Dires, the thought can be tempting. When Vice learned that Gwen's blood contained the power to kill the immortal Dires, he flipped out, not because of the danger, but because of the possibilities. Our lives—theirs, centuries long—could finally end."

"You lived with your powers for much longer than I have," she noted. "Maybe I have nothing to complain about."

"You're not complaining—you're being honest. You've had a lot to deal with in a short period of time. And you've been warrior stoic about it, for the most part."

"So your brothers came to grips with Gwen and what her blood can do?"

"Killing themselves would mean killing Gwen, and she'd been dying for nearly half her life from seizures. She fought to live, found her king and her family. None of us were willing to sacrifice her happiness for our own selfish motives."

"I always did like a good love story. Is there a marriage ceremony?"

"There are different steps. Some of them involve chains and others, the moon."

"Can you tell me more about the chains?" she asked innocently.

"One day, I'd like to show you."

Hours later, the skies opened again. Kate thought of the raindrops as Seb's tears, his anger and pain at having to let go of Lila, and even with that, she knew she'd have no sympathy for him when the time came.

The time is here.

And it was. Lightning flashed, thunder rolled and, hopefully, humans stayed inside where they belonged.

And you're not thinking of yourself as human anymore.

She put her palms to the window, her breath making steam against the glass. There was nothing else out there now. The threat was waiting for them at Pinewood, squaring off, having no idea that the Dires planned on fighting, not running.

They were in for the surprise of their lives. Or deaths, as it were.

Stray once told her that the ragtag army they'd pulled together had to be enough. Tonight she was confident that it was more than enough. With some of the Weres following Liam, the immortal Dires, including Harm and Kill, as well as Jez, they would fight and win.

She and Gwen would stay behind with Rogue and wage their own battle. It was safest that way—and they hadn't given her an option. She didn't argue much, because it was exactly what she wanted.

The best wolves—and witch—would win. There was no other option.

"Want to talk about what's bothering you before we take the field?" Stray asked quietly from behind her. "And no, I'm not reading you—I still can't. I just know you well."

That last part warmed her, although in this case, she'd much prefer not to discuss it out loud at all. But she knew she had to, for all their sakes. She'd been struggling not only with staying, but with keeping her powers.

If she chose to keep them, she would be deadly, and thus there would be another decision to make. But first things first. "I don't know if I can keep these powers. And I've been thinking . . . what if I include something in the powers that will compel the new . . . owner, so to speak, to give them up when he or she reaches the right age?"

"So you're giving the powers to an innocent and condemning them to death, one every ten years."

"Better one than potential millions," she said quietly, finally turning to meet his gaze. It was serious and sad at the same time. None of this sat well with her either, but her options were limited.

"So you're willing to die."

"Yes."

"I won't let you."

"I can't be used against you. I won't." She paused. "I'd be yours until I die."

"You'd die immediately, Kate. There's no way to give back your powers and live out your normal life."

She wrapped her arms around herself.

"I can't tell you what to do with this. I don't know what I'd do if an opportunity presented itself to me to end things. I've been on this earth seventy-five years—my brothers, a lot longer. They struggled when they found out Gwen's blood could kill them, put them to rest. But they'd never use it because they love her. Still, I don't know what they'd do if they found another way out." He paused. "It's not going to be easy, but I think that nothing worth having is."

"I don't want to hurt people."

"Then don't."

It couldn't be that simple, could it? She looked into Stray's eyes and realized that, if she gave away her powers, she'd never know.

"Lila picked you because she knew this was your destiny. Your mother tried to change it. I tried to change mine, and things were worse than they would've been otherwise."

"But then you never would've met me," she pointed out. "I wonder if Lila knew that. She could tell the future."

"I don't need her to tell me mine. She's standing right in front of me."

Chapter 48

Stray stood next to his brother in the cemetery where Rogue said the final battle between the Dire ghost army and the wolves would be fought. Jinx had known the location for days, ever since he'd discovered the ghost corpses and had tried to keep them contained, but when they'd arrived, the iron gate had been ripped from its hinges.

Vice had searched for it, found it in the woods and brought it back. He and Jinx reattached it, because when all of this was over, the ghosts needed to stay where they belonged.

Now even Stray could feel the excess energy from ghosts and spirits. Jinx said they were everywhere, scattered and nattering, and as Jinx tried to turn their talking off, Stray forced himself to tune out his brothers' minds as well.

There was pride and fear and anticipation in all of them. Stray didn't need to know more. They would all fight to the death, as it were.

If the ghost army won, they'd continue on from here, overpowering humans and killing whatever was in their path until Seb—with Leo's okay—called them off.

Leo Shimmin also had several possessed county leaders in his pocket, although controlling them would be difficult.

Stray and Killian would take care of that later, once they defeated the Dire ghosts.

Which was why they couldn't lose. There was more at stake than ever.

Rifter was there, along with Vice, Jinx and Harm, who'd been freed of the silver he'd worn from the time he'd resurfaced weeks earlier since the meeting with Jinx and the vampire. Liam, Cyd and Cain were there along with the Manhattan pack and other recruits. A second and third wave waited in the wings.

Jez was also there, standing next to Jinx.

"You think this is going to work?" Kill asked him.

"We're stronger than they are—we can't die either," Stray said.

"But the Weres can," Kill pointed out, and Stray knew that Jinx was worried about the twins and Liam, like they all were.

"When duty calls, they come," Vice interjected.

"Jameson's mine," Rifter said.

"I might have to help you with him," Harm told him. "Just because I spent time singing doesn't mean I didn't keep up with the warrior ways. It's a part of me—you're all a part of me—whether I wanted it or not. Gwen says I need to accept that. This is a start."

For a long second, Stray held his breath, until Rifter nodded his consent.

"I suppose it's only right to take him out together."

At those words, Harm stepped in front of the pack with Rifter and they waited in silence for the ghost army to arrive.

The ground began to shake like it was being plied by a thousand horses running in their direction. Actually, the sounds came from all sides, like the living Dires were being boxed in by their ghost counterparts.

"Stand your ground," Rifter told them and, as hard as it

was not to swivel and look for something—anything—they waited for the first real signs that it was time to wield their swords.

Jinx saw them first, but thankfully, all the Dires could see them. He didn't know why that was, but he didn't question it as the Dire ghosts came at them from all sides—every angle, swooping and screeching and turning transparent as they moved. They were dressed in full Viking Dire battle gear, which meant chain-link armor and long swords, their mouths open with the whoop of the battle cry and the howls of their wolves.

Jinx wondered if the ghosts had the ability to shift to their Brother Wolves, or if they were trapped deep inside, in pain.

Brother Wolf howled at the ghost army, like he was trying to get a response as well. Silence followed.

"I've got this for us, Brother. Hang tight."

Jinx had given them all silver weapons that wouldn't work on regular ghosts—they'd need iron for those. But for the Dire ghost army, which was an unnatural grouping, what worked on them in life would still work on them in death.

Jameson hovered above the rest, looking down on them. His bearing remained regal, his eyes pure black like his soul. "How dare you try to thwart us? You ruined the Dire existence once before, caused us Extinction. We must rid you from this earth so it will not happen a second time."

"We will fight you to your second death, Jameson," Rifter told him. "Prepare to go back to your afterlife."

After that, there was no more talking as the two armies, living and dead, blended into each other.

Vice took the honor of the first kill, a silver blade right through the heart of a Dire warrior. It was both heartbreaking and exhilarating killing their own.

"Jinx, your left!" Vice called and Jinx ducked and rolled, turned to find himself under the blade of his father. He hadn't seen him in the mix of ghosts, but he'd known it would come down to this moment.

For him and for Rogue, he would do this. He leapt to his feet, circled his father with his own blade poised for the kill.

"You would kill your father again?"

"In a heartbeat," Jinx said through clenched teeth as the battle raged on around them. "But I didn't do it the first time. You were responsible for what happened. Rifter's a good king. Under his leadership, the Dires would've stayed alive and prospered."

"You and your twin are unnatural. Your mother should've let me kill you and Rogue when I had the chance," his father said.

"I'm not going to waste that opportunity and have the same regrets." Jinx lunged, the blade successfully embedding itself in the man's neck. The look of surprise on the apparition's face made Jinx pause for a second. His father hadn't believed Jinx could be a warrior.

"You were wrong again, Father," he whispered as he drew the blade out and sliced through the head, watching the ghost's corpse fall into separate pieces on the ground.

"Jinx, watch!"

Jinx turned in time to see Jez bear down on the ghost aiming for Jinx's back, the blade going clean through from back to chest before slumping to the ground.

"You owe me, wolf," the vamp called as he wheeled around and headed back into the confusion. "Good kill, though."

And there were still so many more. Jinx took the blade and began swinging as the body count—dead and living— began to rise.

Chapter 49

The battle raged on for so long, Vice lost track of time and space, his mind only on vanquishing anything dead that came across his path. And still, the Dire ghost army kept coming, marching, not caring that for most of them, it was to their final death. Cain was able to protect Liam and Cyd as they fought and his prowess as an omega would spread to the other Weres. It would go far in cementing Liam's backup.

But first they needed to win this battle.

Jameson had floated frustratingly too far above for them to get him, directing the ghost army, no doubt with Seb helping from the sidelines. That bastard witch would die if Vice had anything to say about it. He'd kill him every single day for eternity if that's what it took.

Vice took down two Dires he used to spar with back in the day, saw the hatred in their eyes and wondered if it had been there all along and he'd been too stupid to notice it.

Everyone had always known about his abilities. He couldn't hide them if he tried. To his knowledge, no one had ever thought he was dangerous or problematic. He'd always been picked for battle. But now he wondered if maybe they did that in hopes he would be killed faster. After all, the

Elders had been mortal Dires once, killed for their abilities. And even though the Elders told the Dires to be protective of those with abilities, not fearful of them, Vice realized they'd never listened.

He sliced the first and then the second, taking both heads off with the same clean motion and whirled around to see Jameson coming down and headed straight for Rifter and Harm.

"We've got this, Vice," Harm told him, and although Vice wanted to buck that order, the look in Rifter's eyes told him he wanted this kill himself.

Only for him would Vice stand down, but it hurt. Man, it hurt like fucking hell running through his veins.

The warriors circled. For someone who no doubt hadn't picked up a weapon in centuries, Harm swung the blade like nobody's business. And when they had Jameson between them, Harm kept the blade level to the top of the apparition's head, the iron keeping the old king from rising up and away from them.

"Why didn't you take us out on our Running?" Rifter asked. "Or were you scared we were too powerful, so you went after innocents instead?"

That enraged the Dire ghost. He lunged for Rifter, who moved back and repeated the question.

To watch the wolves work together after all the adversity, the anger, all the time apart, made Vice think they actually had a shot in hell to make this work.

He'd said his own prayer to the Elders, one in particular, not because he thought she gave a shit, but because he didn't know what else to do.

"For the innocents you killed, for not listening to the Elders and sparing their lives, for all the injustices you've wrought in this life and beyond, you will die," Rifter said and then there was nothing but a flash of silver and iron blades.

*   *   *

The earth shook as the women waited in the attic with Rogue.

"It's happening," Gwen said, and Kate saw the silver gun tucked into the side of her jeans. "Rogue told me I'm both healer and destroyer. Right now, every bone in my body is telling me to destroy."

Kate knew how badly Gwen wished to be out fighting with her family. But the women had agreed to wait here alone with Rogue. The protection spell Kate wove would save them as long as Seb didn't lure Kate outside.

Letting Stray out of her sight had been hard, but necessary. He and Kill needed to work in tandem.

She and Gwen would form their own coven and do their best to distract Seb from pulling the puppet strings of the Dire ghost army.

Kate stared the mare down several times, reveling in the fact that the bitch never won the eye contact contest.

She wouldn't touch Rogue's hand though—not yet. She had to do it at the most crucial time to distract Seb, who would be pulling the strings for the Dire battle. Until Rifter and Harm killed Jameson, it could never be over.

The floor rocked again.

"The battle," Gwen whispered, hugging her arms around herself. "This has to work."

"You'll know when they kill Jameson?"

"Yes, I'll know," Gwen said. "You will too."

"You realize that you can reach Rogue on your own?" Kate asked her.

The wolf doctor shook her head. "It only happens with Rifter."

"No, Rifter can only do it with you," Kate explained. "That's what Rogue says."

"When did you talk to him again?"

"I realized he was layering his thoughts."

The mare was distracted, anxious, because Seb no doubt was. She was cutting into Rogue deeply now, her fingers scoring the skin. Gwen stared at the bright red blood running off his arms.

"I can only see her during the dreamwalk."

"Lucky you." Kate watched Gwen pat the blood away, even though they both knew it was a losing battle. "It's time."

"I'm here, Kate. You do what you need to," Gwen told her.

Kate concentrated on bringing the wall between her and Seb down. It would also bring the wall down between her and Stray, which would leave him vulnerable. But Killian was with Stray—and that was Kate's comfort.

Almost immediately, Seb called to her.

You picked the wrong side, Kate.

"I'm happy with the side I'm on." She spoke out loud so Gwen could hear.

When your Dires lose, we're coming for Gwen. She'll get to watch her blood poison them. But we'll keep her alive, like a pet.

How could Seb be the same man Lila had professed to love so deeply? Her witch hadn't been stupid or blind—so either Seb had changed so much he was beyond help . . . or he was lying to her.

"You're white as a sheet. What's he telling you?" Gwen asked, tugging at her. Making sure Kate was still with her and not ready to walk outside and find Seb.

Gwen had promised Stray in front of Kate she wouldn't let that happen. Whatever it took, Kate wouldn't go to Seb, even if it meant chaining her down.

The chains lay in the far corner of the room. Kate had avoided looking at them, because they signaled her potential weakness. She wouldn't admit to any for the moment. Couldn't.

"Shimmin wants you, Gwen," Kate whispered, not wanting to give the words more power than they had.

"He can't have me," Gwen said, her voice fiercer than

Kate had ever heard it to this point. It looked like Gwen was trying to halt a shift as the anger coursed through her, but she closed her eyes and held firm.

When she opened them, she had wolf's eyes, but she was still very much ready to help Kate and Rogue. "I'm ready. Let's take away his power."

"Lila would want it this way," Kate said with a certainty she hadn't felt until then.

Kate grasped Rogue's hand in hers and Gwen took the other. Rogue was silent, but Seb wasn't.

You've all miscalculated badly. Weres are dying.

Kate's pulse pounded in her ears. Anger and grief balled up inside of her, and still she managed to say, "Seb, you've got to get out of there. You need to escape now, or else it will be too late for you."

It wasn't her voice coming out of her mouth—in her heart, it was Lila's. And suddenly Kate wasn't scared any longer.

She'd drawn up a spell earlier, a combination of finding a lost witch spell and a binding one, but she hadn't tried it until this moment, not wanting to risk giving away her plan.

Lila, how can that really be you?

"It is me." Kate knew for certain it was, because she had no control over her words at the moment. Letting Lila borrow her body was odd, but if it worked, she'd be forever grateful. Her body felt . . . lighter. Invaded, but she wasn't uncomfortable. It was like she was having an out-of-body experience without actually leaving her body, standing aside to watch Lila talking with the man she'd loved.

The man she still loved. Kate could feel how strong the feelings that remained were, even as Lila said, "I've missed you, Sebastian. So much."

Dammit, Lila. If you'd only stayed . . . none of this would've happened. We could've run away, like we'd planned. Our secret was safe with Rifter.

"We were never safe, and it wasn't Rifter's fault. It was

our destiny as witches. We always knew our time was limited. Should be."

It didn't have to be.

"It shouldn't have come to this. You knew it would and you didn't take precautions. You could've prevented it."

Like you did? You ran. You took the easy way out.

"I died to save you," Lila said and Kate started. "If I hadn't passed my powers on to Kate, she wouldn't be able to help you now."

I'm trapped. The decisions I've made, it's too late, Seb said. For the first time, Kate caught the edge of desperation in his voice.

"You always have a choice, even if you don't like it," Lila said through her.

I was a coward.

"Never, Sebastian. Not until right now, if you don't do what you know to be right."

I can't take back my spells.

"Then simply turn away and don't look back," Lila offered.

And then there was nothing from either of them. Whether or not Seb had taken the advice or simply stopped talking to her, Kate had no idea. Not until she saw Gwen staring at the corner of the room and turned to see Lila there, in full form, a revenant, not a spirit.

"Lila," she breathed.

"I let you down. I stayed away." Lila looked contrite. Her cheeks were wet with tears.

Kate stared at Lila. "I don't know what to do. I have all this power and I still feel powerless. How's that possible?"

"Do what's in your heart. That will always steer you in the right direction."

"Like you did with Seb?"

"There's always sacrifice involved with love, Kate. You know that better than anyone. When I left Sebastian, he felt as though he lost everything. He didn't understand my sacrifice. He thought it meant I didn't trust him enough. The

Dires were the only ones holding him together," she explained. "He'd been with them a long time, made sure they didn't know about me, for my sake and theirs."

"You never got to say good-bye."

"I just did. Now it's your turn to carry on with the powers. Godspeed, Kate. Save your family."

With that, Lila was gone. When she turned back to Gwen, the half Dire appeared to be in a trancelike state of her own.

"Gwen? Are you all right?"

"Rifter and Harm are fighting Jameson," Gwen said softly. She clutched Rogue's hand and then Kate's extended one across Rogue's chest—and, together, right under the mare's face, they waited.

Chapter 50

As Rifter and Harm both sliced Jameson with their blades, the Dire armies, both dead and alive, went completely silent.

Rifter and Harm withdrew their blades almost reverently. Although Jameson was a bastard, he was also a Dire king and, in the eyes of the Elders, disrespect at this stage wouldn't be tolerated.

They placed the killing swords on the ground next to the body of the ghost that wasn't dissipating, but rather, bleeding out, the coloring fading by degrees.

"Is it over?" Vice asked finally. His voice was low and he was acting as second in command, watching over his king and the wolf who'd given up the throne, whirled around to see if the Dire ghost army would fight back.

They weren't.

"Kill them all!" Rifter roared, and his side moved forward without hesitation. All except Stray and his brother.

Come to me, Stray. Bring Killian. Kate's voice.

"We've got to get back to Rogue—it's our only shot."

Killian looked to Rifter, who'd zeroed in on his brother. Rifter nodded his assent before slicing a Dire ghost's head off with a different silver blade than the one used to kill Jameson.

None of this concerned him—this wasn't his past or Killian's, but somehow, it was. And he'd been lucky enough to be a part of it. He bowed his head for a moment and gave thanks to the Elders for letting the Dires find him, for his brother, for Kate.

"Stray, we have to go now." Killian tugged him and they bounded back to the car with the weapons still clanking on their bodies.

Stray drove like the truck was on fire, listening for Kate again and hearing nothing. He called to her but again, no response. And if she'd blocked him out, whatever the reason, it couldn't be good.

When he pulled into the garage, Kill was out of the truck before it even stopped moving. Stray slammed it into park, locked the house back down and followed, coming into Rogue's room behind his brother.

Rogue lay in his familiar position, with Gwen holding one hand and Kate the other.

Seb's gone—left behind his spells and disappeared. Trick the mare, Kate told him.

He turned to Kill. "Need your best witch impression again—that mare bitch needs to be called off."

"Now, Killian. Right now. Stray, block him."

Stray turned to stand in front of his brother, and Killian morphed then, right in front of his eyes. It looked painful as hell, far more so than a shift to Brother Wolf, and Stray swore he heard Killian's cries in his head.

He'd never seen his brother cry.

When the man stood, it wasn't his brother any longer—it was Seb who stood before him and Stray's Brother Wolf reacted violently.

Seb put his hands out to stop Stray. Closed his eyes and Stray heard Seb's voice in his head.

Come to me, now.

To whom he spoke, Stray couldn't be sure. He could only hope it was directed at the right source.

As Kate watched, the mare shifted hard and turned to stare at Kill, who'd morphed into Seb, thanks to his skinwalking abilities.

Come to me now.

Seb's voice, except he wasn't talking to Kate.

Now. I'm calling you off him. Release the wolf.

Slowly, the mare began to climb off of Rogue.

Come to me, Seb ordered, and the mare seemed powerless to do anything else. She walked across the room, directly into the devil's trap on the floor under the rug that had been there for centuries, thanks to Seb's spell.

As the mare sensed the trap, she heard, *Now, Kate— now!*

Stray's voice. She grabbed Gwen's hand and they began to chant the banishing spell for the mare. Now that her bond with Rogue had been broken, they weren't in danger of hurting the wolf.

The mare screeched, held her hands over her ears and tried to get out of the circle. But she was slammed backward and Gwen took that opportunity. She moved forward, in front of Kate as both Seb and Stray moved out of the way, held the gun steady in front of her—and she shot.

The iron passed through the mare and she crumbled into dust on the rug. Gwen collected it into the jar Kate gave her and closed the lid, effectively trapping the mare inside for eternity.

"We need to bury this in concrete," Gwen said, and then they all turned to Rogue, who simply lay there. The women rushed back to him, put his palms in theirs and waited.

"He's so quiet," Gwen said finally.

"Peaceful," Kate agreed.

"He's alive," Stray confirmed. "I'd know if he wasn't."

But whether or not he'd wake up was anyone's guess.

Killian was still in Seb's form. When Stray touched his shoulder, his brother began the painful task of shifting back into his own form.

It left him panting on the floor, weak and shaky.

"You can't do that again," Stray told him.

"I'll do what I have to do to save my kind. My family," Kill told him, his voice sounding as weak as he looked. Stray helped him up and they formed a circle around Rogue as Kate began to chant a protective spell to stop any other evil spirits the trappers might have up their sleeves.

"And the real Seb just left the trappers?" Stray asked when she stopped.

"Yes, when Lila asked him to. She really loved him, enough to walk away knowing it most likely meant he would die. He loved her enough to listen."

"Sometimes the love of a good woman is all any man needs to save him," Stray said quietly. "But I'm guessing the Dire ghost army stopped fighting when Seb left."

Kate came over to him and hugged him and, in that moment, he felt like he could finally rest. But no matter what, it still wasn't over—not completely.

Chapter 51

There was one more step Killian and Stray needed to take together. As the Dires and Weres cleaned up the cemetery and Jinx sealed the graves with Jez's help, Stray and Killian went to the weretrappers' facility several towns over.

Shimmin hadn't been heard from since the battle. Rogue remained asleep and Stray hadn't wanted to leave Kate's side.

She'd wanted to come with them, but he'd persuaded her to stay home and let them take care of this last bit of business.

"Ready, brother?" Killian asked now.

"Let's get this done," Stray said. They moved through the crowds until they got close. With Killian erasing memories and planting new ones that didn't include any knowledge of Weres or Dires or anything remotely supernatural, they were able to walk into the first floor of the facility without issue. Stray read their minds, helping Kill to do what he needed to.

You don't know why you're here. You're a peaceful, loving person who accepts differences in all people, species and races. You want to leave here, go home and get a job helping

*people. You'll never come back here again, and you don't
believe in wolves, witches, vampires or anything supernatural.*

And the trappers were leaving. Weres too. It wouldn't
completely stop the trappers, but it would foil their larger
plans for now.

Kill couldn't erase memories in the minds of Shimmin,
Seb or the demons. He couldn't do it to the ghosts, and unless he and Stray traveled the country constantly in search
of trappers, they couldn't eradicate them all. But for these
trappers, it was perfect. And permanent.

"The politicians are possessed—Seb's lost control of
them," Stray muttered.

"Not our department," Kill confirmed as they stood
alone in the now-empty facility. "Weres are headed back
where they belong. These trappers are done."

"For now. And there are more of them."

"One thing at a time. There will always be predators and
prey. Mortal enemies. The key is balance—too many of one
and the natural order's gone."

"You don't want them eradicated?"

"That's not natural. That's not what the supernatural
world needs."

He stared at his brother, wondered if Kill had always
been this philosophical.

"Brother, there's nothing unnatural about us." Killian
spoke with such fierce conviction he saw Stray's eyes go
lupine again. "We can make a difference. I don't care what
the prophecy says—I believe in us, not words."

Stray swallowed hard. "I do, too."

"Good wolf. Now, let's get you back so you can talk to
your witch." Killian put a hand on Stray's shoulder as he
walked out.

Kill wished he could believe his own words as easily as he'd
spoken them, as an older brother protecting a younger one.

No matter how powerful and dangerous Stray was, Kill believed he was good. Always had been.

Kill himself was another story, but he hoped his general proximity to his brother would help. He'd lived alone for too long, and he was scared of the thing he'd become when he'd killed his parents. It had saved many, to be sure, but in the future, who knew what it would do? For now he remained both Dire and skinwalker, since he'd already been immortal. But he had no idea how, in the future, the curse would twist inside of him, punish him for a crime that had needed to be committed.

What's done is done. If the wolves would have him, he would stay. If they told him to leave for the good of all, he would do that too. He knew how to be alone.

Chapter 52

Rifter and Harm buried Jameson and took the others back to the Dire house, including the dead Weres that Liam was responsible for burying himself.

There weren't as many as there could've been. For that, Jinx was grateful.

He didn't afford his father the same burial rites as Jameson. He allowed Jez to burn him into oblivion on the ground, which was a disgrace, as warriors from that age were supposed to be lit on fire in the water for their funeral pyre.

Finally, when they were done, Jinx turned to the ancient vampire. "It didn't close."

"Did you expect it to?"

"I'd fucking hoped." He paused. He'd known the Dire ghost army wouldn't go back into purgatory. Hadn't expected what escaped to, either. But... "If Seb is gone now... Wait a minute. Just stay there and watch me, okay?"

Jez nodded and Jinx closed his eyes and said the prayer from the old country in the ancient language—because if Seb had used it to open purgatory, now that Seb had abandoned his post, everything would reverse and be put right.

"Whatever you're doing—it's working," Jez said quietly,

and Jinx simply repeated it, over and over, refusing to open his eyes.

"It's done, Jinx. It's done."

Jinx opened his eyes and saw ... nothing. The yowling hole was gone, replaced by grass that looked as though it had never been touched.

But still, what had escaped was out—and it was never going back in. Jinx would have to send whatever freaks escaped back to hell, no matter how hard it was or how long it took him.

He shuddered at the massive responsibility literally thrown over his shoulders, and Jez put a hand out to steady him.

Jez, who was now was all nervous energy, which was odd to see from a deadhead. "This is going to be hell, no pun intended."

"None taken," Jinx muttered. "Mind if I stay with you?"

"I was going to insist, wolf. Need to keep an eye on you."

"Because I'm evil?"

"Because you're the farthest thing from it."

There was no party, no celebration for what they'd done. It was less because it was business as usual and more about whom they'd just battled.

The Dires had lost their destiny to the wolves they'd slaughtered tonight, and what could've been was weighing on their minds more heavily tonight than it had for centuries.

Centuries.

Kate couldn't wrap her mind around it, or the decision she was trying to make.

She'd written the prophecy down, stared at it, tried to figure out a way they could stay together. Killian had already mentioned leaving and she didn't want that for the brothers.

If they don't turn their wrath on each other ...

But they'd already done that, and the world survived around them. She was the most dangerous thing for both of them. She had to find a way to release Stray. She'd been searching the grimoire, the Internet, calling to Lila for help with little luck.

"I know what you're trying to do, Kate." Killian's voice came from behind her, and she turned.

"I'm dangerous with both of you. I can pull Stray and he pulls you. I can't stay."

"It doesn't say that."

"When we're together proves it," she said. "And I don't want you to have to leave again. You've sacrificed too much. You should stay with your family."

"They're your family too."

"I don't know how accepting of a witch they'll be. Not after Seb."

"I know why you're doing it. You think you're helping him by letting him go."

"I don't want him forced to be with me because he'd bound."

"He wants to be with you. He chose this."

"He didn't," she insisted, but Kill explained. "I can manipulate his memory, Kate. It would hurt, but I could do it. I could make him forget the familiar bond. But he made me swear a blood oath to never, ever do that. He chose you, and for him, that bond is as good as the mating bond he can't have."

"He really . . . did that? For me?" she asked, heard her voice quaver as Kill nodded. "I know Stray can only mate with a wolf."

"Only a Dire, in accordance with the old ways," he agreed. "And we don't give our hearts away that easily. He gave his to you, and he wants to love you, serve you. Protect. And you're telling him no."

"I didn't mean . . ." She turned immediately to go find the wolf, but then circled back and hugged Killian first. He stiffened, obviously unused to physical contact. "Thanks, Killian. You were always watching out for him, weren't you?"

Killian glanced at her as if he wanted to crack some wiseass remark, but ultimately, he bit it back. "I wanted to spare him all of this."

"I think he knows that."

Killian looked hopeful. "I hope so, Kate. All these years, I stayed alone. Lived alone, all to keep Stray's secrets and to keep him safe."

"Secrets are never good," she muttered.

"I hear you, witch," he said, but witch was spoken as more of a simple endearment, an acknowledgment of what she was rather than a dig. And then he surprised her by saying, "So why haven't you told my brother that you love him?"

"I thought you couldn't read minds."

"It's written all over your face," Kill said before he left the room.

It's written all over your face.

How to tell him?

Don't run or else I'll chase you.

As Stray's words echoed in her head, Kate smiled. And then she ran, out of the house and toward the woods.

Chapter 53

Stray couldn't control himself once Kate started running. Brother Wolf surged and he fought the shift, instead took off on two legs at a dead run toward her back.

No matter how powerful, Kate wouldn't be able to outrun him. When she learned she could mimic a shift with witchcraft, she might be able to keep up with him. Until then, he had the upper hand and he'd take it.

Within minutes, he closed the space between them. Another thirty seconds and he was on her, waiting for her to give in and stop. But she wouldn't, tried to keep the run going.

He snagged her with a hand around her waist, lifting her up and off her feet. He slowed, pushed her to him, stopping moving when he pushed her against a tree.

"You can't leave me," he told her. "I don't want you to."

"I've caused you a lot of trouble."

"Ditto. That's behind us, Kate."

"I can't go back to who I used to be. I was never that person, anyway. Not since the accident."

"I like who you are now. You soothe me, and I think I do the same for you."

He ran a hand along the brand, the electricity sparking between them. It made him hard and her start against him.

"Suppose it's just magic?" she asked.

"Then hallefuckingllujah for magic," he murmured. "Why shouldn't we let it make us happy? Maybe that's what it's been there for all along."

"I hope so." She nibbled his neck. "I like magic. And I like when you chase me."

"Like?"

"Love," she corrected. "From the start, Stray. I think I knew when you first touched the brand that this was meant to be."

"Me too."

"But what about the mating? I'm not a wolf. The Elders . . ."

"I'll figure something out," he promised. "But first you have to come back and not leave me ever again."

"Never," she swore. "When I met you, everything in my life clicked together for the first time. And you keep talking about being fated. What if that is what this is? I mean, what's a familiar? Something that protects me. I protect you, too, so I guess I'm yours too. This isn't a one-sided thing for me. If it's that way for you, tell me now."

She barely caught her breath before he was kissing her like he was claiming her. It was brutal and sensuous all at once and she had her answer.

But when he pulled away, he answered anyway. "You mean everything to me. I don't care what the Elders say. You are mine. My mate."

"Stray—Brother Wolf—I'm okay. Really. I'm a little scared. I can't deny that. But I'm going to help people." She paused, drew in a shaky breath as her fingers dug into his shoulders, like she was drawing strength from him. "I'm just so sorry. You shouldn't have to be bound again. Not to me, not after the way you grew up."

He jerked his head up to stare at her. Brother Wolf's eyes were Stray's—they inhabited different forms but they were the same.

Stray was all wolf. Animal. And still, somehow, she knew he was the best man she'd ever known.

"I tried to let you go. I'd do anything to make you happy, especially after everything you've done for me. Anything."

"I don't want you to get rid of me," Stray whispered.

She turned, buried her face in his chest. "I know what you did for me—with Kill. He told me about the blood oath."

He didn't sound upset when he told her, "Kate, we're bonded. In a way that's past being a familiar. In a way the familiar bond can't touch."

She looked up at him. "What do you mean?"

"We've . . . you bring out my mating instincts. And I'm only able to mate with another Dire, so I don't understand it."

"It's the magic." Her face fell.

"There's no way you could manipulate my mating instincts," Stray told her. "I can't be spelled."

"So what are you saying? This is meant to be?"

Stray swallowed hard. "My king . . . Rifter . . . when he felt . . . fated to Gwen, things happened. Strange things. And if we can't be mated in the traditional way, I still won't let you go. Can't."

First Stray went to his king and brothers and Gwen. Gathered them around the old oak table without Kill or Kate, because he didn't want to expose her to everything just yet. Not until he figured out some things.

"I think you all know how I feel about Kate, that I love her. She's my mate. And she's a witch. I need to make sure you're okay with that." Stray looked to Rifter first.

"She fought with us—for us. In my eyes, she's every bit Dire," Rifter said.

"Gotta hope the Elders feel the same," Vice muttered. "I agree with Rifter. I'll call Jinx, but I think his answer will be the same."

Around the table, Gwen, Harm, Liam and the twins all nodded their agreement.

"Now, about the Elders," Stray started.

"It's not going to be an easy pitch," Rifter said.

"When we were only exposed to other Dires, it wasn't a problem. How can we be expected to not fall in love with others?" Stray asked.

"Because we never had before," Vice said simply. "Thousands of years and we've never found anyone to be our fated, our mate. And suddenly it's going to happen?"

"Maybe it's because of the Elders?" Rifter suggested.

"Why now?" Vice asked.

"Because they need us. More of us—solidarity to fight to keep humans safe," Rifter said.

"Are humans really safe from us?" Vice asked.

"She's technically—"

"Witch."

"Immortal," Stray corrected. "And she's all fucking mine."

"Yeah, but are you hers?" Vice asked. "What? I like to ask the hard questions."

"Yes, I am. She's keeping her powers. We're staying bonded."

"But, dude, she's not a wolf," the ever-helpful Vice pointed out. "What's she going to shift to? An orgasmic woman?"

"Don't care—she's all mine," Stray said stubbornly, noting Rifter couldn't argue with him—how could he, when he'd been in nearly the same position. He wouldn't have given up Gwen for anything. And if the Elders hadn't intervened, he would've lost her last year.

"And I'd also like my brother to stay as well, despite the prophecy," Stray added, held his breath as Rifter deliberated.

"I think Killian can stay here. Should stay here. I'd feel

better if he was under our watch because of his powers," Rifter said. "Granted, I feel better when we're all here under one another's watch. We all have our foibles, Stray."

"Thank you, Rifter."

"Stray, with Kate, ask Eydis, not all the Elders," Vice said.

"You act like you know her personally. Has she done favors for you or something?" Stray asked.

"Just ask. Go to the oak tree in the middle of the woods that was split by lightning. She favors that tree," Vice said, got up and left before Stray could ask any other questions. Rifter looked as in the dark as Stray was, but there wasn't time to figure it out.

Vice tended to give good council—Stray wouldn't waste it.

Stray waited until dark, left the house alone and went to the tree Vice told him about. The oak was massive, thousands of years old, split clean down the middle by lightning, and still somehow both pieces stood, healthy and ramrod straight. The tree bloomed every spring and stayed lush and green until winter.

Now it was barren, but the bark was dark and healthy. He stared up at the sky with his hand on the tree.

"Eydis, I implore your help," he began. "It's about Kate."

"Speak, wolf."

She was behind him. He turned, expecting the imminent shift, or to see the other three Elders with her, but none of that happened. "You need to be in this form to communicate your wishes to me, correct?"

"Yes." Stray bowed his head out of respect and then continued. "I wanted to come here to ask for something. I love Kate. She is my mate, wolf or no wolf—and I know she feels the same."

"You want me to allow you to be with her?"

"Yes. But I know, most of all, that she wants to be rid of

her power. If there's a way she can have that, even if she remains human and lives a human lifespan, I would wish that for her instead."

When he looked up after a long silence, Eydis was watching him closely. "And you think I have this kind of power."

"Yes."

"I can't change a future."

"You can, but you won't," he ground out.

"Watch your tone, wolf, or I'll shift you," Eydis's voice was soft but steely, and he didn't want Brother Wolf to do this. No, this was Stray's thing.

"Apologies."

"The only way something like this works is a life for a life. And you cannot give yours."

"There must be a way."

"The way is to accept your destiny."

He stared at her. "Like the prophecy. If I stay with my brother . . ."

"If you'd stayed with him," she intoned. "You changed the course of history. You did this. You cannot outrun it again."

It was like a gunshot to the chest. He sank to his knees as Brother Wolf took over . . . and then he ran, away from Eydis, from the fact that seventy-five years ago, he'd set all of this in motion and somehow contributed to Kate being what she was now.

She'd accepted her future as a witch, but Stray loved her enough to release her from that. And if that wasn't possible, he would love and protect her and her powers until the end of time, approved mating or not.

He ran until he reached the crest of a hill and his senses rang out that something was very wrong. He waited impatiently, as his instincts and the wolf told him to, until he saw a man get to the top of the hill and begin to walk through the woods.

It was Shimmin, and he had Kate, was dragging her along with him.

Why hadn't she called to him? He started moving stealthily toward Shimmin, noted that Kate struggled to throw the cop weretrapper, but it appeared that he'd drugged her, because her legs began to drag behind her and her arms flailed less.

He took off on a dead run, heard the howls of the other wolves behind him, all of them well aware that this could be a trap, that Seb could very well be hiding in the woods.

No matter what, he would not let Shimmin have her.

"Dires took my brother, so I'm taking one of yours. I didn't think you'd mind losing a witch, considering your kind doesn't have the best of luck with them." Shimmin laughed, a cruel sound that made Brother Wolf bolt for him before Stray could stop him.

Stray finally pulled the reins and forced himself to shift back. Blinked and hoped none of this was real, but it was. Her worst nightmare, and he knew she was far more worried about Stray than she was about herself.

"It's me or you," Shimmin told him. "And I know you're not going to kill me. I still bear the poison to immobilize you for the rest of your natural-born life."

"Don't do it, Stray," Kate pleaded. She could speak, but her body appeared paralyzed by whatever Leo had given her.

But Stray had to. He went for Shimmin's throat, ripped it out before anyone or anything could stop him, not caring about the poison, not caring about anything but saving Kate.

It had been the only way to ensure her safety.

Chapter 54

Shimmin had thrown Kate to the side when Stray lunged for him. Now she crawled over to Stray's body, the drugs Shimmin had injected her with making it impossible for her to walk.

This time there was no blood, save for Shimmin's, but Stray remained unconscious for far too long.

She wasn't aware that she'd been screaming for help until she saw Vice running toward her, followed by Gwen. Vice was holding her and Gwen was checking Stray.

"I just went to find Stray—to tell the Elders I was ready to pledge my loyalty to them, the way Gwen had," Kate explained. "Shimmin was watching Stray—I literally stumbled on to him."

"I don't know how the hell he got on the property without us knowing," Vice muttered, and then he started to clutch at his chest and breathe hard.

"Our guard was down," Killian said from behind them, his breath also coming too fast to be normal. "What the hell is happening? Why isn't Stray moving yet?"

His voice sounded rough, and Kate noted that Vice was looking very pale as well. "What's happening to all of them?"

"When one of them dies, they all do," Gwen told her.

"I thought they couldn't die?"

"Technically, they can't. And Stray should be waking up soon."

"But . . . Shimmin's blood . . . pure poison . . . to us," Vice told Gwen in a halting voice. "It . . . immobilizes us."

"For how long?" Gwen demanded.

"Forever . . . we were told. We've never . . . put it . . . to . . . the test," Vice managed.

Kate willed herself to pull it together. Went deep inside herself and pulled up a healing chant, even as Gwen dropped her medical bags and placed her hands to hover over Stray's chest. She closed her eyes in concentration as Kate watched and chanted, and she didn't know which one of them had the power, if both or neither, but she believed. And Stray had told her that was all she needed.

Stray, I believe. Finally. Please come back to me.

For a long while, there was nothing. Sweat beaded on Gwen's brow and she began to shake. Rifter, who'd dragged himself up behind her tried to pull her away, but thankfully Gwen had more strength than he did, was able to shake it off. "Rifter, please—I have to do this. I'm the only one of you not affected. Let me."

And he listened, which she knew didn't happen often. It probably had something to do with the fact that he was also feeling the effects of the poison. In fact, all the Dires were on their knees, with only Liam and the twins to guard them. And guard them they did.

Finally something good began to happen. Stray's breathing quickened and he began to cough, hard, curl up like he was in pain. Like Gwen was pulling the poison from his body.

"Now, Kate," Gwen told her. "Trap the poison."

Like it had happened earlier, her mind knew the spell before she could doubt herself—her hands curled and she spoke in ancient words, pictured the black pain rising and catching inside her binding spell, far away from where it could harm Stray or anyone.

Gwen stopped a few minutes later, leaned back against Rifter and brushed some hair from her face, which was flushed. Her eyes were clear and bright, slightly lupine, as though she could shift at any moment.

"You did it—you saved him," Kate told her.

"Finally. I was beginning to feel useless," Gwen said as Stray began to stir between them.

Rifter placed his hands on her shoulders, told her more fiercely than Kate would've thought necessary, "Never. You are never useless, mate."

"Right. Forgot the alpha thing," Gwen murmured, but she seemed anything but displeased. As Rifter carried her away, she called back, "Stray's fine now, Kate. He should wake up fully in a few minutes."

It took about ten minutes for Stray to be up and functioning. He ignored Kate telling him to take it easy; instead, he picked her up and carried her inside the house, up the stairs and into his bedroom.

Vice followed them, threw some heavy silver chains on the floor, where they landed with a loud thump. And then he closed the door behind him when he left.

Stray kept her tight in his arms, kissed her fiercely. It would be so easy to sink into the bed with him and let him take her.

But something tugged at her, something she couldn't deny, and she pulled away.

"What? Did I hurt you?" he demanded, his eyes going to the bruises around her neck.

"No, you didn't. I was just thinking about the mating."

"Second thoughts?"

"No. I still want to be your mate, even if it's not officially recognized beyond anyone but us and your family. But . . . we could still go through the motions," she suggested and then blushed when his head whipped toward her. "I mean, I won't turn into a wolf, but I could still, um . . ."

She looked pointedly at the chains. "If you're into that sort of thing."

"For you, I could be into anything."

He was serious—so serious. She'd never wanted anything more. Her heart raced, because this was within her grasp. Because their love didn't involve magic of the manipulated kind in the least. "So those are the mating chains?"

He went over and picked up a large metal collar from the floor. "You put this on me. Chain me up. And I'm supposed to endure the mating pain as a sign of my love."

"I don't want to cause you any more pain."

"This pain, I'll gladly deal with."

"We've had sex more than twice—the pain must've been excruciating."

"Worth it. And now I get to use this mating tradition. I've known I'm fated for you."

"Even though I can't shift into a wolf? Because that obviously won't happen after we, ah . . ."

"Yes, even though."

"So this is just for show?"

"It's more than that. It's an honoring of my warrior ways. I never got to be a part of them growing up, but now I am. This would be my crowning glory."

"Then I want to be a part of that."

"You already are." He climbed onto his bed and grabbed the headboard. "Wrists, then ankles. Then collar."

She locked him in place, felt herself grow more aroused than she thought possible as he lay bound under her, his cock jutting thick and heavy, his eyes lupine as he watched her. She expected to hear him howl soon. Wanted him to.

"Now this." She opened the last piece of the mating chain carefully—placed the collar around his neck and locked it slowly. It didn't need to be opened with a key, but rather a hand, and Stray didn't have a free one at the moment.

"Now you get naked. And you put me inside of you. And you fuck me," he told her, licked his bottom lip as his voice grew deeper, darker. She noted his canines had elongated and she felt nothing but want. Her sex was wet for him already, and she slid out of her clothes and mounted him, hovering above his shaft before slowly bringing herself down on it.

Later, there would be a time for drawn-out exploration, for stroking and kissing and worshipping. This was for hard and fast, for mating. For joining as one, and she waited until he was fully inside of her before beginning to move. Back and forth, she rocked against him, her hands on his chest, watching his face bathed in pain and pleasure fighting for dominance. She didn't worry about it—this was part of the ceremony.

It was what Stray wanted. He writhed under her, bucked, moaned. She felt him grow bigger inside of her, realized she couldn't pull away from him now because of that, even if she wanted to.

It had happened before, but not like this. Never like this.

"Stray, more," she heard herself moan as her sex contracted around him. The way he throbbed inside of her brought on multiple orgasms and she couldn't have controlled herself if she tried. She raked his chest with her nails, bent down and bit him on his shoulder, hard enough to draw blood, didn't stop when he cried out.

She'd become wild. Feral. A beast, just like him. And she liked it.

Stray had never mated before, but he couldn't imagine it being more perfect. When she bit him, the pain throughout his body had been as intense as anything he'd felt before, and then his orgasm had staggered out of him, a jagged, sharp burst that finally took away any of the previous pain and gave him only a shiver of pleasure as intense as any he'd ever felt.

Kate collapsed on him when he was finally sated. It was hours later—too long for a human to deal with, but not an immortal witch, no matter how inexperienced. She'd gotten nothing but pleasure from the experience, because he'd watched her.

She'd looked happy. She loved him—told him so several times.

He stroked a hand along her shoulder and she reached up and undid the collar around his neck. Stared at him. "Did it work?"

"It worked for me."

She laughed a little, sat up and undid his wrists. Stayed straddling him while she reached back to undo his ankle bindings, and he saw it on her shoulder.

He waited until he was free and then he got off the bed, holding her against him, turned her back to the mirror in the bathroom. "Look over your shoulder."

She did and her eyes widened. "That's . . . a wolf tattoo."

"It's a glyph, like mine. It comes out right before our first shift," he told her.

"It looks just like your Brother Wolf."

"It is."

It began on her left shoulder and went halfway down her lower back. Brother's eyes glowed with a secret they now both knew.

"We share your wolf," she whispered as she stared over her shoulder. "I like it. No, I love it. You."

"My mate," he told her, kissed her until he was hard again.

She pulled back and looked over her shoulder at the wolf in the mirror again. "Should we let the others know? Don't we have to dance under the moon?"

"Plenty of time for that tomorrow. All the time in the world." And for once, that wasn't a scary thought for either of them.

Epilogue

Rogue opened his eyes slowly, expected to see the mare's face, even though he no longer felt the weight of her on his chest.

There was no one there, and he recognized the attic of the Dire house in the Catskills, where they'd been living before the capture.

Fuck me. He sat up, ignoring his complaining muscles, and shook to wake Brother Wolf. The beast was hibernating. Shell-shocked.

Well, get unfucking shocked, he told the wolf. *Gotta deal.*

He fingered several hand-rolled cigarettes, brought one to his nose and inhaled the scent through the paper.

If he lit it, he'd see blue smoke.

Vice.

He'd smelled that nightly for the past months, which meant the Dire had stayed close.

He heard whoops and howls from the slightly opened window, moved to peer out and saw the Dires and some Weres running in the moonlight along with a witch. *Kate.*

It was a mating ceremony, but with no sign of the Elders.

Good. Those fuckers could rot.

He'd heard everything going on around him, more since

the mare left than ever, knew Jinx was still living apart from the Dires—and with a deadhead. And that Jinx had opened—and closed—purgatory. Vice was still Vice, and Stray and Kate had mated somehow. Harm had finally lived up to his legacy.

And he'd seen more in hell than he'd ever wanted to.

Yeah, reentry was gonna be a bitch.

Acknowledgments

Writing a book is never a solitary endeavor, and I'm so grateful to the following for their help and support.

For the awesome Danielle Perez, whose insights and patience are always invaluable and appreciated. For Kara Welsh and Claire Zion, for all their unwavering support; for Erin Galloway, my wonderful publicist; and for everyone else at NAL who helps introduce my Dire wolves to the world. And I'd be remiss if I didn't give a special shout-out to the art department for their most awesome covers!

For my friends, writing and otherwise, and my readers—the support, encouragement and laughter you supply is more important than you'll ever know.

For my family, who understand why I spend so long in the writing cave and who are always waiting for me—usually with dinner—when I crawl out. Love you, Zoo, Lily, Chance and Gus.

Don't miss the next novel in the
Eternal Wolf Clan series,

DIRE DESIRES

Coming in July 2013 from Signet Eclipse

Two days earlier

When she dragged in with the old blanket draped over her naked shoulders, she knew she still wore the wildness in her eyes like the chill of a winter's night.

She hated the daytime the most. The other patients did as well, avoided the sun, hated to be pulled into the fresh air as if they were horses to be exercised in captivity. She wanted the air and exercise, no doubt, but unfettered.

She wanted the moon. The small pad of paper she'd stolen during her last therapy appointment would be in its hiding spot, showing the beginnings of many crude drawings of the orb.

In her mind's eye, it was perfect, beautiful.

She wouldn't talk about it in the sessions with the man with the glasses. For five years, others had tried and failed. He would fail as well, because Gillian had stopped listening, stopped knowing what she once was.

A daughter. Once loved, until something went wrong. She began to talk about wolves, to run in the woods alone. Naked.

That was, apparently, unacceptable. Signaled illness.

Since she continued to escape, that meant the illness was getting worse, not better. She felt it too. But she always came back voluntarily because there was no other place for her. And still, something inside of her compelled her to look for others whenever the moon grew heavy, and lately, when it didn't. The past two months had been a roller coaster of emotions for her. This time, she knew the wildness was too much for her—it threatened to overwhelm her, suck her into its madness, never, ever to let go. Maybe one day she'd allow herself to go all the way in, see that it was for the best.

But today she returned. Last night she'd run and then she'd lain under the stars and she'd dreamed. The dreams were of another time and place—distant, beautiful—and she felt stately and wise despite the way the men looked at her when she strode in.

They shoved her to the ground unceremoniously. Checked her for weapons.

I am a weapon, the rustling in her ears told her. But the men who held her down didn't know that, and she knew better than to tell them.

After she felt the initial prick of the needle, she waited for the familiar poison to work itself through her body. Her muscles relaxed. The rustling in her ears stopped.

But in her dreams, she ran.

Vice swore he heard something slam to the ground in the woods outside the Dire house right after four in the morning. He'd been out running the woods and had just showered and prepared a snack fit for a king, but his curious Brother Wolf wouldn't *not* let him check it out. And since he was the only one either not on his honeymoon or in a coma, he went. Left the house naked and shifted the second his foot touched grass.

The nighttime air was cool and soothing. For an hour, he ran through the brush and remnants of snow, searching for whatever it was that made the noise.

He ended up at the tree he thought of as Eydis's, since he was always drawn to it when that specific Elder called for him. Vice listened when called, because he was compelled to do so.

Still, he couldn't control what he said in front of any of them, but hey, he was immortal, so what could they really do—kill him? That would be a fucking relief.

The tree was a massive, thousand-year-old oak that had been split straight down the middle by lightning. Like the Dires themselves, it had survived centuries, still standing healthy and straight.

The tree blossomed during springtime, stayed green until the worst of winter. Even barren, the tree stood out. It was magnificent.

Now it was entirely destroyed—one half lying on the ground, the other bent and broken—and he felt sick.

It would take something powerful to do that. Or something magical. He saw a hole in the ground close by, shaped as though something—or someone—had been thrown from the heavens.

He looked at the shimmering white glow that lined the hole and sucked in a breath. There was no way that could've happened.

He wanted to call out her name, crawl into the hole and wait for her. . . .

She hasn't come looking for you. And she won't.

With that last thought, he gave a howl, long and loud, the most mournful one he'd ever heard his wolf make. Not since Eydis was sacrificed and was picked to be an Elder.

He'd been sixteen when that happened.

Brother Wolf circled the tree, stared at it for hours, trying to think of a way to repair it. But there wasn't one. Nothing could handle this kind of wrath and survive—no one could.

Except you.

And then something inside of him stirred that made the wolf break into a dead run toward the house.

Something he hadn't felt for six months.

Rogue was awake and at his window, staring down at him. Vice howled with approval and relief, and he saw Rogue smile a little.

He shifted quickly and took the stairs two at a time, all the while trying to tamp down his emotions so they wouldn't be too hard for Rogue to deal with. It wasn't easy. He took a deep breath, then slammed the door open, raced to Rogue and hugged the crap out of him. "Dude, you're really up."

Rogue hugged him back, didn't say anything for a long moment, and Vice was pretty sure he was crying. When they pulled away, Rogue wiped his cheeks. "You look good, wolf."

"You don't look half bad for what you've been through." Indeed, Rogue's chest still bore marks from the mare who'd held him in a supernatural coma for six months. She'd been under Seb's spell—and Seb was a powerful witch who'd once been friends with the Dires. "You know Seb's gone?"

"I heard. I knew what was happening around me. I just couldn't do shit about it," Rogue confirmed.

"Did you call Jinx?"

"Not yet. Just give me some time, all right?" Rogue asked and Vice cocked his head and stared into the wolf's eyes.

Finally he said, "Gotta at least tell Rift. Gwen will need to check you over." Although they were all alphas, Rifter was their king, and they owed him that respect.

"I'm fine. Really. Cover for me, Vice. A couple of hours and then I'll tell them. I want to shower. Clean the hell up."

How could he turn Rogue down after what he'd been through? And of course, that was what Rogue was counting on. "Yeah, all right—coupla hours but that's all. And don't tell Rifter—no need for him to have my head again."

"Deal." Rogue hugged him again and man, it was good to have Jinx's other half back. Although Vice hated to leave him, he did so out of respect, and closed the door and went downstairs.

He rounded the corner to the kitchen and found Rifter and Stray standing there.

"Hey," Vice said in what he hoped was a normal voice. Then again, he'd never been normal, and Stray and Rifter had apparently been trying to fuck themselves to death with their mates, so the last thing they cared about was how *Vice* sounded. And by the looks on their faces, they weren't angry at all. "I was just out running and—"

"Kate's got the wolf—the glyph," Stray interrupted him. "It's my Brother Wolf—smaller, but it's there."

"So she'll run with us under the blue moon," Rifter said with a great deal of satisfaction. "It's a good day."

Indeed it was.

When the dust had settled and the Dire ghost army was put down, they had all been relieved. Shimmin was taken down, and so was the biggest facility where the trappers experimented, along with the castle where Seb was kept.

Seb had disappeared. Vice had blown the place sky high and Jinx had done some binding spells with Kate's help.

For now the trappers were in a state of disarray—in New York, at least. In other parts of the country they were gearing up, and that's where Liam came in.

The young wolf was King of the Manhattan pack. After Linus, his father, had been killed by the trappers and the rogue Weres working for them, Liam had lain low and gained support. He'd taken Cyd and Cain as part of his pack, would take them to Manhattan with him. Those two Weres that Jinx had taken in as moon-crazed and newly shifted teenagers were a far cry from the twenty-one-year-old alpha and omega.

Liam would step up his game now, since the king of the Manhattan pack was also the king of all Weres. He would have to guide them through the upcoming assaults the trappers would no doubt try in order to get some power back.

"For the first time in a while, things are looking up," Rifter said. "Once Rogue wakes up, we'll have more reason to celebrate."

Vice nodded with a smile as was expected of him, but his mind kept wandering back to the damned oak tree. When Eydis spoke to Stray days earlier, she told him that Kate could only mate with a Dire under one condition: *A life for a life*, and the Elders didn't just forget about shit like that. Someone was going to pay—or else someone already had.

And now, the mating had been allowed. Vice thought about the tree and the *life for a life* thing and shook his head. No way. No *goddamned* way.

Jinx was on the highway going much faster than necessary when Vice rang him up and started talking as soon as Jinx answered.

"Listen, two things—Kate's got Stray's glyph on her back. And Rogue's awake."

Jinx gripped the wheel tightly at the last sentence and lost his breath for a moment, until Vice prodded, "Dude, you with me?"

"Yeah, I'm here."

"He's gonna be fucked up for a while. Just gotta deal with it," Vice offered. "If I didn't see him, he wouldn't have called for me. He just wants a few hours."

Jinx could understand that—really, he could. But his fucking twin . . . it was like not calling himself. "So, about Kate's glyph . . ."

"Guess the Elders approved the mating."

"When have the Elders helped us, besides Gwen?" Jinx demanded.

"Kate's still here," Vice pointed out.

"The Elders didn't come down and allow it. It's a trap."

"But they didn't stop it—and they gave her Stray's wolf."

"I don't trust it. They screw us for centuries and now they're nice to us?" Jinx shook his head. "Look, they were

Dires just like us, with abilities and everything. You'd think that would make them less dick-like."

"What do you want me to say? Most people in power are pricks."

"Right. So the Elders can go fuck themselves." And that's why Jinx planned on handling the shit that had come out of purgatory that needed to be put down, since he'd been the one to open purgatory in the first place. That was his ability, the one he was born with—he could see ghosts. Rogue, his twin, could see spirits. But those stuck in purgatory were somewhere between the two—crossed over to a certain point, but not all the way there. Jinx would lead them back into hell. And if Rogue got off his ass and decided to help, that would be great too, but Jinx wasn't holding his breath.

Vice changed the subject quickly. "Liam's going to fight tonight. Twins too. You'll be there?"

"I can't. I've got to hunt. Business as usual." Although it wasn't. Not by a long shot.

The Dire ghost army had actually been laid to rest because they'd been killed honorably in battle, so Jinx didn't need to worry about sending them anywhere. They were finally at peace, even though they'd died at the hands of their sons. And the Dires took pride in the fact that they'd fought and won. They'd used their warrior ways.

But Jinx and Rifter were still at odds, meaning Jinx wasn't invited back to the mansion to live. And that was fine by him. "Keep me updated."

"Will do. You know where to find us if you change your mind."

Jinx hung up and glanced at the vampire sitting next to him in the truck, the one he currently shared the penthouse with in a Dire-owned apartment building because neither supernatural being would give an inch.

"Shouldn't you go with Vice?" Jez asked.

"He doesn't need my help."

"You can't still be worried about this 'Jinx is evil' shit."

"How do you know the evil from purgatory didn't hang around me? Vice is really goddamned susceptible to being possessed without warning," Jinx told him. "If he got too close to what we're dealing with . . ."

"I get it," Jez said. Jinx was pretty sure Vice did as well, but the wolf wasn't any less pissed at him. "Rogue's awake?"

"Awake and not wanting to see anyone for a couple of hours. Fucking diva," Jinx muttered as they pulled up to the gated brick building after their four hour drive and got a visitor's pass for the car. "Let's just do this job and I'll deal with my twin later."

When Marley, a human ghost hunter Jinx had met months earlier on another job, had called him last night and told him that she'd gone to the facility to find a ghost and ended up running from a monstrous being instead, Jinx knew right away what was hiding inside that building.

A psych facility was the perfect spot for a monster from purgatory to hide—and by *monster*, he knew it could be a lesser demon or something worse. If people paid more attention to those who claimed to see monsters instead of drugging them, the world would be a better place.

"Goddamned humans, always screwing themselves over," he groused.

"Your *human* friend gave you the lead," Jez reminded him.

"Since when are you so reasonable about them?"

"They have their uses."

"I haven't seen you feed from one."

"True."

So how was Jez feeding? Jinx wanted to ask but figured it was safer not knowing. He was grateful to have any help at all.

Still, he couldn't help but think about how helpful Rogue would be as well, but he was still too fragile. And probably pissed at Jinx. He wondered if his twin would keep his secret about purgatory, since none of the other Dires, or the Weres who lived with them, knew. Only Rogue and the witch Kate, who promised discretion.

He decided he couldn't worry about that. "Let's get the wolf out first and then we'll deal with the evil later on tonight."

"While you're in, I'll get the lay of the land, so to speak. Check in with a few of the patients about what they've seen."

"How're you going to do that without a visitor's pass?' Jinx asked and Jez smiled.

"Let me worry about that, wolf."

Jez was a deadhead—aka a vampire from an old order—and, if Jinx understood it correctly, Jez had been brought back from wherever vampires waited to die in order to help the Dires through their current messes. That meant he was far stronger than most vamps—the same way Dires were stronger than Weres. Jez could go out in sunlight, enjoy food. According to Jez, there were more like him, but he'd been sent specifically to help Jinx through these current battles.

There was always a goddamned battle. Always would be. But for now, he could kill two birds with one stone: grab the evil being and put him back in purgatory, and save a wolf named Gillian.

He wasn't surprised a Were had been placed in a psych hospital. It had happened countless times before. He was just lucky that Marley picked up on it before she'd been run out by the monster.

Now they got out of the car, and Jez disappeared around the back of the building while Jinx went in the legal way. He showed his fake ID—it read JOSH TODD—and from there gained easy entrance. Stray had already gotten into the hospital's system and given Gillian a brother named John, and put John down on the list of visitors. Jinx figured that there would be so many people there that day wandering the grounds that breaking her out should be relatively easy.

This place was worse than the morgue and he steeled himself as he walked through, ignoring the ghosts that harangued him for attention. They flew at him like incoming missiles with deadly aim as an orderly named Ken came to guide him to Gillian's room.

Jinx kept his eyes akimbo and his fists tightened at his sides. He felt hinky here—the result of the monster, not the ghosts. Whatever it actually was, he was pretty sure it was gone now, but it was bad. Really fucking bad, since his skin crawled as if it were contaminated.

"She doesn't like to come out during the day," Ken told him.

Makes sense, Jinx mused as he nodded and the guy continued, "At least she's back."

"She never says where she's been?"

"Won't tell us, and if she tells the shrink, he can't say." Ken paused outside the locked door. "She took her pills this morning. But it's been a while since you've seen her, right?"

"I'm in the military."

"She can get violent. I'll stay with you."

"That's not necessary," Jinx told him. "I'll be fine. But I would like to try to get her out for a walk."

Ken looked at Jinx like he belonged in the padded room as well. "She can't."

"Why?"

"She's considered too dangerous."

Jinx stopped arguing and instead looked into the small window.

Gillian had her back to the door. She was curled like a wolf on the bed, the T-shirt she wore riding up on her thighs.

"We give her clothes but she barely wears them. The nurse got her into that when she was half asleep."

The door clicked behind her and Gillian jumped up and stared at him. Jinx remained in place, more out of shock than because it was the best way to handle this wild wolf.

She was no Were—he'd known that the second he'd

stepped inside. Gillian Black was a Dire, and she was weeks away from her first shift. His Brother Wolf could smell a Sister Wolf, and his wolf surged in a nearly uncontrollable frenzy. That hadn't happened to Jinx since he was newly transitioned himself.

It didn't hurt that she was gorgeous. Wild, long-limbed, brown hair tumbling over her shoulders. Golden skin and her eyes glowed nearly aqua, like the shimmering ocean that reminded him of the old country.

"Down, Brother," he murmured to himself and she cocked her head and stared at him.

He had no doubt his eyes had begun to change to the wolf's. "Gillian, I'm here to help you."

"They all say that." Her voice was raspy from underuse.

"I mean it."

Sister Wolf is confused, Brother told him.

"Who are you?" she demanded. She might not have been trained in the warrior ways, but she circled him as if ready to fight.

"I'm just like you."

"A mental patient?"

Jinx grinned. "Let's take a walk."

"To remind myself what I can't have? No. Besides, I'm not allowed to."

"I didn't say we were coming back." He barely spoke the words, but the way her eyes widened, he knew she'd heard him clear as day.

Gillian wanted to ask this man with the long reddish brown hair why he'd do that. But really, she was too busy being drawn into his eyes.

Something deep inside of her that wanted the moon was also drawn to this man.

She never trusted, but the rustling said to now.

"How long have you been here?" he asked with a side-long glance out the single window on the door.

He was built like a warrior from gladiator times—she'd seen the show on the TV in the main room. He looked as though he could do anything.

"Does it matter?" she finally asked.

"To me, yes."

"Five years this spring." It was spring already but she wouldn't give him a date even if he asked outright. She needed to keep something for herself, had learned the importance of doing so in a place like this.

A scream tore through the late-afternoon air, sailed in through the window and made her cringe. "It's like that all the time," she told him. "Worse on visiting day."

"Do you get many visitors?"

"You're my first in over a year." Over three years, actually. At some point her parents had given up. There were care packages, clothes she never wore, books she never read. Nothing that could be of any value to her.

"You'll stay with my family," he told her. "They're all like you. I'm like you."

She didn't know what he meant, but the rustling did, was chomping at the bit to be with others like herself.

She didn't ask how he planned on doing anything. He simply pointed to her pants. She slid them on and he knocked on the door.

"She wants to walk with me," Josh Todd said.

The orderly looked between them. "Not without a major dose of tranquilizer."

No choice, Brother Wolf told her Sister Wolf, but Gillian shook her head and backed away. Too many injections made her feel odder than she already did. She could barely get her equilibrium during the past six months to begin with, never mind the last five years that passed in a blur of sameness.

Except for the escapes, the only time she could actually breathe, time had ceased meaning anything at all.

This wasn't going to go well at all. Josh Todd spoke to her

in a low voice, but she lunged past him and threw herself at the orderly.

She hated him and this place. Hated the visitor too, who'd promised her too much and then didn't come through for her.

So what was the point of sitting here like a good girl, telling them, "Oh no, I don't need to go outside—I'll just stay here."

The next time she left, she wasn't coming back. The decision had been made but it would be on her own steam.

The orderly was coming with a dose of tranquilizers and she didn't want them. Even though the other man told her to take them, that they would help with the escape, she wouldn't submit.

Nothing inside of her ever truly would.

Also available from

Stephanie Tyler

DIRE NEEDS
A Novel of the Eternal Wolf Clan

Feared by humans and envied by werewolves,
the Dire wolves are immortal shifters,
obeying no laws but their own bestial natures.

Rifter leads the pack, and his primal instincts have led
him to claim Gwen, a woman seeking solace from the
chronic pain that has wracked her body her entire life.

But whatever future Rifter and Gwen have is threatened
by an enemy of both humanity and the Dire wolves...

"A raw, sexy world."
—*New York Times* **bestselling author**
Maya Banks

Available wherever books are sold or at
penguin.com

facebook.com/ProjectParanormalBooks

s0408